LOCKSLEY

LOCKSLEY

Nicholas Chase

ALLEN LANE

ALLEN LANE

Penguin Books Ltd, Harmondsworth, Middlesex, England
Penguin Books, 40 West 23rd Street, New York, New York 10010, U.S.A.
Penguin Books Australia Ltd, Ringwood, Victoria, Australia
Penguin Books Canada Ltd, 2801 John Street, Markham, Ontario, Canada, L3R 1B4
Penguin Books (N.Z.) Ltd, 182–190 Wairau Road, Auckland 10, New Zealand

Published in Canada by Allen Lane, 1983
Published in Britain by William Heinemann Ltd, 1983
Published in the United States by Richard Marek, 1983

Copyright © Nicholas Chase Productions, 1983

Canadian Cataloguing in Publication Data
Chase, Nicholas
    Locksley
    ISBN 0-7139-1627-3
    I. Title.
    PS8555.H37L62   C813'.54   C83-098489-5
    PR9199.3.C4474L62

Printed in Great Britain by
Richard Clay (The Chaucer Press) Ltd, Bungay, Suffolk

AUTHOR'S NOTE

Richard the Lionheart, King John, Eleanor of Aquitaine – everyone knows that they were real. But the Princess Berengaria was as well; and Maud de Caux, Jacob Mancere, des Roches, Vizier, John Naylor and almost all the rest. And if you go into Sherwood Forest and find a spot not far from the ancient Roman ditch, thinking of those names conjures up one other: Atheling, Earl of Locksley.

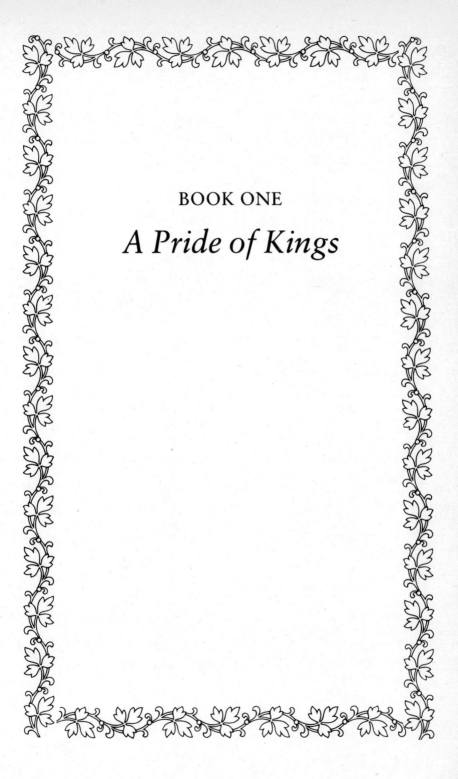

BOOK ONE

A Pride of Kings

CHAPTER ONE

I sit, take up this pen, prepare to tell the story of my life . . . but there are too many places to begin, and so I hesitate. From this attic room I can look beyond the harbour to the open sea, where a thousand curling waves rush here from England – and, in looking out, I look back as well, and my memories are like those waves, rising for a moment, spending themselves against the sun, then curling up again. Which one to choose, and how to hold it in my mind?

Since this is to be the story of my life, I suppose it would be simplest to make a beginning with myself, but even that is difficult. Today, if you wish to find me, you need only ask for François Mèry, merchant in wool, citizen of Calais; but at other times men have known me differently. I've been scholar, ordinand, crusader; a murderer and a smuggler, royal equerry and regicide. I've been Daniel Delore, owner of a stew of whores; Robin Hood, an outlaw; Alwyn White, a sailor. I've been a banker, in company with a Jew; a friend of kings; husband to a queen. Indeed, I've been so many different men that my true name and bearing are almost lost – and yet not quite. I can still tell the world: I am Robert Godfrey Bouvier Atheling, Knight Equerry, Fourth Earl of Locksley, Verderer of the Royal Forest at Sherwood by Decree.

Of course, I could begin like that, and make it a proper chronicle: "I was born on Lammas Day, the Year of Our Lord 1171, the third child and second son of William Atheling, Knight, Earl, etc, and Edwina, his wife, who died within a week of my appearance." The trouble is, if I start like that I'll then be forced to speak of my family and its genealogy, a subject I find more tedious than any other. Like a hundred families, we have a past of dotted lines, bastards, and outright lies that would have you believe that we're connected to everyone from the Pope to Charlemagne. But suppose I skip it all; then I could begin with my boyhood days, my brother Garth, our life at Locksley Hall. That would be more reasonable, for I was a second son and the world reserves some interesting fates for second sons. In any case, my father chose education and then the priesthood – a fact that illustrates his political acumen more than his piety. The monastery of Kirklees and its nearby nunnery lay beside our lands, and by ancient right it was the Earl of Locksley who chose the abbot. When Garth assumed the title, what more natural choice than me? That way, at least, I wouldn't be a burden . . . So, if I began like that, I could go on from my happy childhood to tell you of my student days at Oxford, reminding myself that I've now forgotten everything I learned except my Greek and Latin, and hopefully my manners: *Qui vult potare debet prius os vacuare, Et sint illius labia tersa prius.*

But I wonder, in turn, if all that will interest you. The student life has been lived by a thousand others, and has historians better suited to the task than me. Besides, I shared great times and knew great men, and there are certain tales that only I can tell. I write from duty – I still have debts to pay to history, and have no time or need to detail petty things.

Or do I fool myself?

As I look out the window, I see the cold grey clouds of winter reflected in the cold March sea. A chill is in my bones. It never leaves. This is my seventieth year, and everything begins to feel like cold, damp stone. Let me face the truth: I am an old man now, and I want what old men want – to be young once more and to feel the sun. That is why I write. To remember. To have it all again. To breathe the scent of lime and clover, to fill my mouth with wine and olives, to feel the smooth muscle of a horse beneath my thigh . . . That sun! Where does it come from? But now I know; and knowing, know where I'll start my tale. Fifty years ago, almost to the day, beneath the magic sun of Sicily. With Garth, my brother, and with Richard, King of England, on our way to Acre on Crusade. Yes. The day before the French fleet sailed. That day, in that wondrous light, when Garth and I rode out of camp to hunt.

"Garth, do you think sticking pigs is the same in Sicily as it is in England?"

"God knows," answered my brother. "But I hope eating them is. I can almost taste those chops." He licked his lips and rolled his eyes and laughed. "You know," he added, "the Mahomets are like the Jews – they won't touch swineflesh."

"The Mahomets think that we eat *them*."

Garth laughed again. "The only one I ever saw was much too lean."

4

We both paused now, leaning forward in our saddles, the leather creaking softly. Both of us were nervous beneath our chatter. We'd ridden out of Mate Griffon just after breakfast, sticking to the shore around Messina, then following a narrow path that led us up the cliffs above the sea. Finally, turning inland, we'd gradually ascended a lumpy range of olive-covered hills, and now were zig-zagging down the opposite slope. The hillside was gentle, covered with thick turf and daisies and mushrooms hidden in shady hollows, so it was no surprise to discover the roughed-up spots where pigs had rooted. I looked down the hill. At the bottom, meandering along through the grass, was a marshy stream that disappeared into a small wood at the far end of the valley, a kind of overgrown thicket of oak, thorn and olive. That's where they'd be; deep in shade, resting till the sun moved down. "We need William, Hubert, Robin, old Balderson," I said.

"I know. A dozen men with pikes."

We fell silent, nervously eyeing that thicket. Then I muttered, "We can't take the horses into that."

Garth grunted, knowing I was right. The thorns would be bad enough, but if we did find a boar and it charged, our big Belgians would have no chance – not in brush so tight they couldn't turn. But if we didn't take the horses, we'd have to go on foot; and, on foot, I'd rather face a lion than a boar. After a moment, Garth said, "If we ride *around* all that, I'm sure we'll find game on the other slope."

I smiled. Once there'd been the fiercest competition between my older brother and myself, and though it had died down with the years, it wasn't dead yet. I said, "So is that what we do, big brother?"

Garth grinned. "Ah well . . . It is a question of judgement, or proper wisdom. As a scholar, you should be the one to say."

"Well, as a scholar, I know you'll never defeat my rhetoric . . . So I say: 'On the one hand, there's a certain danger . . . on the other, I prefer pork to rabbit.'"

He laughed. "To hell then, little lad. If it's pork you want, follow me."

With that, he spurred his horse and we trotted down the slope. Reaching the stream, we let the horses drink a little, then continued along the bank toward the woods. Stopping there, we pegged our mounts in the shade of a stunted, twisted oak. Garth unstrapped his hunting lance and I slipped my bow from its leather case. We pushed into the bush, which turned out to be as dark as a cave. Hacking ahead, our leggings caught the worst of the thorns, but nothing stopped the insects: the island was crawling with them except in the breezes near the shore. Now they buzzed about our ears and settled

5

contentedly on our necks to feed. Finally we struck a path, an old pig run, and followed it along till it merged with another.

"This will do," said Garth.

I nodded. There was no sense going further. At this time of day, resting in the underbrush, a pig would be invisible until you stepped on it; lacking dogs and beaters, we could only wait until an animal showed itself. So we waited: Garth on one side of the run, myself on the other, facing in opposite directions so we wouldn't be taken unawares.

Edwin Scathelock, Garth's squire, had made us lunches; an onion, goat cheese, a leather pouch of wine. Finding some ferns, I nestled down like a bird and began to eat. I realised I was ravenous – it had been a long ride – and as I bit into that strange, strong cheese I thought of our route, up those great cliffs beside the blue sea, and thought again how amazing it was to be here. Sicily: where you could pick olives and lemons from the trees, and where the great Caesar had fought more than one of his battles. Above Messina, we'd found an old, abandoned temple to the Roman gods, grottos of fallen pillars and columns where wild dogs lived. If this were Sicily, what must the Holy Land itself be like? And then this question, by contraries, made me think of home. How different it would be: the river would still be skinned with ice and only near the foundations of the house, where the earth was warmed, would new grass be growing. Poor Locksley. Poor England. Before them lay another month of mist and oozing mud. And the boredom of it all. For my father, there was nothing to do but complain of the cold and his taxes, and for the women – I thought of Marian – nothing but sew, sew, sew. Despite *our* boredom – two months camped out in France, now six months here – I decided I was the better off.

Finishing my wine, I got my bow ready. It was a beautiful weapon, a gift to me from Hubert Scathelock, my father's Chief Huntsman and father of Edwin, Garth's squire. The wood was Spanish, which is better, no matter what you hear, than English yew or ash: clear, straight-grained and close to unbreakable in normal use. I took a string from my purse, checking to see that the twist was tight, and stretched it. Then I selected the two best arrows from my quiver; as long as my arm, they were perfectly drawn and fletched, but very light – too light for this sort of brush: even a twig might deflect them from their mark. But there was nothing to do about it now. I was as ready as I could be. Lying back among the bushes, both of us were hidden, though Garth, fully a head taller than myself, stood out slightly in the bracken. Our looks belied the fact that we were brothers. Garth had a Saxon's blondness, my mother's gift, and his high cheekbones, strong jaw and hard blue eyes gave him a Viking cast; by contrast, my own hair was dark and curling, while my brown eyes made people think of Spaniards or Italians. But these differences matched our positions perfectly: Garth seemed every inch the knight, I a perfect squire. Now I waited, my breath merging with the soft rhythms of the air around me and my skin with the dappled shade. An hour passed. And then . . .

We smelled her before we heard her; heard her before we saw her; and saw her so quickly we had no time to think, or else we might have run.

She was a brute. Her odour, low and rank, assailed our nostrils and then we heard the harsh, ragged sound of her breathing only ten paces up the run. Garth hissed. "Get behind me. On the left."

I moved. Behind him, to stay out of his way; to one side, so he'd be out of mine. If she charged, Garth's lance would be our first defence. If not – if she hung back – I would goad her with an arrow.

Peering into the shadows, Garth had her first. "There . . . by the rotted log. A sow."

I stared. She so blended with the shifting patterns of the shade that only her red, beady eyes betrayed her. Yet she was immense. Waist high, enormous at the shoulder. One tusk was missing, but the other curled beyond the thick, blunt snout – a yellowed lance that could gut a man in seconds.

If she had piglets, we both knew she'd charge at once. And in fact she scarcely paused. Stepping forward into the open, she trumpeted – giving us one warning to be gone – and then her small, sharp hooves began a steady tapping on the heavy soil. Garth's lance swung down; he bent forward, braced, like a man about to push some giant boulder. I nocked an arrow, catching another in my bow hand as I eased back the string. She came another pace. Her jowls, shaking with her breath, glistened in a patch of sunlight. And then she charged: digging with her back legs, driving forward, dust billowing around her like smoke and her eyes glowing like hot coals. Then her head dropped down, ready to gore, and Garth's lance dipped, plunged – the force spinning him to one side – and my arrow flew, light as a breeze against my cheek. I never saw it strike, yet she went down like a brick dropped into a pond – legs splayed out, chin scraping, slewing round from the strength of her charge and knocking my legs out from under me.

By the time I scrambled back to my feet, the light was going out in her eye.

Garth spat. "Yours, I think."

I could only nod; I was too busy catching my breath.

There is only one way to stop a charging boar: break its backbone. And there is only one place, the very base of its neck – exposed

7

in the last second of its charge – where the flesh is thin enough to allow it. We'd both been aiming for this spot. Garth's lance had struck too far back, plowing a furrow as wide as your hand along the beast's side. But my arrow, neat as a cleaver, had chopped its spine.

Walking round her, I could feel myself tremble. How huge she was, all sweaty and bristling. I thought of the Caledonian Boar who had vanquished Hector and even evaded Jason and his spears. Well . . . he should have used a longbow and an arrow. Garth nudged her swollen teats with the toe of his boot. "She'll have piglets nearby."

I handed him my bow and quiver. "They should be easy, even for you."

Garth laughed good-naturedly. As a knight, he would never deign to handle a bow, but as a soldier and hunter he knew well enough to respect it. Besides, as old Hubert had once told us, even a knight must sometimes fetch his dinner. Now that I had my full height, Garth and I were equal with quarterstaves, though he was distinctly better with the broadsword – he'd been training since he was five – but when it came to the bow, I always won. Still, he was good enough; twenty minutes later he returned, dragging three piglets behind him and with only four arrows lost from my quiver. By that time, I had my prize – that tusk – and had begun quartering the sow with my dirk. Now we finished the butchering and then, taking two trips, dragged the meat back to the horses. Lashed together, we draped the joints across their backs like saddle-bags, and covered them with ferns and pine branches to keep off the sun and flies.

"Along the shore?" I said, as we got up.

Garth shook his head. "It will be quicker to cut over the hills."

I laughed, but didn't disagree – I could already taste the crackling meat myself. So we headed off, and by late afternoon had reached the top of those sandy, gorse-covered dunes that rise along the shore. We paused a moment, looking down at Mate Griffon; even after two months of living beside it, it was still a sight to behold: the tall wooden palisade, the huge postern gate, the great keep rising up behind. It had more than five thousand joints and ten times that number of bolts, pinions and lockscrews held it together – for, at the end of our sojourn in Sicily, it would be taken apart, to be re-assembled again in the Holy Land. But, as we paused and let our horses blow, our eyes were drawn to another sight, almost as impressive: the great fleet of Philip of France. A hundred sailing ships filled the bay, and between them and the shore dozens of lighters were carrying men, horses, supplies and arms for one half of God's greatest army. Even from here, we could hear the shouted commands as the drivers manoeuvred their carts along the beach, and we watched two hapless ostlers struggling to push a grey Belgian onto a barge.

"I wish it was us," I said.

"Patience, little brother. Soon enough." Then Garth grinned. "Come along. We are owed a hero's welcome."

We got it, too. Riding up, we both hoisted a piglet over our heads like trophies – the poor beasts taking revenge on our pride by dripping gore all down our backs – and the men came running out, cheering the prospect of a feast. Our camp, about a mile beyond the walls of Mate Griffon, was pitched in the lee of a small pine grove, just enough shelter to protect us from the occasional storm. Here we had our tents, latrines, cooking pits, and an old oak stump that Garth, after disposing of me, would sometimes fight. Thirty-two men from Locksley had followed Richard's cross: two knights, Garth and Nicodemus, a cousin who was travelling with us but who wore our mother's family coat; Edwin and Joseph, their squires; three ostlers from the village for our horses; and two dozen footmen, each with a pike, a bow and twenty arrows, all a gift from my father. Now they swarmed around our horses, cutting down the meat and calling for roasting spits and faggots. Within ten minutes, fires were blazing and the joints were spitted. Garth shouted out instructions: "A piglet for the hunters, the rest is yours . . . No! Keep a second piglet for our Frenchmen cousins!"

This brought a groan, but it was in fact a good idea; we had a pair of cousins in the French camp, and the pig would make a decent farewell gift. So, the fires blazed, the meat roasted, and darkness slowly fell. I stretched out in the sand beside our tent, tired but happy, and watched the French fleet loading. Beneath me, the warmth of the day seeped away, and suddenly it was night, the whole shore now ablaze with fires and torches, gauntlets of flame marking the path to the shore and the unending stream of Philip's lighters. Even as I drew near our fire and shared the pig – a dozen happy, fat-smeared faces glistening round me – the clamour from the French camp went on. Armour clanged; horses whinnied and protested; men shouted; and, above it all, borne inland on a breeze, there was the constant groan and straining of the ships as they moved at anchor. At length, as the greedy groaned and belched and dozed, Garth shook me by the shoulder.

"Brother, shall we go down among the enemy?"

I smiled, then looked at him levelly. "Will you take Edwin? Any of the men?"

He thought for a moment, then shook his head. 'If we look for trouble, we might find it." I nodded. "Still," he added, "I'll take my sword."

As he strode into the darkness toward our tent, I let my eyes wander over the thousand blazing lights of Philip's camp. Perhaps it was unfair to call them "enemy"; we were allies, after all. But here on Sicily the alliance had grown uneasy. Though they'd taken the Cross together, the two kings had long been rivals. Old King Henry, Richard's father, had tried to link the realms by marrying him to Philip's sister, Alix, but that had come to nothing. Philip pretended to take this rejection personally – a spurning of his family – but I suspect rivalry, rather than alliance, suited both of them. As well, they had numerous other quarrels: money, for example. Their latest dispute in this regard made a complicated tale, the kind my father always liked to gossip over, ticking off relationships, marriages, dowries and inheritances on his fingers. These sagas usually made my head ache but this one, at least, I thought I understood. A few years before, Richard's sister, Joanna, had married King William of Sicily. Naturally, she'd brought a dowry with her, but King Henry (still alive then) had been promised an inheritance from King William in return. But now King William had been overthrown by Tancred of Calabria, who'd imprisoned both Joanna and her dowry. Richard had been enraged (by the dowry's theft, it was generally agreed, more than his sister's gaoling) and had therefore attacked Messina. Victorious over Tancred, he'd claimed 20,000 marks in compensation: half for the stolen dowry, half for the promised legacy to Henry (which he now claimed as heir). How did all this lead to a quarrel with the French? Because the two kings had previously agreed to divide all spoils from the Crusade in equal shares. The question now became, did Tancred's compensation qualify? At first, Richard had claimed it was the profit from a private fight, and though he'd ultimately relented (generously, I thought) Philip was still sulking. His bitterness had seeped down among his men. Brawls had broken out; there'd been several stabbings; and now sentries patrolled the margins of both camps. So, though I wore no sword myself – just my dirk – I was glad of Garth's.

We set out, Garth leading the way with a pine-pitch torch, I following with the pig – carefully wrapped in jute – hoisted on my shoulder. Despite our fears, we had no trouble. Quickly, we passed among our own fires, nodding to those men we knew, then stepped beyond our picket line into a stretch of no-man's-land, an area of low-growing gorse and rocky beach now all in darkness. On the other side, drawn by our light, the French sentry hailed us, and though he was hardly welcoming, he passed us through. Now we entered a sort of military hell. A soldiers' camp is filth, noise and confusion all mixed together; and a great camp being broken is treble that. Orders were being shouted on every side. Huge tents, suddenly struck, flapped like great bats in the dancing light. A cart had broken at the axle, its load of barrels rolling off the back and smashing on the ground. Men rushed forward – all at once the blaze of a dozen torches made the horses shy, sending them plunging backwards. We hurried on. Garth wore his surcoat, with his English arms, but in that madness no one noticed. Finally, stopping for a moment, Garth pointed: "There's Gisor's pennon."

Following his finger, I saw the tattered flag. It flew above a single tent, pitched at the very margin of the camp, which, I suppose, was a sign of the low favour in which the French king held him. But then Sir Raymond de Gisor had little to offer except his good right arm, and even that was aging. He was very poor. His family, and his family's land, had been ravaged by the plague – and nothing can destroy a fortune faster than a castle with no tenants to support it. In the end, unable to pay his scutage, he'd taken the Cross again, and would have to hope that Saracen plunder could raise the family name once more. But Raymond was my father's age and he probably knew, as Garth and I did, that he was unlikely to survive this journey, let alone return to France with booty.

We found him, with half a dozen men – his entire retinue – huddled round the embers of their fire. They looked more like carters than Crusaders; their armour was ancient, mostly leather, and terribly worn, while their weaponry was a collection of old pikes and javelins. Still, we hailed them cheerfully and brought forth our pig. Their eyes all lit up at the sight of it, and within a few minutes the fire had been rekindled and the pig spitted on a spear jammed at an angle in the ground.

"So you leave on the morning tide, cousin?" asked Garth politely, sipping at a wooden cup of wine . . . or vinegar: it was hard to be certain which.

Gisor nodded. "Tomorrow we'll be throwing up your fine pig into the sea. I've never seen a group of men so seasick as this bunch. We puked all the way from Marseilles, and I suppose we'll carry on to Acre."

Garth, who had his own sad tale to tell, made a face. "I always wonder whether it's the sea, or that food they give us."

Gisor smiled; then, as the piglet roasted, we talked of mutual friends and exchanged those rumours that pass for news with soldiers. How many men had Saladin at Acre? What were Richard's plans? Who would lead this force or that? Since no one knew the answers to these questions – though all pretended to – I found my mind wandering back to the chaos of the camp. We were, after all, two English men surrounded by ten thousand French. The longer I sat, the more uneasy I became – and, as it turned out, we sat too long.

After two hours in Gisor's fire, the pig was roasted well enough for the men to start hacking at it with their knives, but just as they'd begun to do so, two riders came pounding up, and Gisor's men stiffened one by one. Dismounting, our two visitors approached us. One was tall, dark-haired and wearing arms (or, a chevron sable) which I didn't recognise. The other was much shorter, his hair lank and mouse-coloured, his dark eyes deep-set behind bushy brows. As they came closer, Sir Raymond rose from his place and both Garth and I followed suit. As the knight saw the arms on my brother's chest, he raised an eyebrow – and Sir Raymond looked distinctly nervous.

"Sir Garth Atheling of Locksley," he said quickly, "and this is his brother, master Robert Atheling. They are cousins to me." Then, turning to us, he completed the introduction. "The Chevalier St Denis and his companion, Frère Falaise." I looked at this last-named closely; if he were a brother, he was a strange one. He wore chain-mail like a knight, though it was covered by a plain surcoat and a grey tunic. His belt held a long Turkish knife and a short-sword, the pommel gleaming with a jewel. There was only one order I knew that allowed a man to dress this way and carry arms in public: he was a Templar – a man of Christian plunder, as I once heard it put, whose vocation was the butchery of Saracens and other eastern heathen.

"Good evening," said Garth, to both of them. His voice was firm, correct, polite. He even extended his hand, but St Denis ignored it and stepped in front of him to tear a piece of succulent crackling from the pig. Falaise just stood there, watching.

"English pig," said St Denis. "It has a flavour like no other." His French was thick with something else . . . Alsace, I would have guessed, or perhaps he'd simply lived for a long time among the Franks.

"The sow was Sicilian," Garth said, "though the arrow that killed it was English enough."

St Denis, his chin now glistening, turned and smiled back to Falaise. "Shot from behind, I'm sure. Everyone knows that is the English way."

Falaise grinned at this, though Garth stiffened. But both of us managed to hold our silence – there were ten thousand men on their side, and precisely two of us. Nonetheless I stepped a little closer to Garth, closer to the fire – and, as I did, I saw something flash on St Denis' hand. "That ring," I blurted, "where did you get it?"

Slowly, the Frenchman moved his eyes to take me in. Then,

turning his hand better to catch the fire's glow, he glanced down at his knuckle.

Quickly, before he could speak, I tried to soften my tone. "Forgive me, Chevalier . . . I thought the stone was very fine, and it reminded me of another."

Now Garth understood and stared at the French knight's hand. The ring had been given by my father to Hubert Scathelock, who in turn had given it to Edwin, to bring him luck on Crusade. I hadn't seen Edwin, I suddenly realised, since that morning.

St Denis stepped back, flicking a piece of meat from the end of his dagger into the fire. Then he shrugged. "I took this ring from a dead boy sprawled in the doorway of a stew. Not that I owe you any explanation. The stone, as you say, is a fine one and bears the arms of an earl. I assumed the boy had stolen it."

"Dear Christ," said Garth. "You killed him!"

"I killed no one, seigneur. Everything happened exactly as I said."

"You lie."

We froze, all of us – and I think even Garth was shocked at his accusation. I could see that his hand was trembling, but he'd loved Edwin. St Denis smiled slightly. "You will take that back – or I will take your tongue."

Sir Raymond looked hastily between us, thought of intervening; and then thought better of it.

"You are a liar," said Garth, "and a murderer – and I'm the one who's taking. Your life and that ring!"

Then everything happened very quickly. St Denis, taking one step back, flung his cloak aside. Garth's hand went to his own sword, but even as he drew it out, Falaise reached to his neck and with a flick of his wrist something flashed in the night: as though by magic, the flat hilt of a dagger appeared in Garth's shoulder. Blood blossomed on his surcoat. With a cry, he dropped down to one knee – and then St Denis drew his sword.

I jumped forward. I had a five-inch dirk against a yard-long sword. I needed a weapon and took the only one at hand, the javelin holding the pig above the fire. Pulling it from the ground, I used it to launch the remnants of the pig at St Denis. He staggered back. Then, before he could recover, I kicked the embers of the fire toward the horses and the tent. The horses reared and plunged; in a moment, the dry canvas was burning like a torch and men were rushing everywhere shouting for help.

In the confusion, I got Garth up. "Can you stand? Walk?"

"I think so."

"Backwards then! Not through the camp – back among the dunes!"

Sir Raymond's unfavourable position in the French camp was our salvation. St Denis and Falaise had looked to their horses, and by the time they turned round to find us, we'd been swallowed by the darkness. Treading backwards, steering clear of even a Frenchman's shadow, we soon reached the shelter of the dunes.

There, flinging the javelin to one side, I turned to Garth and whispered. "Are you all right?"

"Those bastards," he muttered between his teeth, "those fiendish sons of whores!"

"Yes, I know. But can you walk?"

"Of course," he said.

And then, in a dead faint, he collapsed against me.

CHAPTER TWO

It took Garth a week to heal.

He'd lost a lot of blood; for three days he lay in fever; and for another day he was too weak to stand. I was worried enough, God knows, but even at the time I wondered if this wasn't for the best. Edwin's body had been found, foully murdered – a sword thrust in the back – in a stable in Messina. There's no doubt that if Garth had been able to get up, he would have sought revenge, and revenge against an experienced knight like St Denis could well have cost him his life. As it was, the French fleet sailed without incident, and by the time Garth was out of bed a hundred miles of ocean separated us from the Chevalier and his loathsome friend.

Which did nothing to still Garth's fury. When I told him what had happened, he stormed about so angrily I thought his wound might open.

"A mere boy! And to gore him in the back. What sort of devils must they be?"

"And only for a ring," I said, not much less angry myself. "The stone is valuable, but not worth a life – or the shame of taking it."

Garth shook his head. "It wasn't the ring. With a man like that, murder is sport."

Was that the explanation? Or had Edwin died merely because he was English? In any case, there was nothing we could do about it – for now, at least.

Slowly, Garth mended. The sun seemed to give him strength and ease the stiffness in his shoulder. After a time he was walking; then riding; and one morning I awoke to the *whump, whump, whump* as, once again, he defeated that old oak stump near our camp.

"So you're well again, brother?" I called.

He grinned. "I'm one of King Richard's knights, you'll remember. I must be ready to defend his new bride."

The King's bride: for days, both Messina and Mate Griffon had been buzzing with rumours about her, and even in the camp we'd taken a little trouble to clean and ready the place for her arrival. For a group of soldiers, I sometimes thought we took a great deal of interest in our leader's social life – though, after months of lounging on that shore, I suppose there wasn't much else for the men to talk about. Everyone, I believe, had sympathised with the King's rejection of Alix, Philip's sister. She'd been mistress to old Henry, King Richard's father, and I know that if *I'd* been the King, I wouldn't have wanted her. Did he want anyone? The King's fondness for his own sex was well known, and bothered many people, though I remember one old campaigner muttering: "As between a filthy whore and a clean lad, I'm not sure which a man should choose." Still, even a Sodomite king was obliged to marry, and the real question was why he had chosen an unknown Princess from Navarre to be his bride. According to most people, the answer was political, though the explanation was as tangled as a skein of wool. It went this way: King Richard had made a great enemy of Raymond of Toulouse which put all his southern realms, especially his mother's home of Aquitaine, in danger. Thus, he needed an ally in that region. He chose Alfonso of Aragon, because he was an enemy of Raymond's also; and this led him in turn to Sancho of Navarre, for Navarre and Aragon were already allied against Castille. So, by attaching himself to a minor Spanish king, Richard strengthened his ties with a greater one and covered his southern flank. But beside these political considerations, there were personal ones as well: for this marriage, *any* marriage, could only please King Richard's mother, Eleanor of Aquitaine, and the rumours claimed she was bringing the bride herself, and was prepared to conduct her son, at knife-point, to the altar.

For once, the rumours proved right.

Two days later, when messengers proclaimed the news that the ship had been sighted, Garth and I decided to join the curious crowd that thronged the harbour. By the time we arrived, a guard of honour had already formed along the dock, two dozen of the King's greatest knights, with their armour shining and their mantles rippling in the breeze as though before a tournament. A brace of yeomen, each wearing a surcoat with King Richard's stalking lions, stood by the poles of two sedan chairs, awaiting their royal passengers. The only thing missing was the King himself.

"He'll have to come," I said.

"I'll wager he won't," said Garth. "To a king, a marriage is merely a treaty like any other. There's no love or feeling in it."

It was a wager I took up, the stake being a mug of the wine which hawkers, passing through the crowd, were selling from casks strapped on their backs.

And it was a wager, I soon realised, that I was going to lose. The King still hadn't arrived as a little ship sailed round the breakwater and a shout rose from the crowd. The ship was only a common trader, and I was surprised at how small and plain she was: clinker-built, big-bellied, her hull tarred and patched in a dozen places. But her crew was skilful; smoothly, gently, they warped her in along the dock. Standing on fish boxes, we craned our necks for the first glimpse of the royal personages, though for a moment there was nothing to see but a sailor furling a tattered sail. "What a scow," I said, "you'd think a king's lady would deserve something better."

"Aye," said Garth, "it's not Cleopatra's barge, and that wine isn't from Champagne – but you owe me a cup just the same."

Pushing through the throng, I fetched us some, and by the time I was back, and on my fish box, the gangplank was down and men were bustling about on deck. Finally a shout went up. A lady had appeared, and though I'd never seen her before, I needed no one to tell me who she was. This was Eleanor of Aquitaine, the most powerful woman in all of Christendom; she'd survived two royal husbands to tutor her son in the governance of the world. Even then she was very old; almost seventy. Yet only her ebony walking stick betrayed this; she was still tall, erect, and firm in all her movements. Her presence overshadowed everyone, and it was a moment before I noticed the little figure – the Princess Berengaria – beside her. Yet, as soon as the crowd grew aware of her, a hush fell. She looked so small, scarcely more than a child, her jet black hair done in a long braid that made her seem even younger than she was. Lovely? Stunning? Beautiful? It was hard to find the word. I was young, though not entirely a stranger to women and their charms, but never had I seen a lady as lovely as this. A dozen different feelings filled my breast. I felt desire, and shame that I should feel it – for this woman was the bride intended for my king. I felt frustration, almost anger. Here was a woman, young and beautiful, about to marry a king who would prefer any man to her – indeed, some said that he really loved her brother, another Sodomite, with whom he'd often jousted. But mostly I felt pity. She was so young, so innocent, but would now be subjected to the corruption and deceit that surround the courts of all the greatest kings. But, if she had any doubts, she bore them bravely – that was the word I wanted, she looked so *brave* – and indeed, with a brave little smile, she took the hand of the Captain of the Guard and came down the gangplank; and when the crowd, almost nervously, began to applaud, she smiled again and

17

gave us a modest wave. Following her future mother-in-law, she pushed through the curtained entrance of her chair and assumed her place. At once, a trumpet sounded. The procession of mounted knights, their horses clattering on the stone of the dockside, began to move off. And the crowd, with a great cheer, fell in behind.

"So," I said lightly, trying to hide my feelings, "she'll be our Queen."

Garth, I think, had been impressed by her as well. He nodded slowly, "Unless the King changes his mind again."

"Do you think he will? With his mother right here?"

Garth laughed. "I see what you mean. I wouldn't like to cross *her* myself."

It was now after noon. Rather than following the mob, we elected to walk home through the town. After so long we knew every inch of the place – there wasn't that much to see – but there was something pleasant in watching ordinary people go about their ordinary tasks. Slowly, we strolled along the harbour front. Most of the fishermen were out at sea and the docks were now in the possession of those ancient men who sit, in every harbour, and warm their bones in the sun, watching the ceaseless movement of the waves and remembering. Behind them were sheds, where the boats were pulled out and worked on – a few men now were repairing their nets; and behind this, in a small square, lay Messina's small market. Here, sheltered from the sun by tattered canopies, wrinkled old peasants peddled their wares. There were barrels of fish and olives, and clay vessels of oil; lemons and bitter oranges; walnuts and hazelnuts, of the sort called filberts; cheeses swathed in damp cloths or swimming milkily, in the Greek fashion, in vats of brine. We bought nothing, just looked; and when we grew tired, we turned into the network of back alleys that ran toward the camp.

It was in one of these alleys, near an ostler's, that we saw them. Or rather, Garth did. He'd seen that boar, too – perhaps he had an eye for dangerous animals.

"My Christ," he murmured.

"What?"

"There. Riding out of that stableyard."

I stared: at two mounted men, urging their horses to a canter. I only saw them for a moment, and then they disappeared behind a wall; but even if I'd had a chance to study them longer, I would have found it hard to believe. St Denis and Falaise. Definitely. Certainly. Unmistakably. "But it can't be," I said. "They're with Philip, at sea."

"If they are, they both have twins . . . They must have stayed behind and hidden themselves, or . . ." Garth swore. "Of course. Why didn't I think of it? They're hostage knights to Richard."

Hostage knights: left by one king, Philip, with his ally, Richard, to ensure that their alliance would be kept. And we would have a few knights travelling with the French.

"Come on," said Garth. He began to run. We reached the stable and peered down the intersecting alley, but it was empty and so wet with slops that there wasn't even a puff of dust to prove that anyone had passed. I was almost relieved, I admit. I would never have said so openly, but the prospect of Garth fighting a man like St Denis – especially as his shoulder wasn't perfect – didn't please me. This thought, however, must have shown on my face, for Garth smiled. "Never fear, little brother," he said. "I'm not being hot-headed. If he *is* a hostage knight, I'll let my quarrel die rather than cause more trouble between the King and Philip. But there's something you didn't see."

"What?"

"That St Denis was wearing no arms. And if he truly *is* a hostage knight, what would he be doing here, dressed like that? And why haven't we seen him around Mate Griffon?"

"You mean he's hiding something."

"Himself, if he has any decency, or . . ."

What? There was an obvious way to answer the question. They'd ridden out of the stableyard; either they'd paid for the use of horses here, or stabled their own mounts. We stepped around the gate, into a courtyard. A bearded, heavy-set man was cleaning out one of the stalls with a wooden fork. He turned as we came up, setting down his fork and wiping his hands on a leather apron. I thought he was none too glad to see us, though the sight of Garth's arms made him doff his cap, and half a denier even bought a smile.

"My lords," he murmured.

"The two men who rode from here just now – were they lords too?"

He looked uneasy. "They might be, sir . . . but they don't call themselves that."

"What *do* they call themselves?"

"I'm not sure I ever heard them use a name, my lord."

"'Ever'? They've been here before, you mean? How often? What for?"

He turned to one side then, and spat. When we looked up his eyes were steady.

"All I know, my lords, is that they take horses from me one day and bring them back early the next."

"And where do they take your horses, ostler?"

"I've never asked, my lord."

"But you know. And if you don't tell me, I'll fetch half a dozen of

19

King Richard's best knights and we'll ask them when they come back."

He thought for a second. It was obvious he wanted to lie – but had no courage for it. Finally he said, "Sir, someone told me they'd seen two of my horses on the shore path to the south the day those gentlemen would have been riding them."

The shore path, south. This was the route we'd taken on our boar hunt. Returning to camp, we saddled our own mounts, swung west of the town, and picked up the path on the far side. For a time, there was no separate track to follow – the path was too well travelled – but six or seven miles along two sets of prints departed from it, heading away into the hills. We slowed, following carefully; letting our horses pick the way, trusting them to choose the same path the Frenchmen's animals would have taken. The hours passed. We sweated like pigs. Only a Norman, I thought, or a mad dog, would willingly ride out in the Sicilian sun. But finally, as dusk was falling, we reached a stream beyond which lay a long, slanting ledge of rock. My heart sank. There was no way to follow any animal across it. Stiffly, we clambered down from our saddles, letting the horses drink a little and splashing water on our own dust-caked faces. Then we looked around wearily. The landscape was unfamiliar, for, in our hunting, we'd never come so close to the sea. Now, in the distance, we could hear the deep pulse of the surf while further to the south, but also near the shore, the great brooding cone of Mt Etna spread a delicate pink glow across the darkening sky.

At length, Garth said, "This must run into the sea."

I thought for a second. "Yes. So if we follow the stream, then ride along the beach?"

"Yes, but not quite that. Hurry, though. It's near dark."

We allowed our horses to walk along the bed of the stream. Their hooves clattered and splashed, but with each step the stream itself rushed more noisily, drowning out every sound. We went on for a mile like this. Then Garth stopped ahead of me. I moved up alongside him, and followed his pointing arm: before us, in a V formed between two dunes, I could see the stream rush out to the surf whose bubbling line of phosphorescence now seemed suspended in the dark.

"Left or right?" Garth whispered.

There was no certain way to tell. I shrugged. "To the left?"

He nodded, turned his horse away from the stream, and led us along behind the dunes. If St Denis and Falaise had crossed them, to go down to the beach, we were bound to see their tracks, but remain hidden ourselves.

Perhaps ten minutes passed before Garth stopped again. I waited, then realised why, for my horse blew and his ears began twitching; he'd scented the Frenchmen's mounts. Awkwardly, Garth leaned back and down to slip off his spurs, then carefully dismounted. I did the same, and we led our animals away from the beach, into a patch of gorse, where they immediately grew calmer.

"They can't be far," I whispered.

Garth nodded. "But the wind's blowing from them. It could be half a mile yet."

We debated briefly, then hobbled the horses; if we had to make a quick retreat, we'd regret it, but we were more worried that they'd give us away. I took my bow; strung it; but decided to leave my quiver behind for sometimes the arrows rattled inside; instead, I stuck three under my belt. Quietly, we set off. It was now very dark. The surf sighed softly and a gentle breeze blew in from the sea, chilling our sweat-damp skins. With the heavy sand under our feet, we moved as silently as ghosts – but not far. After a hundred yards, Garth slowly sank to his knees, and pointed. And I saw the big, splashy tracks left by their animals, the hooves throwing up the dry, white sand to expose the darker, damper ground beneath.

We paused then, undecided on what to do next. But all at once the breeze lifted, rustling through the marsh grass that grew along the tops of these dunes, and carrying to us the sharp scent of a fire. They must be right on the other side of the hill. Garth swung his scabbard round in front of him, where he could hold it quiet, then motioned me down. Side by side, like two lizards, we wiggled up to the crest.

They were only thirty yards distant: two silhouettes huddled close to a blazing orange fire. Beyond them stretched a broad, sloping, sandy beach. Further down, untethered, their horses stood calmly. Beyond them, and beyond the white line of the surf, was the deep purple sea.

I pulled my head back. "What are they doing?" I whispered.

"The fire's a signal, or will be. Look beside it. There's a great heap of dry grass. They'll throw that on when they see a light on the water."

Garth was right; and it wasn't long before we knew it. Both of us saw it, a pinpoint of red far, far out on the sea. Then we even heard St Denis' command, and both men moved to the pile of grass. It blazed up like a torch, throwing their harshly drawn features into relief and spreading their vast shadows along the beach. But just for an instant. As quickly as it flared up, the grass burned down. And then, like St Denis and Falaise, we waited.

I think only twenty minutes must have passed, though that wait seemed much longer. We peered into the darkness, till our eyes ached. Yet, long before we saw the boat, we heard it: the creaking of oars, the pinching squeak of an oarlock. St Denis and Falaise heard it too; leaving their fire, they went down to the water. Five minutes later, one of them called out, and a moment after that we saw a shadowy movement as someone jumped from the boat, seized its painter, and dragged it onto the beach.

Voices rose and fell in the rhythms of greeting. A man laughed. Then three figures walked into the light of the fire.

St Denis . . . Falaise . . . and another. Whose face we couldn't see, but whose arms we both knew instantly: *argent, a lion rampant gules* – the field and charges of Sir Guy de Gisbourne.

Garth reached out, squeezing my arm; telling me to hold silence. But I knew his mind must be whirling with the same questions as my own. Was that Gisbourne himself, or merely one of his men? What could he be doing here? For Gisbourne, we both knew, was an *English* knight hostage to *Philip*.

For a few minutes, the men talked round the fire and then, crouching together, passed a flagon of wine. There was no way we could have heard what they said – we were too far away. But we were close enough to see the English knight reach inside the surcoat and bring something out – a cylinder – and hand it to St Denis.

Then all three men shook hands and moved back toward the water.

"A messenger," I whispered.

"Yes. And I think the King would like to read his message."

He pressed my shoulder then and we slid back down the dune, sending little skirts of sand ahead of us. At the bottom, Garth kept his voice low. "No argument now. We go back to the horses. Lead them to the stream. Then, just as we came, back to the path."

I thought for a second. "I'll give you no argument, but how does this give *us* the message?"

"Very simply, little brother. We reach Mate Griffon before St Denis, gather half a dozen men, and meet them at the ostler's." His teeth flashed in a smile as he said this – and I smiled back, for I knew it would work, and I knew there'd be a certain pleasure in settling the matter in the ostler's yard.

A thought pricked me in some fashion, and nagged as I struggled along through the sand. And, then, just as we came up to the horses, it came clear in my mind.

"The ostler – the stableyard. That's where they found Edwin!" I didn't mean this directly as a warning, and yet that was how it worked. For Garth stopped in his tracks – and was at least fully alert when a figure, crouched behind a hummock of grass, leapt upon him. It was the ostler himself. Who could only have followed us all the way from Messina, watched us tether our horses, and then hidden himself. Now steel glinted in his hand, and the man's arm clenched round Garth's throat from behind. I jumped to one side, nocking an arrow in a second, but knowing even as I drew back the string that a shot would only risk hitting my brother. In a flurry of sand, the two men rolled over: Garth desperate to keep the man's knife hand pinned, the ostler fighting to keep Garth from drawing his sword. Finally Garth gambled. He let go the man's knife hand and, with all his strength, pushed him away. Staggering back, the man slashed upwards, but his backwards momentum made him flail in vain. And now Garth was free, swinging his sword in a slanting lunge that sliced across the fleeing man's thigh. He screamed. A terrifying sound which rang in our ears. Then a huge spurt of blood shot up from the wound and I knew his life was done: Garth's thrust had cut the great artery that runs up through the hams. With a horrible bubbling groan, the man fell dead between us.

But we knew his scream must have alerted the Frenchmen, and as Garth caught his breath, we heard the pounding of their horses' hooves. Then we saw them, charging across the dunes. But now it was fully dark; with no sound to guide them, they were briefly uncertain, reining in their horses on the last hummocky dune above us. Their horses reared; and for an instant, with the sky and a few stars behind them I had the two riders in a faint silhouette. In that instant I loosed two arrows. One I knew was full on its mark; there was the *thunk* of the shaft driving home and a groan, a grunt, of life lost in total surprise. But the other must only have struck one of the horses, for I heard a high-pitched whinny of pain. Then both animals plunged into the darkness of the slope and thundered on toward us.

I had killed Falaise. His horse carried him along like a bouncing sack of grain, then deposited him not ten feet from where I stood. Quickly, I nocked another arrow and turned toward St Denis – but Garth raised his hand and stopped me. I watched, half-sickened, half-enthralled, as the two knights shuffled cautiously through the sand and began to duel.

Steel rang and flashed; the sand flew up in a kind of storm; the two figures, like dreadful shadows, leapt about. For a time it was all confusion, but then, as my own eye cooled, I could see that their styles of fighting were as different as night and day. Garth moved with the classic steps I'd watched our father teach him: first a few quick feints to judge your adversary's speed and competence, then more deliberate thrusts to find a point of weakness. St Denis, on the other hand, moved as a ferret moves, jabs and thrusts coming from all directions in a blinding flurry. I knew what this style meant. St Denis had recognised that Garth outweighed him by a stone and stood over him by at least a head. This disproportion in their strength meant that St Denis would tire first; if he was to win, he must strike quickly. Garth's best strategy was obvious. And yet he spurned it. I'd seen my brother fight at many tournaments and none ever said he was less than chivalrous – he'd win by skill and bravery, not by the chance of height and weight. So they both fought with a brutal, desperate, reckless fierceness . . . until St Denis made a fatal blunder. I saw it, even as Garth must have, and sucked in my breath – a stroke from the Frenchman that went much too high. Whirling away, Garth held his blade outstretched from his waist, his sword a kind of scythe. The blow sliced through St Denis' left leg, and from the gout of black blood that spurted up, I knew it must be mortal. He sank to his knees. But Garth never paused. Raising his sword above his head, he brought it down between St Denis' neck and shoulder, the heavy steel slicing through flesh and bone, splitting the Frenchman's chest in two. He spilled upon the sand . . . and Garth sagged down beside him, though it was I who was trembling, and could barely speak.

"Well done . . . ," I murmured faintly.

Sweat glistened on my brother's brow; his chest was heaving.

"He'll have the cylinder," I said.

"And Edwin's ring," he panted. "Take them both."

I knelt, eyes half-closed, felt through warm blood and cooling flesh. Beside me, Garth was rising. I looked about. Falaise's body had come to rest in a little patch of gorse. "Should we bury them?"

Garth shook his head. "They're no Christians. Besides, it's a barren spot and birds must eat."

CHAPTER THREE

Beginning with the lowest clerk, we ascended the ladder of nobility at the Court – knees knocking, slipping on several rungs, but climbing ever higher – and eventually gained an interview with Sir Jean DeVaux, one of King Richard's closest advisers. He heard us out, examined the cylinder (though Garth was careful not to let it leave our sight) and finally agreed that we could see the King the next morning, though only briefly. But we knew we were lucky to see him at all, for now the great camp was being struck. When we woke that next morning the beach was a mad carnival of men, horses, flapping tents and fluttering pennons. Long lines of carts, loaded with provisions, stretched along the beach and even longer lines of men, braced against the surf, passed their cargoes to the lighters that shuttled back and forth to the fleet offshore. Everything was being moved: wicker cages filled with chickens; goats, trussed up and carried along on poles; hay for the horses, salted fish for the men; and barge after barge of rocks and boulders, ammunition for the mangonels, because King Richard had heard that there were no quarries near Acre. The noise of the shouting men and screaming animals was deafening, and then, with a thunderous crack, the vast forge of Mate Griffon was doused. As we made our way along the beach, I said, "Hell must be like this."

Garth laughed. "Then I shall strive to be a saint."

The King had already gone aboard his flagship, and at DeVaux's instructions we boarded a wherry that sculled us out toward the fleet. And what a fleet it was. Thirty of the vessels were new, built and crewed by men from the Cinque Ports; forty more had been commandeered in Marseilles and Normandy; and there were even ten old tubs, rescued, judging by their stench, from the Flemish wool trade. Before leaving for France two years before, the only boat I'd ever sailed on was the ferry-barge at Kirklees ford, so I found them all impressive – at least until we approached *Rex*, King Richard's ship. She was like an island floating on the sea. Larger than any vessel in the fleet – larger than any ship King Philip had – she stretched two hundred feet in length, her huge prow forming a beak-shaped ram. Beneath her towering side, in company with half a dozen barges and lighters, we were like so many children tugging at the aprons of a cook. Our mouths agape, we stared above us. Ladders slapped down; a guard bawled out instructions. Someone pushed behind me . . . and before I knew it, I was two hands up and climbing higher.

Feeling more relief than I would have cared to admit, I reached the top and one of the crewmen pulled me across the gunwales. At once, my nose prickled with shipboard smells: pitch, warm canvas, wet rope and sawdust. All around me, men were rushing to and fro, setting sail, swinging through the rigging. A hatch had just been opened, and beneath it I could see rank upon rank of empty stalls. Once I'd listened to a drunken knight boasting about *Rex*, and now I found myself believing all he'd said: that she could carry King Richard and all his Court, three hundred knights, their horses, food and armour – enough power in this single vessel to conquer most kingdoms.

"My God," said Garth, who now tumbled down beside me, "I would never have believed a ship could be so big. Look there . . ."

I turned toward the prow. On the forecastle, a group of men were lashing shields against the gunwales. "For the archers," I said.

"Yes. At least fifty, I would think."

Fifty archers: enough to defend the largest castle. But just then a courtier, probably recognising Garth's arms, came toward us. He was a small, dark-haired man with the tight-faced features that mark a clerk. "Locksley?" he enquired. Garth nodded. "Then follow me."

Smiling at his pigeon walk, we trailed him along the deck, beneath a canopy, then down three steps to a small ante-chamber. There were benches on either wall, and a pair of doors – guarded by two sentries – at the back. "Wait," ordered our little clerk; and then, without so much as a glance at us, or the guards, he pushed between the doors which, swinging open, gave me a glimpse within. There was a single room, large and airy, filled with patterned sunlight, probably from a skylight overhead. A tapestry was draped across one wall. Against this, sitting in a high, carved chair, was a single figure: dressed in black silk, a small ruffle of white lace about her throat, an enormous ruby ring glittering on her finger. Queen Eleanor: I knew her at a glance, but then the door swung shut.

Still, we didn't have long to wait. Soon His Majesty the Clerk beckoned us inside. Staying right on his bony heels, our eyes fixed

26

rigidly ahead, we crossed the room, almost knocking into each other as he stopped to announce us: "Sire, Sir Garth Atheling of Locksley and . . . his brother."

Then he stepped aside and I saw – for just an instant – Richard, known as The Lionheart, King of England, Duke of Normandy and . . . But the instant wasn't long enough to get through even half his titles, for at once I was on my knees, head bowed, closely inspecting my boot. As a sort of after-image, I had an impression of his height and the blondness of his beard and hair. And of his beauty: if he loved other men, and other men loved him, it was easy to see why. Yet there was nothing womanly about him; his beauty had a rugged edge and his voice was deep and strong. Perhaps, I thought, his disdain for women was simply the result of seeing them so little. He was a man who lived his life among other men; a warrior who was happiest among his fellow soldiers. I thought all this as he spoke with Garth, exchanging pleasantries and asking after my father. But then he turned to me – and his cold blue eyes seemed to read my thoughts. Praying that they weren't quite able to, I put on my best smile and drew myself up beside my brother.

"So you are Atheling's other son?"

"Yes, Your Majesty . . . Robert."

Flustered, I'd pronounced my name in the Saxon manner and at this the King smiled gently. "One of my English subjects . . . whom I so rarely see. But that's all right. I like them well enough. I'm glad you're with us, and only wish your father had come as well. He's always been a good man, and a loyal knight."

This, in fact, wasn't altogether true. During the feud between King Richard and his father, Henry, *our* father had maintained a strict neutrality. "Stay out of family squabbles," he'd told us, "especially royal ones." Good advice – though, as later events showed, I never took it. But now I carefully accepted his comment with a dutiful nod. "I'm sure, if his strength had permitted, he would have wanted to serve Your Majesty."

At the sound of a soft chuckle, we all turned. It was Queen Eleanor. Her smile was kindly, but there was a knowing twinkle in her eye. "I think, my Lord, that in your recent troubles William Atheling was a *wise* man as well as a good one." At once, Garth and I both blushed: and, though I could hardly know it, this was not to be the last time in the old Queen's presence that I'd feel naked as a child. But King Richard merely laughed and, seeing our embarrassment, ushered us to a table at the far end of the room where he offered us wine. Now, with a moment to collect myself, I realised that there were three other people in the room, whom I'd barely noticed before. Beside Eleanor, with sewing in their laps, sat two other women: a small, slight Sister, almost hidden in her wimple, and another girl, also darkly dressed, whom I immediately recognised as Berengaria, Princess of Navarre, King Richard's bride-to-be. Everything I'd felt at my first sight of her, I felt again – but doubly. And I realised, with a certain pleasure, that something joined us: we were the two youngest people in the room. As well, we were both essentially spectators. What did she think about this scene? These people? The life that lay before her? Carefully, I watched her – watched her watching, if you like. For she missed nothing. Her large dark eyes flicked about the room, taking everything in; and though she worked at some sewing in her lap, I think her ears were following a dozen separate conversations. But always – like myself, like everyone – her attention came back to Richard. What did she really think of him? And what did I? I watched him as a clerk came in to consult about provisions. He listened carefully, thought a moment – then decided. And once he spoke there was no argument. He was a king. A great king. His presence, a kind of strength, radiated out from him, touching everyone. I felt it touching me . . . and for just a second felt uncomfortable. He was a Sodomite. Yet, undeniably, it was his person that you felt, not only his position. If I wished to serve him, it was not simply because he was my king, but because he was a special man. Did Berengaria feel this too? For it was the man, more than the king, she'd have to live with . . . But all at once, switching my attention from the King to her, I realised that she'd been watching *me*. Suddenly the room seemed very small and the Princess very close. Only the King's distracting voice saved me from a blush:

"Well, Sir Garth," he said, "it seems you can tell me something about two dead hostage knights – one hacked in two by a broadsword, the other skewered by an arrow. Both men, I believe, were personal friends of Philip."

All eyes in the room now turned to us. Garth cleared his throat. "I was . . . responsible for St Denis, Your Majesty. And my brother dealt with Frère Falaise."

King Richard, frowning, swivelled on his heel and stared at me curiously. "You shot him with an arrow? An odd skill for a nobleman, don't you think?"

"Perhaps, Your Majesty," I replied. "But under the circumstances I was grateful for it."

Garth paled, and I suppose my irritation at this slight of my favourite weapon showed. From the corner of my eye, I saw a smile flicker on Queen Eleanor's lips and then King Richard laughed. "I fear Falaise might not have shared your gratitude – and I'm not sure I do either. I knew St Denis, and I doubt that the world will much miss him or his friend, but you realise that King Philip will demand an explanation."

Garth stepped forward. "We can give it, Sire." Then, at King Richard's nod, he told the story of all that had happened, from our first encounter with St Denis at our cousin's camp to the final skirmish. I was proud of my brother as he spoke: Garth was a soldier and spoke like one: directly, with no words wasted, but leaving nothing out. I could see that the King was impressed; he never once interrupted or questioned, but merely stroked his beard and took everything in with a gathering frown – especially as Garth reached into his purse and brought forth the cylinder, its seal intact. The King examined it thoroughly, then asked, "You're sure, Sir Garth, that it was Guy de Gisbourne who gave this to St Denis?"

Garth's voice was firm. "I am certain, Sire, only of what I said. The man was wearing Guy de Gisbourne's arms."

"Well, no matter. Let's see what this contains." Reaching to his belt, he unsheathed a small jewelled dagger – but as he was about to cut the wax, his mother spoke. "Call DeVaux, My Lord," she said. "Let there be a witness that the seal is intact, and that we are not responsible for its contents." Eleanor of Aquitaine: she'd survived two kings, a dozen wars, a thousand plots – and not by being careless. King Richard hesitated, but then nodded. The clerk was summoned; having duly entered the cylinder into his record books, he broke the seal and tapped its contents onto the table before us.

Garth and myself, forgetting ourselves, bent forward as eagerly as the King. Then, the King included, we all looked at one another curiously: for, lying on the table-cloth, were three small chessmen and a roll of parchment, sealed again with wax. Picking this last up, the King broke the wax with his thumb and unrolled the paper on the table. We read – or tried to:

```
DQIRDMZODGYMZSXVMQDQSVEMXGFQEBXGDVY-
MEPMFDQSVPVOACGAPZGZOQEYVVAMZZVE
DVOMDPGEVZEVOVXVMZGZOVMOFEQPVZOKBDG-
YPQSQNVFGQTVGFMPFQDDMYEMODMY
BQDGQZVMFVZEGXMQDQSQYBDMQPAZQYCGQYP-
MYOAYBMDMGVGVOXMEEQYDVOMDV
MPADVMFGDVFMCGQXQAZQYVXXGYPAYVFVNVYG-
ERDMFQDFGGEYADFGGEQDVF
MZFQCGMYTVOZGZFVGEFVNVNPGQZQDVFEQPEVY-
GXMOYQVOQDFVQDVZFRMOFV
NXVGYYVFFMZF
MYVOEFGGEQFEAOVGEQSABTVXVBBGEFQGMX-
QPVOA
```

The King stepped back. "And what do you make of this, Sir Garth?"

"Nothing, Sire."

"And you, young bowman?"

I took a breath. "It must be a sort of message, but written in a . . . cipher."

He looked at me, and was about to speak — but paused: for his mother now came forward and took up one of the chessmen. "These are my arms," she said. "The arms of Aquitaine."

I picked up another of the pieces myself. All three were rooks, swordsmen with the arms of Aquitaine painted on their shields. But then, as I examined them more closely, I saw that each was armed in a different way as well: with an arbalest slung across their backs. I said, "Sire, I think these come from France."

Queen Eleanor smiled. "In truth, Aquitaine is Aquitaine, but sometimes the ignorant claim it as a part of France."

"I know, My Lady. But your arms could have been painted on any chess piece — these, however, were probably *made* in France."

She looked at me curiously now. "And how do you know that?"

"If the piece was English or Norman, My Lady, this figure would more likely have a longbow, not an arbalest. Some of our men do use them — I know the King has one — but the weapon is much more popular with the French."

King Richard had been listening carefully, quietly stroking his beard. Now he said, "You are saying, then, that a Frenchman sent this message?"

"Most probably, Sire."

"Then you must mean . . . ?"

I hesitated. "I *suggest* it, Sire. I'm not certain."

He smiled. "You *are* your father's son."

"And none the worse for that," said My Lady Eleanor. "William Atheling is no one's fool."

"Nor am I. And if that message was sent from Philip, and if it was so important that St Denis was prepared to die for it, then I must know its meaning." Quickly now — how many other problems must have lain before him on that day? He turned to the clerk again. "Tell DeVaux. This man, Robert Atheling de Locksley, is to join our Household as the Royal Cipher Clerk."

"Sire —"

I think the man was trying to object, but King Richard hurried on. "Further, both he and his brother, Sir Garth of Locksley, are hereby made My Lady Berengaria's Equerries." He turned to Garth. "You will join her ship, and sail to Cyprus with her bodyguard. You understand?"

"Of course, Sire. You do great honour to our family."

He nodded then. "I do. And see that you do not dishonour the honour that I do you." Then, his eye shifting to me, he added, "I must know that message. The trip to Cyprus will take two weeks – have it for me then."

"Sire," I said.

But, from across the room, Eleanor's soft chuckle came again. "Remember, My Lord, your new clerk is scarcely older than a boy – you'll frighten him."

I was about to reply, but then I had no chance: because now, for the first time, Berengaria spoke – her voice so soft it was little more than a whisper though it stilled them all. "Never fear, My Lady, my new equerry won't fail us."

She looked at me and smiled, and then – I couldn't stop myself – I smiled back.

"Thank you, My Lady," I said.

And then, with bows, we left the room.

CHAPTER FOUR

At dawn the next morning – 10 April 1191 – King Richard's great fleet sailed forth from Messina.

Garth, myself, and all the men who'd taken the Cross under the Locksley pennon – along with the Princess Berengaria's not inconsiderable retinue – were berthed on a small galley, the *Bellefleur*, which Richard had specially outfitted for his bride. Standing at the foreward rail, I watched the dawn spread like gold over the swelling sea as the huddled shapes of the fleet and the dark line of land slipped away. Being smaller and slower than Richard's warships, we sailed before the rest, but in the end I knew we would be the tail of the dog, for it was inevitable that the fleet would pass us long before we reached our destination. But slow or not, we were on our way, and now, as equerry, I was wearing Richard's arms emblazoned on my tunic. What more could I ask?

On the voyage from Marseilles to Messina, I'd discovered the tedium of a long sea journey; during the next ten days, I learned it all over again.

Once out of sight of land, we barely seemed to move; there was only the sun and the sea and the endless creak of the rigging to mark our slow progress. By the seventh day, all but two of the slowest ships had passed us, and now, like a duckling paddling after its mother, we chased the main body of the fleet. For Garth and I, life fell into a routine: the bell that woke us each morning for breakfast, our noon-time visit to the captain to discover our course, a glass of wine in the shade of the cabin as the hot sea sun finally set. Garth, who hated the boredom even more than I did, spent much of his time training our men, setting up contests for our archers, drills for the pikemen, and playing at mock battle with our best swordsmen, Nicodemus and Ranulf, once a page at Locksley Hall who had replaced Edwin Scathelock as Garth's squire. As for myself, I worked a little at my archery, but otherwise stayed away from

Garth's simulated brawls. My duties as equerry were almost non-existent; the Princess, apparently prone to sea-sickness, spent most of her time in her cabin, attended by Carlotta, the little nun who was her favourite servant.

Still, if the Princess did not keep me occupied, the ciphered parchment did; indeed, as the days passed, and I came no closer to discovering its secret, it was even with me in my dreams. In a way, I was grateful. As Garth paced up and down the deck, he could only count the waves and passing birds while I had a truly Royal Puzzle to pass my time.

In truth, I understood little of ciphers. I knew that the ancients had sometimes written messages across the joins of a scroll wrapped round a staff so that, unrolled, the letters would all seem to be broken in the middle, and only someone with a staff of the exact same size could piece it together again. I also remembered a story that Herodotus tells: Histiaeos, governor of Miletus, planned an insurrection against Darius, King of Persia. Wishing to summon allies, he had his plans pricked out in ink on the shaved head of a slave, who was kept within the town until his hair grew back and only then sent through the Persian lines. Caesar, I knew, had sometimes written secret writing, replacing one letter by another – so "b" was written as "a", "c" as "b", and so on. Augustine had done something similar, as had Charlemagne. But had the author of this parchment? Day after day I laboured in my cabin – until, so Garth said, the crew began to call me "the youthful hermit" – and day after day I got nowhere. Systematically, taking each letter of the alphabet in turn, I substituted it for another; the combinations seemed infinite, the results gibberish. I then assumed that the last letters of the message spelled King Philip's name; and, using this as a key, I thought that here and there I could discern a little sense. But not much. Though I've never been the sort of person who'll admit defeat, I confess that by the tenth day out from Messina I really had no idea what to try next.

In the early afternoon of that day, feeling a trifle sorry for myself, I came up on deck to get a breath of air, slumping down dejectedly on a hatch cover. Garth saw me and came over. Slicing a lemon with his dirk, he handed me half. "Any progress?"

"None, I'm afraid. It's as bad as . . . I don't know. Tickling trout." I scowled; then, sucking on the lemon, I decided that it precisely matched my mood. After a moment, for I'd missed our noon-time meeting with the captain, I asked, "What about *our* progress?"

"Little more than yours, I fear. According to the wind-rose and the stars, we're two days from Paphos."

Thinking of the captain, I said: "Do you trust that man?"

"No. He's a greedy fool, who drinks. The crew all hate him. But the mate is much respected and evidently he's the one who does the navigation."

I smiled. "You've been sampling shipboard gossip."

"What else to do?"

Just then, from behind us, a small voice whispered, "I beg your pardon, Master."

Turning, I saw Carlotta, Lady Berengaria's attendant. She couldn't have been more than fifteen, but dressed in the full black robes and wimple of a novice Benedictine she already looked a widow. Her eyes were lowered, and she fingered her beads nervously.

"By your leave . . . Her Highness, the Princess Berengaria, would see you on the after-castle deck."

I nodded. With a quick curtsy, she turned and fled, disappearing beneath an awning. Garth grinned. "One day, when you're a bishop . . ."

"I know," I said. "You'll be my constant guest."

He laughed. Then, more seriously, I straightened my clothes. I was more than a little nervous. Garth might laugh, but I was hardly happy that my feelings for the Princess had become so obvious. Admiring a lady from afar was safe enough – the sort of thing minstrels liked to sing about – but now we were sleeping just three small rooms away. I told myself to remember who she was and would be; and who I was. But it made no difference. She rarely came on deck; but my ears were so tuned to her step on the companion-way that I was always there to help her to the rail. And when one evening, seeking the privacy of dusk, Carlotta had used the deck pump to wash the long raven fall of her lady's hair, I'd tried mightily to look away – and failed. I knew, then, what I felt toward her. But did she feel anything for me? At night, lying on my sweat-drenched pallet, I told myself that this was a question I'd no right to ask, that I *dare* not ask. And when, having asked it anyway, I sometimes answered that certain looks and glances, the fact that her visits to the deck always seemed to coincide . . . But no, I couldn't think that. Not now, especially, when I was going to see her face to face. Composing my expression as best as I could, I set off across the deck.

Climbing the ladder to the after-castle, I skirted the two men who were working the long rudder pole. Beyond them, in the farthest corner, an awning of white sail cloth had been set above a simple table and two large chairs. The Princess, her back to the sea, was sitting in one of them. Her dress and blouse, both simple, were of

Phoenician blue and her hair hung across her shoulders like a jet black wave, set off by only a single gold circlet. I bowed; then, lifting my head, noticed that the table was arranged for chess.

The Princess smiled. "Do you play, Master Locksley?"

"Yes, Your Highness. My father taught me and I played at school."

"Ah, well, we're equals then, for my father taught me too. He always said that chess was as close to life as any game could be – kings in jeopardy and queens attacking. Would you agree?"

I wasn't quite sure how to answer – and guessed, from the glint in her eye, that my discomfiture was entirely intended. "Perhaps he had a point," I said with care. "I suppose it depends on who the players are."

"Now don't be too much a diplomat; I like you because you're not. In any case, since I have no king with me to attack, perhaps you'll take his place and play a game or two?"

"Of course, My Lady."

"Please then . . . take this chair."

Opposite her, I was struck, as I'd been in Richard's cabin, by a mixture of pride and shyness that marked her apart from others. Now, picking a white and black piece from the board, she said, "Who shall hold and who shall choose?"

I smiled, suddenly picturing her as a little girl playing with her father. "As you wish, My Lady."

At my deference (though how else might I have spoken?) she cocked her head a little to one side. "All right. I shall hold – *that* is my wish. But I have another."

"My Lady?"

"Play fair, Master Locksley. I'll have no pandering to my position – I've had enough of lick-toe courtiers to last a life-time. In the game, we can be equals. If you try to lose, I promise you'll be an equerry without a head."

I nodded. Then, bending forward in her chair, she hid her hands behind her back, shuffled the two pieces, and held her arms toward me. I chose black, which gave her the advantage, and seeing the colour of the piece she scowled, as though I'd allowed her white on purpose. Nonetheless, she advanced her king's pawn. I countered – and ten minutes later mated her. As easily and as quickly, I won the next three games. Frowning down at her last defeat, her lips pushed forward in a pout and I wondered if my fairness had been well advised. Then, suddenly, she laughed.

"Ah well," she said, "chess has never been a woman's game."

"You play very well, Your Highness."

"Not half as well as you, Master Locksley. But it makes no

difference. My father taught me the game only to give him company – and I thank you for giving it to me."

"My Lady, it was my great pleasure."

Taking one of the pieces from the board, she studied it and then glanced up at my face. For a second – just a second – I thought there was something in her eyes that asked me for something different than the formal chatter of an equerry. Or was that my imagination? But then, almost with relief, I saw her eyes falter and look away. Putting the piece back on the board, she spoke: "As I said, my father always claimed that this chessboard mirrored life, but I don't believe it. The king is weak and can scarcely move but castles run about at will and the knights hop like fleas." She laughed then, very softly. "And I mustn't forget you, Master Locksley. They tell me you want to be a priest – then, being all spiritual, you'll move the way a bishop does, passing through the other pieces."

"Your Highness, I'm not a bishop yet."

"But come, you must be something . . . If you're not a king or queen or castle, knight or bishop, then you have to be a pawn, the little piece that is sacrificed to the whims of all the others. Anything is better."

"I'm not sure, Your Highness. Most men are pawns. They're sacrificed, as you say, by greater men – that's their fate – but they don't have to be unwilling."

"Yes . . ." For a second, absently, she looked away and murmured: "I suppose that's why there's no piece for princesses upon the board, because they're pawns as well – moved by others, traded for advantage . . ." Her mind, just playing, had led her here, but as her eyes moved back to mine, a trace of bitterness tightened across her lips. Carefully, I said:

"But a princess can marry a king, My Lady, and become a queen."

She smiled – the briefest instant – then shook her head. "No, Master Locksley. Kings and queens ally themselves, men and women marry . . . and since some kings aren't men, some queens are spinsters." Then, taking a breath, she smiled more easily and glanced away again. "Have no fear, Master Locksley, I know the stories. They say the King is a Sodomite, but he's not even that. He's like my brother, a warrior with a warrior's vanity. He only loves his face reflected in a sword, and his pleasure spends itself in blood."

"My Lady –"

She smiled quickly now. "Come, you mustn't be embarrassed. Some day you'll be a priest and priests hear everything."

"My Lady, I'm no priest yet."

"No? What are you, then?"

What was I? I was a man, but that was the one answer I couldn't give. So I murmured: "A pawn, My Lady, as you said." But, in saying this, I held her eye. And now she didn't look away. Faintly, as though in a dream, I could hear Garth's voice badgering at Ranulf to bring more practice swords for the men, and the awning over us flapped in a gust of wind. The deck creaked; the ship rolled gently in a swell . . . and then Carlotta arrived with a tray of fruit and wine and the moment ended. The Princess poured, and as she handed me a cup, I realised I was holding a chess piece, clutched tightly in my palm. She smiled, a cool, proper princess once again. "Are you thinking of your puzzle, Master Locksley? It's still unsolved?"

I nodded. Most mornings, she'd asked after my progress. Now I said, "I only hope I deserve the confidence you showed in me."

She coloured slightly, remembering her boldness in King Richard's chamber. Then, picking up one of the pieces herself, she said, "What do you think they mean?"

"I'm not sure, My Lady. I've spent more time thinking about that parchment . . ."

"Yet they must mean something?"

"Yes, I agree. They're so carefully made. And they can't be there by accident. They must mean *something*, but what that meaning is . . ."

She leaned back in her chair. "Could they not be a sort of password? A signal that the message itself is genuine?"

"I've thought of that, My Lady. In fact, it's the only explanation I can see. Still . . ."

"Yes?"

I sighed. "They were *inside* the cylinder. A password, or some sort of talisman witnessing that the message was genuine, would be better shown before the receiver of the message accepted the cylinder itself."

Her forehead furrowed – and I saw the sort of frown that must have been on my face these past ten days. Then she said, "And why *three* rooks – surely that's another question? Three rooks bearing My Lady Eleanor's arms . . . and were they not all black?"

"Yes, Your Highness."

"But, in a game, there would be only two. It makes no sense." Except, I knew, it did make sense, if only I could see it. Looking up, the Princess added, "Did you bring them with you? Could I see them?"

"Of course, My Lady. They're in my cabin. I'll go and get them."

She nodded, but as I rose, she stopped me. "Wait. We'll all come with you." With a gesture to Carlotta, she led the way across the deck. With the crew watching us a trifle curiously, we went down the ladder, then along to my cabin. It was very small; as we pushed through the curtained doorway, even the Princess had to duck her head. And, once in, there was scarcely room for three of us to stand around the little table that folded down from the wall. It was here I'd spread out the parchment, the three stone rooks holding it in place. The Princess picked them up, one by one, and turned them in her hand. In the days since I'd come aboard, I hadn't looked at them closely, but now I did again. They were, indeed, very carefully made. Even in the dim light of that little room they were impressive: beautifully carved and polished, Queen Eleanor's arms painted on the soldiers in exquisite detail.

"Do you think," said the Princess, "that these men were made especially for the message, or were they simply taken from an ordinary set?"

I thought for a moment; it wasn't a question that had occurred to me before. Then, slowly, I replied, "As you said, My Lady, there are two black rooks in an ordinary set of chessmen . . . so these must have been specially made, or at least assembled from two separate games." I considered a moment longer. "And I'd say the latter because most of the details are carved but the arms are merely painted on."

"You mean, if the arms had been part of the original set, they would have been carved as well?"

"Exactly."

"Then the arms themselves must have significance. Or else why bother?"

Why indeed?

And then a thought began to nibble at my mind.

"My Lady, if you would . . . Could I bring your chess set here?"

"Yes, most certainly." She turned to the little nun. "Carlotta, if you please . . . ?"

For an instant, the girl hesitated; and, once she was gone, I think we both knew why. For now we were alone. I stiffened a little and for a moment she glanced nervously at her hands. But then, with a toss of her head, she looked around. "Your cabin is very small, Master Locksley."

"I am comfortable enough, My Lady."

She smiled ruefully. "Sometimes I wonder if my comfort isn't purchased at the expense of others'."

"My duty, Your Highness, is my comfort."

She smiled again. "You are well spoken, Master Locksley . . . and kind as well."

I wasn't sure how I should reply – but then I didn't have to, for now Carlotta came through the doorway. Taking the board from her, I set the men into their positions. And as soon as I'd done so, the thought that had been forming in my mind was suddenly clear. I must have grinned, for the Princess reached out and touched my arm. "What have you found?"

"The answer, My Lady. Look. As you know, every square on a game of chess has its name. For your first move, you put your pawn on square *King three*. Now, our trouble in looking at these three black rooks was forgetting about the board. Why *three* rooks when the game has only two? And why take the trouble to paint them with a queen's royal arms?"

She gasped. "*Queen's rook three* . . . on the black queen's side." Her finger pressed the square. "But what can it mean? How does it help you solve the cipher?"

"Because in a cipher one letter is substituted for another – for 'a' we write the letter 'b', for 'b', 'c', and so on. What is important is the key, and now we have it. Watch . . ." I took up my slate and chalk, drew the diagram of a chessboard and then wrote out the alphabet, a letter in each square. "You see? In square *Queen's rook three* we find the letter 'x' – which is used in the cipher to stand for 'a'."

"And 'b' is written 'y', 'c' is 'z', and 'a' is 'd' . . . The black rooks are the key – they tell us where to start."

Quickly, moving the chessmen aside, I took up the parchment and with my slate before me began transforming its gibberish into . . . more gibberish.

After ten lines, I was almost sick – it didn't work.

The Princess, peering over my shoulder, groaned. "But you *must* be right."

But I wasn't, clearly. I'd missed something vital. Staring at the board, I tried to put myself into the mind of the man who'd devised the scheme. What had I overlooked? Three black rooks . . . marked with a queen's arms . . . a chessboard . . . It *had* to be. But then the whole business began to swim before my eyes: black, white, black, white. And all at once I saw it – literally.

"It's the *colour*," I exclaimed. "It doesn't mean just the black queen, but the *black* squares. The alphabet isn't written on every square, but only on the black ones."

"So – every second one?"

"Exactly . . . which changes everything." I began to scribble the twenty-four letters of the alphabet on my slate, but only on the black squares. Now *Queen's rook three* on the black was "m". This is what the code would use for "a"; and so "n" was "b", "o" was "c", "p" was "d" and so on. When I reached "z", I went back to the beginning and quickly made up the entire alphabet both as the code had it and the message read. Or so I hoped. And as I began to translate, the long, garbled string of letters at last made sense:

Rex Francorum Angliae Regi salutes plurimas dat. "Regi" dico
The King of the French greets the King of England well. I say
quod nunc es, mi Joannis. Ricardus in Sicilia nunc jacet, sed in
"King" because that is what you now are, my dear John.
Cyprum debebit vehi ut ad Terram Sacram perveniat. Insulae
Richard is in Sicily, but he will have to go to Cyprus in order to get
regem, praedonem quemdam, comparavi ut classem Ricardi
to the Holy Land. I have bribed the king of that island, Isaac
adoriatur. Itaque leonem illum domitabimus. Frater tuus mor-
Comnenus, who is a kind of pirate, to attack Richard's fleet; and
tuus erit antequam hic nuntius tibi advenerit, sed simul ac mei
thus we shall tame that lion. Your brother will be dead before this
certi erint facti, alium mittant.
message reaches you, but as soon as my men have certain report of
the fact, they will send another message.
  Amicus tuus et socius, ego Philipus te valedice.
  I, Philip, your friend and ally, bid you farewell.

"Dear God," the Princess whispered. "John – that must be Richard's brother?"

"Yes, My Lady."

"And he's in league with Philip?"

"So it seems. And if we don't warn the King, you'll lose a husband before you're married and a kingdom before you're crowned."

And, I could have added, as a reward for unravelling the secret of this code, I might lose my life.

CHAPTER FIVE

It took a moment – or perhaps it was the look on my face that told her – for the Princess to understand the full meaning of what we'd discovered.

And then, I saw, she was afraid.

Her eyes faltered, and I realised again how young she was. So young, so far from home, so much alone. And who could she trust? I even saw her dart a glance at me: Could I be trusted? But she recovered herself at once. She *was* a princess, after all. The fear fled from her eyes before determination and a flash of anger.

"Master Locksley, we must warn the King immediately. Send the captain to my cabin. I'll command him to make all haste. Carlotta, go –"

I raised my hand. "My Lady, I would advise against it."

"Why? If what that message says –"

"I know, and I agree. We must warn the King, but tell the captain nothing. Consider a moment. By hastening to the King, the captain will only put himself and his ship in danger. Why should he bother? He was only paid to transport us, not to fight. Besides, even though he's from Marseilles – ruled by the King of Aragon – I know he favours Philip."

She frowned, and then for a long moment her eyes looked into mine. What did she see? A boy, a man? A servant or a friend? A stranger or a countryman? Perhaps she didn't know herself, for finally she asked, "Can I truly trust you, Locksley?"

I tried, then, to look at her as frankly as she had looked at me. "My Lady, how can I answer? If you don't trust me, anything I say is meaningless."

Her face reddened. For an instant, she glanced away. Then, when she met my eyes again, she said, "I'm sorry. I *do* trust you. If I can trust anyone, it's you – I feel it. Forgive me. And tell me what you would advise."

"Return to your cabin, My Lady, and act as normally as possible – don't arouse suspicion. Meanwhile, I'll find my brother and tell him what we've discovered. In an hour, have Carlotta summon us – in the usual way – and we'll work out a plan together."

"An hour? But we haven't time to waste!"

"No, but the King's ship is a day ahead of us, no more . . . An hour one way or the other makes little difference. We must act quickly, but not so quickly that what we do is foolish."

She thought for a second, then nodded. "All right, an hour." With a last, anxious look toward me, she gestured to Carlotta and left my cabin. Quickly, I went back to the message. Now was no time for error. But there was no error. Writing King Philip's words on a separate sheet of parchment, I erased my slate, then stepped back on deck. Everything looked normal . . . but then, I told myself, why should it not? The wind had dropped a little – just when we needed it – and the sea seemed flatter, the ship wallowing in a greyish, greasy swell. I knew just where to find Garth, but wandered casually about, so I seemed to discover him by accident – leaning on the foreward rail, staring straight ahead, as though the very strength of his gaze could draw the horizon closer. He smiled as I came up.

"Ah, the young chess player – a game for princesses, I hear, as well as kings."

I shook my head. "No. Here's the game kings prefer to play." I handed him the message.

"The cipher?"

"Yes."

He read the message through – then read it through again.

"My God . . . no wonder St Denis and Falaise were so ready to die! Hostage knights, conspiring against the King . . . Damn Prince John to hell!"

"Yes. But you remember what father always said?"

"'The sickliest whelp becomes the meanest dog.' How right he was."

And the dog had bitten our family before. Richard had been Henry II's eldest son – and the favourite of his mother, Eleanor – but John had been much closer to his father. Using that influence, John had induced old Henry to grant a large section of our lands to Hugh Fitz Stephen, one of his closest friends. As soon as King Richard had ascended the throne, we'd gotten it back, but only at the expense of what little favour we still held in the Prince's eyes.

"What do you know about this Isaac, King Comnenus?" I asked.

Garth shrugged. "Very little . . . and what I know is only rumour. He's some sort of vassal king to the Byzantines, not much more than a common pirate. His ship – 'his great ship *Imperator*' – is the source of his strength. It is said to be enormous, oared by three hundred galley slaves and with a monstrous ram. He uses it to prey on the shipping that travels round these coasts."

"So he *could* attack the fleet – he has the power?"

"Yes," Garth said, "though only if he could be assured that there'd be no retaliation, assurances that Philip must have given him."

So the Holy Alliance was broken. There was, we both knew, little reason to be surprised. It had only been put together when Christendom had learned that the Saracens had driven the Frankish kings from the Holy City. Till that very moment, King Richard and Philip had been bitter rivals and Leopold of Austria, the Alliance's third leg, had made a career of balancing back and forth between them. Now, it seemed, the fragile restraints of piety, and the prospect of shared plunder, had vanished. For Philip, the temptation had been too great: at one stroke, he would rid himself of his ancient rival; avenge the insult done his family by the rejection of his sister; and set his own man, John Lackland – a weak, poor king he could easily control – upon the English throne.

"We must warn him, Garth,' I said. "It's the King's only chance."

"But how?"

"I don't know. We can't tell the captain – he'd only sail us round in circles until he was sure the danger had passed."

"And in any case," Garth said, "now that we need it, the wind has died."

We both turned our faces upwards; the air was still – even the constant creaking of the ropes had almost ceased – though a little rain had now begun to fall.

"What about a bribe? You claim the man's greedy, a drunken fool. The Princess must have some silver."

Garth shook his head. "He'd only be suspicious."

"But money buys suspicion."

"Yes, but think. He'd want to know the reason for our haste. If we didn't tell him, he might sail anywhere – and how would we know? Are you a navigator? And if we *did* tell him, or if he guessed, what would he do? Philip wants Richard dead. So what might he pay for Richard's bride?"

I hadn't thought of that, but now I thanked God that I'd spoken to the Princess as I had.

"So," I said, looking cautiously about me, "we have to take the ship. That's what it comes to."

"Yes, dear brother . . . and I'm not sure the exercise won't do me good."

I smiled. "Well," I said, "you're the soldier. How do we do it?"

43

But, instead of answering my question, Garth gave a quick shake of his head. I turned. The mate was coming toward us, at a run. He was a tall, sturdy fellow, also from Marseilles – clear-eyed, with a look of intelligence about him. He nodded to me, then doffed his cap and turned to Garth. "My lord," he began, "by your leave . . . Could your Lordship station a few of his men with the horses?"

Garth frowned. "Why? The ostler should be with them, or at least one of the boys."

"Yes, my lord, but shortly now it will begin to blow –'

"The wind is calm. We were just cursing it."

He smiled – with a hint of the humour a sailor finds in a landsman's ignorance. "My lord, soon you'll be cursing it for different reasons. Look, sirs, behind us. Those clouds off our stern. On these seas, you get sudden gales like this. Sudden, short, but bad enough while they last. We're not far from Cyprus, sir, and a good anchorage, and we should get there before the worst of it reaches us. But if we don't, and one of your horses breaks out of its stall, he could kick our bottom out with fear."

"Just a minute," I said. "You say you're heading for port?"

His eyes looked nervous. "Yes, My lord. Those are the captain's orders. The wind should drop in a day or so. Then we'll go on, along the coast."

Garth looked at me, then grabbed the mate by the arm. "I don't care what the captain says. We must close up to the King with no delay."

The man, held in Garth's grip, began to look truly alarmed. I cut in. "Don't be afraid, just listen. If we don't reach this anchorage, would we be in any danger? What would happen if – how do you say it? – if we ran before this storm?"

"Well . . ." He licked his lips. "The King's ship should be just off Paphos and we'd reach him quickly. The wind's taking us in just that way. There'd be no great danger. Your Lady, the Princess, might be sick and we'd perhaps lose a little rigging, but nothing more."

"So you'd not be afraid to do it?"

"No. But by your leave, my lords, I must take orders from the captain – who is a very . . . cautious man."

Garth squeezed his arm more fiercely. "Never mind that coward – we'll take care of him. Hold to your present course and there'll be ten marks for you when Paphos comes in sight."

"We order you," I said, "in King Richard's name."

For a second longer, the poor man hesitated; but then he gave a nod of assent and moved away. Garth slapped my arm. "Get your dirk, little brother. I'll fetch Nicodemus and meet you by the captain's cabin."

I nodded and dashed across the deck, which was now alive with men who were hastening to take down all but the smallest stretch of sail. My dirk, in its scabbard, I shoved under my belt, then threw on a cloak to cover it – a cloak I would have needed anyway, for as I stepped outside my cabin the rain began to fall in earnest, pelting down from a black and swirling sky. Lightning flickered on both horizons; sails, sliding down the rigging, snapped and flapped like enormous pennons in the rising wind. The crew was already scattering sand around the deck, but even so I slipped and skidded as I ran across it.

Garth, Nicodemus, and two of our men were waiting outside the captain's door.

"Is he inside?" I shouted, lifting my voice against the wind.

"Of course," said Garth. "In a gale, the captain's place is always in his bunk." He turned to Nicodemus. "Wait here. If we call, come to our aid. Meanwhile: no one passes."

The little Spaniard nodded. Garth, motioning me to step aside, hammered on the door with the handle of his sword. "Captain! This is Locksley! A word with you!"

A moment passed. Garth called again. There was still no answer, and he lifted his foot to kick the door down. I touched his arm. "Wait," I said. "You keep your sword at the ready."

With my shoulder, I drove against the lock, once, a second time; then, with a splintering sound, the whole frame gave way. I staggered back. Garth pushed past me. The captain, a greasy apron slung round his heavy belly, stood inside the fetid cabin, his red eyes watering with a mixture of drink and fear. Yet, to give him credit, he was prepared to defend himself. Perhaps one of the crew had warned him, for he had a sort of sword in his hand, and even raised it. But with one wide-sweeping swing of Garth's great broadsword the man's puny weapon was sent flying to a corner. At once, with a groan, he dropped to his knees. "My Lord, have mercy! I beg you!"

For an instant, I wondered if Garth's contempt hadn't overcome his knightly training: for he lifted his huge sword above his head – wood splintered from the cabin's ceiling – and seemed to slice the man through the parting of his hair. But, swinging down, he turned the blade flat and it hit the captain's skull with a tremendous clang, as though he'd struck a stone.

With a groan, the captain toppled forward, unconscious, his mouth working like a fish.

"Tie him up," said Garth, "and lash him to his bed."

I did so – though, as I made the knots, I wondered to myself whether he wasn't the luckiest man aboard. For now the storm was raging. By the time I finished, and we'd told the mate that the ship was ours – or rather his – the sky above had turned into a roiling mass of cloud and the moaning wind was sucking long lines of spume from mountainous, crashing waves. Garth had already told the Princess what we'd done, and she'd given him three marks in silver to show the mate that we meant to keep our word. Pocketing them on the after-castle, I wondered if he still felt he'd struck a worthwhile bargain. Exerting all his strength, he wrestled with the steering oar as we nosed down into a cresting wave that smashed against us with a hammer blow that shuddered through the ship. Rain streamed down our faces, stung against our skin. If you lifted your eyes, the wind was blinding.

"Get below!" he shouted. "You'll do us no good here!"

Now it was our turn to obey, for the mate was right: any aid from us would only come through prayer. Drenched, staggering, we careened across the pitching deck in search of shelter.

What is a storm? Wind and water, furiously mixed – and mixed with fear. What a potion! That night, for the first time, I drank it down. At times – perhaps it was my youth, perhaps it was the novelty of the liquor – it seemed to make me drunk, and I felt within myself a sort of frenzy and excitement that matched the world that seethed about me. The sky raged, the sea boiled, and when night fell and you could no longer see their separation, it was as if we'd been lifted up into some unworldly sphere. Yet, standing my turn at watch (for we provided more than silver to keep the mate's courage up) I felt an excitement that I'd never felt before. So much power swept against us – but it only swept us on. Shouting against the wind, I called for more. And yet, at other moments, that same power made me shrink with horror. I watched as three men struggled to secure a hatch – one of its wooden bolts had loosened – and I watched as a gigantic wave, splitting the bow, carommed down the gunwales on each side, sweeping them to oblivion. Later, just as the mate had prophesied, the horses gave us trouble, one snapping its halter and breaking from its stall. Terror blazed in the poor beast's eyes; he bucked and lunged. A great wave sent him plunging to his knees. Struggling up, he began to flail and kick – and would have kicked the ship's belly out if Nicodemus had not dodged between its slashing hooves and slit its throat. A bloody rain sprayed everywhere, soaking through our clothes. But what could we do? What could anyone? Indeed, by midnight, there was nothing to do. With Garth and half a dozen of his men the mate could barely hold the steering oar steady on its course. The few sails he'd tried to set were tattered rags. Rigging and spars were scattered everywhere. One

46

corner of the foreward castle had been sheered away. The foreward hatch, beneath the impact of gigantic waves, had split, so now we were taking water. No, there was nothing anyone could do but hope and pray and wait for dawn.

And at last dawn came.

With it, an abatement of the storm; it didn't cease, but the wind steadied and the seas no longer fought each other but tumbled the ship onward with a kind of grace. With pikes and axes they cleared away the wreckage of the night. Around seven, we hoisted sail – now we seemed to fly – and a little later the galley fires were lit once more so we even got a breakfast of mealie porridge and hot wine. Returning to my duties as equerry, I bore two portions below.

The Princess smiled as I came in, though her face was pale and her hair dishevelled; it was clear she hadn't slept.

"Master Locksley. It is very good to see you."

"My Lady. You may not be so pleased after you've tasted what I've brought you, but it's the best they can do for now.'

Carlotta, sprawled on her bed, groaned at the very mention of food, but the Princess managed to spoon a little down, then sipped the wine. Colour came slowly back to her cheeks, spirit to her eyes, and she smoothed her hair into some kind of order. Then she smiled. "I'm afraid, Master Locksley, that this is the best *I* can do."

I smiled in return. "My Lady, you do very well."

"How is the ship?" she asked. "Where are we?"

"The ship is in no danger. We're not sure where we are, the mate hasn't had time to check. He thinks we might be off Curium – a while ago he saw some ruins, a temple in the hills."

"And King Richard? How far behind are we?"

"Not far. The wind is with us and we have a look-out posted."

"Then you – we – all of us – have done all we can."

I nodded. "Including our friend the mate, My Lady. I was wondering if you might give him the rest of his purse yourself . . . and it might be politic, I think, to spare a few coins for the captain's pocket. We've set him free, but a little silver might pacify his temper."

She smiled. "Were you raised at court, Master Locksley, to know politics so well?"

I was wondering how to answer when there was a knocking at the door. I opened it. Nicodemus stood there, grinning. "Sails, my lord! The horizon is thick with them. We've found the fleet!"

I turned, hastily bowing my leave, but the Princess rose. "Master Locksley, I wish to come."

"My Lady, the seas –"

"On your arm, I'll be safe enough."

We hurried out. The wind whipped her hair against her face and pressed her skirts against her body. Her cheeks grew flushed and I smiled at the pleasure she was taking. Clinging to my side, she staggered to the rail. By now the sky had cleared, the sun was out, and white clouds tumbled overhead. On the horizon, a dozen white sails shone like tiny silver birds. Garth came up, still looking exhausted but smiling broadly. "There they are – we've done it!"

"You're sure it's them?" the Princess asked, shading her eyes and squinting against the sun and wind.

"It could only be the fleet, My Lady. But they're still nine or ten miles off. We'll have to get a little closer before we can run our signals up."

"And how do you know King Richard's ship will see them?"

"My Lady," I explained, "he probably won't. But each ship will be ordered to pass the message on until it reaches him."

She nodded, and clung more tightly to my arm – seized, I told myself, by the excitement of the moment rather than by any affection for myself. The ship, like an enormous porpoise, plunged from wave to wave, spray flying up like a prickly mist against our faces. The masts groaned with the weight of the wind, and as we changed course slightly the billowing sails, swinging on their arms, cracked like whips. The fleet drew nearer; and now, on our right hand – or starboard, as I'd begun to call it – we saw a long spit of land, a cape of rock and pines. Then I heard the mate call out – he'd found a current that pulled us in toward land but which, with the wind, drew us even faster toward the fleet. Sucked between King Richard's ships and the shore, we soon made out the shape of the nearest vessel, and at once our signal flags went streaming up the mast. It was a simple message: red for *danger*, yellow for *attack*, black for *enemy*, a blue stripe for *acknowledge and repeat* – but it was enough. The first ship replied at once, and a second later we saw its own flags run out.

"It's done, My Lady," I said. "Even if he's miles from us, the King will soon be on his guard."

Indeed, within ten minutes the whole fleet veered off, heading for the open sea, and as they sheered away, one huge set of sails stood out: *Rex*. All our eyes turned over the portside bow, staring toward her.

After a minute, the Princess said, "He's coming closer."

"And look," said Garth, "she's flying *our* signal flags."

An acknowledgement of the message? For a time, that's what I thought. But then, from high in the rigging, we heard the look-out shout, "Sail! Sail! Off the starboard quarter . . . !"

We all swung round, peering down the ship, but our view was

48

blocked by the masts and after-castle. Just then the look-out called again – a call that was near enough to screaming. Yet I didn't understand. The *stern*? We'd come a long way, and very quickly, but the main body of the fleet still lay off our bow – and *starboard* was the *landward* side, that cape . . . But then the mate came running up. "An enormous ship," he gasped, "heading directly for us."

At once, Garth took command. "Robert – help get the Princess to her cabin. Nicodemus – our men, the archers, get them out on deck."

He ran off down the ship, but as I went to take the Princess's arm, she pushed my hand away. "Go with your brother, I'll make my way." I hesitated. "Go," she said – and then, before I could stop her, she hoisted her dress around her knees and ran back toward her cabin. I watched her reach it safely, then followed Garth, joining him and a dozen other men who were staring, in horror, over the after-rail.

"Dear God," I murmured. But it wasn't God, nor quite the Devil – just the *Imperator*, King Isaac Comnenus' killer ship.

"Look at her," said Garth. "She's twice *Rex*, ten times us . . ."

This was nothing more than the literal truth. Though she still stood more than a mile away, I gasped at the size of her. Like some gigantic bird of prey, she'd been lying in wait behind that cape, pulling out to sea even as the fleet sheered off: our warning had been just in time. But now, it seemed, the messenger would pay the price. The view we had of her was broadside, the hull curving up at least thirty feet above the water. Two rows of oars gleamed wetly with each stroke, rising and falling like the legs of some loathsome insect. Three masts soared above her decks, each carrying an enormous triangle of sail. With this vast stretch of canvas, together with her oars, she was bearing down at us at lightning speed – and indeed she had the look of lightning, for her prow was a huge brass ram that flashed against the sun.

Garth again began issuing orders, and for the first time I saw the hope that a commanding presence can create even in a hopeless situation. Buckets of water were set in position against fire-arrows; axes were distributed to the crew to cut away grappling hooks; and two of the huge hatch-covers were wedged against the gunwales to provide cover for the archers. But, as the ship grew closer, I saw it *was* hopeless, and after a moment Garth took me to one side.

"This ship is finished, little brother."

"Of course. They know that coast – that current is drawing us right to them. They'll grind us into tinder."

Garth calmly surveyed the men, who were still rushing about

49

their tasks. "I'm glad you see it – but I hope they don't." He turned to me. "You understand your duty, then?"

"My bow is in my cabin." With a grin, I squeezed his arm. "See what use your broadsword is across twenty paces of open sea."

He didn't return my smile, only looked me grimly in the eyes. "Listen. There's no time for foolishness. You have to get the Princess clear. Take the water-boat. You'll get wet in a sea like this –"

"Garth –"

"*I command you.*" Then his voice softened. "You *have* to do it."

Inside, I felt myself trembling, but I could still think clearly enough to know he was right. "Come with me then."

He shook his head, then looked toward the crew. "If I leave, they'll go to pieces. Besides," he added – and now he *did* smile – "I'm the better swimmer." He slapped my arm. "Take Ranulf to help you. I want Nicodemus with me. Go now – you'll need time to get well clear before they hit us –"

"Dear brother –"

But with a shove – the sort of blow he'd dealt me a hundred times in boyhood – he sent me sprawling toward the Princess's cabin, then turned away, hurling himself into a group of men who were rolling a water-cask across the deck. I staggered to my feet, then almost fell again as the Captain brought us hard about, the booming voice of the oar-leader calling out the order from below-decks. The group around the water-cask went flying every whichway, the barrel itself thundering to the rail and bursting through it with a splintering crash.

Making my way across the heaving deck, I groped down the companionway to the Princess's cabin. The place was a total shambles – furniture, bedding, chests and clothing lying helter-skelter. The Princess herself was on the bed, comforting Carlotta, who was whimpering with fear, her wimple and dress askew.

"My Lady, quickly, we must leave the ship at once."

"Leave . . . ? Dear God, Locksley, I can barely move and poor Carlotta –"

"Don't argue, just get something on over your dress – a cloak, a blanket, anything." Then I stepped forward and grabbed Carlotta, shaking her hard and dragging her to her feet. "Stop your snivelling. Gather up your lady's jewels –"

"Locksley –"

"My Lady, if we don't move now we're all as good as dead." For a second, her eyes were furious, but then she nodded. "All right. Carlotta . . . Quickly now . . . we must do as he says. Get my box . . ." But now I wasn't listening. Whirling round, I dived back through the door, climbing the steps two at a time and shouting for Ranulf to come. Somehow, in the clamour that now filled our little ship, he heard me and came running. "Do you know the watering-boat?"

"Yes, my lord."

"You're to launch us in it."

By then the women had readied themselves and I steered them across the confusion of the deck. Garth, I saw, had been thinking well ahead of me: two Locksley men were standing guard by the portside rail where the little craft was lashed. "Hurry, my lord, she's almost on us."

Carlotta was weeping and almost paralysed with fear – Ranulf just threw her in. The Princess, for her part, merely took my hand and stepped nimbly to the bow. Ranulf I sent to the stern for balance, while I got myself amidships – if that little craft could be called a ship. Taking a firm hold of the oars, I signalled to the men above us, "As smoothly as you can . . ."

In a series of jerky, giddy drops we descended to the sea. Carlotta screamed; the Princess pressed her hand against her mouth. Ranulf, who I suppose had never rowed across a stream in all his life, looked round wildly, turning white. And then, with a slap, we struck the surface. Using one oar, I pushed us away from the hull, then got the other into the water just in time to turn the bow into a swell. Like a cork, we bobbed to its crest, then, with a sickening lurch, slid down the opposite slope. Desperately – fearing we'd be dashed against the *Bellefleur*'s side – I stroked. The next swell hit us. Up we went, jerked forward as though from a mangonel's arm, only to be dropped the next instant like a bucket down a well. I dug down with my back, strained forward with my shoulders, and in a moment my hands were raw. I looked around for help. But somehow, in our violent launching, Ranulf had hurt himself and was sprawled across a thwart. Alone, I tried to pull in rhythm. Forward, back, up and down; then up and down again. For a full ten minutes, all I saw was the bottom of that boat, a glimpse of sky, then my boots again. But at last, as we drew ourselves beyond that current, we finally rested. To my surprise, as I glanced round, I could see that we'd edged a little closer to the shore and that the *Bellefleur* was a good eight hundred or a thousand yards away. *Rex* was still well out to sea, though drawing ever nearer, while *Imperator* . . . For an instant, we couldn't see her, And even as I forced my brain to accept what this must mean – that *Bellefleur* was directly in her line – we all drew in our breath. For there she was. Beyond *Bellefleur* and yet *above* her, the great brass ram came like an enormous beak snapping down across the middle of her body. The sound of the impact, like that of a huge tree crashing down through the forest, spread across the water and we watched in horror as our little ship was split and gutted. Men flung themselves into the sea, I saw a horse spin like a leaf through the air, and all the time *Imperator* kept coming on, her double rank of oars beating the water into froth, smashing down through spars and planks and men in time to the deep, booming beat of the galley drum.

"Dear God, Robert . . . your poor brother." The Princess stretched her hand toward me – but suddenly she pointed and cried out: "Look . . . there he is! Three of them; floating there!"

I squinted, and with a sudden burst of happiness realised she was right. *Bellefleur* was lost but Garth, at least, was saved. I longed to go to him, but forced myself to look to shore. "Pull!" I cried. "Pull on!" Again I picked up the rhythm, pulling with all my strength, pulling until the blood rushed through my ears. At last the Princess, reaching forward, grabbed one oar and looked anxiously into my face.

"Master Locksley . . ."

I glanced up: and realised that there was more than the sound of blood booming in my ears. We'd come across a bar, where the surf was breaking, and now glided into a wide, calm pool about a quarter of a mile from shore. I leaned forward, panting. If this coast was safety, then we were safe.

Ten minutes passed as I slowly caught my breath. Sweat burned my palms; it was as though I had a yoke upon my neck. Then, gently, the Princess touched my shoulder. "Look," she said, "the King's ship . . ."

I turned; and if I'd had any breath to lose, I would have lost it in that moment. The two great ships were closing: closing in an eerie silence that, like the now brilliant sun, enclosed them with a crystal clarity. The Princess gasped. I heard Carlotta pray. And we all stared ahead, our hearts urging our King to victory though I could scarcely see where that victory might lie. *Rex* was enormous – yet she was only half the length and breadth of the Byzantine ship, and the *Imperator* stood three times as high above the water. Each of her masts possessed a watchtower and even from this distance we could see that each round turret held a dozen bowmen waiting to fire down upon the English decks.

Yet, as we watched, I realised I had underestimated my King's sea-going skills. He had recognised his problem and used his one advantage: namely, that *Rex* was a sailing ship while the sails of the *Imperator*, a galley, were almost useless unless the wind was perfectly behind her. Thus, as the two ships drew on, apparently on a collision course, *Rex* suddenly swung a fraction seaward and sheared alongside the behemoth ship. Now, sharp but faint, we heard a clattering sound drift to us across the water: the sound of a hundred English shields being lifted above their heads as *Imperator*'s archers loosed their shafts. But then – like a strangely louder echo – a different rending sound carried above the pounding of the surf: the crunching of *Rex*'s hull against *Imperator*'s starboard oars. Now, as if caught in some gigantic eddy, the Cypriot ship swung in a helpless spin. In an instant, *Rex* was past; and if she'd taken some casualties from the Cypriot archers, they didn't stop her own for suddenly a thousand arrows darted toward *Imperator*. The two ships separated. But *Imperator* now had one broken wing. King Richard, using the still strong wind, darted round her, poking, prodding, and then finally catching the wounded monster off her guard. Helplessly, her stern drifted toward *Rex*'s bow, and though her ram wasn't the terror of the *Imperator*'s, it was enough. Both ships shuddered; locked; and when they slowly swung apart we could see the jagged rent torn in the Cypriot's hull. Worse: other ships from the English fleet had now drawn closer, like dogs around a wounded stag. Arrows pricked her skin on every side. Her sails began to burn, curling upwards like enormous flakes of ash. And at length she began to founder, settling slowly on her haunches, her great brass prow swinging round in rage. Her crew gave her up then, flinging themselves into the sea, where, I knew, the English archers would calmly pick them off. Then I imagined the horror of those who wouldn't even have that slim chance at life: the galley slaves, at least three hundred strong, naked, faint with heat, screaming as the water thundered between the decks, reaching the ankles of those chained up in the lower rows, then rising higher, above their waists, their chests, their necks . . .

At the last, I looked away and picked up the oars once more. The Princess continued staring out behind us, while Carlotta sobbed, curled up below the gunwales. From Ranulf, there was no sound. His face was very pale, his eyes were closed, and blood from a long gash in his leg dripped into the scuppers. His right arm was broken, a white tip of bone at his elbow having torn right through the flesh. Without help soon, I realised, he'd lose his arm and perhaps his life; and so, when we reached the beach, we wasted no time in celebration, but carried him into the shade of a few scraggly pines. At once, the Princess took command.

"Carlotta. Go back to the boat and fetch my jewel box . . . Master Locksley, take your cloak and lay it over him . . . He must be kept as warm as possible."

As I did this, Carlotta returned with the brassbound jewel box that was the only thing the Princess had salvaged from the wreck.

Opening it with a key strung round her neck, she dumped its contents across the sand – a fortune in gold bracelets, glittering emeralds, ruby rings and diamond brooches. Then she handed the empty box to her whimpering servant. "There's a stream along the beach. Fill this up and bring it here – and don't dare spill a drop!" As Carlotta hurried off, the Princess began tearing long strips from the hem of her dress and carefully bound up Ranulf's gash. She looked up at me. "Do you have a knife?"

"Yes, here . . ."

But she shook her head. "Take it, and cut two lengths of wood – long enough to run from his shoulder to his wrist."

I nodded – and was somehow not astonished at her coolness. When I returned with two trimmed branches, she took my knife and cut away Ranulf's jerkin, then – with gentle care – took that awful splinter of glaring bone and pushing it into place. Coming from his swoon, Ranulf screamed in agony – I had to hold him – but she kept on, ignoring the spurts of blood that splashed across her from the wound. With the bone replaced, she then tore at her dress again, tying my two twigs on either side of his straightened arm.

"He'll be all right," she finally said, "unless the rot sets in. But we must be careful when we move him."

"My Lady, I thank you for him."

She smiled slightly, but then sagged back against a tree. She was exhausted – and looked as though she'd passed through a charnel house. Her face was streaked with Ranulf's blood, and her dress was drenched with it. But for me she was still beautiful – too beautiful – and deliberately I looked away, and gazed off-shore.

Rex, and the other English ships, were still grouped around the *Imperator*'s grave, waiting as small boats searched the waves for survivors from *Bellefleur*.

I said, "We should build a signal fire. I'll get some wood."

The Princess rose. "Here, I'll come. There's driftwood near that stream."

Together, we walked along the beach. We said nothing, but with every step her tired body brushed against mine and I had to slow to match her pace. She was here, I thought: which made this place a perfect spot. But I knew that I should truly wish to be a thousand miles away. Or would that make a difference? Even when I closed my eyes, I could see nothing else. She was so beautiful – even more beautiful in rags than finery. Her dress had been torn to half its length, the soaking cloth drawn tight against her body. When we reached the stream, she waded in at once and began to wash herself, splashing the frigid water across her face and arms and legs. Beneath her tattered gown, her flesh curved and swelled. As she washed, the blood, all pink and watery, flowed down her thighs and legs, swirling in the current. She looked up then, and feeling my eyes upon her, her breath came hard, her small breasts swelling.

"Dear God," she whispered.

And then someone strange – someone who was not myself – reached out and took her by the shoulders – felt their firmness pressing in his palms – and drew her close. Her mouth met mine, her body pressed against me. For a single instant there was nothing but the salt taste of her lips and the burning of her hip . . . and then she moved away.

"My Lady, I beg you –"

"Shush," she said. "Not 'beg'. That's one thing with me you'll never have to do." Then she smiled and took my hand. "Let's find some wood and build our fire."

CHAPTER SIX

It wasn't until early evening that we were taken off that sandbar – a receding tide trapped us behind it – and as we clambered onto *Rex*'s deck, dusk was already falling. Attendants hurriedly led the Princess and Carlotta away; DeVaux, greeting me warmly, took me to Garth while Ranulf was carried below deck to the infirmary.

My brother greeted me with a mocking laugh. "A beached fish, I hear."

I replied in kind. "A drowned rat – I see."

He grinned; but then, as this faded, his face looked very weary and serious, and I asked, "How many?"

"Six. Two when we were rammed. Four jumped but never got out of the water."

"Nicodemus?"

"He's all right. A boat took him to one of the other ships."

We both slumped down onto benches loosely covered in straw. The ship, at the best of times, was crowded; now, packed with survivors from *Bellefleur*, there was almost no room at all and we'd been given a cubbyhole not far from the stables. I could hear the horses stomping and with a nod in that direction I asked, "I suppose . . . ?"

"All gone. And all our armour – most of the men don't even have their bows." He sighed with resignation. "We may get to Acre, but we won't be much use to the King."

For Garth, I knew, this was a very dark moment, but thankfully his misery was soon dispelled. Now that we both knew the other was safe, we each fell asleep, slumped like two stable boys hiding from their master: a sleep that lasted several hours, though it only seemed like a moment before a hand was shaking me by the shoulder. It was a messenger from DeVaux; the King wished to see us. We both looked incredible: a beached fish and a drowned rat, but now with straw stuck all over us. Still, there was nothing we could do but follow the messenger onto deck, where we saw that the stars were out and the ship was getting under way. As before, we saw the King in his cabin, but this time everything was different; this king was no diplomat, worried by rumours of intrigue, but a general surrounded by the trappings of war. He wore his surcoat over a heavy, quilted tunic and an unsheathed dirk was stuck under his belt. Having destroyed Isaac's terror-ship, the King was now determined to raze his kingdom; as we waited, messengers were being dispatched to other commanders in the fleet and Guy de Lusignan, King of Jerusalem, who was already in the Holy Land. Perhaps because of all this activity, our meeting itself was brief, and for a dozen reasons I was glad of it. I told him about the code and how it worked, then gave him the message, which I'd been able to remember almost word for word. I watched his face as I did this; I was, after all, telling him that his brother and his chief ally were betraying him together. Yet his face showed little reaction – a slight tightening of the lips – until the very end when he looked between us, his eyes flashing, and swore us to secrecy. We agreed, of course. He seemed to relax then, and his glance became kind. Speaking formally, but with true feeling, he next thanked us, both for himself and on behalf of the Princess. Finally, as a token of his gratitude, he told us that his armourers would replace everything we'd lost and that four chargers and eight horses of march would be provided for us from his own stable. Garth, I could tell, was overjoyed.

"Sire, I would ask for nothing more – you have made it possible for me to live again."

The King nodded, and then, with an appraising look, turned to me. "I know," he said, "that you will share in your brother's pleasure, but you've served me specially well, Master Locksley. Surely there's some boon I can grant you?"

Given what had happened between the Princess and myself, I knew what I had to say. But it took me a moment to blurt it out. "Your Majesty, I would like to ask one thing . . . but I'm afraid that you'll misunderstand."

"I'm a king, Master Locksley, but not so foolish as that might lead you to believe. If I don't understand, I'll tell you so, and then you can simply explain. Go on."

I nerved myself. "Sire, I have been equerry to the Princess Berengaria – a great honour – but we are about to make war and the Princess will be kept far from danger while I desire to fight." Did I? I suppose so. But I knew I couldn't be alone with the Princess while the King was absent; I didn't trust myself, or her.

Richard frowned. "Do you have a horse?"

"No, Your Majesty. But I could use one of Garth's."

"Can you use a sword?"

"Not so well – but I'm excellent with a bow."

"You mean, you'd rather be a foot soldier than an equerry?"

"Your Majesty, yes – by your leave."

He smiled sceptically. "Your training as a scholar hardly suits you for it . . . though, I confess, I've been gaining the impression that you know more than books."

"Your Majesty, I beg you – grant this wish."

He shook his head. "I can't. A foot soldier? Think how humiliated your father would feel. No, if you're to fight I'll have to knight you – and for your service to the Princess and myself I'll give you arms and armour."

I was dumbfounded. And just a touch ashamed. To be rewarded in this way by a king whose bride I'd dared . . . But then there was no time to feel anything, for I was kneeling, with Garth beside me, and the King gently laid his sword upon my shoulder – once, twice, three times. Then he intoned the accolade:

> Itel valor deit aveir chevaler
> Ki armes portet e en bon cheval set.
> En bataille deit estre forz e fiers . . .

Reaching down, he slipped his hand beneath my arm and helped me to my feet. "Rise, Sir Robert Atheling of Locksley . . . Avencez . . ."

I couldn't quite meet his eyes, but at last I found my tongue. "Sire, I will by God's good grace so act that I may win your regard and high approval."

He smiled. "Thank you, sir. I trust you will. Indeed, I think you'd better for I know I'll not gain the approval of the Princess. She'll miss you greatly."

As he said this, his voice was light and I could see nothing in his eyes that gave me any hint of the thoughts behind them. Did he know anything? Would he care, even if he did? To him, just as she'd said, the Princess was a pawn, to be sacrificed in the interests of his alliances. He didn't want her as a woman. But what did he really think of her and what sort of life could she find with him? For an instant, I felt another sort of shame – for I was abandoning her. More: this was betrayal. For as I stood before the King, as I felt that power which radiated from him, I knew that this really was my wish – to serve him in every way I could. But then Garth touched my hand, and with bows and final courtesies, we left the room.

We went back on deck. The night air was fresh but pleasant, the stars brilliant. With all sails set, Rex's great hull hissed through the water. Walking to the starboard bow, we stared out toward the dark, bulky forms of the land. A line of phosphorescence marked the shore and golden splashes in the hills, huge bonfires, showed that the Cypriots were closely watching our progress.

After a time, forcing a joviality I could scarcely feel, I clapped Garth on the back and said, "Let's get some wine. We have an excuse to celebrate. We've both been rescued, and you'll be wearing the King's armour and riding one of his chargers."

Garth grunted. "I might celebrate, Sir Knight. But you, I suspect, would only be drowning your sorrows."

At once, I looked away. I had told him nothing of what had happened, and I said nothing now. But Garth, I suppose, knew me better than anyone alive and after a moment, when I still hadn't answered, he put his arm round my shoulder. "You know what the fishermen say about the sea, little brother?"

"No. What do they say?"

"Just that it's full of fish . . . If one slips your hook, only wait. You'll soon catch another."

I stared out toward the Cypriot coast, the same curving beach where we'd stood today. A memory; that's all it could be. A dream, that must never be real.

I murmured into the darkness, "But what if you don't *want* another?"

Ubique bellum parabamus: on all sides we made ready in war.

And there is nothing like war to make you forget love. For the next two days, I lost myself in the clang of armourers, the bustle of ostlers and carpenters, the constant excitement and rumour as messengers passed between the ships. What was happening? Would we attack? Where? When?

All our questions were answered soon enough. Sailing north, *Rex* led the fleet past Cape Arnauti, Kokkina and Morphou Bay. Then we struck inland, at the port of Kyrenia. As we entered the small, crescent-shaped harbour, it was obvious that the population had long since fled, hiding in the hills north of the town, or making their way inland toward Nicosia. We landed with no opposition, the fleet careening close to the beaches, and off-loaded soldiers, horses, supplies. This was all madness – I kept wondering why Isaac Comnenus, if he had any army at all, didn't strike; we would have been pushed into the sea without lifting a sword since no one really seemed to know where they were. But by evening we'd grouped ourselves into some sort of order, and with a flurry of excitement received word that we were all to assemble in the square.

We marched in by torchlight, rivulets of flame snaking through the steep, narrow lanes of the town. Huge shadows raced up the walls of the deserted houses. Armour glinted like gold; pikes flashed; and the horses, edgy in the press of bodies, reared and plunged, striking sparks from the cobblestones. Garth and I were both mounted now, and as we reached the open square we peered across the sea of men and fire to the King and his chief knights, who'd grouped themselves beside a fountain in the centre. What a fearsome sight they were! If we were an army of the Lord, we looked that night like Viking devils or the Goths who swept away Rome. Pitchy smoke coiled upward from the torches as though from Hell, and the shields of the knights flashed like dragon's eyes. I recognised their arms – Sir Gavin Hursey: argent saltire sable, sword piercing a mullet or; Sir William Fleetwood: per pale nebuly or and azure, six martlets counter-changed; Geoffrey Corbet: azure two ravens argent; Sir William Chambers . . . But then, irresistibly, my eyes were drawn to King Richard himself. He had mounted the edge of the fountain, and DeVaux was holding an enormous torch above his head – a light that seemed to turn our king into a statue of gold that could only make me think of pagan idols. His hauberk flashed like a serpent's scales – even his hands were gloved in mail – and as he lifted his shield, with its two golden lions, and brandished his huge axe above our heads, our army roared. Soldiers began thumping the butts of their pikes on the ground, and beating their shields with the flat of their swords. Then the call went up – "*Christo duce!*" – as though from a single throat. Finally, as this mighty roar echoed away, the King waved us all to silence and began to speak. "Friends," he cried, "Normans! Men of Poitou and Anjou! Men of England! Listen to my words! We have come far together, and have endured much, but when we left Messina, I felt certain in my heart that our true journey had at last begun. But God has willed that our cause be interrupted once again, this time by a man who is surely as much a heathen as Saladin himself. He calls himself a king, and a Christian, but he has attacked an army that intended him no harm, an army whose only purpose is the Lord Our God's. This is blasphemy – and for that blasphemy we shall punish him. He has fled from here, like the coward he is, into the mountains, where he has a nest. It is called Nicosia, and is guarded by a fortress called St Hilarion. Tomorrow we shall meet him there – and there tomorrow he shall die!" Then, lifting his axe again – his hair flying around his head like a wild halo against the night – he gave his great battle cry, "Remember the Holy Sepulchre!" which we answered as a man, our mailed fists smashing on our shields in salute. With the sound still echoing in our ears, the marshals formed us into ranks and we marched from the town.

No army likes to march by night, but in this case there were few difficulties. The road was straight and well-marked, so it was impossible to get lost, and though the hills above us could have been used to lay a dozen ambushes, it would have been difficult to deploy a substantial force against us; in fact, we met no resistance at all. Slowly, we trudged onwards and, increasingly, upwards, perhaps making a speed of two or three miles in an hour. We managed to maintain reasonable order. Garth and I stayed at the head of our men, while Nicodemus – who'd now rejoined us – herded them along from behind. The hours passed. Muscles began to ache. Soon, our undershirts were drenched in sweat (armour is the hottest clothing known to man) and mist, forming against the metal, ceaselessly trickled into our eyes. Gradually, however, dawn broke against the cliffs, casting a silvery light that threw lurid purple shadows among the cedars, and after a time I could see a large building clinging to a slope ahead of us. At first, I took it for Isaac's fortress, but it turned out to be a large abbey, as deserted as the town. We turned in, grouping ourselves in its courtyard, and ate breakfast – a meal consisting of porridge, herring and bread, washed down with a cup of wine, that was doled out to us from the back of the kitchen carts.

When we'd finished, all men with banners, including Garth, were ordered into the abbey to receive their orders. Seeing no reason against it, I went along, placing myself at the edge of the mob that crowded into the refectory. After a time, King Richard entered and mounted a table at the front of the room. Now, very carefully, he began to outline his plans. There was no hot oratory, I noted, only logic – and great detail. This, I knew, was his strength as a warrior. Everyone knew precisely what had to be done, and why. His strategy, he said, was based on both geography and history. The main city of the island, Nicosia, lay inland, where it was relatively safe from attack by sea. Most of its defences lay to the south, along the coast, and to the east, where fairly easy ground invited invasion. For years, the islanders had paid relatively little attention to Kyrenia and the northern coast because the city was protected here by rugged hills. Only one road cut through these hills, and that could be protected by the castle of St Hilarion, which overlooked it at a narrow pass. In fact, however, this was the weak point of the island's defences, and twenty years earlier a brigand named Reynald had successfully attacked from precisely this direction, calling the road the keyhole to Nicosia. If that was true, then St Hilarion was the lock: if we could take the castle, or by-pass it, then the island would lie within our grasp. To capture it, using no more than two thousand men, King Richard intended to attack on both flanks. Archers and infantry would approach from the north; the King, leading ten battles of knights, mounted archers and infantry, would strike in the south. As the heralds read out the order of battle, we heard that the Locksley pennon would fly behind the King's.

At eight that morning, after a little rest, we marched out from the abbey. The sun, already, was scorching hot. By noon, our throats were parched and I felt the trembling weakness in my muscles that comes from too little water. Finally – thankfully – as we approached the pass, the King's marshals came riding down the line, ordering a halt for food and water. Sliding from my saddle, I followed Garth – his spurs jangling, his scabbard slapping at his thigh – to the water pot. As we took our turn at the dipper, we both looked up toward the high-sided pass, half-blocked by a towering pinnacle of rock. "Just beyond there," said Garth, "and we'll see it."

But it took us two hours to travel that final half mile. We waited as stragglers caught up the pace, and then the men were ordered to drink their fill and shelter as best they could in the shade of the carts and trees. Ahead, in fact, the King even pitched his tent and retired inside to sleep. As he saw me frowning at this leisureliness, Garth grinned and pointed upwards. "Look at the sun."

"I don't need to. You can't escape it."

"Yes you can. See how the pass runs north and south? All morning, and for a few hours yet, the sun *must* shine from behind the castle into our eyes – as it is doing now. So the King waits. But soon enough the archers will have it in *their* faces and we'll feel it on our backs. Those are the small details, little brother, that win great battles."

Is that why we won? Then, I didn't know; later, I didn't care. When the trumpets finally blew, and we re-mounted, I felt a strange detachment overcome me. At the time, I assumed it had something to do with my peculiar situation, the *absence* I had so deliberately created in myself. But later I came to understand that this was a general state. It was not fear exactly, but rather a state that rendered fear unreal. It was there, but as though in a dream. And indeed everything had the quality of a dream, each scene very vivid but unconnected to the last . . . The sunlight shimmering in the dust before us. Echoing trumpets, swords pounding shields, pikes thumping the earth. Shouts, half-heard; orders, half-understood. The great pressing weight of the men at your back . . . We surged forward. Then, high above us, we could see the castle rising up on one side of the pass: battlements, enfilading towers, bailey wall and portcullis gate. The men on the ramparts were black dots, their arrows jabbing needles of light. We thundered ahead, and then the long, plaintive call of the Signalman's horn filled the valley. Now, in front of us, the infantry quickened their pace to a run and the archers drew two arrows each from their quivers, nocking one and placing the second between their teeth. I heard the King's voice, *"They cannot see you!"* he cried, and then they moved onward, infantry first, two men deep and staggered in line, their shields chest high and then higher, forming a wall of iron and wood behind which the archers dashed in a crouch. We saw them reach the northern wall. Then, with that ghostly sound, that sound like no other – the sound of tearing silk, the sound of a bird's flight in the night – a thousand shafts leapt up. And as soon as he saw them go, the Signalman sounded his horn again, the King shouted his battle cry and my saddle jolted beneath me. All at once I was galloping. Dust swirled up around me. Garth, half a length away, seemed lost in a mist. Then I heard – saw – felt – another volley of arrows climb into the air, and realised that our own mounted archers were giving us cover as we dashed through the pass, directly beneath the walls of the fortress, to its southern side. Somewhere close by a horse groaned in agony, and I felt an arrow slice past my face. Then, all around me, men and horses were dying, as the archers on the ramparts found their range. But they were too late. Too many of us were past. Following Garth, I cantered up the slope of a hill, and stared down at the castle's southern wall.

We drew up, our horses snorting loudly, and gasped for breath ourselves. Then Garth grinned and shouted wildly, "They have lost! They have lost!"

I could see he was right. On this side of the castle, the walls were vulnerable, the ramparts poorly defended, for they'd never expected anyone to make the dash we'd just made. From the knoll where we'd stopped, we could look down, beyond the walls, and see the panic that was beginning to build. The townspeople from Kyrenia who'd taken refuge inside the castle were flying in all directions, holding their hands over their heads in a pitiful attempt to ward off the rain of arrows that continued to fall from our archers on the northern flank. I knew what those arrows were like: triple-barbed, with loose heads that came off in the flesh – even a small wound could be fatal. As well, our men had now begun to use flaming pitch, and even as we watched smoke billowed from a granary near the keep. Then a rumbling sound made us look round; the ram had made it, though the cart was stuck with arrows like a pincushion and one of its traces was empty where a wounded horse had been cut free. But it was there: a huge millstone mounted on its axle which we'd taken from a mill in Kyrenia. "Come on," said Garth. Wheeling our horses about, we trotted down the slope, joining the rest of our forces.

King Richard himself now took charge. The horses were led away – a horse can pull a cart, not push it – and a score of esquires, fully armoured, took up position behind the ram. Then, at the King's signal, the mounted archers moved forward, and though I couldn't lay claim to their great skill, I gave a wave to Garth and trotted ahead to join them.

"Be careful, little brother!" he called.

"Save your sympathy for them," I returned, pointing to the distant ramparts.

In three ranks, we moved up to the castle; then, just as we came within enemy range, the King shouted and our first rank sprang forward. As their first volley went up, the second rank charged and finally – the air now thick with arrows – the third rank, including myself, made its dash. As I loosed my first shaft, I groaned with disgust – it would scarcely reach the castle wall – but my second, let go just as I pulled up, flickered away to the ramparts; if someone didn't keep their head down, he would feel its sting. Wheeling, I dashed back, crouched low in my saddle and steering between the horses of the first rank, which was now charging again. As I pulled up, out of range, I could see that the esquires with the ram had advanced, beneath the protection of our fire, to the base of the wall. Now I could hear their sing-song shout as they began to swing the great ram in its sling, and as the archers on the ramparts turned their attention to this new danger, we advanced more boldly, firing as we went. I stared upwards. On the walls, directly above the cart, I could see men passing boulders in a line – like buckets to a fire – and I aimed a shaft. It flickered overhead. I aimed again . . . but to pause for even an instant gave the archers on the wall a chance to find you and an arrow thudded to the earth just in front of my horse. Swerving, I galloped away to the left. But then, reining in, I found a target – indeed, we all began to do so – for in attempting to shoot straight down at the base of the wall, the Byzantines were forced to expose themselves more and more. I watched one of my arrows take a man high in the chest, toppling him straight back off the wall, while another, catching its victim in the arm, sent him twisting away in agony. For twenty minutes, we maintained this lethal harrassment, losing among our own forces only two horses and one man wounded. By this time, every blow from the ram was raising a huge cloud of dust, and the King had rallied his knights just out of bowshot, waiting for a gap to appear. Waving to Garth, I saw the flash of his sword in return. Then the ram crashed again, and a shout told us that a breach had been started. I now had two arrows left in my quiver. Making a last dash, I loosed both of them and as I wheeled my horse round a huge section of the wall collapsed – like a dyke crumbling before the sea – and with a tremendous, thundering roar the King and his knights surged forward. Pouring through the gap, they leapt over the fallen rocks of the wall and tore into the hordes of soldiers and townsfolk within. Turning my horse, I charged after them, and in a second I was lost in a whirl of smoke and dust and flashing steel. The noise was awful; men and animals cried out in agony. All at once my horse faltered – for a moment, I didn't understand that his belly had been sliced open beneath me and his guts were dragging behind us like the tail of a kite. Clinging to his neck, I crashed to the ground. Shaken, I rose to my feet – just in time to see a Cypriot charging me with a studded ball and chain. He stopped. He swung. I stepped forward. The chain wrapped round my shoulders. I embraced him, dirk in hand, stabbing his back often enough to kill a dozen men, and finally pushed him away, into the steaming offal of my poor dead horse. The scene around me was madness. I stood in a pool of blood, and as I wiped the sweat from my face I saw that was blood too. Except for the knights, with their arms, it was impossible to tell friend from foe. I looked round for Garth, and saw him, still on his horse, near the wall. Then I held my breath. A Cypriot, in leather armour, leapt down behind him and began to throttle him from behind. But with a terrific wrench Garth dug back with his elbow, driving the man down the horse's rump and another of our knights, wheeling about, hacked the man through the shoulder. I saw the King then. He too was near the wall, with a group of knights who'd surrounded a cart where a dozen Cypriot soldiers were making a stand. What an awful sight that was. With their little short swords, the Cypriots couldn't even get close to our knights; and, because of the height of the cart, our knights couldn't properly strike them. So, in a grisly harvest, swords flashed like scythes, literally chopping the Byzantines off at the knee.

As best I could, I now made my way through the mêlée to Garth. All around, men were falling. The ground was black and slippery with blood, and now smoke was added to the huge clouds of dust. For our men, I saw, the battle was now a form of labour, a sort of butchery. But, in a final, desperate move, a small group of Comnenus' men charged toward the King, driving Richard and his leading knights back against the castle wall. Together, Garth and I saw the King's predicament: his great figure stood there above the rest, his axe whirling in the air, threads of blood spinning from its gleaming edge like rain. Yet, despite his incredible strength, he was cut off and far out-numbered, and with a cry Garth lunged toward him. Running at full tilt, leaping across the fallen and parrying a dozen blows, I followed after him. I was a knight; and if I'd not truly earned my spurs before, I did so now, a dozen times. My sword became a steel extension of my hand, catching flesh and blood and slicing through. Finally we reached the tangled, flailing pack of fighters, and if I'd turned half-mad with fear and blood-lust, the madness I now saw in my sovereign's eye stopped mine, like a greater pain that cancels out a smaller. He was death alive. He lived for this, the carnage and the horror; he revelled in every mighty swing, relished each blow as it struck home. But there was no time to think. The tide that had enveloped Richard now swirled round us. I beat off two men, slashed another across the arm. Then – God only knew where he'd come from – an enormous figure reared up before me. He was a Turk, with swarthy features and a turbaned head. His axe was as tall as I was, and though I managed to parry his first awesome blow, it knocked me sideways, slicing a gash along my cheek. I staggered. For that moment, my sword arm limp, I stood defenceless. The axe came up . . . I felt nothing, truly. Not terror. Or horror. For a moment longer, my life just went on. I was exhausted, so I heaved a breath, as naturally as though I'd breathe for evermore. But then I saw the Turk's eye flicker to the left and my heart went out of me. The axe, changing its flashing course, descended just as Garth lunged forward – lunging with a sword two hands shorter than the Turk's huge axe – and the massive wedge of steel caught my brother beside the neck, tearing his body open as easily as fruit. I screamed . . . or perhaps I didn't . . . perhaps it was all inside of me . . . I only knew that in living, I had died. My head began to spin. I had no breath . . . And when the Turk, now like a Delivering Angel, raised his blade again, and as my brother's lifeblood drained into the sand beneath my feet, I watched his face grimace with the force of the coming blow. Which never came. For the sun, behind the man's shoulder, was suddenly blotted out. In its place flashed a halo of golden hair and a russet beard. It was the King; and even as I began to faint, his axe swung down as if to fell the largest tree in England. The Turk's chest split like kindling. A gout of heathen blood splashed over me. And then darkness folded in and I thought that I had died, that the Locksley name would never carry farther than a mountain pass in Cyprus.

CHAPTER SEVEN

We used to swim in the River Don, which swings in a wide, glistening arc behind Locksley Hall, and I never forgot the day when, for the first time, I opened my eyes under water. The light was dim, but magical, the strange silence like a spell, and the shapes of rocks and swinging fronds beckoned in an almost frightening way. I'd been frightened to go in, and Garth had held my hand, and when I turned and saw his face, it seemed the strangest sight in all the world: his hair streaming above his head, his skin a ghostly white, his features trembling mistily . . .

Now, in Cyprus, it was as though I was swimming in the Don again. Lights and sounds and images swayed before me, and there was Garth, just as he had been, and it made no difference to say that he was dead for he was only floating, drifting weightless, slowly turning somersaults to show there was nothing to be frightened of. Or at least that was what I saw in my delirium. There were other shapes as well, different faces and strange voices. A man who smelled of camphor. A lady, whom I knew, but whose name I wouldn't, couldn't, say. And another whose name I must have said, as she stared at me, her head cloaked round in black. Carlotta. Yes, and every time I said her name, something cool would press my cheek . . .

For two days I swam in that world of strange lights and fancies but then, my fever broken, I at last awoke. I felt very weak but my mind was clear. It was mid-afternoon. I was in a tent: there was that smell of canvas heated in the sun. Shadows moved beyond the wall and someone, far off, laughed. And the woman, the little Sister, was dozing in a chair. I whispered her name again.

"Carlotta . . . ?"

Her eyes opened; she began to rise.

"It's all right," I said. "I'm better."

At once she smiled. "I thought, today, you might be."

"Where am I?"

"In a tent near St Hilarion, or what's left of it. You were much too weak to move. Just a minute . . ."

Drawing her habit close about her, she slipped outside. A moment later, DeVaux pushed back the canvas. He smiled; a smile, I think, as friendly as the man was capable of giving. "It's good to see you better, Locksley. The King will be glad to hear it."

"Where is the King?"

"In Nicosia, accepting their surrender."

"So we won?"

"Here? Oh yes. We chased Comnenus up the valley, caught him, and put him into fetters: silver ones but fetters all the same. When the news spreads, the whole island will be ours."

"And our men? I mean – the Locksley men?"

"They're with the King . . . as part of his own guard, in fact. Under a Captain Nicodemus."

I nodded, then eased back against my pillow; even this little effort had left me weak. But there was one more thing I had to know, and DeVaux read it on my face. Gently, he touched my shoulder. "We had to bury him. But it was done with great dignity and honour. We laid him in with his shield, and all his armour on and the King himself placed the Cross in his hands." His eyes flickered toward the back wall of the tent. There I saw the Locksley pennon, my brother's spurs, his rosary. I nodded. Whispered, ". . . very tired . . ."

"Then sleep," Carlotta said, "that's all you have to do."

And that was what I did, only awakening the next morning, when DeVaux appeared again. Another man was with him: the man who smelled of camphor. He also had a heavy red beard and the thick accent the wild men from Scotland affect. I had never met him, but knew who he was: Macdairmid, the King's Physician.

He bent down and touched my cheek. "You'll have a scar," he grunted, "but the blade was sharp and clean." Pressing the wound with his finger, he made me wince. "Never mind, boy, it's not rotting. Have you stood?"

"No."

"Try today. And eat. Build up your strength." He turned, gesturing behind him, and Carlotta entered with a bowl of awful gruel.

Forcing myself, I ate a spoonful and then – I suppose ungratefully – turned to my attendants. "Why is it that the sick are always given loathsome food?"

Macdairmid snorted. "You'll be well by nightfall, then," he said, and pushed out.

His prediction, however, was not quite right. I did stand, but my knees were weak and wobbly and the single step I tried set off the greatest roaring in my ears. But the next morning, with Carlotta's help, I managed to leave my bed, then the tent, and even walked a little through the cooling ashes of St Hilarion. At noon, feeling truly hungry, I insisted on eating a proper meal; then, as the sun climbed higher, I abandoned the tent for the shade of a grove of cedars. There, an hour later, Carlotta found me. Now that I was strong – no longer nurse's fodder – she was shy again. Eyes cast down, her face hidden in her wimple, she softly murmured, "I think, my lord, that you are now recovered."

"Yes. Thanks to you, Carlotta."

Her eyes, then, did look up. "And thanks to my Mistress, my lord. Who sent me to you."

"Of course."

"She would wish me . . ." But then she paused, and her eyes faltered and looked down. "She fears for you, my lord. And grieves deeply for your brother."

I waited. She said nothing more. "Tell her," I began . . . But tell her what? What could I say to her, or she to me? In a few weeks, she'd be King Richard's bride, and whatever she felt for me would have no meaning in her life.

Before I could continue, Carlotta spoke again. "She would always want you safe, my lord. As I would . . . But she knows that you will do – what you will do. So please take this, from both of us, for luck . . ."

And then, before I could stop her, she removed a small silver locket from around her neck, pressed it into my palm, and dashed away through the trees. I watched her go – wanting to run after her, to catch her up, to give her some message . . . but knowing there was no message I could give. Delicately, when she was gone, I prised the locket open. Inside, preserved within a golden drop of amber, was a small white flower, a lily-of-the-valley blooming now as it had done a century ago in some forest in Navarre.

I took it, and slipped it round my neck; and perhaps it did bring me luck – though good or bad, I couldn't yet have said – for as soon as I walked back to our camp, DeVaux summoned me to his tent and gave me orders. If I felt strong enough, I was to return to Kyrenia, find quarters for myself, and await the King's pleasure.

Since there was nothing to keep me in St Hilarion, I paid a final visit to my brother's grave and left the next morning, joining a number of carts that were going back to the harbour for supplies. On the road, you could see that life was returning to normal. People were straggling back to their homes. In the olive groves, peasants were working; and everywhere now smoke was curling from chimneys.

In the town, I found a room overlooking the harbour, and from my window I could see our ships, pulled up on the beach or riding gently at anchor. Their crews fished, or swam in the sea, and in the evening they came into town and got drunk on wine. My own pursuits weren't much more ambitious. I walked, rode a little, built up my strength. After two days, I removed my last bandage: the gash had healed cleanly, though my cheek was still badly bruised. My first wound. A soldier's wound. And now, if I wanted, that's what I could be. While I walked through the town – as, slowly, I accepted Garth's death – I realised that my future had now totally changed. I would be the next Earl of Locksley, not an abbot or bishop at Kirklees. But was that what I wanted? To be a soldier? To lead the men of Locksley against the Saracen at Acre? Only a year before, the course of my life had seemed a simple one, ordered, without complexity; now, by a few twists of fate, it had become a tangled skein of questions. Garth's death brought on the obligations of my family, yet there was also the question of this Crusade and my place beside the King. Barely a man, I was also heir to an earldom and a knight in the service of God. Still, I told myself that just as fate had posed these questions, so she would answer them. And one thing was certain in my mind; whatever course the future took, it must lead me away from the Princess Berengaria. I must accept within myself the fact that the chasm of position and circumstance between us was impossible to bridge and that my desires must remain within me, unspoken and unrequited.

My desires ... even to think the word made my gaze turn seaward, to *Rex*. Every day, since my arrival, lumber had gone out to her each morning, and all day long the carpenters had hammered away. Now she was all a-flutter with pennons, and a huge canvas canopy had been erected on her after-forecastle deck. The town was full of the rumours. The King would return, sail the ship round to Limassol, and there marry his Princess whom I watched every evening as she paced back and forth along the deck.

And then, on the fifth day of my stay in Kyrenia, the King did arrive, thundering through the town in a brilliant, dusty display with half a dozen of his knights. This was early morning: they must have been riding all night. In any case, that afternoon, the King's messenger summoned me: King Richard's pleasure was to see me within the hour.

It felt strange to have a deck beneath my feet again. I was led below, to the same cabin where I'd now been twice. But it was changed again, laid out with large banquet tables, covered in white cloths ... all for the wedding feast, no doubt. In fact, as I arrived King Richard was eating, though in a smaller way: a plate of cheese and bread, a dish of olives, a cup of wine. He was dressed in a long white gown, belted round the middle; I realised he must have just awoken. His face looked strange.

I bowed. "Your Majesty."

He nodded, gesturing me forward, then squinted. "My Scotsman says your wound has healed – though I'm not sure you could tell it by your face."

I said, "Your Majesty . . . I pay you homage as my King but I wish to thank you as a man – you saved my life."

"I returned a favour. You saved my life, my ship, the Lady Berengaria." Then he grinned. "But in battle, Locksley, try to avoid men who are bigger than yourself – and if you can't do that, attack them from behind."

"In future, Sire, I'll try to remember."

He made me sit, and poured me some wine, which we then drank to the memory of my brother. "He was a fine knight, and you can tell your father that he died a true knight's death." It was, I knew, the sort of thing he'd say to anyone; and yet I felt he meant it. Then, setting down his glass, he brought up a bundle from the bench beside him. It was wrapped in cloth; loosening a tie, he opened it, revealing a device I barely recognised. It was a bow, though a very strange one. Short, no more than half the length of my old longbow, it was twice curved, the shaft was wrapped in strips of hide, its tips were horn. The King pushed it across the table to me.

"That Turk was carrying it – it makes a more useful trophy than his head."

I picked it up; it was slippery with oil. "You're very kind, Your Majesty."

He held up his hand and smiled. "Don't thank me yet. I'm trying to bribe you." Then, with a sudden frown, he got to his feet, turned his back and walked away from me. "We've saved each other's lives, Locksley, and perhaps that makes a bond between us. But there's another. You hold a secret that men have died for – and one that I would kill to keep."

Unconsciously, I touched the ring on my finger: the ring my father had given Hubert Scathelock, the ring they'd taken from my brother's finger. If I hadn't seen it flash on St Denis' hand . . .

"Since we last spoke," the King went on, "I've thought a great deal about that message and what it means. I could pretend it wasn't true, but Isaac Comnenus attacked just as it said. So . . ." He turned round then. "You loved your brother, Locksley. Do you believe that I love mine?"

"My Lord . . ."

"Do you believe I would forgive him . . . even now?"

"My Lord . . . yes, I do."

"Prince John is weak, devious, spiteful, arrogant – but I love him anyway. I admit, part of the reason why I can love him is because he *is* weak. He's a great one with words, my brother. Words, conspiracies, and subterfuges – no wonder they use chessmen in their messages. But words are not power, Locksley, and wars aren't fought on checkered boards. Power is an army and the money to pay to keep it in the field, and I assure you that the sight of my brother on a horse, a sword in hand, would set the world to laughing. So, in truth, I don't care what he does or thinks."

"But King Philip, Sire . . ."

He looked at me, and cocked his eyebrow. "You're no fool, are you?" He smiled. "I said I'd make you bishop – and I will – but you might make yourself the Pope." Then he turned round. "But you're right again. Philip I *do* fear. Not his army, but his greed. It must be such a strong temptation. Kill me, sit my brother on the throne, then one by one . . . Poitou, Anjou, Normandy . . . You understand?"

"Yes, Sire. I see the danger very well."

"And would you act to stop it?"

"Your Majesty, I will do as you command."

He turned round again and shook his head.

"You've come too far – you've lost too much . . . I can't command. But I would *ask* you to return to England, in my name, with letters for the Court to make you a Royal Clerk in the Treasury answerable only to myself. Those letters would give you access to every room at Westminster, permit you to study any document, and could only be revoked or tampered with on pain of death. If my brother is in alliance with King Philip, I must know it – and by your seeking it, you might put it to an end."

I stood for a moment, speechless. In all my thinking about my future, I'd never considered such a quick return to England. I used a question to delay. "Sire . . . If I discovered something – something you should know – how would I send the message?"

"On your return to England, go by Aquitaine and see my mother's castellar. Arrange with him that any message sent from you will come at once to me."

"And my men, Your Majesty?"

"They would stay, with their own banner, but under my protection."

He'd thought it all out. For a moment, my thoughts swung back and forth, as though on a crazy balance. I'd never see the Holy Land; yet, in England, I'd serve my King. Our men wouldn't have an Atheling to lead them, yet the honour they'd enjoy could not be greater. At home, I'd be a world away from this ship and all that she carried – but then, wasn't that all for the best?

Finally, hardly knowing what my answer might be as I opened my mouth, I said, "I'll do it, Sire."

King Richard smiled. "So, I'm in your debt again – and never fear that I'll forget it." He took my hand. "Everything is ready. We only needed your agreement. DeVaux has found a ship that will take you as far as Crete. From there, go on to Brindisi and then travel overland to Rome. You'll have money and should have no trouble after that."

"Your Majesty."

"You'll be my eyes and ears, Locksley, and I'll have to trust yours as I do my own."

"You can, My Lord."

He showed me out himself. What a scene it was – a King in his nightshirt, despatching his spy, his *instrumentum vocale*, as the ancients used to say. My head was in a whirl.

For that day, and the next, it kept on spinning.

That same afternoon, I met with DeVaux and received a packet containing my letters – one to the Court, another to Queen Eleanor's castellar – along with a number of maps, and a quantity of money. Then, over a long meal with the clerk (such a strange man he was; I now wished I'd come to know him better) I was given a quick education in the mysteries of the Royal Household, the King's Treasury and its various keepers; I heard tales of the Prince and his advisers, William Longchamp, the Treasurer, and a dozen other great men whose comings and goings I should carefully observe. Finally, that evening, I packed my things, though I had so little they scarcely filled a leather trunk: Garth's spurs; his dirk; two fresh tunics and a cloak; hose that a woman in the town had darned for me; and lastly the strange bundle formed by the Turkish bow.

The next morning I arose alone, and in darkness. The air was cold; the cobbled road leading to the harbour-front glistened blackly in the mist. Looking across the water, I could see the shadowy shape of the vessel that was to carry me home; a xebec with slanted, lateen sails. I would have to get out to her myself, but expected that to prove no difficulty for half a dozen fishing boats bobbed beside the quay, the men who sailed them talking quietly together, sipping warmth from wineskins. Adjusting my trunk on my shoulder, I made to approach them, but just then a liveried figure emerged from the gloom and stepped toward me. He was no bigger than a boy and moved with quick, lithe movements. Holding up one hand, he blocked my way.

I hesitated.

He smiled and made a jerky, bobbing bow.

"What is it?" I demanded.

He smiled again, pointed to his mouth and shook his head – I realised he was dumb. And then, with quick, cupping motions of his hand, he beckoned. I paused a moment longer; but then, recognising his arms as Eleanor's, I nodded and signed that I would follow. Turning quickly, he led me back along the shore where I slipped and staggered on the dew-slick stones. It was still very dark, but now the night was lifting, and after a time I saw we were following a path that curved around the bay and ended on a little, cedar-covered spit. At the end of this, planted in the cleft between the rocks, a smoky torch was burning. Its sputtering, orange light revealed a boat, a small skiff, a fringed canopy erected above the stern. A single figure sat there: a knife-like shadow. I knew it was the Queen.

"Lord Locksley?"

Her voice, in hailing me, was soft, and made me whisper.

"Your Highness?"

"My lord, my servant is called Vendar. He'll take your chest." Her fingers moved, quick darting gestures as intricate as a spider's web, and the servant turned toward me and extended both his arms. I slipped my trunk down to him. Carrying it easily he waded to the boat, I following, the water icy round my knees. As I pulled myself across the thwarts, the Queen smiled and patted the seat across from her. "Sit here, my lord. We'll take you out. By the look of that ship, you'll have no easy journey; you may as well begin it comfortably."

Awkwardly, I sat. "There was no need, Your Highness. It's cold and early –"

She waved my words away. "A Queen's wishes are always needs, My Lord – and sometimes hard to deny, as I think you may have learned."

She could only have been referring to the Princess: my face expressionless, I held my tongue. Deliberately, she pretended to mistake the reason for my silence. "Don't fear poor Vendar. He's the perfect servant, a head filled with secrets he can never tell. In any case, my needs are simple. I only want to thank you and give you some advice." Looking beyond me now, her fingers moved again, and the boat rocked slightly as Vendar settled between the oars. Slowly, we began to move; then more quickly; and in a sudden, girlish gesture, the Queen reached down, letting her fingers trail across the water. When she looked up again, I began to speak, but a gesture stilled me. "I do need to thank you, lord; please don't protest. You've lost so much, and gained so little. The mission my son has sent you on is no compensation for your brother. And a knighthood isn't worth a love. – No, don't speak. You'd only have to lie, and above all else, it's your honesty I want. It's the rarest gift a queen can get and if you give it to me I can reciprocate. Why shouldn't I, besides? You know all our secrets now. The King can't love a woman – what others hint at, you know for truth. His brother, my husband's favourite, has become a traitor, conspiring with our family's greatest enemy. So thus our throne – the throne I sat on – lies in the gravest danger. We have no heir; no unity among ourselves."

As she'd talked, the dawn had begun to flush across the sky, tinting the gentle waves with rose. With reluctance, for I had no idea what to say, my eyes met hers. I murmured, "Your Highness, in all this I can only seek to serve you."

"Indeed, you serve us well, honouring us by doing so. But I want you to understand that service, Locksley. The King, I think, has been your hero, and John, the Prince, you've seen as something opposite. But all that's false. Both of them are my sons, and I know both well. Richard only finds his strength by fleeing his loathing of himself – his sex, his body, all that it demands. This, precisely, is what John embraces – and never listen to the priests, for it's no weakness. He understands himself and other men. He thinks. He has a mind. Yet, because he is a coward, his actions can never support his thoughts, so he plots and conspires ceaselessly but never strikes. You see?" She smiled then. "Perhaps you don't, but never mind. One day you will – just listen and remember. What I wish to say is this: my sons are men and nothing more. They have men's weaknesses, their prides and vices. You must, like a mother, forgive them in advance. For good or ill, dear Locksley, you're now allied to their separate fates. That is *your* fate. And you'll only survive that fate if you remember this: It is not the men but their blood you serve; not their power but the Crown that gives it to them."

My Fate . . . So, it seemed, I truly had one. But didn't every man? I'd come here half a scholar, half a priest; now I was a knight. I'd come here as my brother's second, now I left an earldom's heir. The little world of my own thoughts and feelings, my own poor memories, had touched a larger one and now I was transformed. Yet, despite all this – and despite the sadness at all I left behind, all the bonds of love – I suddenly felt at ease and smiled.

"Your Highness, if that is my fate, I accept it gladly."

She smiled; her voice was soft. "So I see you do . . . and only pray that you may not regret it."

"Never, My Lady, I promise you."

She said nothing more; indeed, there was no time, for already Vendar had edged us up to the xebec's side. A command was shouted, a rope came tumbling down, and hastily I took my leave and scrambled up.

My fate ... What did it mean? I leaned against the rail and wondered. But found no answer. And as the anchor chain came splashing up, I told myself the only thing we can tell ourselves, that what would happen could only be God's will.

The sails filled; the prow swung sluggishly to the shifting of the steering oar.

I was an agent of the King, and from this time forward – come what may – his business would be my only thought.

BOOK TWO

A Snatch of Thieves

CHAPTER ONE

Slowly, darkness falls. In the distance, a shutter slams and far away I hear the fading rumble of a barrow. Now the beacon fire is out, for the last of the fisher ships are anchored in the bay and the dock is quiet. Soon, I will light a candle. Soon . . . but now the darkness only seems to brighten memory. The Mediterranean sun is almost blinding and I linger for a moment beneath its rays; it will be a long time before even my remembered self will feel its warmth again. So, reluctantly, do I watch Kyrenia and its golden coast shrink to nothingness behind me, smell that filthy ship and feel again my heavy heart. Peering into the darkness of a Flemish winter, I see the last moments of that southern spring and follow myself as I travel half a world to reach an English autumn. What a trip it was . . .

"Youth," Procopius says, "is a terrible illness only cured by time and wisdom." No man is wise, at least I'm not (perhaps it is only folly that keeps us youthful and alive), but by the end of that voyage I'd taken half the cure. Six months it lasted. Not so long, you'll say; but time is a currency in which each day is a separate coin, with a different weight. And those days had the weight, if not the gleam, of gold. I slept in ditches, rode carts piled high with dung, lost a toe to frost as I took the lepers' route across the Alps. And every step I took alone, for with every step I saw my brother die again. But then, as I drew nearer home, my mind grew anxious for another reason. While I had come to manhood (too proud a boast?), England had descended into madness: or so the roadside rumours claimed. The archbishop of York, King Richard's bastard brother, had been thrown into prison; Longchamp, his Chancellor, had fled to France. To pay their taxes, men sold their sons as serfs, and even the smallest breaches of the law were punished savagely – which is the greatest breach of the law itself. Without its King, the country suffered a Prince, and even the nobles had now divided: some sided with John, sweeping up his leavings, while others opposed him, fearing they'd be those leavings soon enough. I continued on; yet every day, bringing me nearer home, made me more uncertain. I had a commission from the King, but would his brother honour it? Twice in the King's name I had asked for help along the way, but was met either with indifference or, in the second instance, a surly threat. And then, one night in a rough hostelry beyond Lyons, I heard a group of English wool merchants talking together. They spoke in Saxon, no doubt assuming that what they said wouldn't be understood, but from what they told each other, it seemed England was a madhouse. Prince John had virtually assumed the throne, and anyone who interfered with his rule was treated brutally. Whole villages had been burned, their inhabitants murdered wholesale, new taxes were being levied every day, and to mention Richard's name with favour was enough to have you drawn and quartered. Growing wary after this, I travelled in disguise and decided to consult with my father and his friends before trying my luck at court. Thus, as I sailed for Dover, I saw a thousand shadows darkening my path, and five days later, lying in a bracken bed only a few miles' ride from home, I stared into a night still blacker – blacker even than the old man's night that surrounds me now. I thought of my land, my King. And then I thought of Garth. How would I tell them? What words would I find to use?

A false dawn spread its watery light across the sky.

Birds awoke. A squirrel chattered. My horse, untethered, clumped down to the stream.

Shivering, I rolled out of a blanket that had stiffened like a shroud. Last night, I'd gathered twigs and slept with them against my body, so now they were tinder dry. Burning, they made a smokeless fire; though here, I thought, well away from the Roman road and hidden in a gully, I should be safe enough. I warmed my hands; then, fetching a cup of water from the stream, I mixed some meal and nuts together and made myself a porridge. My horse grazed, my bones unthawed; then, though both were still reluctant, I eased us up the gully's rim. The night had been cold; in the gully, the fold of earth had warmed us slightly, but here the grass was grey with frost. A mile away, beneath some oaks, blue-fleeced sheep huddled together seeking warmth; in the woods, smoke curled from the charcoal burner's kiln. But nothing else was moving. I tapped my heels and the horse and I trotted into wakefulness.

Last night, riding hard, I'd crossed into Yorkshire; now, as the true dawn flickered behind the trees, I pounded across the moors of Hathersage into the scattered stands of beech and ash that lay between me and the rising ground of Locksley Tor. A mist rose with the sun, trapping the light and turning the air to gold. As the horse's hooves drummed along the turf, the sun slowly crested the trees and warmed my wind-taut skin. Thus, keeping off the roads and taking pains to put trees and hedgerows between myself and the horizon, the miles sped safely on. At length, the ground beneath me rose; a gentle slope, then steeper. And finally, reining in, I found myself at the top of Locksley Tor, looking into the valley that had been my childhood universe. I smiled then, despite everything, and whispered comfort in my horse's ear. This had been the first hill I'd ever climbed, Garth and my father standing below, laughing and urging me on. When, on tottering legs, I'd finally reached the summit, I'd looked about me, marvelling at the world, Sherwood Forest and its mysteries away to the east, familiar Locksley and the river to the north.

Now, loosening the reins and letting my horse put his head down, I followed the river with my eye, picking out landmarks and finding the stand of oak and alder that blocked my view of Locksley Hall itself. The river was a silver band; beside it ran the narrow, beaten track that followed it to Sheffield. Beyond both lay the bottom meadows, always lush, and then Preester's Hills, henna-coloured now with autumn leaves.

Memories hovering round me like my misty breath, I urged the horse ahead and we edged sideways down the hill. Reaching the valley floor, I saw that little had changed since I'd last ridden here; in the coppices of beech and yew, there were swathes from recent cutting, and in the distance – the first human landmark – I spied the low, grey mound of John Hoade's cottage: Tom, his son, had been a companion of my childhood while his wife had taught Marian how to sew and cook. Which brought more memories back: hunting wild pig with my father and Garth; visits from the neighbouring lords; my first adventures with the local girls – good days filled with happiness and laughter, when life had seemed a single, brilliant afternoon. Then, passing through a grove of oak, I picked up the trail to Locksley Ford and here every turning seemed to take me back in time – the first deer I'd ever seen had bolted across this path, the first time a horse had thrown me, I'd tumbled just here, where the path dipped down towards a huge old willow, bent across the river. That spill had been hard enough, but the Ford was easy: a broad, shallow gravel pan. My horse, unfamiliar with it, picked his way across, a misstep splashing a spray of jewels into the rising sun. Then, with a heave, we clambered up the steeper, opposite bank, across the Sheffield track, and cantered into the springy meadow grass. A mile now, I thought; a mile and a screening wall of oak was all that separated me from home. Ducking my head, I entered the shadows of the trees, warding branches off my face, leaves rustling beneath the horse's hooves. Ahead, as the trees thinned out, the sky was bright and clear; and then, emerging, I finally saw it . . . Locksley Hall.

There was a moment when my mind, so well prepared by now for the old, familiar sight, saw nothing wrong, memory and desire defining the shape that rose against the sky.

But then my heart thumped hard and my breath froze in my chest: for the stone walls at either end of the Great Hall stood by themselves, licked with soot and bridged only by charred rafters that had once supported the great slate roof but which now rose over the gutted remains of my home like the cracked ribs of some giant beast. I was stunned. It was a shell. A ruin. The narrow windows of the North Tower stared blindly down and the stables and forge, which had leaned up close to the east wing of the house, were nothing but black smudges against the earth.

In a daze of horror, I nudged the horse along. The sun sparkled; dew splashed silver, but as soon as we'd crossed the meadow, the horse's hooves stirred up sooty dust and I was looking down at the blackened litter of my life: tables, chairs, chests of clothes and tools all scattered and charred as though by a dragon's fiery breath. I drew the horse up; slipped from his back; stood on the huge cobbled step before the door and looked round aghast. What could have happened? How could such a disaster have struck this place? But even as these first questions formed in my numbed brain, I saw the answer. Oddly, the enormous frame of the entrance door still stood, apparently untouched, and it seemed as if the doors had been thrown open, to welcome a stranger. Then, stepping closer, I saw the truth. One of the doors, battered and splintered, still clung to its hinges; the other, lying inside, had been chopped to kindling. Axes had smashed them down, men had forced their way into this hall; and as I stepped over the threshold, I could almost see their torches blaze.

I waited, holding my breath; the air was still. I heard the silence of a crypt.

I lifted my head, and the charred rafters seemed to stretch like a spider's web against the sky.

I moved my foot: a flake of ash drifted on the breeze, then was sucked suddenly higher and disappeared, the remains of . . . what?

Cold ash, charred wood and splintered bone. Behind me, the horse stamped and blew, trying to rid his nostrils of the stench. I could smell acid in the air; my eyes grew moist. Yet I didn't cry, not now, for I was still too numb with shock. Coming two thousand miles to bring the fatal news – prepared to comfort others – I'd been swamped in death. Marian, my father, this whole household – forty souls at least . . .

Who? When? Why? The questions started; and as they began racing in my mind, my blood raced with them and my heart began to pound. Horror, fury and despair – I felt them all at once.

Then, like a cold breeze against my neck, fear touched me.

Behind, the horse, still restless, tossed his head, the steel of his bridle jangling. I stepped back and stroked his neck and looked around. The horse had felt it first, but I knew we were both right to feel afraid. The men who had put a torch to Locksley Hall would show no mercy to its rightful heir. But they couldn't have expected me; no one in England had known I was coming. Besides, if they had, men would have taken me at the Ford. Still, if there was no reason to panic, there were many to be cautious. They might well have left behind a sentinel, a vulture to overlook their carrion. Reaching behind the saddle, I unlashed my bedroll. Within it, carefully wrapped, was King Richard's Turkish bow. I stretched it now, then fitted it across my shoulder, and tucked three arrows – all I had – beneath my belt. I mounted, my eyes searching beyond the ruins, in the woods and hills. Nothing . . . and a watcher, if there was one, might well not know me. Pulling the horse around, I slowly retraced my steps, like some disappointed visitor, and crossed the meadow to the elms. In their shelter, I stretched low against the animal's neck, urging him ahead, but then jerked him hard on the leftward hand just before we reached the Ford. There was no path here; with difficulty, branches slashing at my face, we picked our way along the river bank. For half a mile, the elms still hid us and when they thinned I turned him to the water's edge. The river broadened a little here; but though the current was slow moving, it looked black and deep and for a moment the horse baulked, dancing back. I dug my spurs in: and though he panicked when he lost the bottom, he managed to swim the twenty yards that put the ground beneath his feet again. Plunging, fighting for every inch, he dragged us up the bank. There, once more hidden by some alders, I reined him in. Both of us were soaked; but to anyone waiting at the Ford, we would have seemed to have disappeared.

Moving from thicket to thicket, I now let the horse walk and rest. For the moment, I had no plan; I'd merely wished to run, instinct had taken me to safety – but now that I was safe, the reins slack in my hands and the horse moving easily beneath me, I scarcely knew what to do or to think. And so I wept. I wept for them all. I wept for Garth, my father, Marian – I wept for all the dead – and then, I suppose, my tears were for myself. All the memories that had quickened in the air this day, the very familiarity of this ground I travelled, now seemed to mock me and make me feel all the more alone. I had lost everything; my family gone, my home destroyed, my future dissipated. What could I do? How could I live – live within myself, live upon this earth?

Then, perhaps, I was not so far from death myself – temptation flickered like the shadows among the trees – but I had no will, not even strength for that. My horse, indeed, became my will, carrying me where he wished to go. Perhaps he even understood, for at length, all on his own, he stopped and stamped and snickered softly.

I lifted my head.

The woods, I saw, had ended. Beyond, the morning sun was glistening on a farmer's field.

This halt – the sun – the change – all served to rouse me. I drew a breath. Then – I'd been so unaware – I considered where we were. This took a moment, but then I knew. Of course: these were the lower acres of John Hoade's farm: broad, lush fields of grass, unharvested; I supposed he was letting it go to fallow.

Now, gently, I eased my horse's head around. As life and breath stirred in me, so did my questions. Who had done all this and why? If anyone could tell me, John Hoade could and I turned my horse along his meadow. After a moment, as we topped the rise that sloped up from the river's edge, his cottage came in view. It was large for a tenant's cot, but Hoades had tended these acres as long as Athelings had owned them. The original wooden hut had long since been changed for stone, carefully chinked with mud and moss, and each generation had added on a room. Now, everything looked as it had always . . . but then I paused. Why was there no smoke curling from the chimney? Then, drawing closer, I paused again. Where were his animals? His flock of hens? His swine?

The cart, usually stowed beneath his lean-to shed, was gone. The pile of manure he so carefully husbanded was scattered . . . Without thinking, my hand reached up and touched the bow, still slung across my shoulders. Yet, if anyone was waiting here, they'd have horses, and I saw no sign of them. Slowly, cautiously, I let my own mount walk on, drawing him up ten yards from the cottage threshold. Nothing stirred. There was no sign of danger; no sign of anything; but I stayed in the saddle, ready to spur myself away, and called, "John? Mistress Hoade? Are you there?"

I stared at the cottage. Still as the grave it seemed . . . though there'd been no fire here, no obvious mark of pillage: with its thatched roof, the place would have flamed in seconds. So was it abandoned, as it looked? But that was madness. Hoade had eight acres, nothing more, but they were among the richest on my father's land – *my* land – and were enough to support his family and two others.

"John Hoade!" I called again. "Come out! Is this the way you greet your friends?"

Then, with a sudden creak, the door swung open, and a figure stood there.

A woman. Her face hidden in a shawl, her body in a grey wool cloak. Then a hand emerged and pushed back the shawl, revealing a pale face and a wisp of reddish hair. I knew her – yet I didn't. "Megan? Is that you?" Megan . . . the Hoade's little slavey girl: the first girl I'd ever lain with. She frowned and I smiled despite myself. "Don't you know me, Megan? It's Robert – Robert Atheling."

Her mouth dropped open; and then, on some account, she blushed. "Oh dear Christ . . ." She turned. "Mistress! It's Robert, coming home . . . little Robin . . ."

I swung down from the saddle then and a moment later old Mother Hoade, as round as a dumpling and just as soft, was pressed against me while Megan stood aside and smiled. Finally, as the good old woman shook her tears away, I said, "Where's John? Your animals –?"

"Dear martyred Lord," she said, "he doesn't know. The Hall – you've not seen . . . ?"

I squeezed her to me. "Yes, I've only come from there. My father . . . ?"

She shook her head. "Dead. All of them . . ."

But I scarcely heard her. With a creak, the cottage door was swinging open, and inside I saw a row of candles flickering in the gloom. Slowly, entranced again by horror, I stepped inside. Death had visited here as well. Wrapped in a blood-stained shroud, with only his face exposed, John Hoade was stretched upon the table, the pale light of the candles glistening on his waxy skin.

I crossed myself and knelt.

Rising, I touched Megan gently on the arm. "How . . . when?"

"Two days ago, in Nottingham." These words were whispered: but then she hissed, "They cut his belly open while he yet lived, then pulled –"

"Hush now, Megan," said Mistress Hoade. "He's gone and now it makes no difference how. Whatever they did to him, I know his soul is ready for the Lord."

In bewilderment, I turned around to face her. "Dear God, who has done all this?"

From the threshold, the old woman bowed her head and whispered. "De Caux," she said. "They were Maud de Caux's barba-

rians . . . She did it all. She killed my John, she killed young Tom —
he's gone too — and all the people at the Hall . . ."

"De Caux . . . But I've never even heard the name?"

"She's wife to Ralph Fitz Stephen, Robin — though which is
master and mistress is sometimes hard to tell. Six months past,
Prince John disallowed all your father's titles and made Fitz Stephen
Keeper of Sherwood. Your father fought them, so they burnt the
hall, and then they raised the rents of all his tenants. None of us
could pay — we would have starved. Our men had no choice but
poaching. They hung Tom for snaring a rabbit and all John did was
take a fox."

How could I believe it? How could any of this be true?

I stood there, stunned. Death, death, and more death; I'd come
home to the death of everyone and everything I'd ever known.
Slowly, I turned away from John Hoade's gutted body, stepped past
his wife and Megan and sought the sun. Yet, once more, its
brilliance mocked me; its light remained the same, but the world it
shone on had so completely changed. What could I do? Where could
I go? My mind spun round. And I'm afraid, though I should have
been comforting them, it was John Hoade's women who helped me
now. They made me see that none of this was accidental, some mad
mistake. They forced me to accept that my commissions from King
Richard would mean nothing to his brother — except an excuse for
hanging. And finally, when I told them Garth was also dead, they
insisted that I had to flee.

"Little Robin . . . once Fitz Stephen hears you're in the Shire, your
life is forfeit. You have no choice. You have to go."

Struggling, I got my wits together and nodded. "All right. I'll
return to France, then back to King Richard and tell him what has
happened."

"God knows what he can do . . . but yes, anything . . . Just be far
from Nottingham by nightfall."

Megan touched Mistress Hoade's arm. "Should he not see
Marian?"

I looked between them. "*Marian?* You said —"

With a darting hand, Mistress Hoade now crossed herself. "The
saints forgive me, Robin. I thought you knew."

"Knew what? Just tell me — is she —?"

"Yes, yes, she *is* alive. She wasn't in the Hall when they burned it
down. Two months before, she'd gone away to Kirklees. She's safe
there now, but . . ." She looked at Megan anxiously. "Would it be
safe for him? Maud de Caux and the abbess are thick as thieves. If
they see him . . ."

But I shook my head. For the first time now a little joy was in my heart. "Don't tell me of your Maud de Caux. I'm not leaving without seeing Marian even if the Devil tries to bar my way."

With her anxious, woman's frown Mother Hoade turned back to me – but just then we all looked round.

From the cottage yard you could barely see the river and the track to Sheffield on the farther bank. There, something moved. Metal flashed. I squinted . . . "It's just a cart."

With relief, Mother Hoade took her breath and nodded. "Malcolm Greenleaf, then, come for us. We'll bury dear John in the parish ground – they'll allow us that – and then go on to Cuckney Green. My sister's there . . . But he'd best not see you, Robin. He's a good man, but ale can loosen any tongue."

"I'll go then, now. I'll ride for Kirklees, see Marian tonight, and then go east, toward Lincoln. No one can expect me there."

Megan touched my arm. "Robin . . . Robert . . . Take me with you." I looked at her, then to her mistress; but before either of us could speak, Megan quickly added, "You'll be safer if I come. No one would think you'd travel with a woman, and I know the abbey well – I'd be able to find a way to Marian."

"Megan, dear . . ."

She turned now toward the old woman, taking her gently by the shoulders. "We both know that my aunt can find a place for you, but I'll only be a burden, another mouth to feed, another bed to find. There's no work in Cuckney Green, but if I go to Kirklees I might find something in the abbey, perhaps the laundry or the kitchen – they can always use an extra pair of hands. And if there's nothing there, I can always find my way to you again." She turned back to me and blushed. "My lord," she said, "if you could . . ."

"Megan, I'm not lord of much except this horse, but if you wish to go, I'll take you willingly."

We both turned to Mother Hoade, who, making up her mind, nodded quickly and glanced toward the river. "All right, then. But hurry. Get your bundle – Malcolm can't be far."

Megan dashed into the house; I mounted my horse. And then, taking a silver denier from my purse, handed it down to Mistress Hoade. She took it with a blush; thanked me; curtsied; and then, despite herself, bit into it.

I smiled. "It's from King Richard, Mother. His silver's good enough."

"I'll thank you, little Robin, and let you thank him. It could save us all when winter comes."

Then Megan appeared again, a small cloth bundle in her hand. Getting up behind me, she kissed her mistress farewell and with a wave, we galloped off. By the time we reached the river, Malcolm's cart was at the Ford; and as we swam across – at the spot I'd found that morning – I suppose Mistress Hoade was on her way to Cuckney Green. We too went north, but swung west as well; travelling slowly, avoiding every road and farm, letting the deer paths lead us through the woods. We crossed the Don at Hunter's Ford – it was too broad to swim – but did so without anyone seeing, and quickly lost ourselves in the lush forests that grow round Cannon Hall. By then, it was early afternoon. The horse, with his double burden, was tiring, and twice we'd heard other riders travelling near us. It seemed best to stop and rest.

Hobbling the horse, I rubbed him dry, then let him graze around a patch of bracken. Megan and I, between us, had enough food to make a little meal, though we lit no fire. As we ate, we talked. We shared our memories, of the Hoades and of each other and our childhoods – of the farm and Hall, of harvest bonfires; of Marian and Mistress Hoade who'd taught them both to cook and sew. In this, it was natural enough that she should cry, no less so that I would comfort her, and in its turn, or so it seemed, natural that we would kiss. The embrace was like the breaking of a spell. I'd been dead before – grief and rage and horror had frozen me in a trance. Now her warmth released me. Her mouth pressed up against me and I pulled her roughly to the ground, pressing her to the forest floor and pushing her clothes aside. She cried out as I went in her; thrusting forward and clutching me, her sweet breath caressing my cheek. As I looked into her face, she smiled acceptance – but then turned away, tears glimmering in her eyes, and as we moved to age-old rhythms, I knew that both of us were whispering in our hearts for all of them . . .

CHAPTER TWO

At certain times I've felt a strange sensation, for which I've never found a name; a feeling, as I stood in a certain spot, that I'd stood there long before: that I knew it, intimately; that what lay around the bend was as familiar as my hand. A face . . . sunlight on a wall . . . the roots of an ancient tree bulging through the soil . . . It is as though I might have seen them in a different life, and have only now remembered, or perhaps when I was still a babe-in-arms, before memory began. Bewitched in such a manner, I always stop and ponder, for what is not least strange about this feeling is the certainty, even as I feel it, that the feeling isn't true. I know, in fact, that I've never stood here – never seen this face – never watched the light fall against the wall in just that way – never made those roots a shape . . . I know this; so it's a sense of being very near but very far; close, but completely separate.

The next evening as we rode out from the forest and looked down the slope of Mirrins Vale, that feeling, or a cousin to it, swept over me.

Below lay the River Calder; beyond, the Monastery of Kirklees and the nunnery in the farther distance. I knew, in truth, that I'd seen the sight a hundred times before but now my memories might well have come from a vanished life and time. Then, I'd been a second son; standing here, with Garth beside me, I'd looked across the valley to my future and the peacefulness of the scene had been a natural part of me. Now, the vision was no less gentle, but utterly remote. Flocks were grazing in the northern meadow; a boat swung lazily in the river's current; a cart rumbled across the narrow bridge toward the gatehouse, the logs across the span jumping up behind its wheels with little puffs of dust . . . All of this, I thought, made for a tranquillity I might never share again.

"It's so grand," said Megan, her voice a breath against my ear.

She was right enough; grand – a grandeur that could have been my own. Had I truly wanted it? I wondered idly – for indeed the answer to the question made no difference now – and gazed below. The nunnery was just a pool of shadow in the dusk, but from where we stood, I could see the monastery plain enough, the two long wings of the almonry and pilgrims' hall separated from each other by the iron gate, with the cobbled courtyard in behind. Now, at sunset, this was filled with bustling people. Beyond were the cloisters, flanked to the south by the refectory and, to the north, by the beautiful little priory church. Yes, I thought, it was grand indeed. There were more than twenty buildings altogether (once, in secret, childish pride I'd counted them), each made of quarried stone, with pitched slate roofs and glass windows, rather than oiled paper, which now glinted with the lowering sun. *Had* I wanted it? For some reason, the question now made me smile, and then I murmured, "Did you know I was supposed to be a priest?"

Megan chuckled and reached round to pinch my belly. "I heard that once. I suppose since then you've had a different calling."

I laughed – perhaps the true answer was just that – and tapped my heels, trotting us down the gentle slope. Crossing the bridge, we joined a ragged file of travellers and pilgrims who were gathering at the gatehouse. Taking our turn, we paused as the porter stopped us. Dawlish, he was called: a squinty dragfoot wreck who'd had his post as long as I remembered. He saw so many faces there was little chance he'd know me – and I don't suppose he'd ever seen me when my beard was full. He squinted up. "Not pilgrims, are ye?"

I shook my head. "Travellers on the way to Bolton Abbey. I'm to deliver my sister there for service."

He leered at Megan, then looked back to me. "And what's your names?"

I had this ready; something simple, I'd thought, and easy for us both. "Robin. Robin Hood of Doncaster. The maid is known as Megan."

With a nod, the old man now mumbled, "You get your supper in Refectory Hall, matins at midnight if you've a mind, and breakfast on bread and ale at eight. Women to the right as you come in, men above by the outer stairs. Stable your horse just there and God bless you both within this house." Holding up a clawed hand, he gave me a beady look that softened as I handed down a quarter of silver.

The courtyard was thronged with people, all hurrying to get their places in the Hall: pilgrims in wide-brimmed hats and widespun cloaks, men-at-arms, minstrels, one sullen knight with a bloody bandage round his arm and a juggler, brightly clothed in blue and yellow, who was already spinning three clay bottles from hand to hand. Slipping from the saddle, I helped Megan down and said,

"We should hurry if we want to eat." In the stable, she helped me with the horse – another bit of silver for the almhouse boy bought some hay – and then we took up our bundles and joined the last stragglers going into the Hall. This was very large, a hundred feet long and half as wide, laid out now with more than fifty tables – from the long benches where the paupers sat to the glittering candles and cloth of the Bishop's dais. Like everyone coming in, I glanced there instinctively. The lords and ladies were already in their seats, ranged on either side of the abbot's chair. He, in fact, was absent, though the prioress's place was filled, for she often left her nunnery to visit here. Lecia, she was called, according to Megan: this was the woman who was so close a friend to Maud de Caux. I scanned the other faces, searching for Marian. She should have been at the abbot's table, and well above the salt, but I couldn't see her.

"Will anyone up there know you?" Megan whispered.

"DeVincey would . . . and Cullen. That's his lady, in the cloth of gold . . . But never fear. We'll not get close enough."

Indeed, we didn't. One of the monks showed us to a table, took a coin, then squeezed us in between two heavyset men with the leather aprons and sooty faces of wandering smiths. Brothers, they grunted; from Leeds; on their way to Nottingham in search of work. I grunted back, saying as little as I could—my accent might betray me long before my face – and then grabbed the platter as it came around. Hare; chicken; stewed vegetables. Having had nothing hot for two days now, I took my share and perhaps a little more. I ate hungrily; then, as my belly began to fill, I watched and listened. For the first time since I'd been in England, I was now among a large group of King Richard's liegemen: and his vassals, under his brother's stewardship, seemed low and sullen. Like a greasy flame, grumbling and complaint flickered round the table. No one spoke of kings or princes – their worries were work and bread and taxes – but the discontent was plain to see. In the shabby clothes men wore; the cheap crockery we ate from, the sort that usually graced the pauper's table – for even the abbot had to pay his taxes; and the few, paltry coins that people had to spare for the minstrel's hat. *Thy market dispatched*, he'd sung, *turn home again round, Lest grasping for penny thou losest a pound.* Beside me, the smith had laughed. "That moral's lost on us, singer. We've none a pound to lose."

The whole table joined in the laughter, and even the minstrel grinned, but beneath it all you could hear their fear: none had the pound – worse, they hadn't the penny to grasp. What had happened to Richard's kingdom, I saw, not only affected great families like my own, but everyone else as well. Yet what could such men do? Only what they did: grumble, drink, and travel even further from their homes in search of work. Well, I quietly told myself, I *could* do something more – I could tell their king. And if a king isn't concerned with his subjects' welfare, he's a fool, for his own depends on it.

As the minstrel began another verse of his song, I nudged Megan and we squirmed out of our places at the table. By now, a few others were leaving too; enough, at least, that we didn't look conspicuous. Passing along the noisy aisle, we made our way through the eastern door, into the vaulted tunnel of the cloister beyond. It was now dark and cool, and while we'd been eating a drizzle had begun. Few people were about.

I whispered, "You're sure you want to do this?"

"Yes, I'm sure."

On the upper floor of the monastery, above the Monk's Parlour, lay a few private apartments for Monastery Donors – of whom the Locksleys were one. If Marian was in this place, she should be there, but Megan would have to fetch her. A single man, especially one looking as unkempt as I did now, would be instantly thrown out, while she might pass as a servant or messenger.

"Remember, though. If you're challenged, just say you've lost your way."

She nodded. "I'll be all right. No one fears a woman."

She slipped off, along the passage. I let her disappear, then continued along the cloister to the slype, the narrow passage that led to the monks' scriptorium, the little rooms where they copied out their books. These, each with a window facing north, would be empty now, and locked – except that the locks were simple, and on the door that stood second from the end, the bolt had never worked. I stopped in front of it, looking round. Behind me was the "little cloister" – the court where the monks would sit and rest their eyes – but now it was deserted. Using my knife, I worked against the door. The bolt slipped back, and I stepped inside.

The room, barely large enough to turn around in, was dark and smelled very musty. A table and a rush stool were set below the window, the table laid out with parchments, though in the darkness there was no way to read them. I waited, listening; but there was no sign that I'd been spotted. Someone passed the door, then hurried on. A pigeon cooed; the drizzle fell . . . And in the church, visible through the window, a light flickered briefly and then went out.

After some time – I'd just started to worry – steps came along the passage and stopped before the door. *"Robert."*

I worked the latch, stepped back – and in the darkness embraced a woollen cloak, damp hair, soft skin . . . my sister.

"Marian – thank God you're still alive."

"Oh, let me thank God . . . though I've prayed enough already. It's really you . . ." In the dark, her hands flitted across my weather-beaten face. I squeezed her hand. "Where's Megan?"

"Hiding, further down the cloister."

"All right. We should get down a little . . . below the level of the window."

"Yes. We must be very careful. *You* must be. Even now they're looking for you."

I was startled. "Who?"

"Fitz Stephen . . . Maud de Caux . . . The Prince."

"They know I'm here?"

"Just that you're in England. They learned today. They're sending men to watch the Hall and they're guarding me . . . It was a piece of luck that you sent Megan on ahead." Then, again, she hugged me to her. "But you're safe now, little brother! Thank God for that."

We held each other, awkwardly, half crouched down. In some ways, as children, we'd been closest, Garth separated from us both by his age and the shadow of his inheritance. And at least with me, in all the rough-and-tumble games we played behind our father's back, she had a chance of keeping up, and even sometimes winning. We even looked alike; her hair was dark and curling like my own, and her honey skin contrasted with our dead brother's Saxon cream. Her figure was slight and boyish – and I couldn't help likening her to the Princess. We'd always confided in each other, as much like friends as blood relations. Now, despite my absence, that feeling was renewed – and since we only had each other left it was another gift to thank God for.

Finally, crouching there on the stone, we let each other go and told our news – a sort of horrible barter, death for death. Our father. Balderson, the steward. Old Scathelock, poor Edwin's father . . . She'd guessed at Garth.

"When I heard you'd come back alone, I knew. And that's why they'll kill you, Robert. You're the Locksley heir. They *must*."

"And yet they don't harm you?"

"No. Listen carefully now. You must understand what's happened. To increase his treasury – for King Richard's Crusade, or so he said – Prince John sold our father's title."

"*Sold* it? But it wasn't his to sell."

"So father said. He wouldn't buy it back. And so the Prince sold it to Fitz Stephen. He murdered father, or at least his wife did it in his name. Yet, you see, she's worried. By King Richard's decree, a Locksley should be Keeper of Sherwood. So she wants to murder you and marry her son to me – her son not by Fitz Stephen but by

93

another man, de Birkin. She hoped my blood will give her family a tincture of legitimacy. That's why I'm alive – the only reason."

"But have you married him?"

"No. My God, no. I put them off, saying I have to grieve a year for father."

"And when is the year up?"

"I don't know. Even to save my life I don't think I could let him touch me." She squeezed my hand. "But don't think of that. Or me. I'm safe for now. It's you they're hunting. You have to get away."

"Yes. To France, and then King Richard – he'll be in Acre now."

But Marian shook her head and her grip tightened on my hand. "Robert, you mustn't. Listen – their spies are everywhere, in every port. If you try to leave England now, they'll only catch you."

"But I have to go. The King must know what's happening."

"All right. You have to go – but don't go *now*. Delay a little. Even Maud de Caux and Prince John's watchers will grow tired in time. Wait a month or two."

"It will be winter then. If I wait a month, I'll wait till spring."

"Then wait till spring. Or send your message another way. If you don't, they'll kill you just as they murdered father. You have to stay and hide."

I tried to think. I could stay and hide till spring . . . but by then there might be no kingdom for the King to save. Yet, if I tried to escape and failed, I'd give my life for nothing. And who would protect my sister then? I listened. I could have begged for a sign. But there was nothing but a cold seep of water beneath the door, against my hand.

At last I said, "All right. I'll stay."

"Thank God!" She bent forward and kissed my brow. "Thank God, thank God –"

But then she hushed; from the church came the tolling of the compline bells.

As they echoed through the night, I whispered, "We have to hurry."

"I've already been too long."

"If I'm to stay," I said, "I'll need a hiding place. Somewhere close by, but not too close – not if they're already watching you."

She leaned back, sitting on her heels, her cloak sweeping down across the floor. Reaching out to me, she took my hands. "You must go to Sherwood. The Forest has become a sanctuary. Since these troubles started, even before our father died, fugitives have been hiding there. Tom Hoade was one."

"Yet they caught him."

"Yes. But there's more danger in the towns. And now bands have

94

formed in Sherwood, groups of men . . . men who refused their taxes or simply couldn't pay them . . . men who would have gone to bondage otherwise. They had a leader. I know him. His real name is Jean Neuilly, but they know him only by his Saxon name – John Naylor . . . He was a King's Messenger, but he quit the Prince's service in disgust."

"And where could I find this Jean Neuilly?"

She shook her head. "I don't know that. But just go into the Forest and he'll find you. I know you can trust him if he does."

"You say you know him?"

She drew back a little; then so far that her face was scarcely visible in the gloom. "Yes . . . I won't lie, Robert. I know him . . . well. Several times he came to father, warning him – his father knew our father – and I met him at the Hall. *Father* trusted him . . ." She looked up then, and I saw her smile. "Don't scold me, Robert. I'm still your sister, but I'm no maid. Jean Neuilly is another reason why I'll never marry Ralph de Birkin."

I waited; and then, when she said nothing more, quietly leaned forward and kissed her cheek. "All right, then. I'll find him. But if you and I should need to meet – or send a message . . ."

She nodded, and took my hands again. "I've already talked to Megan. She'll stay with me and pass our messages. You know that oak, the big one that you and Garth used to climb – the one you fell from?"

I smiled. "How can I forget?"

"Well, we'll hide our messages in its fork. I'll arrange for Megan to pass that way once or twice a week."

"People will grow suspicious."

"Only that I've found a lover." She quickly squeezed my hand. "We'll say it's this Robin Hood that you've become."

"Ah, such a lucky man."

She laughed. Then, gathering her cloak around her, she stood up. "I must go. They'll miss me." She kissed my cheek. "We'll meet again in a week or two, when it's safe."

I nodded, then hurriedly hugged her to me, and then she broke away and eased the latch. I held the door; reaching back, she touched my hand for one last time, then vanished in the darkness. I waited, listening to her step . . . then Megan's . . . and then there was nothing but the rain.

I slipped out, pulling the door quickly shut behind me. My own route was easy. Along the slype; a gated wall; then through the gardens. Nothing moved. The monks had a little vineyard here, and once among the trellises and vines, I was invisible. I reached the river, working along the edge till I found a shallow spot. From the opposite bank, I looked behind me. In the crevice of the valley, Kirklees was just a thickening, a gathering, of the darkness. For a moment now, I thought of King Richard and what Queen Eleanor had said that morning in Kyrenia's harbour. Fate. *My* fate. Was it possible that my father's death, the end of Locksley Hall and the threat against my sister were part of it? Had it brought me here?

But then I turned and hurried on, toward the safety of the forest.

CHAPTER THREE

Sherwood Forest, my childhood Eden; where, at least in memory, I would lie beneath the greenwood tree, listen to the wind breathe among the branches and watch the fluttering leaves playing with the sun.

How different it now became.

For eight nights and seven days I hid alone – not in a forest, but a wilderness; not an Eden, but a Hell. Yet, I would swear by all the Saints, it was a Hell that not even Lucifer could imagine, for there was no heat or flame, only a constant murky darkness and bone-deep, shivering cold.

I expected none of this when I set out from Kirklees, and in truth that first night was only misery, rain dripping through the bracken where I lay. I was uncomfortable, but not uneasy. The Prince and Fitz Stephen might know I was in England, but England is large enough, and they'd missed me at the Hall. But a fool always underestimates the enemy, and that night I was more than foolish. Where else would I go but Kirklees? And once they'd tracked me there, they'd have no trouble learning I was "Robin Hood", a stranger who'd disappeared in the night and even left his horse. Before first light, the baying of brachets awoke me; by dawn, I knew it was my scent they'd taken. I began to run, the ragged horror that berselets and liamhounds would make of me before my eyes, and within an hour my heart was pounding beneath my ribs and my tongue was lolling from my mouth like a wolf or fox's. And it was like a fox I ran: doubling back continuously; keeping to the rock every place I could; leaping ditches; scrabbling over scree; hiding my stench in streams and marshes, splashing through their muck and mud until I found a little rest among the reeds. Even looking back, that first day was the worst. It was a wonder I survived. I was tired to begin with, and had no food, not even a handful of berries, and the trees were already losing their leaves so that only in the deepest thornscrub could I really lie up safe. No doubt – though I cursed it often – the rain saved me. Cold and drizzling, falling from an endless, leaden sky, it chilled me to the bone, but as long as the curs didn't strike directly on my trail I knew an hour would wash my scent away. That night, wedged in the fork of a willow, I watched the light of my pursuers' fires flicker through the trees, and prayed and tried to catch my breath.

But the next day – and the next – I ran and ran again.

I ran in circles; up hill; down dale; I skirted valleys and crossed rivers only to cross them time and time again. Running like a fox, I learned the forest the way a rabbit must. A winter birch grove gives no shelter – but love the prickly holly for the cover of its leaves. Yet, fox or rabbit, I could never go to earth. Where was my lair or burrow? And even if I dug one, I knew the dogs would only seize me by the neck and drag me out. So I could only run; run, and hope that the hounds would drop before I did. My mind dulled; even my memories of the time remain a blur. On the third day, I knew, they almost had me. I stumbled across one of the wagonways that are used to haul lumber from the forest, and a moment later a troop of cavalry, spent dogs trailing after them, came wearily along. They'd been after me all day and must have been almost as exhausted as myself. But once they struck my scent, the howling they put up raced down my spine and I could almost hear the dogs' slashing yellow teeth against my flank. But I was lucky; it was dark; and even as they had my trail, dusk deepened into night and I was able to slink away, across a stream. On the fourth day – another memory – I found out what would have happened if they'd caught me. I was starved by then, half dead. I'd eaten nothing but a few currants the blackbirds must have missed and a kind of reed which, if you pull it carefully, brings up a root like an onion's. But I was very weak; I decided to leave the Forest, find a farm and get real food. I stopped at the third I came to. It stood all alone, a little steading of mud and grass roughed from the forest's edge, with a lean-to byre, a wattle hut, a single heifer to pull their plough – the home of villeins, I blearily conjectured, who might well be mine, though by this point I was too exhausted to know quite where I was. Panting, I crouched in a muddy ditch. The rain hissed down. A smudge of smoke drifted from the roof-hole of the hut and my mouth watered at even this faint hint of food. I tried to think. I had money; I could easily pay for what I wanted. But such payment might be so memorable that the villein would head for the nearest village – nearest taverner – to tell the world about it. Yet if I stole what I wanted or even killed them . . . It was a decision I never had to make. Even as I lay there, four men rode up, their hauberks covered with the green surcoats of

Foresters, but with the addition of the Fitz Stephen badge. They had no dogs; were, I guessed, just a random patrol, hoping for a lucky strike. They were the first of my trackers I'd seen by daylight and, hidden in my ditch, I eyed them curiously. Normans, or at least the captain was – he rode a sorrel destrier while the rest had smaller palfreys. Their shields were oxhide over limewood, they carried swords, no bows, and on his offside the captain slung a lance. The hooves of their horses thudded and squelched in the midden heap before the hut and the captain bellowed. A moment passed. The rain fell, sputtering into a sort of sleet. The doorway of the hut was a hole, covered by a skin, and finally this parted and a man emerged: small, cloaked, with a Saxon's beard and filthy, straggling hair. Another bellow brought forth his shrew, a woman dressed in tattered cary cloth and bearing a wicker basket – their child, no doubt. Both of them stood there, cringing. The soldiers shouted. They wanted me, of course – but these poor creatures couldn't have betrayed me if they'd wished for they had no idea I was hiding nearby. Finally, the soldiers, swinging their horses round, enclosed them in a circle. One of the palfreys plunged and danced. I was about fifty paces distant, too far to see but easily close enough to hear the screams – the woman's – and then the circle parted and one of the soldiers, reaching down, dragged the villein by his hair across the yard. He slipped away, belly splashing in the mud and ordure. Two soldiers grabbed him. They dragged him, screaming, to a stump where the man chopped kindling and laid his hand across it and lopped it at the wrist: a jet of blood brightened a puddle for a moment, then trickled away in the muddy yard. My stomach churned; I swore. But there was nothing I could do. I still had my bow, wrapped in my bedroll, but an arrow will not cut mail and, besides, I'd only three of them. Heartsick, I rolled away. Heard another scream – the stuck-pig squeal we all make when a sword-thrust runs us through – and then scrambled to the shelter of the forest's edge. I lay there till nightfall. Then, like a carrion dog, I skulked out, sniffing across the yard. I felt ahead. My feet slipped and slid in mud and gore. The baby, like an egg crushed between your fingers, lay in its basket. The mother, dead, was a huddled heap beside it, the man was gone . . . or at least I didn't find him till I pushed inside the hut. It was a filthy hole. The floor rushes were deep in mud, the bed was a pallet of branches covered with a single hide. The fire, smouldering on, filled the place with a choking smoke. The villein was beside it on the floor. Perhaps he hadn't found the courage to push his stump into the embers and cauterise the wound, or perhaps he'd simply decided that the life of a one-handed man wasn't worth this pain. In any case, he now lay dead, his life's blood curdling round him. I leaned across his body. By the fire was a thick clay pot lined with crusted, half-burnt beans: a feast on which I gorged. Then, looking round, I found a basket of dried bilberries on which I supped more daintily. There was nothing more. I pushed outside. I needed clothes. My tunic was in tatters and even my thick gambeson was torn in places. So, in no good conscience, I looted the poor dead woman who was huddled in the mud. They'd stabbed her; her cloak was rent and bloodstained. But the cloth was strong. I cut it in half across the width – making a sort of chape – then made leggings of the rest. Thus, fed, and a little warmed, I the fox disappeared once more into the drizzling night.

The days passed. I survived them, one by one, although my bones ached, my nose streamed like a wretched child's, and my head grew light with fever. But soon it grew easier. On the sixth day they called off their hounds and by the eighth day the Foresters' patrols were much reduced. Why? I never learned. Perhaps the dogs, or their fewterers, were needed elsewhere; perhaps they'd just grown tired of the chase; or perhaps they'd concluded that I'd left the Forest altogether. But to me the reason made no difference for I now knew, barring some terrible mischance, that I'd won the battle, at least for now. I could rest. Hunt. Risk a fire and cook food. Yet I remained careful. At the height of the search, the Forest had been deserted; now, as the soldiers left, travellers returned. Keeping off the roads and wagonways, for I still moved ceaselessly, I took great care that none should see me. Yet, inevitably, they did. A monk, alone, treading a pathway as silently as myself – he crossed his forehead as I dodged away. A wood-cutter, wearing Fitz Stephen's green but not a soldier – I passed him calmly by and I think he took me for a half-mad pilgrim. Later, that same day, a knight: shield I didn't know, hauberk, ventail open, helmet with a massive nasal – he scarcely deigned a glance as I scurried from beneath his destrier's hooves. But, at last, on the twelfth or thirteenth day – I was beginning to lose count by then – I had a meeting of greater consequence.

It was late afternoon; an afternoon as cold and wet as any other. I'd just killed my supper, a rabbit, and was now looking for a place to build a fire: for I always built my fires before dark, ate, then moved to another spot before night fell. Following a pathway, I'd come to the Dyer's Stone which has stood for ages past on the edge of a nameless brook. I knew the spot well. The stone was scratched with runes, prayers to some savage, vanished god, and as children Garth and I – like everyone else who passed this way – had tried to puzzle out their meaning. Despite my weariness, I remember, those memories made me smile, and as we'd always done, I touched the stone and crossed myself for luck, though it now occurred to me that I was thereby blaspheming every god who might be looking down upon me. No matter; I already felt deserted by all the gods who'd ever ruled. I stepped ahead. Almost as ancient as the stone, a huge elm had been felled as a bridge across the stream, its upper edge adzed flat and then polished by ten thousand passing feet. Now the rain had made it slippery, and since the last thing I needed was a twisted ankle, I set my foot upon it cautiously.

Just then, a man emerged from the bushes on the opposite bank. I halted.

He'd blundered out, head down, pushing through the scrub; on that side, it grew to the water's edge. So he hadn't seen me. Perhaps, indeed, I could have escaped unnoticed, for he was buried in a hooded cloak. But I froze, standing where I was. And then his head came up and we eyed each other.

The man was enormous – to this day, I still don't understand how I could have been so foolhardy as to fight him. He stood only a head taller than myself, but had three times my breadth; and if that breadth was fat, it had been laid down so long ago that it had turned to gristle. His arms were long and sturdy and his wrists and hands were huge. Even his head was large: a rough-hewn log set upon massive shoulders. Yet, I admitted to myself, if he had a brute's size, he didn't have a brutish look. His face was handsome: broad forehead, large dark eyes set pleasantly beneath bushy brows. He was clean-shaven and close-cropped – a Norman's mien in contrast to my Saxon shagginess – and though his cloak was worn it was woven from good Canusian wool. Like myself, he carried a bow and quarterstaff, and I assumed a dirk beneath his cloak.

It was he who broke the silence. "Good day," he said.

He spoke in English – I answered in French. Which made him raise a bushy brow. Then I added, "It seems we both need this bridge."

He smiled. "Then it is a bridge we must judge too narrow . . . since it is only wide enough for one."

His accent was northern, I thought: perhaps Artois. I eyed him. Kept my voice even as I spoke. "I think, sir, you must grant my precedence."

He stepped forward then, and set his right foot on the log. "I grant you nothing."

I hesitated. I knew it would be best to yield. I was too weary for a fight, and this cause was senseless. Yet, perhaps I was not weary enough – and had lost my senses long ago. Indeed, I'd been wandering so long I could scarcely remember a time before this, and the original reasons for my coming here were lost in a blur of misery.

Now something stirred. A memory. I had other tasks in life than plain survival, other skills than cowering.

So, saying nothing, I stepped up on the log and began across.

I caught him off guard; he'd assumed his size would drive me back. But then – his weight so great that even the great elm upon which we stood shuddered – he leapt up, strode forward, met me just beyond the mid-way point. He was holding his staff by one end, his other hand held ready to grasp it in the centre on the parry. I lifted my own wood high, whirling it above my head, and feinted at his ears. A feint he took. Backing off, he slightly lost his balance; ducking beneath his guard, I whacked his ribs. He grunted. Grinned. "So, little man, you've fought with staves before."

I neither smiled, nor spoke. Quarterstaves: they were the one weapon, if you grant that it is a weapon, where I'd always leave Garth bested. I waited, panting. Wondered suddenly what I was doing here. It was utterly senseless. I had skill, but the hulk before me could win on strength alone. Indeed, one clean blow to my skull and my head would split like a rotten melon. And now he came forward again, his staff held like a lance. I leaned away, parried, jabbed his thigh. But he recovered quickly and clubbed his staff upon my own, the sound of the blow ringing through the woods and its shock racing from my hand to my shoulder. I almost dropped the rod. Seeing my disadvantage, he lunged again, but I thrust low with my staff and rattled it between his knees, sending him backwards in a hopping dance – he was surprisingly nimble for a man his size. At the end, he teetered. I tried a lunge – too desperate – which he parried bringing his staff up against his chest, then whirling it out, nicking against my elbow. I yelped aloud. At once, I lost all feeling in my hand, and though I caught my slipping rod with the other, I now awaited what must be the final blow.

It didn't come.

Panting, he gave me another grin. "Wait a moment. The feeling will come back."

I smiled then. "A gentle knight . . . with a cloak for armour, his sword a quarterstaff."

"That's me. Sir Gentleness."

All at once I realised something – fighting with this giant had brought me back to life. I was no less tired, no less wet: but despite my rags and hounded heels, I was myself again. I flexed my fingers. "In that case, when I have you at my mercy I must give you quarter."

He laughed. "Villein – I'll make you remember that."

Then he was on me. We jumped together. Blow after blow was swung and parried. Back and forth we went, he using his size, I my greater skill and speed. The woods rang with the crack of wood on wood, the duller thud as a blow was landed. Soon, we were both bruised and staggering. He slipped down once and I had a chance to return his earlier courtesy. Another time, he almost had me, but with a quick leap backwards I regained the bank, then bounded back to the log before he could seize possession. But the end was never in doubt. To give him proper credit, my enormous adversary gave a lovely feint, his staff driving low as though to clip me on the knees. I dropped, and brought my own staff down, holding it with both hands across myself. Then, with so much speed I scarcely saw the movement, he swung directly upwards, hooking his staff under mine between my hands. With a great wrench, he sent my staff spinning through the air. I waited. He reached out – and, with a certain delicacy, toppled me into the stream.

The stream, frigid and swollen from all the rain, was swift, but didn't come above my waist. Spluttering, I hauled myself to my feet, then staggered to the bank – *his* bank, I might say, the side I'd been trying to reach. He laughed at this, reaching down to help me up. "You lose the battle and gain the day. And deserve to do so, little man."

I slumped down against a bush and blew. "I thank you for your mercy. You could have cracked my skull."

"No. I want to find what's in it. What are you called?"

I thought. Who was I? But then I remembered. "My name is Robin Hood."

He shook his head. "But it's not – no Robin Hood ever spoke your French."

"A man can learn. It's what I'm called. And who are you?"

"John Naylor – so they say."

I laughed – louder, as I saw his grin. "I never could pronounce these stony Saxon names."

He squatted. I smelt warm wool; felt, even from a pace away, the warmth of his great body. He looked up, across our log. "Few come this way."

"Today, I think, one too many."

"Perhaps," he grinned. "But a narrow path can have its virtues. For instance, a troop of soldiers would never pass by here, and this last sennight the Forest has been thick with them."

I looked away and grunted. "I hear they coursed a man."

"Yes. Atheling. The heir to Locksley."

For an instant, the hair prickled on my neck. But then I said, "I think not. They seek an outlaw, Jean Neuilly."

Silence stretched. The rain continued; the brook ran out. Marian had said he'd find me, and so he had. Then I grinned; so this was the man who swived my sister. If he was her first, as I supposed he was, she had great courage. He must have seen my thoughts for his face turned red. He grunted in his turn. "So we are well met."

"It seems so . . . Jean."

He shook his head. "In this Forest I'm always Naylor, or better still, call me Little John – just as you are always Robin Hood."

Why not? I was an outlaw: should have an outlaw's name. I said, "Marian . . . you've seen her?"

"No, but there was a message. She's frightened but all right. They tracked you by the horse."

"The girl?"

"Oh . . . they never noticed her. Marian said she found her in the kitchens, and needs a maid."

Then, suddenly grinning again, the big man stood. "So then, Robin Hood, I hear you're seeking sanctuary?"

"God knows I am."

"We've not far to go then. Follow me."

We set off, eastward, following the brook's upstream course, then slowly ascended Wharncliffe Crags. We walked for an hour, and though I didn't remember this ground, I knew more or less where we were, for we always stayed west of the Great North Road. The rain continued; pushing through bracken and thickets, we made our own path – if any part of me had been left dry after my ducking in the stream, the dripping leaves now soaked it. Finally, ahead, Neuilly paused.

"Stay close," he murmured, as I came up. "From this point on, we're watched."

I scarcely knew it; a rustling among the elders might have been a bird, a glistening spear point in an elm seemed merely a glossy leaf. But I stayed at Neuilly's shoulder as my surety. Then, with no warning, we broke through an alder thicket, found a beaten path beneath our feet and a hundred paces on stood the rim of a dell. It was large, scoop-shaped: perhaps an old stream bed, it opened into a broad gully further on, but was sheltered all around by a thick screen of pollard willow. A camp, crude but permanent, had been set up on the grassy floor. In the centre stood a dozen cruck-built huts, thatched across the lodge-poles, the walls plaited with willow strips, then daubed – the daub now a glistening, muddy slime. On the far side, built against the bank, there were even two stone enclosures with timbered roofs. Before one of these, steaming and hissing in the drizzle, a fire burned.

A fire: therefore men. But no one stirred.

Like a child clinging to his mother's mantle, I followed Neuilly down the slope. We crossed a midden: bones and flies. A cutting stump: faggots neatly bundled. Slowly, my eyes moved from hut to hut. But uselessly. As we reached the middle of the dell, Neuilly stopped and lifted his staff above his head. Instantly, faces appeared among the willows, looking down. Then men appeared. Long-haired, clothed in skins and rags. Most were armed with spears, but some had bows, and I guessed that twenty arrows were pointed toward my heart.

Slowly, they stalked toward us. They stood half crouched. Eyes gleamed behind filthy, shaggy hair. Lips, curled back with tension, revealed their fangs. Someone cackled. No one spoke. Some of their filthy skins were smeared with grease, other smelled of feverfew – to ward off insects – and hovering round them all was a sweaty stench. Finally, when they'd encircled us, Neuilly – Little John – calmly said,

"Ease your strings. I've brought a fresh recruit. Robin Hood of Doncaster."

They eyed him, sullen glances flicking up. Two bows were lowered – but the others stayed.

One, a cur laced inside a deerskin, muttered, "Another mouth to feed – you had no right."

At once, the staff whirred out, a serpent's tongue, and the man toppled to the ground, blood leaking from his ears. For a second now, all eyes were turned to Little John. One licked his lips . . . I waited for an arrow's strum. But just then a shape, like a furry dog, came scrambling through their line. A little man. A broken, hump-backed dwarf. He tumbled up and grabbed my arm.

His voice was oddly gentle, almost cooing. His fingers stroked my palm. "A smooth hand, Robin Hood of Doncaster. What can it do?"

I swallowed. Heard the fire hiss. Felt eyes moving over me.

I said, "I can fletch an arrow."

The dwarf's hand dropped mine, and he pranced away pulling a tall lean man from the stalking circle. "Perhaps you can," he said, "but not as well as Alan here."

"Then, if you have no need for fletchers, I know medicine."

The dwarf laughed then, turned a somersault and hid himself behind me. He whispered, "Perhaps you do. But I know magic – which is more healing than any herb or potion."

I looked over these men, watched them watch me. I was the goat; the mouse the cat tormented. When they grew tired . . . I turned to Little John and saw his anxious face. What skill could they value here? How could I earn my way among these savages? I gave the only answer.

"If you do not want me as a fletcher or a healer, then there's only one thing more I have to offer you. I know killing. A hundred ways. A lance. A sword. A bow . . ."

A bow: at once, with a laugh, the dwarf spun off, leaping up like a happy dog and snatching a bow from one of the stalker's hands. He brought it to me, with a single arrow. "Show us," he said. "There – that willow. You see where the fungus grows?"

I saw. It was barely thirty paces off. Perhaps, I thought, this midget man was on my side. But the bow he handed me was hazelwood, its limbs unbalanced, and the arrow, I thought, was aspen, too stiffly spined – no doubt inclined to yaw. Yet I'd shot with worse. I stretched and loosed in a single motion, the shaft blurring through the rain, then entering the fungus with a gentle plunk. Someone murmured, "Such a shot means nothing." Ignoring this, I turned to my little interlocutor.

"Dwarf, what is your name?"

"Mercury, they call me."

"Then so will I. Mercury – can you shoot a bow?"

"I can."

"Then take this and fetch that shaft. And from that spot, shoot it further on, along the gully. Strike that oak – high enough so all may see."

Taking the bow, he lurched and scrambled through the camp. As he did so, I undid my bedroll. Seeing my strange bow, a few necks craned. I bent it; took an arrow; caressed its fletching until the feathers, taken from a single mallard's wing, were smooth. Mercury, by then, had tugged his arrow from the willow. Angling the bow across his body – clearly an accustomed stance – he stretched. The arrow leapt. We watched its gadding flight, but it struck the oak square on, at shoulder height of a normal man. Now, all eyes turned to me. I took a step, motioning the circle to part around me. The oak, a hundred paces off, lay beyond the dell, beyond the screen of willows. More light fell there, which helped. I took a breath and let it go. Nocking the arrow, I felt its feathers touch my cheek. And loosed. The air was rent. And then, with a splitting sound, my steel broadhead sliced the previous arrow like a stick of kindling.

They gasped; as, by Christ's thorns, they should have.

Little John, the big man, grinned. "So then – do you want this Robin Hood as friend or foe?"

Mercury, the dwarf, put up a cheer. Then they all did. And thus, God help me, I joined their Godforsaken band.

CHAPTER FOUR

Autumn curdled into winter. Breath rimed on beards, blood thickened in veins, and inside leggings stiff as iron our bones creaked and cracked. As for my spirits . . . at first, I will confess, they froze too: a skin of ice at the bottom of the deepest well. But then, despite everything, they thawed. The cold was bitter, but at least I could huddle close to the fire's warmth and put hot food in my belly. I'd lost everything, or so it seemed; and yet, restored to me was a gift beyond price – the freedom to act. I was no longer cringing from the hounds. And I was no longer alone. For, to my surprise, I gradually became reconciled to my strange companions.

Even as a child, I'd always known that the Forest had been full of homeless, speechless creatures who roamed wild as wolves. They seemed joined to an ancient time when the old Saxon gods had lived among the trees – nightmare figures useful to frighten children to obedience. But these men were different. Many, if they'd but known it, were my own villeins: driven from *my* lands by Prince John's taxes and Fitz Stephen's soldiers, they had poached to eat and now hid to live. Others, formerly freemen, were escaping bondage while still others fled brigandage of a more ordinary sort: Much the Miller, Arthur Bland, the tanner, Gilbert White Hand, formerly a butcher – Fitz Stephen had driven them all from business, installing his own minions in their place.

Of all these men, it was naturally Little John whom I came to know the best. He had Norman blood, like myself, and at times, alone together, we'd speak in French. And we shared each other's secrets – our true names, histories and purposes. He was an easy man to like. Strong as an ox, but gentle in his heart, as so many big men are; I had no fear for my sister on that score. Everyone recognised his qualities. Indeed, to this point, if the band had had a leader, it was he; and I certainly had no desire to displace him. Yet, as time went on, he constantly urged my claim, even when I resisted.

"You're a soldier, professionally trained —"

"Not true. My training, as Marian must have told you, was for the priesthood. I'm better with Latin than a lance."

"You quibble. You're the finest archer in these woods, you've a strong right arm — and the brains to go along with it."

"You underestimate yourself," I said.

"Perhaps. But I would rather advise than lead."

I smiled. "All this is flattery. You know I'm the Lord Locksley now. Marian can only wed with my approval."

He merely grinned. "Knowing her, my lord Robin, you'd never have the courage to refuse it."

So, Little John became my friend, and a sort of lieutenant; gradually, as the years went by, he even became something like a brother. Yet, if I learned to love him best, I befriended many of the others too. My favourite weapon had always been the bow: so it was natural that I should draw near to Allen — Alan-a-Dale, as the others called him — for he served as our bowyer and fletcher. He'd been born at Woodhouse Warren close to Mansfield. Tall and lean, his face was brutally scarred, for he was the only member of his family to survive the pox. Orphaned, but with a little money — his father had been a freeman farmer — he had apprenticed himself to Hallam of Trent, a famous bowyer, and when his seven years were up had practised his trade in the little towns and villages between Nottingham and Worksop. I never knew what had forced him to take to the Forest — he never said; I never asked — but I often thanked God he'd come: without his skills, we would have all been lost. He made bows the way the Welshmen do: two pieces of elm, close grained and straight, jointed with hot horse glue and wrapped with hemp and linen. His arrows were turned from birch or ash — heavy enough to carry through brush and drop a deer — and his piles were honed from whatever scraps of steel or iron we could bring to him. In the camp, he was always busy, and I think he found his solace in this constant occupation; for there was always something sad about him. His scarred face made him shy. It was a face, in truth, that might have drawn some women but discouraged men, and I always believed he practised the same vice his monarch did.

Whatever the truth of that may have been, Allen's afflictions were nothing beside Mercury's. But even though I've never understood why we ask the crippled to amuse us, it was this little man, with his twisted back, who was our jester. His spirits never seemed to sag; he found laughter as natural as breathing. He was neither English nor Norman, for he had been born in Rome, and for the first time since Sicily I heard a little of that tongue. Trained as a *jongleur*, he travelled from court to court across Europe, chased from one to another – or so he claimed – by cuckolded husbands drooling for his blood. He blamed this, not on his own lechery, but on that of women: their loathing of his broken body only made them long to touch it, and they spun the most amazing theories about his member's size.

"But surely," I once chided him, "true virtue demanded that you resist temptation."

"Not at all," he replied, turning a somersault at my feet, "for surely I only did God's virtuous work by providing it."

Our jester and magician – he could pull a coin from behind your ear, eat fire from a burning brand – Mercury was our healer as well. He had potions to lessen fever, salves that healed cuts when they began to rot, and knew how to boil up comfrey to make a cast. In addition, his prowess with weapons was considerable. In knife fighting, his size actually seemed to work to his advantage, and though he was somewhat awkward with a bow, he'd learnt to throw a seax with more skill than any man I've ever known. He had powerful wrists, and, at least with his little axes, could use either hand: with a quick flick they'd tumble twinkling through the air, striking marks thirty paces distant. Four were always on his belt.

All in all, these men, with perhaps a dozen others, formed the pith of our little band. Their exile was complete and permanent; if they showed their faces outside the Forest, they were as good as dead. Around us, however, was a larger group of varying size; men who still had contacts with their families, but joined us for the larger hunts, and others in the villages who helped us either with goods or information. That first day, there'd been about forty men in camp, and I was to learn that this was normal. At harvest time, the umber dropped; if a big hunt was on, it grew. Mostly these were men, but sometimes they brought their women: simply to hide if Fitz Stephen's hounds were out, or, if our kill was large, to help cut the meat and carry it and boil up tannin to preserve the hides. Most of our time was spent in hunting, but from time to time, I will admit, we took to thieving. We had no choice: we needed silver money. The villages could give us grain, but we had salt to buy, and cloth, and above all steel and iron. Still, we kept our consciences passably clear. We attacked strangers, never local people; tried not to kill; and left all pilgrims and villeins alone. This last, admittedly, was no great sacrifice. Only the rich had money – merchants with their trains of rounceys, fat abbots on their mules – but at least within the Shire the common people never learned to hate us. Which was as well. We needed them. They were our eyes and ears, warning us of Fitz Stephen's raids. When they came, we had to flee, slipping down the narrowest paths into Sherwood's darkest depths, for his soldiers, with their armour and horses, were too strong for us.

But then we could flee no longer.

The crisis, when it came, was sudden. At Candlemas, we learned that Fitz Stephen had died: news, however, that brought us no great pleasure. He'd been brutal and rapacious, determined to squeeze every muid of wine and sack of grain from his peasants, but at least he'd understood that his wealth, ultimately, derived from them. His wife, Maud de Caux, who now took his Reeveship in both fact and name, wasn't even bridled by that restraint: it was as though she felt spilled blood was a sort of gold that could fill her coffers. Within a week, her soldiers swept the Forest like a bitter wind, slaughtering half the peasants in a village suspected of aiding us. Before this onslaught, we had no choice: we fled to our camp. There, timorously, we cowered, and for one bone-cracking week even doused our fires. Finally, however, starvation forced us out. I led a team of hunters south, Arthur Tanner took another north. I returned with a scrawny fawn – Arthur not at all.

For two days we waited.

By the third, we all knew what must have happened.

"They have them, Robin, they must," said Little John.

"But do they know *what* they have? A poacher is nothing remarkable . . . and if Arthur had found no game the soldiers might only be suspicious."

Little John shook his craggy head. "Will Copley was with them and he bears a brand. They'll know. And Maud de Caux, I think, is a woman who turns suspicions into certainties."

I pondered. We had our fires now, but kept them small. Shrugging my cloak closer round my shoulders, I stretched stiff fingers toward the flickering flames. Under torture, any of us would talk – talk, scream, blubber, everything we knew. I had no illusions. If Arthur's group was taken, we'd lost our greatest secret: the location of the camp.

Beside me, Little John now murmured, "A doubling of the guard?"

I decided, and shook my head. "It's no time for half-measures. We move – everyone, everything. At once. You lead them. And while you go I'll take Mercury and two others and try to find Arthur's band."

He nodded, rising. "If there's anything left to find."

There wasn't, much.

As Little John led the others into the Manor Hills – to a small camp there we sometimes used – Mercury and I scoured the woods for miles around. We found them two days later. North of Barnsley, a little south of the Calder River, a number of paths ran together into a narrow road leading to a stream whose current raced so fast it never froze. In winter, two villages drew their water here, carrying buckets back and forth on yokes.

Now, every trip, they'd pass our carrion.

From irons around their necks, they were staked by chains to the roadside. Their eyes were slimy pits – two knots in a rope looped round the head, twisted tight, then tighter, till the eyeballs pop. Their hands and feet had been axed off, the stumps plunged in boiling pitch. And from the mewling sounds they made, I guessed they had no tongues. Yet they lived. They sucked the snow, and even had bowls of oats before them they could mouth like dogs. They'd live until the winter slowly killed them – long enough, that is, to tell the world what happened to the men that joined us.

Behind me, now, one of my own men retched.

I touched Mercury on the shoulder. "When the road is clear . . ."

He nodded; blessedly, I had to say no more. We stood; approached in silence. Then, in the space of two heartbeats, my arrows, his small axes, mercifully stilled four others. We hacked them free, dragged them to the woods, and buried them as best we could.

The next day, our old camp was razed and pillaged.

The next week, another village burned.

"It can't go on," I said. "She's making war on her own estates."

"Maybe," said Little John. "But it won't have to go on much longer. Soon, where will we be able to get our grain? Who will help us? Trust us? Even the strongest of castles can be undermined. That's what she's doing."

Mercury murmured, "Ah yes. Fear turns love to hate in the twinkling of an eye. Soon, the people will be blaming us for Sweet Maud's sins."

He was right. I looked around. This camp was safe, but primitive; primitive even in comparison to the one we'd left. Our shelters were patched from boughs and skins. Allen had no forge or anvil. Behind us was a cave, a storeroom perfect for hanging game . . . but there was none to hang. With help, I knew, we'd be able to re-build, but who would help us now?

Little John, watching me, gave a fleeting smile. "You see, Robin, why I'd rather advise than lead."

"There's no decision here," I shrugged. "All we can do is kill some of them before they kill all of us."

"What do you mean?"

"What I say. They have plucked eyes from our men – we will pluck eyes from theirs."

I convinced Little John – he saw we had no choice – but our men didn't like it. They had never fought the soldiers willingly. They were villeins, after all; men on horseback terrified them, for they knew that a soldier, with his palfrey, could ride them down with virtually no risk to himself. As well, the soldiers all wore chain-mail and our arrows, with their soft iron tips, would scarcely penetrate it. Talking to them, explaining my plans, I could see the fear in their upturned faces. Or not so much fear, I decided, as disbelief. I told them that: standing on a rotted stump, my cloak drawn round me against the bitter wind. "You do not believe you can win," I said, "just as the villeins in the villages believe that they have no hope. And because you don't believe, you lose; and because they don't believe, they end with nothing to hope for. I tell you: you will win. And when you do, the greatest victory you will gain, will be in your own hearts." When I convinced them, it was only because – for some strange reason – they believed in *me*, which, I feared, was no great weapon. In *my* heart I knew that our victory, if it came, would have more conventional origins: total surprise and overwhelming numbers.

Still, four days later, I was crouched in ambush, hidden in the bracken beside the road that runs south from Clipstone to Fountain's Dale. It had been a day of bitter cold; easier to hide our bodies than our misting breaths. But now dusk was falling, grey as ice, and we hid within the gloom like the last breaths inside a dying man. The road was narrow here; coming off a curve, rising to a hill. When the soldiers came – the day's last patrol, riding home to Clipstone barracks: tired, careless, thinking of the tavern's steamy warmth – we would have them trapped. Along the road, beside me, were nineteen men; hidden beyond the hill, thirteen others. And across from us – worth a troop of cavalry – was a little pond, a frozen swamp, its razor-sharp ice cutting off retreat for mounted men better than the highest cliff.

A frigid hour passed. I prayed to God to bless us. Hands pressed to crotch or armpit, we waited for the look-out's whistle: when it came, it was like the single sound in a silent dream. Then, an instant later, we heard the horses' hooves ringing on that frozen road as though from iron. They came swinging round the bend. Four grey soldiers, four sorrel palfreys. They loomed like monsters, their grey cloaks flying out like bats, breath misting round their heads, ice glittering on their helmets. Drumming hooves: bodies jolting in the saddle: the terrible swish that only moving chain-mail makes . . . I wondered if they wouldn't terrify us all and, like some ghostly army, pass by unscathed.

But then, ten paces from me – bless him – Much bellowed out a war-cry and nineteen arrows, tensed on strings, were loosed. The silence of a sucked-in breath. Then shrieks as though from Hell. The horses screamed and plunged, twisted, reared about, their legs breaking under them like kindling wood. Three went down, skidding on the icy mud, feet flailing. But the fourth, the Captain, stood: enough, in himself, to rout us. I stepped from cover and he saw me, checked his rein and wrenched his horse's head around. But his shield was still twisted to his back. Drawing one of those precious arrows I'd brought back from my Lost Crusade, its pile the finest Spanish steel, I loosed, pinning his belly to the cantle of his saddle. He screamed his agony; the horse plunged and bounced him, like a loosened sack of wheat. Meanwhile, his men were staggering up, struggling to re-group. But they had no chance. Their eyes already glittered with the crazed despairing look of men about to die from steel. Like pointed, snarling wolves, we were all around them. In an instant, a hundred shafts were loosed. Some men, forgetting themselves, aimed at the soldiers' upper bodies, and merely prickled shields and dented chain-mail. But enough remembered. The soldiers' haubergeons came only to mid-thigh. Arrow after arrow sliced their knees and calves – fangs tearing at the haunches of the stag – until, one by one, the soldiers became St Sebastien's blasphemed image. One staggered, dropped; one tried to run and slipped and couldn't rise. The last, defiant, sword in hand, finally began to sway . . . and then we were on them with our spears and axes, thrusting and stabbing until the road ran red.

Two minutes? Three? That's all it took. Then, exhausted, we stood about our kill. From our mouths, the blood, our heated bodies, there rose a cloud of steam. Our gasping breaths rasped on the air. Someone coughed. I felt a trembling in the knees. Ice cracked a branch behind us in the woods. It was almost dark . . .

"Strip them," I croaked, "take everything. Little John – I want the Captain's horse."

Kites on carrion. Grasping, tearing hands. A muttered curse . . .

We left them there, stripped naked, gutted at eye and crotch, then vanished in the woods.

In three weeks, we struck six times; on the roadways mainly, but twice luring the soldiers to the woods. We killed eighteen men of theirs, lost one ourselves. Our booty was considerable: much armour (two ancient, mascled hauberks; four haubergeons of ring-mail, the others chain), swords, dirks, steel-piled arrows, four horses with equipage. But we gained much more as well. Now, our men had confidence and skill, even the beginnings of a soldier's discipline. With our victories, the villeins respected us again. And so did the enemy. By March, the soldiers were patrolling in groups of twelve: but because the patrols were strengthened, they were far fewer, and because of our skill at ambush, they kept to the main roads and wagonways, leaving us the Forest. In this fashion, the bitter winter dwindled to a spring of grudging truce, giving us a respite we welcomed. We built our new camp – called Eagle's Nest – and re-stocked our larder. Allen set to work repairing mail and dented helmets, Little John drilled a dozen men with swords. As for myself, I took on a different task, teaching half a dozen of our number how to ride. They were all villeins so horses only frightened them – they were the Lord's great weapon – but patiently I schooled them on our captured palfreys. By April, I would not have called them knights, but they made an excellent corps of messengers: stationed by turns at strategic passes in those hills, they would give us many hours' warning of attack.

Thus, the spring brought a sort of peace. The rivers flooded; hawthorns came to bud. For a time, as men slipped off to plough and seed, our numbers dwindled. There was less to do. Slowly, lying in the sun, we thawed, stretched, remembered former pleasures. I shaved my dark, curling beard, fattened on pheasants' eggs, enjoyed several trysts with Megan. But as the weeks passed my conscience stirred. Relieved of the winter's pressure, my thoughts moved again to the King, to Prince John, his brother, and to all the reasons that brought me to the Forest in the first place.

It was clear that we had to warn King Richard about what had happened to his kingdom. But how to do it? Little John was firm: if we needed to send a message to the King, I couldn't be the one to take it. "Robin Hood" was needed here – this whole corner of the shire depended on him. But the obvious choices, beside myself, were all too risky: Little John, Allen, Much amd Mercury would all have trouble travelling, for their faces were even better known than mine, since they'd been in the forest longer. And our lesser men were unsuitable for different reasons. In Sherwood, they were shrewd enough, but they knew little of the world outside and many had never been as far as Nottingham. How could I expect them to find Richard in the Holy Land?

"What we need," Little John said one day, "is a merchant or perhaps a minstrel. Someone who's used to travelling and wouldn't arouse suspicion. Even an old man of court – if you could find one who was loyal."

"Marian might," I answered. "She knew all the families in these parts."

"Well," said Little John, his voice studiously neutral, "I suppose we should ask her then."

I smiled at this: he was always looking for excuses to go and see her. I didn't blame him. Their opportunities for meeting were rare and risky, for Marian was watched continuously, but two days later we sent a message asking her to come to the usual spot, a small wooded dell not far from Kirklees. I sent Little John ahead, giving the pair a chance to be alone, and rode up later as twilight fell. Golden shafts of sunlight slanted through the trees, and at the top of the vale I drew my horse up, waiting for a moment, half-hidden in the shadows. I smiled, seeing them below: they sat on a hollow log, hands clasped, heads bent together. What an odd sight they made – my enormous friend, my little sister – but their feelings for each other were apparent even in the trusting, restful forms their bodies made together. Not for the first time that spring, I thought of the Princess Berengaria. Was the frustration their love brought worse than the pain my love's denial caused in me? I wondered for a quiet moment; and then, making as much noise as possible to warn them, I rode into the dell. Little John grinned as I came up, and seemed so happy and complacent that I had to tease him: "Well, well. It seems you take great pleasure in my sister's company – one of these days, perhaps, we'll have a little talk."

He shrugged as if he didn't understand. "Dear Robin, this is only work. I've been tracking down our messenger."

"And?"

Marian smiled. "What about Richard Lee, the son of the wool merchant in Doncaster? He's often travelled with his father and I know they support your cause."

"He's very young."

"But you can trust him," said Little John. "And if you wrote your message between the lines of the writ Richard gave you, that would identify him well enough."

"All right. One problem solved."

But now Marian frowned, and gently touched Little John on the arm. "I'm afraid I have another." We both looked at her as she went on: "My time is up. De Caux has insisted on my answer within a week."

Now we were very silent. With the setting of the sun, a little rain had started, pattering on the leaves, sprinkling the shoulders of my sister's cloak, shining in her hair. At last Little John murmured, "Dear Christ, I'll kill that woman with my own two hands."

"What about the annulment of de Birkin's marriage?" I asked.

"They're getting it. At first they applied to a young bishop, Fitzherbert of Devon, but he refused them. Maud was furious so she went to Prince John, who's now actually thrown Fitzherbert into gaol in Nottingham."

"A bishop?"

"Yes – he'll do anything. And somehow he's kept it secret. Now John has personally interceded with the Pope and documents have already gone out to Rome."

Little John was recovering from his fury: "But that might take months yet."

"Besides, your year of mourning isn't up," I added. "And if you tell Maud you'll marry her son, we'll gain more time still."

"But she'll want to announce it publicly, and once that's done they can force me to go through with it."

Yes; once the contracts were arranged, there was no chance of turning back. "All right," I said, "tell her you refuse – you won't announce it while you're still in mourning. But convince her. Change your tune. Make her believe you're eager for de Birkin –"

"Dear God, Robin, that would be beyond me."

"No. Listen. Doesn't the Prince usually come to Nottingham for Christmas? Tell Maud that she can make the announcement then. On the last day of Christmas. Surely that would satisfy her – and that gives us the most time to plan."

A plan . . . But what could that plan be? Gloomily, as darkness fell, we said good-bye and I rode back to Sherwood while Little John led Marian back to Kirklees. But her news had changed everything, and I scarcely noticed, the following week, when we dispatched Richard Lee with our message to the King. The weeks slipped by. Buds blossomed; the fields turned green; the summer came. We fished and hunted, fought three skirmishes with Our Lady Sheriff's men – while all the time, inwardly, we wrestled with the problem of my sister. If worst came to worst, she could always live with us, but for a woman we knew our life was terribly cruel. As well, it would put an end – in public – to all the Locksley claims. Our family, in the great world outside the Forest, would be finished. In the end, of course, we'd make that sacrifice, but was there no way to avoid it? If there was, we couldn't see it, at least throughout that summer. The autumn came. Then, after a great argument between us – for Little John wanted to keep it a purely private matter – we told the men and they all agreed to help; and would have agreed all the more if they'd known Marian wasn't simply Little John's lady love, but my sister too. But willingness was not the problem – we had to have a plan. And it seemed they could no more discover one than me.

The days passed by. The first great snow drifted through the woods. And one day the Prince's train – knights, ladies, carts and wagons, two hundred heavy-burdened rounceys – slowly stretched its way through Sherwood. By the first day of Christmas, the Court was all assembled in its usurped glory, and two nights after, Allen rose before our central fire, and announced that he was speaking for all the men.

"We must do something, Robin – you two have done so much for us – and we feel there's only one solution. Even if we kill Maud's son that only means they'll kill John's maid – if he's left her such – which scarcely seems an honest bargain. So we must take de Birkin hostage: hold him to prove Maud's word that the lady will be safe."

I stood beside him, feeling the flickering flames leap up to warm my cheeks. "But how can we do it?" I asked. "We're not magicians, after all. De Birkin, the whole Court, is now in Nottingham, which is the Prince's strongest castle, even stronger than the Tower."

"Aye," said Little John. "Even for a hundred men, main force would just be suicide. We must use stealth; get in and out unseen. But how? What can we use as our disguise?"

Allen, still on his feet, looked round him: and then the broken shape of Mercury came waddling to the fire's edge. Across from me, the glow of flames between us, he squatted down on little haunches, smiled and held one finger up. "You say we're not magicians, Robin . . . and yet I am."

"Mercury, real men aren't captured by sleight-of-hand, even if the hand is as cunning as your own."

"Maybe. But, in truth, what is our problem? We must get into this castle, and get out, unseen."

"More," said Little John. "We're to return with an unwilling prisoner."

"More yet," said Mercury. "It would do our souls good, we've all agreed, to have a priest among us. Why not this honest bishop, Fitzherbert?"

"So now," said Little John, "we break into the dungeon too."

"While," I added, "we snatch de Birkin from Christmas revelry in the Hall. It can't be done. We couldn't get in, let alone get out."

"You give up too easily," Mercury grinned. "If you think, it's just a riddle. Ask yourself, dear Robin: what passes through a castle's walls unseen?"

"The air. You'll turn us into birds."

"Not quite – but not far wrong. I'm thinking of two things only, both of which are carried on the air. One you smell, the other hear – but both you rarely see. One will lead us to the dungeons, the other to the Hall." He rose then, and turning toward the others, opened his little arms:

"What passes through a castle's walls unseen?
One hides its face from others' sight,
The second flashes teeth in candlelight.
Both from the rumbling belly come –

> One is falling ordure,
> The other laughter's rising hum."

He turned back across the fire. "You see?"

I thought, and then I did. By God's bowels, the little man was right.

CHAPTER FIVE

I held my breath and tried not to gag.

"Our Blessèd Lord," I murmured. "Mercury truly is the Devil's spawn."

Allen coughed. "Aye. And then, spawned, he swived his mother and got his Evil Father horns."

Oswin laughed behind us and we heard a hinge squeak. The shed door opened. Beyond, the night swirled with snow. Much, who'd wisely waited outside, now caught a whiff. "Dear Jesus," he muttered.

Oswin propped the door open against the wind and drew closer. He grinned in the darkness. "Robin, if you're going to be a true gong farmer the first thing you have to do is lose your sense of smell. Next comes your prudish pride. Just remember: turn any man inside out and this is what he smells like."

He was right. And his cart, I told myself, was just a cart – this one, indeed, had been scrubbed out and he even called it "clean". There was no sense in fussing; in fact, standing here now, smelling this stench, I began to believe that Mercury's plan might truly work. In castles, the privies are set within the walls, the ordure falling down between the inner and outer stones, preferably to a moat or stream; if not, it heaped up in chambers that men like Oswin mucked out. "Gong farmers" they were called; and they were part of the answer to Mercury's riddle. *What passes through a castle's walls unseen?* These men did. All the world looked down on them: no one feared them, or saw them as a threat. In their disguise, we probably *would* pass through Nottingham Castle gates without being closely questioned.

I looked inside Oswin's cart and inspected his tools: wooden spades, paddles, and folding leather buckets on long handles. "Everything's there," said Oswin, "and the clothes are on those hooks."

Breeches, leather aprons, gloves – they smelled no better than the cart. Yet they too were clean. I said, "You know you'll lose everything?"

"Aye, but your money will buy it new again, and better. Just break the door down, and make it seem the cart was stolen. I'll report it in Alfreid tomorrow night. No one will hear of it in Nottingham until next week."

He helped us drag the cart out, then harnessed his two horses. Stomping, restive, they didn't enjoy the prospect of such early work – it still lacked three hours till prime. Then, as Oswin returned to his bed, we dressed in his clothes, made our final preparations and clambered aboard the wagon. Much took the reins; Allen and I huddled down behind the seat. The stench, this close, was awful, but it was far too cold for jokes. Slowly, clattering away from the little steading, we moved along the road that joins Alfreid to Nottingham. The track was frozen mud, and the horses' hooves slithered on the icy ruts. The snow kept falling; twisted, like writhing snakes, across the fields. We shivered, rubbed our hands, then gave up these meagre protests and simply froze. For a hopeless period we jounced and jolted. We seemed to make no progress; there was nothing to see but flat black fields and blacker woods. This was the week of the Winter Solstice, and even when prime rang out from a little village church, the sky was black. Finally, however, the sun squeezed above the flat horizon and we drew over.

Oswin had a little brazier. We lit it, stomped our feet, and broke our fast on dried meat, an oatcake each and a big mug of heated wine. Winter fields, a sea of muddy waves, stretched on either hand. After a time, to our left, I saw another cart creeping down a lane toward us, and a moment later we all caught sight of spears on the road ahead: the morning's first patrol heading north from Nottingham. They cantered toward us, mail glittering in the rising light, their horses snorting clouds of mist. Huddled round our coals, we didn't give them a glance, nor did they look at us; and as they disappeared from sight, we too resumed our places and went on our way.

The road, the day, both stretched gloomily before us. Oswin's scrawny nags were worse than mules, and I wondered how many steps they took to travel a league – more, I suspected, than the Romans had numbers for. The snow continued. The sun, behind a smudge of clouds, was as pale as the moon and not much warmer. But, as the hours passed, we at least gained a little company; carts and wagons pulled by everything from dogs to oxen; pilgrims on foot; another of Maud's patrols; and the mesne of a great knight, wagons, destriers, a dozen palfreys – the arms and banners sparkled like brilliant beads along our road. Except for those on foot, few of these travellers were content to tag behind us; most gave a warning shout and trotted past. Noon came and went, then none, when we stopped again for more warm wine.

It was shortly after this stop that two travellers appeared on the road behind us.

Both rode palfreys. One was a very large man; beneath his cloak, he wore a priest's robes – and he was a priest, judging by his belly, who might have confessed to the sin of gluttony. The second was a dwarf, dressed in a yellow jerkin brightened by patches of red and blue.

As they pulled even with our wagon, and moved around, I called to the dwarf, "Could you tell us, sir, are we fair on the road to Nottingham?"

He grinned and wrinkled up his nose. "On the road, yes . . . but hardly 'fair' . . ."

"Don't complain, little man. Our work would be less needed the more your friend controlled his appetite."

"If he was my friend, good sir, I would apologise indeed for the labour his great belly causes. But he's my father – and no man can choose his parents."

Now Allen called, "Could that be true, good Father? Would you accept this wretch as your begotten son?"

"I must," he replied, riding closer. "I got him on a whore, but then, seeing the lamentable issue of my fornication, I at once took Orders and now we travel the world calling men to follow my example and repent from sin."

All this – so Mercury claimed – was a common *jongleur*'s turn in Italy: Father Tuccolo and His Son, the Dwarf. They'd rail each other as we'd been doing and then – the bigger man the platform for the smaller – turn their tumbling tricks. Now, twisting round to see that the road was clear, Little John grinned and said, "Do you think we'll earn our supper at the Hall?"

"The choicest cuts."

He laughed. "We've not been questioned once. Everyone believes us."

"You're only too believable, good Father Tuccolo."

"Well, I wouldn't say the less of you. The smell, I mark, convinces . . . Mind you hurry, though. They'll close the gates at sunset."

I nodded, then he gave a wave and trotted on ahead.

In fact, despite Little John's caution, we timed our arrival perfectly, joining the final rush of carts and people pushing within the city's gates to join the Twelfth Night celebrations. No one questioned us. We lumbered slowly through the mud-churned streets. The snow grew heavier: piling up in eaves, whitening slates. Now, for an hour or so, we huddled in a narrow lane, for gongers worked by night, the less to disturb their noble patrons. In the houses around us, candles and rushlights flickered. A woman, cloak pulled round her, lamp before, raced her shadow along the road . . . A lone rider cantered past, snow steaming on his horse's haunches . . . We froze and waited. I thought of Marian; memories of Berengaria warmed my limbs. I told myself that even though a castle wall and this nauseous stench that plugged my nostrils separated me from a Prince, who was false brother to my King, our destinies were nonetheless woven all together. I dozed a little. And then – like everyone else in Nottingham that Twelfth Night – my eyes were lifted up: up to the hill on which the mighty castle stood, then higher still to its topmost battlement where now a pitch torch blazed against the night . . . then another and another until the entire outer wall was ringed with fire, a star as bright as the one that had led the Three Wise Kings.

Beside me, Allen grunted, "In honour of the Prince?"

"No," growled Much, "to light the way for his Royal Gong Farmers." He shrugged, snow sliding from his cloak. "I say we go: as well to perish there as here."

I reached ahead, and slapped him on the shoulder. He took up the reins and the horses sleepwalked down the street, wound through a maze of lanes about the market, then pulled us higher to the castle. The final slope. Rushlights blazed on either side. Our guts slowly tightened and we muttered prayers, as Much pulled up the horses before the double towers of the gate-house. In the light – and that patch of snow and cobble held the whitish glare of noon – we could see that the castle guard was royal, their breasts emblazoned with John's lions. An advantage – none of them could possibly know us. Much did our talking; the captain passed a lamp across our faces; then waved us on. Wheels grinding across bare stone, we clattered through the gates.

We had now entered the castle's Lower Ward, a broad court of cobblestone. Our eyes moved up: on the battlements the torches blazed, the sentries' long black shadows tramping back and forth between them. Below, to our left – against the northern wall – was the castle's chapel; to our right, on the south, lay a wooden guard house just inside the gates, then a large residence for visiting knights and another building for lesser dignitaries where Marian would be staying. Finally, directly in front of us – a great lump of blackness – there soared the cylindrical tower of the ancient keep – with the dungeons, and Fitzherbert, underneath. Two torches burned in cressets by its door revealing guards with gisarmes on the steps.

I swung up beside Much, who murmured, "So far God is with us, but is that where we wish to take Him?"

"He'll forgive us. But swing right, around to the side, and draw in there."

He clucked the horses up. Slowly, we moved along. With the Prince and his Court in attendance, it was obvious that the castle was overcrowded; along every wall temporary boxes had been erected for the extra horses. We saw varlets working there, spreading straw, but otherwise few people were about. The soldiers kept their pickets along the battlements; an esquire clattered up the steps outside the residence of the knights. But at least, within this Ward, there was little other sound. Much pulled up; then, with difficulty, turned us round so we were pointing back toward the gate. We were now within a passage between the keep's southern wall and the apartments where Marian would have her room. Behind, on the far side of the keep, was the Upper Ward and, at the rear of this, Nottingham's Great Hall. Here there was more light and bustle; figures flitted across the snow; spurs jangled; and, as the door swung open for an instant, we could hear the sound of music and laughter, as Mercury's doggerel had predicted. The Prince and his attendants, it seemed, were happily at their Twelfth Night Feast.

We got down, off-loaded our tools: and, after a nudge from me, Allen began to whistle and I grumbled to Much about the tardiness of Oswin's nags. Thus, in normal order, we paraded round to the keep's front entrance. Once, in a time even beyond my father's memory, this massive stone tower had been the castle's heart: residence of the lord, site of his Holy Chapel, haven for his villeins in time of war. Now, it was little more than a jail and barracks for the soldiers.

The guard knocked for us, the Chief Warder opened from within. He was a heavy, red-faced man, bluff as the evening's weather. "I've had no notice," he grumbled down to Much.

"Aye, well, we had little either. We're to do you first, then the Hall when the entertainment's done."

He squinted in the torchlight. "Where's Oswin?"

"Sick in bed. I'm Alaric, his cousin."

For a moment longer, the Warder delayed; but we so looked, and smelled, our parts, that he finally turned on his heel and strode inside. We followed after. Beyond the doors, we were within a porch or vestibule that protruded from the keep itself. A dark hallway stretched before us – except it wasn't a hall, but a drawbridge, its heavy planks echoing with a hollow *clump* beneath our feet. Memory flickered: as a boy, I'd come here with my father and they'd pulled it up for me, revealing the dark pit beneath. Now, on its far side, a cresset burned revealing a gloomy passage glistening round. The Warder bade us wait and disappeared. We heard a bellow and a short time later he returned, accompanied by another man. "He'll take you down."

Much nodded. The second man, very short, with a massive head that seemed to sit directly upon his shoulders like a frog's, marched us on: down the passage, then down a narrow, twisting staircase that uncoiled to the gloomy cellars underneath. These were the dungeons. Tallow candles lit wet, glistening walls; beneath our feet were ancient, mouldering rushes. Without a single glance behind, our frog clumped along till he reached a crosswise passage. Then, lifting his candle up, he croaked, "I'll leave you then. You'll know the way."

I called, "Aye . . . but open up your pigswill door . . . On the southern side. That's where we left the cart."

He grumbled something in return, then disappeared: his lamp revealed the dungeon doors and, further down, a bench, a table, a jug of beer – our froggie's lily-pad.

We continued on, along the outer wall, following Oswin's instructions but scarcely needing them. A candle burned directly opposite the chamber door and the odour of the spot foretold what lay within. We set down our tools, tugged kerchiefs round our faces. Then Allen drew back the bolts and lifted up the latch . . .

The stench, the horrid hum of flies: a heap of excrement the depth of two men high . . .

Much moaned; I gagged; Allen crossed his forehead and murmured, "By the thorns of Christ . . ."

A rat squeaked along the passage.

Black and compacted at the base, a lighter ooze swam up above, and began to seep beyond the chamber door. Grimly, we set to work, digging at this filthy mountain. Spadeful after spadeful, we loaded up our buckets, then hooked them onto yokes; Allen, with the first, staggered down the passageway. We didn't talk; tried not to breathe: my teeth clenched like a portcullis across my mouth. Finally it was my turn to heave up my burden and stagger off, but aching shoulders were a paltry price to pay for sweet fresh air. Pushing through the small side door (when this place had still had kitchens, it would have opened to the midden), I slopped my load into the back of the cart. Then, for a second, I panted happily. The snow, still falling, was cold against my face, but welcome. I looked around. Sentries still shuffled on the flaming battlements, but the Wards seemed even emptier than before. Lights glimmered from the hall; I heard the strains of music . . . And then, like a mole, I scuttled back along my burrow.

Gradually, the loathsome mound was transferred from keep to wagon; minute by filthy minute, the hours passed.

Finally – Allen was just returning from the cart – the Chapel bells began to ring: compline. This, at long last, was our signal. Within the Hall, the entertainments were now scheduled to begin. And on the dais, as we'd arranged, Marian would call for wine, fill up her glass, and begin to sip it slowly. When she was finished, she'd then ask her future husband, de Birkin, to conduct her to her rooms. With a nod, Much set down his tools, though Allen, with a purposeful clatter, kept on loading buckets. I now turned to a special spade: my Turkish bow, and two arrows, had been wrapped around its handle. I unlashed it, slipped on a string, then followed Much along the passage. Reaching the corner that turned toward the cells, he called, "Warder! My men will have some water. A fresh bucket if you please!"

The frog slowly blinked, then rose . . . and stepped into the light. I loosed: at this close range, the arrow passed right through him, clattering out behind. He fell forward with a gentle thump. Quietly – we didn't want to arouse the prisoners – we ran to him, snatched him up at head and heel, then dragged him back to Allen. We stripped his keys, pushed him within that awful chamber, and slammed the door. "All right, Allen, you know what to do. Much: with me."

We ran along the passage, then out the pigswill door. Much clambered aboard the cart, while I pressed myself into the shadow of the visitors' apartment, directly across the passage. How long would Marian take to sip a glass of wine? Huddled beneath those stairs, it seemed like hours. My greatest fear was that someone else would decide to forego the evening's entertainment and return early to their chambers. But no one did. And finally the Hall door swung open and I spied Marian's silhouette. I held my breath. Slowly, almost lazily, the two figures strolled across the Ward. I'd told Marian to pretend good grace before her fate (to be announced the next day) and she was acting her part to perfection, for now I heard her gentle laugh. A smile glimmered in response, then glinted more brightly as it caught a leap of light from the torches high above. De Birkin. For the first time now I saw him. A tall man. Well set up. They stepped a little closer . . . He had a cold but handsome face, vain enough to believe he might have made this conquest.

Marian whispered, "The torches are like the stars."

"They are, my lady, though I fear the sentries –"

I hit him then, my dirk held like a club. He groaned, half twisting round toward me. I struck once more. As he crumpled, I caught him beneath the arm and held him up.

Marian gasped. "Thank God. I couldn't have kept that up much longer."

"You did wonderfully – even now he's dreaming of your love. But remember: he left you at the stairs and turned back, towards the Ward. That's all you know."

She squeezed my arm. "Yes, sweet brother. God go with you."

Holding de Birkin up like a drunken sot, I dragged him across the snow-filled passageway to the cart. Then, from within, Much reached down and grabbed him. "Throw me his cloak," I whispered, "then bind and gag him. Where's Allen?"

"By the door. You get clear, then he'll lead Fitzherbert out."

In the shadow of the cart, I took off my gonger's clothes – their stench could too easily betray me – and put on fresh. De Birkin's cloak was vair, trimmed with weasel; rich enough to get me past the guards but not so rich, I hoped, to mark me once I was inside.

I stepped into the light and whispered, "How do I look?"

"Very lordly," Much returned.

"The bow?"

"Under that cloak, no one will see."

Quickly, I stepped round the Keep and into the Upper Ward. For two strides in that sudden flood of light, I was uncertain: but then, feeling the lick of fur against my cheek, I told myself to remember who I truly was and simply be a lord. So I hurried forward to the Hall, appearing natural enough – I'd been summoned away; my mistress, my lady, had fallen ill; or I was rushing to order an even greater lord from merriment – and when I reached the steps I dashed straight up, not pausing, assuming that the double guard would do just as it did: throw the doors apart so I could enter.

But then, after this brave show, I stood there, stunned.

The flame of rushlights, the curling smoke of torches, the glitter of gold and glass, the rippling sheen of silk – the light, leaping and reflected, was almost blinding. And the sound pounded on my ears: piping music, from the galleries above; shouts and laughter everywhere; the roar and rumble of a thousand conversations. Recovering myself, but with my eyes still dazzled, I looked around. Here, indeed, was a Great Hall, a Prince's Court, the Glory of the Realm. Twice a hundred tables stretched before me, a thousand feeding noble mouths, and at the Hall's far end, a hundred paces distant, stood the dais where, like a tapestry woven of ermine, gold and sendel – indeed, like the tapestries and banners that fluttered down from the gallery above them – sat the Prince's High Court. The Prince himself; his lady, Isabel – William Fitzrobert's daughter. Great dukes, mighty knights. Their ladies . . . bishops and archbishops . . . I tried to pick out faces, arms. Geoffrey: bastard brother to the King and Prince, now archbishop of York . . . The Earl of Chester. Longespée, another bastard brother: now Earl of Salisbury . . . Lesser names: Maud de Caux herself, happily glistening with grease. There was a man beside her with a face not unlike de Birkin's, so presumably he was another son . . . And then I even saw a coat of arms I remembered from a beach in Sicily: Sir Guy de Gisbourne. What treachery was he plotting now? Or was he simply savouring its rewards?

But just then someone brushed against me and the spell was broken. I stepped back, letting myself join in the anarchy; kitchen sluts, varlets, esquires serving knights; a drunk, snoring on the rushes; jugs of wine upturned; dogs growling happily beneath the tables. Then a great roar went up as two huge boxers, their hands bound up with cloths, made their way toward the dais. With no difficulty, in this mêlée, I made my way toward the Hall's southwest corner. Here was a wooden door. I pushed past an esquire with a tray of spicy beef, opened it and stepped through. No one had seen me – or, rather, a hundred people had, but not one had noticed. Indeed, this place was innocent enough: it was the cistern tower, with a narrow staircase winding round the conduits that led down from the roof. I felt ahead; climbed higher; stumbled on the landing. Then I stopped, felt along the wall, and my fingers found a door. After a wrench, and with a creak, it opened.

Many years before – again, before my father's memory – this level would have been the true "Great Hall" – below, where people were eating now, would have served as storage, while the level above, where the musicians were scraping away, would have been the lord's own bower. But long since, these floors had been cut away, and turned into galleries. This one, traditionally, was called "The Ladies' Walk", though few could have walked here for many a year, for it had been blocked off by a great display of tapestries and banners. I stepped ahead. Light passed through the cloths, letting me see well enough, but I was perfectly hidden from everyone below.

Suddenly, from below, a great roar went up, a tremendous groan. Then, from the gallery above, a musician slapped his drum and there was another roar, this time of laughter. The boxing show was going on.

Sticking closely to the wall (for I was worried about a rotten board) I edged around to the back of the gallery. Here lay much rubbish, left from the dismantling of the floor: old planks; pegs and wedges; heaped up, rotten rushes. In the midst of this, I discovered a rusted, broken adze: a hearth on which I lit a speck of tinder. Then, lifting up de Birkin's cloak, I unslipped my bow, snapped the piles

127

from two arrows, and whittled their shafts to points. Lastly, I wrapped these round with pitch-soaked cloth – which, touched to the tinder, would blaze as brightly as the torches on the battlements.

Thus, prepared, I waited.

The boxing ended; child carollers sang; tumblers turned their somersaults . . .

Slowly, curious, I crept closer to the screen of cloths that enclosed the gallery. Like sails, they billowed and luffed in the smoky, gently moving air, a tapestry of Nottingham at market; Prince John's standard – two lions to replace the Lionheart's; the Shire Reeve's; others I didn't recognise. From behind, indeed, they were more colour and light than meaning, like tattered mantles at a tourney. Through the cracks between, I stared down at the multitude below: benches, tables, platters, flagons, heads bowed down to plates – a map of reverent gluttony. Then, as I crouched and waited, looking down upon that scene, a strange sensation passed over me: for, even as I was revolted, I felt drawn toward those sweaty, glistening necks. De Birkin's cloak caressed my cheek: furs, good wine, rich foods – there was the life, not outlawry, that was my due. More: there was the power. For what had become of my destiny now? What had happened to my fate, its promised intertwining of my life with kings? I thought now of Richard, of all the doubts this last cruel winter had so richly nourished. Once, he'd been a vision – more than a man, a hero – whose radiance had drawn me like a moth before a flame. But where was he now? A vision, unseen, is useless; a dream, forgotten, has no magic . . . So now temptation flickered. I even conceived a treachery. I had de Birkin. With that counter, surely I could make my peace, bargain for a place at the Prince's dais. Why not? My birth gave me the right. And more – so might conscience: for if Richard was now unhorsed, placed on the same muddy footing as his brother, what gave me the right to kill and burn tonight? But even as I asked these questions, I knew their answers – though perhaps only temptation and its shame made me truly understand them. *My sons are men and nothing more; they have men's weaknesses, their prides and their vices. You must, like a mother, forgive them in advance* . . . Now, as I crouched above the weakest son, his mother's words came back. *For good or ill, dear Locksley, you're now allied to the separate fates, and you'll only survive that fate, your own, if you remember this: it is not the men but their blood you serve; not their power, but the Crown that gives it to them.* Yes, I thought, now I truly understand her meaning – and thereby understand what divides me utterly from those below. They only serve a man, not a rightful Crown. And from their usurpation all the sins that now spread across the land are grown; the murder, greed, rapacity. Thus, to myself, I whispered, "What I do tonight, dear Prince, is not done to your person or because of it – but only from allegiance to the Crown you have no right to wear."

It would have been fitting, given this determined resolution, if Mercury and Little John had appeared immediately below; in fact, the tumblers were replaced by dancers, then by minstrels, and then a bard recited. I grew hot; smoke and sweat prickled in my eyes. Yet I didn't worry. No one would be much troubled by de Birkin's absence, and there'd likely be no change of Wardens before the Matins bell. So, with occasional forays back along the gallery to keep my tinder glowing, I merely watched the show. At length a man, mocking a royal herald, stepped forward and blew his horn: and then, with much gravity, announced "The Italian Father, Tuccolo, and his son, a Dwarf". Applause and guffaws echoed through the Hall – and only increased as Mercury and Little John strode down the aisle, for the whole world is prepared to laugh at a dwarf in a funny hat beside a great fat priest. My gallery shook with hooting. They paraded round, Little John taking Mercury's hand as though he was a little boy, or hoisting him on his shoulders. Then, setting down his son, and approaching the Prince's dais, the "Good Father" explained his tragedy and mission – whose details of whoredom, fornication and repentance, unbeknownst to him, were mimicked by the little man behind. The crowd shouted out their favour; and then, as though to dispute his father's tale, Mercury rushed up and began to shriek his story, teasing the audience with obscenity and even treating them to his mother tongue – which was cunning, for everyone knew that the Prince had a little of that language. Happily, the crowd jeered and taunted both of them. A hunk of bread was launched. Mercury caught it, sneered, and tossed it to the dogs. Then a hunk of chicken arced toward him – which again he caught but this time, with a happy shrug, popped into his mouth. Finally (before the air grew thick with missiles) he waved his cap, at which signal the musicians above me began to play and the little man to tumble: bouncing, bobbing, spinning, hopping from floor to table, swinging from his monstrous father's neck as though it was a tree. When he was done, Little John took his turn, attempting a somersault that left him belly up among the rushes on the floor. Everybody roared – then gasped. For now, at the front of the Hall, they could see the implements for the last, most thrilling part of the performance. Mercury pushed a little cart down the centre of the aisle. Beneath was a shelf of glowing coals; above it, an iron cauldron; around, rush torches dipped in pitch. Quickly, bobbing out before this, Mercury now began to juggle: first three coloured balls, then four, then six, and then three knives that glittered and twisted through the air – and finally dropped in a quivering row, stuck in the table before a great lord's lady. Even as the crowd applauded, Little John had the torches blazing, handing them up to his broken son who immediately sent them tumbling toward the slates. In perfect, awe-struck silence, he filled the Hall with brilliant, lovely, fluttering flame – princes gawking upwards like young children – then caught them one by one and was seized by Little John, at wrist and ankle and whirled round in a flaming circle. Set down to great applause, he tossed the torches to his Holy Father and stepped discreetly to the cart – while Tuccolo, with frightening clumsiness, taught himself to juggle. The crowd gasped in horror as the flames almost fell among the rushes, then almost dropped down an old Earl's neck: and so they never noticed Mercury quickly sipping from a dipper that had been heating in the coals. Oil. Oil so hot it would scald his mouth. And then, as Tuccolo tossed the torches high – as high as I was sitting – he rushed beneath them caught them; and, spraying oil like mist from out his mouth, seemed to eat and breathe the fire. The crowd roared with pleasure and excitement . . . while I, at last, got to my feet. Looking down, I could see the cauldron. Water, for safety's sake – or so everybody thought. In reality, more oil – which had already begun to smoke.

I slipped to the back of the gallery; blew tinder into flame; and waited.

Looking out, toward the tapestries and banners, I could only see the glow of light behind them; but I imagined everything. Gradually, step by step, Mercury would back down the aisle so freshly, thickly strewn in honour of the Prince with glazing torches tumbling above his head and flames spewing from his mouth. Then Little John, portly Father Tuccolo, would move beside the smoking oil. But now, in fact, there was nothing to imagine: Mercury torched the cauldron which, like an Etna, sent a gout of flame and sooty smoke toward the roof and then, tipped up, set the Hall alight with a rushing roar. There was a sucked-in gasp of horror: then shrieks of panic, fearful bellowings. "Fire! Fire! Guard! The guard!" Calls of terror shook the Hall as straw and rushes turned to a flaming sea beneath lords' and ladies' feet.

Calmly, I dipped an arrow to my smaller furnace.

The cloth smouldered, flared. I let it fully catch: notched; and then loosed at the tapestry. It was old and very dry; at once the flames spread up. I loosed again: John's banner . . . Now, seeing what was happening, the shrieks below grew even louder. The Hall, from floor to roof, seemed filled with flames, flames enfolding like the flames of hell. And then the tapestry broke free, but didn't fall: instead, like an eagle hanging in the heated air, it soared and drifted, twisted, gently flapped and circled slowly down upon them. The princely banner followed: and one by one, the others, so that the air was filled with flaming monsters.

With my covering screen destroyed, I looked down upon the tumult. Dogs raced about the floor in yelping agony . . . ladies, in their trailing, silken gowns flared up like torches . . . men leapt upon the tables which, unsteady, tipped them headlong into the roiling conflagration . . . And, at the door, there was a different horror. Such a great assemblage needed perfect order to disperse, but here was the confusion of rats flooded from their runs. They clawed and scratched; died screaming beneath their neighbours' feet; and I even saw the flash of dirks . . .

But then, turning away, I made my own escape, down the narrow, twisting stairway: as dark now as when I'd entered despite the burning sun a wall away. The musicians had descended by the other tower; or perhaps climbed up, for the higher levels of the Hall opened on the battlements. And no one within had remembered about this exit. The door by which I'd entered remained shut; the door leading from the tower to the Ward was locked. I slipped the bolt; lifted up the latch; and stepped outside.

Cold air struck my face; shrieks of horror stabbed my ears. The burned and burning were rolling in the snow, people clung together as before the day of Doom, and everyone screamed out their terror. Within the Hall, timbers now fell like hearth logs, sparks flying up in swirling clouds; the sheds and barracks round about began to catch. We had wanted chaos; and we had, in every sense, a noble chaos. Indeed, even as the immediate panic passed, the chaos worsened. The lords and ladies, in their silks and ermines, their dainty hose, now began to run across the Ward, slipping and sliding through the snow. And even those who paused to think only made things worse; for these men were knights: their thoughts went to their horses. Shouting for esquires and varlets, they cut loose their mounts who then panicked before the soaring flames. When I reached the cart, even Oswin's ancient nags were on the verge of bolting. Hands reached down and pulled me in, and then Much let them go: through the castle gates, already jammed; down the slope, waved on by soldiers through the town; then beyond Nottingham Gate itself, thrown open to let the frightened crowds spill out.

For a league, we galloped through the darkness, then drew off the road to the shelter of an alder thicket. Snow and silence drifted through the trees; softly, darkness turned around us. No one spoke, but I think we all looked back towards the golden ball glowing on the horizon.

Then I heard a groan.

I whispered, "De Birkin? He's well bound?"

"Aye," Much panted, "half-buried in our labours."

"And Fitzherbert?"

A strange voice said, "I am here, and safe."

Planting a hand on Mercury's stomach, and another in Little John's lap, I heaved myself up. The Abbot, I saw, was jammed beneath the seat: thin and wasted beneath a greasy robe, his hair long and flying round his face. "Are you sure, good Father?"

He lifted up his head and nodded. Then, "Do I know you, lord?"

I smiled. "Hardly a lord, Your Grace. I am an outlaw. My name is Robin Hood."

He had enough life left to smile. "Then I know you well. Everyone does. At least your name. . . . But why have you saved me?"

"You are a friend to my friends. And your worst enemy is ours – Maud de Caux."

With an effort that left him gasping, he sat up, and gripped my arm. "Maud de Caux is the Prince's Sheriff."

"She is."

"So you serve King Richard?"

I thought then – thought of all my thoughts crouched in that gallery. And then I murmured, "Yes . . . I serve the rightful King."

"Then I must tell you – tell you what I heard in gaol."

I felt him tremble; held his hand. "Rest, Father. You're safe here."

His face strained with the effort, but he shook his head. "They whisper it among themselves. There's news from France, of Richard. They've seized him. Leopold of Austria holds him captive, keeps him for an enormous ransom."

CHAPTER SIX

As we nursed him through the next few days, Fitzherbert told us the story of Richard's capture a dozen times; with my knife laid across his throat, de Birkin confirmed it all.

It was a story, I will admit, that made me regret a little of what I'd thought about our King. But only a little. He had received our message, it seemed, and many others like it: but quarrels among the Christian Princes of the Holy Land had interested him more than the disruption of his own kingdom. And always – always – there was the glory of Jerusalem to lure him on. Finally, however, he knew he had to act. Thus, on 2nd September 1192, he'd made a peace with Saladin, the Mahomet King, who now promised to allow all Christian pilgrims to travel unimpeded to the Holy Places. Then, on the 29th, he ordered Berengaria and Carlotta to depart for Rome, and ten days later sailed himself. His own objective was Marseilles – a long passage – and a Christian homecoming, but on his way he learned that Prince John, conspiring with Philip of France, had arranged with the Count of Toulouse to seize him as he stepped ashore. He doubled back, toward Italy; was shipwrecked twice; but finally started overland through Austria. For this journey, he adopted the guise of a merchant, but how could a merchant's cloak hide the radiance of that golden head? Almost immediately, he was recognised. Fleeing with only a servant as companion, he twice narrowly escaped his pursuers, but had to go to ground in a village near Vienna. There he lay sick, with fever; helpless; and on December 20th, the shortest day of that mournful year, Duke Leopold took him captive. The Duke hated him for a hundred excellent reasons (not least because Isaac Comnenus, of my own brief acquaintance, had been his vassal) and I wondered if the King could really be alive. But Fitzherbert was sure he was. "That's why the Prince's men want it kept a secret, at least for now. Until they decide what they wish to do."

"Does the old Queen know?"

Fitzherbert nodded. "They say she's sending emissaries through the German lands in search of him – the abbot of Boxley, many priests, even knights disguised as pilgrims."

De Birkin confirmed this, but had few other details: only a rumour that John, rather than raising a ransom, was prepared to pay Duke Leopold to keep his brother prisoner, or even kill him. This seemed likely enough, though I wasn't sure it would really happen. Leopold was a vassal of Henry, the Holy Roman Emperor; eventually, he would take charge of the King, and would have to decide whether he preferred John or Richard on the English throne.

One night, as we talked about all this, Mercury said that he had no doubt that the choice would be for Richard.

Little John grinned. "Believe him, Robin. I have a friend, Père Tuccolo, who says he could be the finest Chancellor in the world."

"Don't laugh, my friend. Remember: I know those lands. There, England seems very far away, and people don't care who sits as King in London. But Paris . . . now that is different. If John takes the English throne, Philip is strengthened. And a strong Philip would worry Henry. So . . . he will get as much money as he can for Richard, but then he will release him."

There was sense in that and comfort, assuming it was true. But I said, "Whatever happens, Fitzherbert's news has changed everything. A week ago, we had an absent king; now we have a captive king and soon, perhaps, no king at all."

"And no king," said Little John, "means anarchy."

"Yes. If no one holds the crown by right, then everyone will try to claim it by force of arms – and that is anarchy indeed."

Later, when the others were asleep, I lay wrapped in my sheepskin, my toes edging toward the fire, and watched the stars moving overhead. That scene I'd witnessed from the gallery . . . Fitzherbert's dire announcement . . . speculations about the Holy Roman Emperor . . . All this seemed to speak of different, greater worlds, utterly distant from my own, and to mock the fate I'd thought was mine; and yet, in my bones, I now had the feeling that my world might be moving closer to that larger one. At least, in those next weeks, the problem ceased to trouble me. Perhaps I had too much else to worry over. In the first place, we had to decide what to do about our own captive. Originally, we'd intended holding de Birkin as surety for Marian's life and perhaps, a little, for our own. But if the country was swept by anarchy, a prisoner of that sort would only be an encumbrance; and if the world truly lost its senses, Marian's life might well be forfeit anyway. So we devised a different scheme.

By this time, Richard Lee, our messenger to the King, had returned to Sherwood and now we packed him off again: this time to France, with a personal message to Queen Eleanor. God knows she had other things to think of, but I explained what had happened and asked her to accept Marian at her court. Her answer, as I'd hoped, was quick and positive. So, one bleak day in February, Allen fashioned a message arrow, a reed, hollowed out, painted red, then loosely fletched. Inside this, we stuffed a letter to Maud de Caux written on a strip of de Birkin's tunic: her son, we told her, would be returned in exchange for 100 marks of silver and a safe conduct to Aquitaine for Marian and Megan. Maud was staying in the little nunnery just beyond Kirklees till her Hall could be re-built. One noontime, from a field nearby, I loosed this missile toward the Refectory Hall, where it must have clattered among their dinner dishes.

A few days later, as Lent began, we got back word that Maud accepted our conditions and at Easter Marian and Megan, with Little John as bodyguard, set out for France; I travelled as far as Dover to see them off. It was a fair day – or at least the winds were. My own feelings were less steady. Even Little John, who was travelling with them all the way, had tears in his eyes as we wrestled their satchels aboard the little ship. In all of Sherwood, he was the only one who knew she was my sister. But she was more than that, for she was my entire family now, and my sole connection, except for memory, to the world that had once been Robert Atheling's. Still, I told myself: she'd now be safe at least. So I smiled through my tears and hugged her.

"Don't keep Jean too long," I said, "we need him here."

"If I had my way, you'd never get him back."

"I know. But you'll like Queen Eleanor, and her court will make for better company than Maud de Caux's."

She kissed me. "I'm almost afraid to meet her."

"Don't be. She sounds fierce, but she's very kind."

"I hope so. And I'll remember you to her."

The sailors were shouting now, and Little John and Megan – with my bastard in her arms – were waving from the deck. I kissed Marian again; and then, as she turned away to step aboard, I held her arm. The sails were going up, cracking in the breeze like thunderclaps; I had to shout. "There's someone else you may meet with Eleanor. Richard's Queen. Tell her . . . tell her that I think of her." She shouted something back, but I didn't hear; and then the ship slowly eased away from shore.

Five weeks later, Little John returned. I knew what he felt inside – now his love was almost as distant as my own. But despite his sadness, he was grittily cheerful to the rest of us, and God knows we needed it: for, if one problem had been solved with Marian's departure, we were now faced with a hundred more.

The winter had been hard enough – by its end, few had more than groundmeats and shrivelled turnips for their table – but the spring began with terrible rains that turned the fields to quagmires and made it impossible to seed. Now there was no food, nor the prospect of any; and many lost their homes as the Don and Locksley flooded. Summer finally came, and the villeins struggled to put in what crops they could. But even as people dared to breathe and hope, we learned the full extent of Richard's ransom – 150,000 silver marks. The new levies to raise this sum fell like an axe across the half-severed neck of the countryside. From each knight, an added scutage of twenty shillings was demanded, as well as one-fourth of all laymen's goods, and a tenth of all income from the churches and monasteries. As well, all plate belonging to the monks was forfeit, while those under vows of poverty were required to pay over their wool crop for the year. With autumn, we had a meagre harvest – the crops, put in so late, were pitiful and much perished with the frost. Now people plainly starved and disease and pestilence swept the villages, foot-rot, blackmouth, ague and other fevers. And these, of course, were not the only plagues: Maud, holding the Sherwood fief, collected all the Prince's taxes throughout the Shire, and those who couldn't pay faced her judgement at the monthly curia. By the hundreds, people fled before her soldiers, and those who didn't escape could be seen hung by their heels from trees, eyes burnt out, their bellies gutted, their offal trailing to the ground. Inevitably, all these horrors swelled our ranks; indeed, people now took to the Forest in droves. Most, ignorant of woodland ways, simply perished; some, barely surviving, turned into wild-men, half-mad and almost demented in their suffering; and a few formed bands not unlike our own. The woods were crowded, game scarce; inevitably we skirmished with several of these new arrivals, but with one at least we formed a kind of alliance. About two score strong, this band was led by a man named William – usually "William of the Wold" – who was scarcely taller than Mercury and had a face like a wizened apple. He came originally from Sheffield, but we knew little more about him. He had no interest in the wider world, just meat for his stew pot, and keeping clear of Maud's men, but when he and his band settled a little west of Mansfield, at least order returned to that section of the woods.

Order: there was, in fact, not much of it that year. God and nature all seemed conspired against us, and as for our rightful King – I could feel, a steady pressure within my breast, all my doubtful musings coming back. All spring and summer as his ransom was collected, I could only wonder: was he, even with all his glory, truly worth it? And then, at Advent, escaping the frozen mud and stench of camp, I wrapped myself in a tattered sheepskin, and rode off by myself, letting the horse choose his own way: a way that ended at Locksley Hall. Since that first day I'd not been back. By now, the ruins were just a dirty smudge beneath the snow, the timbers long since gone for firewood, the stones for hearths and walls. Again I thought of Richard, for this was what my loyalty had cost; and yet, as soon as the thought entered my mind, I flushed with shame – others, with so much less, had lost such a great deal more. Could a king be worth it? 150,000 silver marks . . . A man, if he was lucky, could earn two pennies in a day. Thus, if a man rested at Sabbath, at Christmas, at Easter and on his Saint's day, he might make four marks in a year, perhaps 150 during all his life. So by such arithmetic, Richard was worth a thousand ordinary men – but was it true? Could it be? Yet I thought, it *must* be so. The proof was plain to see: without its rightful king, anarchy *did* descend upon the land. If Richard did not return, if we didn't pay his price in silver, we'd pay it a hundred times in blood.

With a gentle twitch, I turned my horse away, walking him through the crusty snow. And perhaps my faith, even this fleetingly renewed, shaped fate a little, for when I returned to camp that afternoon, William of the Wold awaited me.

He was standing with Little John beside the huge fire we always kept roaring in the centre of the camp; a small tough man in shaggy skins leaning on his staff – a careful sign to our sentries that he'd come in peace. We exchanged greetings, a cup of warmed mead, and then he said,

"I have news, Robin, that you'll not much like."

I smiled. "Then it will only be like most of the other news I hear."

"Perhaps. But I think not. You know the soldiers' barracks in Mansfield Town? There's a sergeant in the guard there, thin as a bowstave, with a reddish beard?"

I nodded. "Yes."

"Well, we have corrupted him. We give him venison, enough for himself and a little to sell, and he warns us when the troops come out our way."

I nodded. We, too, had such arrangements, though not at Mansfield. "Go on," I said.

"A sennight ago we talked, this man and I. He began to joke: he said that if I wanted, I could probably sell my skins to Maud for she was intending to dress his whole troop as forest men. He was going to call himself William of the Wold, as men call me, and the other sergeant would be Robin Hood."

"I don't see the joke in that."

"Nor did I. Then, he'd say no more, but yesterday I told him he'd get no meat unless I had his story. You would know, I think, that the King's great ransom is being gathered together at Conisburgh?"

"Yes." Conisburgh Castle was in the honour of Hamelin, lord of Lewes and Reigate, half brother to King Richard's father; he was loyal to Eleanor if not the King himself.

He nodded. "I'd heard the same. Well then, according to my sergeant, it's all together now, and will soon come south, to Windsor, guarded by the old Queen's men. But just below Budby, where the road turns, the Sheriff's men – all dressed as we are – will attack the train. You see the beauty of it. The Prince will get a great horde of gold and be King besides –"

"While we get all the blame."

"Aye. Which is why I tell you. When it happens, don't think those men are mine."

For a moment, this news filled me with alarm and anger; but then, as William left, I sensed a strange excitement. It made me think of Sicily, and the moment when those three strange chessmen had tumbled out of St Denis' secret pouch. Then, I'd had a secret in my hand that might topple kings; now . . . Had it come at last? Was this the moment when my little world would touch the larger one?

Perhaps it was; but for several days, the precise manner of that touching was hard to see. We had to act – but how? To warn Eleanor's guard was the obvious choice, but that would only lose our one advantage, gained so luckily: John would simply strike again elsewhere. It would be better, in fact, to disrupt the ambush, seize some of Maud's soldiers and force a confession from them; this might so shame John before the country that he wouldn't dare to try again. Yet that would be an enormous gamble. In skirmishes, our men could hold their own with Maud's soldiers, but not in full-pitched battle – which is what it would be: the "outlaws" would strike in strength, and be wearing armour under their skin. So what to do? Undecided, we debated back and forth . . . and then Mercury saw it.

"What happens *afterwards*?" he asked. "That's what I don't understand. These soldier-outlaws have their treasure, but what then? If they take it back to Nottingham dressed as forest men, all their deception will be wasted. And if they change back to soldiers, and lead a pack train in, everyone will know it's the treasure. So . . ."

"So what, my little genius?" said Little John.

138

"It's obvious. They'll either hide the treasure in the Forest and guard it inconspicuously, or transfer it to someone – merchants, for example – who could take it into Nottingham without suspicion."

Little John looked toward me. "At least," he said, "that sounds devious enough."

Yes, indeed. It was a conception possessing just the devilish ingenuity that marked both the Prince and Maud; and its execution, when it came, displayed their ruthlessness as well.

By then, five days had passed.

We had posted look-outs on the Great North Road to give us warning of the train's approach: just before noon, two of these came breathlessly into camp.

"They're coming, Robin. At least two score rouncies, heavily burdened."

"The guard?"

"Ten are mounted, and many infantry. Most wear the arms of Conisburgh you drew out for us, but two men at the front are different – I think they're the Queen's own men."

"But none are the Queen herself?"

"No. I'm certain of it."

If she'd been riding with the guard, we would have been forced to warn them. As it was, we now put our plan into effect, Little John leading our fighting strength into the Birklands, an area of thick forest, craggy rock and bramble south of Budby: there they'd lie up until we could determine precisely what Maud's "outlaws" intended once they had the treasure. This was my task. Taking our quickest mount (we now had six: of all the bands in Sherwood, we were still the only one that rode) I headed south, along the road to Mansfield, then turned off it, east, across the Meden River toward Budby. I was certain I knew where the attack would come: just north of a crossroads, near the old mile pillar. Here, the road sank slightly and – more importantly – the forest was dense, dark pine, able to hide a hundred soldiers even in winter. About a mile back from this spot, I slowed the horse and came carefully through a thicket of elm and alder. Then the ground rose sharply into a craggy headland. This was bare of trees except for a dead and twisted oak occupied by a single, glossy raven. I off-saddled, let the bird move on, then shinned up the smooth, weather-beaten trunk and took his place.

It was a cold, crisp day; the air was clear, shadows sharp and black against the snow. I looked out and down, as though upon a map.

Beneath me, the land fell away into a tumble of rock, an icy stream, then forest: which, unlike the bare, shaking elms I'd been riding through, was here grown from green-black pine, all thick with boughs and concealing shadow. Beneath this lay the frozen road itself, like a plait of chestnut hair, and on the farther side a swampy stretch – dead reeds and rushes, greyish snow – and then the pines again. North, I could see the common ground belonging to the village and a few twists of smoke from peasants' huts; south, the highway curled on toward Nottingham, the forest briefly opening to admit the crossroads.

Altogether, I thought, it was a good place for an ambush, though not perfect. Because of the swampy ground on the far side of the road, the "outlaws" could only strike from this side; and some of the guard was almost bound to escape north, to the village, or even fight clear and scatter along the crossroads. Still . . . escape would mean abandoning the treasure, the real objective, and a few survivors would be useful in spreading the "outlaw" story. Besides, the spot had one great advantage: perfect concealment. A flock of sparrows about to settle among the pines but suddenly veering away; my horse's restlessness as the wind swung round; a single flash of steel – as I lay, stretched and shivering upon that limb, these were the only signs that danger lurked below.

Time passed. The sun rose high and shadows shrank; then, slowly they stretched again.

And at last the rounceys came: so many that they moved in a little cloud of mist; so heavily burdened that they travelled at a walk. Most were fitted with wooden saddles, each carrying two iron chests, others were weighed down with heavy bolsters, the rest bore bags of feed and the heavy leather water bogets. As they came on, I could see the guard, the cold sun glinting on their spears and armour. As our look-outs had reported, there were ten knights and substantial infantry: the strength usually called a "conroy". It was a formidable force, and well-trained, for as they reached the pines, they halted and two of the knights cantered on ahead. But Maud's men were too well-placed. The knights pulled up, turned, and waved the others on.

Distance stretched. Every sound was slight but very clear: hooves ringing on the frozen mud, stirrup chains and bridles tinkling. I held my breath. For a second, in the stillness, I witnessed a scene of perfect peace, a lazy, gentle progress beneath the winter sun . . . Then a squall of arrows swept across the road and death came pattering down. They stood no chance; if an ambush succeeds, it succeeds at once. And this succeeded. Horses reared and plunged; a rouncey bolted. Two knights wheeled about, shields tucked beneath their nostrils, eyes and lances searching. The road became a charnel house. All around, horses and men assumed the awkward, twisted poses of the dead. Blood froze slick on the Roman stones. Limbs broken at their joints twitched and flailed about. Screams: calls: shrill shrieks. Silence. A knight and three soldiers fled toward the town, then disappeared. And then nothing moved except a single horse that slowly shuddered into death.

Behind me, my own horse, catching the scent of blood and fear, blew softly.

The wind plucked a tear from the corner of my eye and froze it there.

Two sparrows fled across the air like frightened souls.

I waited. Watched . . .

And then, at last, they came. Dark shapes with flat black shadows creeping across the snow, like wolves. Tentative at first, they circled: then swarmed across the road, running between the corpses, scrabbling for the rings and coins that were their treasure for the day. Could I feel horror at the sight? Did I deserve, in fact, to feel anything at all? For so many times I'd been among those men.

Their scavenging was quickly done; a shout, a spear waved high, brought them back to order. The rounceys were collected – one had bolted to the swamp – and a long, tethered line of their own mounts was led forth from among the pines. As they set off, in double file, I wondered for a moment if Mercury's theory had been right, for they continued straight down the road, toward Nottingham. But then, just above the junction, they swung across the ditch, toward me. I remembered: a path ran there. And a short time later their route was clear: they were heading southwest across the Birklands, more or less toward Mansfield.

Quietly, at a safe distance, I followed them along the winding trail.

I had no difficulty; they, too, could only move as fast as the struggling rounceys, and their slots might have been done by a herd of cattle. We passed through the band of pines, their boughs weighed down with snow, scrambled up a rocky headland, then entered more open ground: oaks and elms, wide-spaced like frozen fingers. The sun flickered behind the trees, remote and cold. A deer bolted through the brush in terror of our progress. Every twenty paces, I drew rein and stopped and listened: the heavy thudding clop of hooves continued on. I wasn't worried that they'd see me, but as we drew level with Major Oak I wondered if we wouldn't stumble across my men, for they would have laid up nearby. Indeed, did I not have that sensation of being watched? Had a sparrow really set that bush a-trembling? Digging in my heels, eyes straight ahead, I moved along. Once more the forest thickened – choking briars; spurs of broken rock; a frozen swamp – but at length the trail broadened into an easy, snow-filled ditch. It was almost like a road. In fact, some claimed it was an ancient Roman road, still haunted by a legion that had lost its Eagle standard here. Winding through the scrub, it carried us gently into Woodhouse Warren, a desolate gilsland cut with briar patches and ravines. Now, I hung back further. We were drawing close to Mansfield, and directly south lay the Clipstone Road. I listened. Stopped. Edged forward. Two hundred paces on, just within a deep ravine, the train had halted, and resting horses blew contentedly.

I got off the trail – they might send pickets back – and led the horse across a rocky outcrop to hide his tracks. Tethering him behind some briars, I then wiggled through an alder thicket and pressed down among the bulging roots of an enormous oak: from there I could see the ravine, or part of it. The "outlaws", still in their skins, had off-saddled; and though a few sentries had been posted, with spears set, they obviously weren't expecting trouble. Most were laughing, plucking at the strange garments they were wearing, while others gathered wood to feed a fire. This blazed up hugely, a swirl of copper colour against the snow. At length, a sergeant shouted – William's informant, by the look of him – and his men sauntered round in the easy way of soldiers not worried about discipline. Roughly, they formed a line, shuffled toward the fire; and there, one by one, pulled off their rags.

The players were changing costume.

As if by magic, they were soldiers of the sheriff once again: for beneath the skins they were wearing mail and dear Maud's arms.

One by one, with a hiss, the skins fell upon the fire, and greasy smoke smudged up. The evidence of their treachery was being destroyed. Or part of it, at least. But what about the ransom? Would they bury it? Take it on to Mansfield? Or perhaps Mercury had been right – perhaps they'd pass it on.

A short while later, I had my answer.

Most of their strength re-mounted, and moved down the trail toward Mansfield. A few others, a dozen men warming themselves around the fire, remained. The ransom, it seemed, would definitely be transferred to someone else.

This was our time to act.

Slipping back to my horse, I made him earn his feed, driving him hard along the trail. But our men couldn't have been placed more perfectly: the animal was scarcely warm before Little John's hands were at his bridle.

"We saw you pass," he said.

"I thought you did. They're barely a league away, among The Warrens."

"How many? We counted three score and more."

"But most have left. Now there's scarce a dozen." Slipping to the ground, I drew out their position in the snow. Rather than attack them now, we decided to let them pass the treasure on and then attack the "merchants" – who would be soldiers in disguise, but hopefully a smaller force. Thus, carefully, we worked back to the ravine and lay in cover. The scene had little changed. The rounceys now had nose-bags on; a soldier paced before the fire, slapping his hands against the cold. We waited, pressed in snow, our warm breaths forming little skins of ice before our mouths. I watched the sun move round and then, within my head, rang the bells for nones.

Shortly after this, one of the look-outs inched up to me: there were horses on the trail, coming up from Mansfield.

"Who?"

He was a young boy and he looked perplexed. "Monks, Robin. Monks and nuns . . ."

My mouth dropped open. If I hadn't been so shocked I might have laughed. Yet it was so cunning – because so obvious and natural. Virtually every day, a little pack train set out from Kirklees, passed through Mansfield, then continued along the Clipstone Road to Nottingham. Indeed, it had been just this trip that had allowed Megan and Marian to leave their messages in the oak. A train of monks and nuns . . . what more innocent way to bring the ransom into Nottingham?

We waited, crouched and watching, and then we saw them, cloaked against the cold, plodding piously on scrawny nags and asses. Eight monks, four nuns: a slightly larger company than normal, but not so large that anyone would comment. A small train of tethered rounceys came along behind, lightly loaded with bags of wool. Turning into the ravine, they mustered round the fire and one of the nuns slipped down; and, as she did so, I saw her wimple flash and then her narrow face – it was Lecia, the Prioress herself. While she warmed her hands at the fire, another nun, much heavier, twisted in her saddle and called orders to the soldiers. But they were already at work: unloading the sacks of wool, then lashing them across the ransom chests. This disguise wasn't perfect, but it would do; people who noticed them at all would only see what they'd seen a thousand times before.

"It's lovely," murmured Little John behind me. "I swear the Prince and Maud must have planned it out themselves."

"You recognise the Prioress?"

"Aye. And feel truly honoured . . . But I have a fear. What if the other soldiers stay, ride on as escort? That would make a larger force, not a smaller."

"They won't. Subterfuge has taken them this far along, they'll trust it to the end. Monks, with a soldiers' escort? That would only draw attention to them."

In the event, I was proved right. When the rounceys were ready and checked, the last of the original "soldier-outlaws" resumed their mounts and trotted down the trail, one more patrol returning to the Mansfield barracks. The Kirklees party waited, watching them move off; and then two of the monks got down and kicked the fire out – their gestures parting their cloaks enough to let us see the scabbards swinging underneath. The rounceys, tethered together, were formed in line; the Prioress clambered aboard her ass; and, with a wave, the procession of religious started down the ravine.

As the last rouncey rejoined the trail, Little John gave his signal: an owl hooting in the middle of the day.

Once more I watched the stealthy horror. Arrows darted. Stuck. Black blood carved patterns in the snow. A donkey brayed. The "monks" struggled to draw their swords, but we were on them with our spears. Now the men were experts in this cruel technique: one jabbing, just out of range in front, a second goring from behind. The last of them tried a break, straight down the trail. That boy who'd been our look-out stood there: and calmly stepped clear of hooves and flashing sword and almost gently tossed his spear through the poor beast's throat. Twisting, half-rearing, the wretched animal skidded down, tumbling his rider in the snow. Before he regained his feet, three men were on him, gouging him through the back and side.

Misting breath and steaming blood. That dazed moment when you try to find your life again . . .

Allen, acting as captain, went between us, counting off, then called "all safe".

Reassurance and a signal: at once men crouched among the bodies, stripping swords and chain-mail. I took Allen by the arm. "Post pickets then line the horses up again. What about those nuns?"

He pointed, a little off the trail. Three asses – one bleeding, squatting on its haunches – were grouped beside a clump of pines, two of our men tugging them back toward us. "A stray arrow found the fourth . . ."

"The Prioress?"

"Aye. She's safe. On the dying ass."

"All right. Leave them alone but kill their mounts. We'll make them walk to give us time."

I turned round then, found my horse, and trotted back to Little John. Forty animals. Somehow, we were going to have to lead them back to Eagle's Nest without leaving tracks like a troop of cavalry.

"We can't take them off the trails," I said. "They're too heavily loaded. They have to have good footing."

"Let's gamble then. This caravan wouldn't have reached Nottingham till dusk. At this point, there'll be no alarm. If we go north, to Market Worksop, we can simply use the road."

"Aye —"

But then the screams came. A scream of fear and horror — a scream torn from a throat that now tore the air. I pulled my horse's head around. But the rounceys, stretched along the trail, blocked out my view. I spurred up the trail. Reaching the ravine, I saw a mob of men, bent over, as though scrabbling for something on the ground, a mob of howling men in skins like a pack of berselets tearing at a fox.

"Allen!"

He came running up and held my bridle. "Robin! That nun, the fat one. It was Maud."

My stomach turned. I dug my heels in and drove my mount across the snow, rearing him up above that screaming circle. As the men saw me, their faces turned, and I looked down into them. Pale, haggard faces; dull, glazed eyes; broken teeth, all yellow. I thought of the first time I'd seen them coming into camp with Little John . . . Gilbert White Hand: his fingers torched at Maud's explicit order . . . Owen Wys: his father drawn and quartered . . . Guy Conan, one eye poked out by Maud's torturer . . . And if I was to find a mirror and search my own face, what would I see?

The circle parted before my horse. A hush fell. I looked down upon a bloody heap of rags. Watched it squirm. Watched it slowly drag itself across the snow. I made out her face at last, all torn and clawed, one eye dangling across her cheeks like spittle. Then, as she stopped and tried to catch her jagged, panting breath, the other stared fiercely up at me.

"Maud?" I said. My voice was almost gentle. "Maud! Who am I?"

She spat. Blood ran out from her mouth. "You are Robin Hood —"

But I shook my head, and then, quite calmly unslung my bow and notched an arrow. I sighted down the shaft. My fingers, breath, my cheek, all quivered: but I softly whispered, "Now . . . what is my name?"

She clung, for a second longer, to her life. She screamed: she screamed my name: she screamed it over and over until the woods rang with the sound. Finally, she could barely gasp it out. "Your name is . . . Locksley . . . Locksley . . . And you are a lord and so must grant me mercy . . ."

I felt my men's eyes upon me then, but didn't meet them. I could only see the wretch who now crawled toward my protection.

Then, suddenly, swinging my horse about, I stared at the faces that turned up toward me.

"You heard her!" I shouted. "That's who I am! Locksley! A lord, a knight. Required by King Richard to enforce his law throughout these lands . . . So I do so, and you shall be my witnesses! I try this woman, Maud de Caux, and I find her guilty – of theft, of murder, of treason against our King. And therefore, with God and the King to judge me, and before you all assembled, I sentence her to death!"

The cold air threw back the echo of my words. Then all was silence. Maud, whimpering, struggled to her feet. She began to run. She ran, up the ravine, to where her soldiers had built their fire. I drew up my bow . . . but before I could even notch an arrow a dozen others ripped the air and toppled her face forward in the snow.

I jerked my horse around, rode him back along the trail. They watched me go in silence. Let me go. I rode on ahead. Rode past the pickets, even past the trail and climbed a craggy headland where I stood sentinel. There, a time later, Little John – Jean Neuilly – found me.

Side by side, we stood in silence, looking out across the Forest. Maud was dead. My family was avenged. And I'd revealed myself. Did this make an end? Once more, just as in Cyprus, the King's life was in my hands. I'd sworn to serve him, and that oath, like an endless echo, had pursued me even here. Did I still wish to hear it? Looking out across the frozen land, I wondered. In these past months, I'd seen so much tragedy: the tragedy that Richard refused to see. But if *his* fate had led him to neglect his kingdom, I wondered if I had the right to blame him. For just as Richard's fate had drawn him away from England, I knew that mine was tugging me away from my own small realm.

Quietly, Jean murmured: "Why did you tell them now?"

"Dear friend, I think our little world has touched a larger one where Robin Hood does not exist, but where Locksley must. They have a right to know."

He smiled. "I suppose you know your meaning."

I raised my eyes; watched a lonely raven lumber across the muddy sky.

"I only know," I said, "that I'll never see this sight again."

CHAPTER SEVEN

The winter sky was grey and overcast, low clouds huddling together against the cold, and beneath this the river had the oily sheen of pewter. A light snow had fallen overnight. By this time, eleven in the morning, it had melted on the tow-paths while higher up, on the banks, last year's dead grass and leaves poked through the frost like a stubbly beard. Beyond the banks lay a line of oaks, their limbs all bare and stiff; then a ditch, very broad and clear, and finally the road. Conforming to the river's course like a frozen shadow, its yellowish muddy ruts rose and fell like waves, spilling into the farther ditch. Beyond this, at least here, there was another ragged line of trees, then a rough stone wall, then farmers' fields – dark furrows of frozen earth where they'd been winter ploughed, or dappled with dead, bent grass and snow if they were pasture land.

The river and the road, the mirror images, formed the centre of the landscape.

The river was the Thames. Thirty miles above London, it was still quite narrow, but already it bristled with the importance that the city and the sea would give it: its traffic and their cargoes were like a stream of boasts. Lumber, wool, hides and bales of every sort of produce were borne by rafts, a hundred styles of lighter and the endless barges that the wretched, plodding donkeys tugged along. The road was no less busy, its custom no less various. There were pilgrims, knights, great men and merchants riding everything from dog carts to sedan chairs and destriers. Every one of these conveyances creaked and groaned and splashed; from dawn to dark, the clatter of their passage never ceased. To a person standing at the wayside, no single note stood out from this cacophony and the ruts from a hundred passing wheels all merged to one. For such an onlooker, a wagonload of wool and timber, pulled by two white bullocks, would be nothing memorable . . . or so we hoped: for this wagon, and disguise, was carrying us on to Windsor.

That cold, drear morning, as we arrived, Mercury was sleeping among the wool-sacks, Allen was huddled in his cloak on the wagon's seat, while Little John and I – now Owen Ovens, merchant, and Daniel Delore, his clerk – were riding up ahead, pacing the bullocks' progress. Our mounts were the last of Maud's palfreys, the others having been sold in Boston to buy our gear and cargo, and for a week now we'd splashed along in muddy misery. Today, so "Owen" claimed, should see the end of it, and as the road began to climb before us, he gave me a little wave and we trotted on ahead. Cresting the rise, we reined in, and I found myself looking into a gentle valley.

"There it is," said Little John.

"At last," I grunted. I was weary, cold and saddle-sore. Why did merchants own horses at all when they never took them faster than a walk? But then, squinting into the valley, I changed my tune – for there, atop a low cliff rising from the river, was Windsor Castle, seat of England's kings. "An impressive sight," I murmured.

"I'm surprised you've never seen it."

I shook my head. "We came to London and Westminster. Garth rode out here many times but for some reason I never bothered." And why should I have done? Castles were for knights; 'prentice priests rode the other way, toward Canterbury . . . But how long ago that seemed! I squinted again, looking beyond the huge, whitewashed walls of the castle to the buildings inside. "I count three wards," I said.

"Aye. Guard house at the foot, the old bailey in the centre – Duke William built it – and the Royal Apartments beyond."

"Much like Nottingham, then."

Owen nodded. "But Windsor's five times as large. It has to be. The garrison's five hundred strong, there are three hundred Knights of Court, sixty clerks for the Exchequer and more than seven hundred servants. We even have permanent apartments for the Archbishop and the Papal Legate."

I smiled. As Royal Messenger, he'd spent most of his former life riding from Windsor to Westminster and there was still a little pride in his voice. His knowledge of the place, of course, would be useful; because of it, he'd lead us through it. So I said, "Well, Master, how do we proceed?"

He laughed. "We're merchants, clerk, so we'll find an inn. That's the first thing merchants always do."

You would have thought, in a town with more than thirty inns, that our task would have been easy, but so many people came to trade with the Court, to plead all manner of cases before it, or simply to gawk, that every inn was jammed. We finally found a spot

– Mercury's badgering did it – though we had to sell the tavern-keeper some of our wood at a bargain price. This was a little after noon. We ate lunch and then, in our room, confirmed our plans. If nothing else, these had the virtue of simplicity. Using his knowledge of the castle and the Royal Apartments, Little John would steal a suit of livery from the company of King's Messengers and make his way to the old Queen. Pretending to deliver a document in the ordinary fashion, he would give her three chess castles – Allen had been whittling them along our way – and a simple message from myself: "Like a mother, you must forgive them in advance." I was certain she'd recognise this; how she'd see us, we'd leave to her discretion.

Little John departed an hour before nones; Mercury, Allen and myself found stools in the tavern hall – pleasant, high-beamed with fresh rushes on the floor – and drew them close around the fire. The supper stew bubbled there, and an old hound stretched his muzzle toward the flames. As we waited, we drank the inn-keeper's brew, diced among ourselves and listened to the gossip buzzing all about. Most of it concerned the Court, cases being tried before it or rumours of bribes to stewards to secure fat contracts. The room was full of merchants: Flamards, French, Italians, several Jews. They had cloth to supply, special smeltings for swords and armour, spices, fish and a hundred other foods; everyone had come to sell, or, if they had a case before the Court, to buy – Royal Favour, that most expensive of commodities. No one talked of politics. Here, I thought, the Realm was only business, the King merely its excuse: essential, but inevitable, and thus taken for granted – as farmers take hunger for granted or vintners thirst. There had to be a king and always would be, and John and his friends were as good for doing business with as any other. As Mercury put it, "In this place, the hum of bees around the honey is enough to wake the dead."

Sometimes, we were included in the buzzing. "You men look like merchants," said one fellow, pulling up a stool, "so tell me what you sell?"

"Wool and timber," I replied.

"And what is your price for pine?"

"A penny below the others."

"And what do others charge?"

"My friend, judging by the pine-pitch on your smock, I'd think you'd surely know."

My answer set the room to laughing and earned us a round of ale. Indeed, in the hurly-burly of the place, we fitted very well and no one suspected us. Here, like ourselves, everyone had at least one secret – the price of what they sold – and their favourite weapons were no different from our own, a friend at Court. Perhaps, in fact, we blended in too well. Allen, at least, grew discomfited. After a time, when the air by the fire grew heavy, we retired upstairs and there he said, "By all the saints, I hate such men. They think only of money. No wonder they flock to this Court. They are no different than their Prince."

Mercury laughed. "Just like, indeed. Both they and the Prince have discovered that blood may be thicker than water, but bullion is heavier than both."

"Aye, a discovery that leaves them no true friends, not even among their kin. I'll take a good countryman any day."

"I wouldn't be so sure. Before a tally stick, every man is equal, and with money even a dwarf can stand fifteen hands above the earth."

"Spoken like a true Lombard – which I suppose is only what you are. Just remember what they say: everything the Italians know about money they learned from the Jews."

Mercury laughed again. "We had to, my good man. Our popes were beggared to them."

I did not join in this conversation, but as they bantered at each other I wondered what I thought about this world we'd stumbled into, and which, in a strange way, so readily accepted us. I understood what Allen said. How could men, with no land – with only the cargo they carried in their carts – have true loyalties at all? Were they not all Jews, homeless, without a country, tied only to their money-chests? On the other hand, Mercury was no less right. If merchants flocked to John's Court, they also came impartially to every other. And more and more, I thought, money was the stead of everything, including knightly service. Many lords, indeed, preferred to pay a scutage than actually arm a knight, and wars were fought with gold as much as steel – waged by mercenary armies who gave their strength to anyone who paid. I thought then of the true contents of our wagon, and wondered whether any of the men downstairs would think the bargain worth it. To them, in their calculations, what would Richard's value be? Not high, I considered ... They marvelled at his deeds around the fire, but almost as though they were hearing of some ancient hero, from a half-forgotten time.

Yet, whatever they thought – or I – he *did* exist today and the silver beneath our wools and lumber was real enough. As dusk began to fall, feet came clattering up the stairs and our door swung open. It was Little John and we all gawked – now he was wearing the livery of the Queen.

I grinned. "The leopard has changed his spots again?"

"He has, but the skin has shrunk." With a grateful sigh, he unclasped his tunic. "The King's Messengers are all chosen for their size, but the pages to the Queen must all be Mercury's cousins. Still, it worked out well."

"You weren't recognised?"

"No, no, they've all changed in the years since I was here. I reached the Queen with no trouble, and she is anxious to meet with you. She's even sent a chair."

A chair . . . When I went downstairs, passing through a hundred envious looks, I saw he was right indeed. Pages, with a chair – carved with fleur-de-lys and gilt-work lions – were drawn up before the inn, a sight sufficient to draw a modest crowd. A page bowed as I came up. "Master Delore, clothier to the Queen?"

"So I am."

"Then I beg you enter, sir."

He held the curtains for me, and I stepped inside a darkness as gentle as a lady's bower. The scent was clean, of oil and cedar. There was a seat, covered in the softest leather, a silk bolster for my head and even a cushion at my feet. Hoisted up, I was now carried – rocked gently in this cradle – through the town, which I only glimpsed in snatches through the fringes of the curtain: but then, I told myself, this was how *I* was glimpsed as well, and though every eye was turned my way, I could not have been safer. At the guardhouse by the Castle Gate we didn't even pause, and as we moved across the Upper Ward the crowds made way before us. And crowds there were; even from my obscurity, I could see that a whole town, or at least a market-place, was enclosed within the castle walls. There were dozens of merchants seeking licences from the clerks for trade; nobles wrapped in silks and velvet; knights in brilliant surcoats and gentle ladies gowned in sendal cloth. They all milled together in the winter sunshine and bowed gently at the passing of a Regal Outlaw.

Just beyond the guardhouse for the Royal Apartments, the chair set down. The curtains parted; I stepped forth: and a herald bowed.

"Master Delore, the Queen will see you presently. I will conduct you to her."

With a nod, I fell into step behind him. Passing down a broad hallway which sent the ringing echo of our steps before us, we then climbed an open, winding stairway to the Royal Rooms. It was cold; pale light fell in patches, grey on stone, leaden on the steel of armour and hanging shields. At length, the herald stopped before a large oak door strapped with massive brass hinges. There were no proper guards, only two pages with dirks. One of these knocked at our approach, then swung the door open to admit the herald. Hanging back as he announced me, I could see beyond him into a room whose austerity would have been surprising had I not known the Queen. To the left a fire roared in a huge stone hearth, but only a stool was drawn up to it; behind, in the outside wall, slit windows let in bars of chilly light that fell across a simple table and a plain wood chair. Then the herald stepped aside and I could see the Queen. She was in the centre of the room, seated in a tall chair, another like it drawn near her, a low table between. Her dress was also plain, a gown of heavy blue wool, and shawls lay across her shoulders and lap. In her right hand was the black walking stick I remembered from our previous meetings; on one finger, her ruby ring. But, beside that ring, the only sign of luxury within that room was the size of her fire and the rugs and skins that were spread about the floor.

I approached, knelt, heard the doors swing shut behind me. Then she gestured me up and smiled. "Come closer, lord. My vision fails a little now and you are a sight for tired eyes." She motioned me to the second chair. As I sat, I thought she did look older, her skin more tightly drawn against the bone. Yet, if anything, her face was more beautiful, like the smooth, carved image of some ancient goddess. She smiled again, seeing me more clearly. "My lord, I fear that your journey from that harbour in Kyrenia was longer than either of us imagined, or intended."

"By almost three years, Your Majesty. But the last mile, at least, was travelled comfortably."

"Ah well. I thought boldness might be the greatest cunning. Still, keep your voice low. I know my own servants but there are always spies about. Your friend, the one you sent – you trust him perfectly?"

"I do, Your Majesty. There are few men I esteem more highly."

She cocked her head a little. "He is well recommended, then. And from your sister also, if he's the man I'm thinking of."

"He is."

She smiled. "I like your sister, Locksley. She knows her mind and always tries to go her own way, which is never easy for a woman. When she was at Poitiers, we often talked and now she and my daughter, the Queen Berengaria, are very close. They are together in Le Mans. I came here from Limoges but stopped to see them, and your sister was very firm. 'When you see my brother,' she said, 'give him all my love.' *When*, not *if*, you see . . . and she was right, for here you are."

And had there been no message for me from the Princess? Perhaps. I couldn't know for sure – even if there had been, Eleanor might not relay it. I replied, "My sister knows my fate, Your Majesty – as you once told it to me."

"Ah, yes . . . your fate. Despite everything, you don't regret it?"

I hesitated; only for an instant, but she saw it. Then, "I no more regret it than I do my life."

But she'd already looked away. I thought she was about to speak, but then she stopped herself. At length, her left hand moved from beneath the shawl draped across her lap, withdrawing the three chess pieces and my letter with its single line. She set these on the table, then leaned her stick against it. And then – still not having spoken – she rose and crossed the room, opening the door of a large ambry against the wall. From within, she took a tray, two goblets and a flagon of wine. Bringing these to us, she poured out our measures, her movements being all so quick and natural that it was a moment before I felt astounded: the Queen was serving me. She raised her glass; we drank; a sip, for her, that barely passed her lips. And then, setting down her wine, she took up my letter. She read it through, and turned to me and smiled; and when she spoke, her voice was the gentlest whisper. "'Like a mother, you must forgive them in advance' . . . Am I right, my lord, in thinking that you understand me now?"

"Your Majesty –"

"No, listen. I beg you, my lord, be honest with me. Here, within these walls, these chambers – within my life – it is what I lack the most. From you, it would be the greatest gift."

"Then, yes. I understand. But I do forgive."

"Yes. Except there's so much to pardon. I sailed from Rouen and came to Dover, then travelled overland – not here, but to London and then north, to Hamelin in Conisburgh. So I saw the country. I saw a little of what my son's freedom costs. Is that what troubles you?"

I flushed then – I'm not sure with what. Shame. Anger. Agitation . . . Perhaps it was just the rush of thoughts I'd kept so long within me. Forgetting myself, I stood and paced toward the fire. "It's not the silver, Your Majesty –"

"The blood?"

"Not even that. Only . . ." I turned back, toward her. "Only that this kingdom is paying out its treasure, and its blood, to a king who doesn't value it half so highly."

"Indeed. You're right. Or, we might say, he values it *only* for its silver."

I looked at her, amazed.

She laughed. "Do you think I will defend him, Locksley? To you? I wouldn't dare. No. He is my son, my favourite son – you know it, as the world does. Thus, for me, his worth is measureless, but for you? That's a bargain you must drive within yourself."

I looked toward the fire. "He saved my life, Your Majesty. That alone –"

She only laughed again. "By the Rood, my lord, that's a debt he would count as nothing. A thousand men must owe it him."

"I am his liegeman, then. My family has sworn him fealty and homage, as they swore it to your husband."

Again she laughed. "Yes, but so did all this kingdom – so did his brother – yet now they revolt against him. Why should your loyalty be greater?"

I thought then of that evening in the gallery when all these temptations, like the flames below, had flared within me. "Is this what you wish me to say, My Lady? Richard is worth nothing, or no more than any other lord held for ransom at a tournament. The worth of a suit of mail, a sword, a shield, a destrier . . ."

"A handful of silver?"

"A fortune to most men! To the men I've lived with these past years, more money than they can dream of. That's all *he's* worth, Your Majesty, but the crown he wears and his right to wear it – that is worth his ransom. And my life."

For a long moment now she looked at me, and I wasn't sure whether her expression – so full it was – showed love or anger, joy or sadness, worry or relief. All those feelings moved within her eyes; and then, as they passed, she simply smiled, a smile of modesty it seemed, and stepped away. She crossed to the window; looked out. And in that harsh bar of winter's light she at last looked old to me. Now, fearing that I'd hurt her, I did feel shame.

"Your Majesty . . ."

"Shush," she whispered. "I'm not angry . . . I asked for honesty and you gave it to me. Indeed, I see now that you've learned a great, great truth. Kings rule by the Grace of God – at least we can pray and hope that it is so – but even if they didn't they would rule because they must. Those people there, scurrying like ants about their business – they would demand it. To find *their* place, they need a mark, a headland, some kind of light. And if that mark is taken or its position in dispute, then the world becomes as disordered as the flames within that fire, and ends the same, as cold, grey ash." She smiled again. "That is your reasoning?"

"Yes, My Lady."

She nodded, turned, and stepped toward me. "I accept it, Locksley. But I ask you this. Is reason everything? You have risked your life so many times – but only for what do you think?"

I pondered then. Was she right? Was it all a calculation, as with those merchants in the inn? Could a king's worth be measured in silver marks, however many or few?

Now, with three quick steps, Eleanor stepped before me and took my hands in hers. "Locksley, I beg you . . . Just say his name. Whisper it in your mind. 'Richard, Coeur de Lion, Richard of England' . . . Say it and then tell me: do you not love him still? A little?"

"Your Majesty, if he was to step into this room —"

"Then bring him here. In your mind. With your eye. See him now. You say it is the Crown that is important and not the man who wears it, but are you entirely right? Listen. I am old, my lord, older than any other person that I know. So time plays strange tricks with me. The past is like a vivid dream; the future – which I can never hope to know – is already memory. This kingdom now breathes with rebellion but no one quite dares cry it out. Why not? Even as they hesitate, men don't know why, but I do. It is only the old Duke, 'The Conqueror'. His frowning shadow still frightens them a little. And I can see a time in the future when my son's shade may do the same – when his memory, though men think it forgotten, will steady them before peril and strengthen them against adversity. But that can only happen if we love him. And you do, Lord Locksley, you love him but are ashamed to confess, even to feel it. That's what I ask. Rescue your love and mine, and all the world's. Help ransom back the King and save a little of ourselves."

Behind me, the fire crackled; before, the old Queen's eyes held mine. Softly, I felt my breath pass out of me and then I smiled. "I think, Your Majesty, that you know me better than myself."

She squeezed my hands. "I've had five sons, my lord, which should be enough for any woman, but seeing you I feel I must have had another. I always knew you would serve me faithfully, but I want you to do so with all your heart."

"I do, My Lady."

"Good, then." She smiled, let go my hands, and stepped back. "Tell me: you have the silver?"

"Yes, it's safe. Here in the town."

"Safe. But only for a moment."

"You think the Prince will try again?"

She smiled. "Oh, yes. I know all my children, Lord Locksley. One of John's greatest qualities is his persistence. He'll be undaunted. He'll try again, here or in Normandy or in France." She cocked her head at this last thought. "After all, it wouldn't be the first time he'd conspired with King Philip."

"The ransom must travel across King Philip's lands?"

"Yes . . ." But then she thought a moment. "Or perhaps it doesn't

. . . Listen. In secret, the news that the silver has been stolen reached the Court three days ago, but the Prince still claims it's only been delayed. Why not agree with his pretence? I will leave here, just as planned, pretending to have the silver with me. But you keep it – you've kept it safe so far, why not go on? I'll go north, the shortest way, but you can travel south . . . Continue as a merchant. Sail to Avranches, then make your way from fair to fair and meet me at Verdun."

"My Lady . . . that would be a cunning plan, but you realise it will endanger you. If an attack should come, you'd be its target."

"But I will have a guard, and a large one. Besides, we'll simply flee and let them take our empty train. In fact, when I think of it, you'll be most in danger. If you're discovered . . ."

"Soldiers would only draw attention to us."

"Yes . . . But go to Le Mans, to Epau – the monastery, near the town, where your sister's staying. I'll send a messenger on ahead and a small guard will meet you there. They can travel separately but close enough to call to. Agreed?"

I hesitated. Then, "All right, My Lady. If they're discreet."

"I'll tell them to be." We both paused; and then, reaching out to touch my hand again, the old Queen smiled. "We've talked much, my lord, but our business has been quickly settled."

"Yes, and I should go. As a travelling merchant, I've enjoyed your presence much too long."

She nodded, turning away; but then, with a frown, checked herself and looked back to me. "Yes, you must go. Yet there's one thing more, my lord. I wasn't going to tell you, but now I feel I must. I said I was in Le Mans, and saw your sister. But I saw someone else as well, who also sends a message . . . to be remembered to your affections. You understand?"

"Your Majesty . . . Will she – the Queen – be with us when the King is ransomed back?"

She shook her head.

"By your leave . . . may I know why?"

"I've had a message from the King, my lord. He expressly asked that she not be there."

CHAPTER EIGHT

Days of merchant misery resumed.

From Windsor, in our bullock cart, we creaked south through winter's mud toward Southampton; from there, by fishing boat, we reached Barfleur. Then, slowly crossing Normandy and entering Maine, we moved from town to town and fair to fair: Bayeux, Caen, Falaise, Aregntan, Domfront. These all seemed the same; "fairs" we called them, but many were little more than farmer's markets with a few stalls for cloths. Yet the best were something different, and by their colour and excitement – their reaching out to the great wide world – I grew to understand what drew merchants to their life. It was a life of adventure and excitement – different from a knight's, but just as real – and it brought a special gleam of envy to people's eyes: you were from beyond the hill and would travel beyond the river, see all the places they would only dream of. Half the time, that's what people bought, in fact; wandering down the straw-laid pathways of the fair and peering beneath the bright canopies of stalls, they would purchase talismans of dreams: perfume; mace; pepper (always under heavy guard); indigo; alum from Egypt and cordivan from Spain; camphor; musk, rubies and diamonds and lapis-lazuli; pearls; great tusks of ivory. Of course, between themselves, merchants were less dreamy. Men from Genoa haggled brutally with Flemish dyers, who then exchanged their bills with Jewish money-lenders, shouting out their anger at the rate in the vilest French. Fortunes were made; and lost; and stolen. And then a new day dawned and it all happened once again. At first, still a stranger in this world, I was more than cautious, but gradually I learned to play my part: learned the rules of buying and selling, of money-changing and of interest rates, even learned the Marshall's law by heart:

No manner of persons may make any congregate or affrays among themselves whereby the peace of the fair shall be broken. All unsealed wine, ale and beer must be sold by measure, gallon, pottle, quart or pint. Bakers' bread must be wholesome for a man's body, and no manner of cook, pieman or huckster is to sell or put up for sale any manner of victual but that which is good. No manner of persons may sell or buy except by true weight or measure, sealed according to statute. No man may make attachment or summons of execution but by me, the Chief Marshall of the Fair. No person within the Fair will break the Lord's Day by buying or selling, nor by sitting, tippling and drinking in any tavern, ale house, or cook's house, nor do anything to break the peace thereof. And lastly, any person who finds themselves grieved, injured or wronged by any manner of persons in this Fair, they are to come before the Steward of the Fair and no one else. Therefore, now, upon this hour, begin in the name of God and of the King, and may God send everyone luck in this Fair and the Fair a good continuance . . .

By Le Mans, as I say, I had learned all this by heart, and was becoming a merchant in fact as well as name. Mercury was a wizard with our tally-stick, Allen had a craftsman's eye for workmanship, and Little John could keep a dozen bargains in his head at once; so we made a good team. More than good, perhaps: our wool and timber disappeared, then the cloth we'd bartered it for was gone as well, and all at a handsome profit. No one followed us, or suspected us; after a time, in fact, we were just more familiar faces on the road, our place secure in the flowing river of carts and wagons that wound from town to town.

For me, this was just as well: I had enough to think of. The old Queen, like some Captain in Caesar's legions, had rallied her troops – myself. But by so doing (a deliberate cunning?) she'd perplexed me terribly. The disillusion I'd grown to feel toward Richard had simplified my feelings about the Princess. We loved and wanted each other. If I no longer honoured the King, why not let our feelings run their natural course? During those Sherwood winters, as my love for Richard had perished in the cold, I'd often thought of that Cyprian beach and cursed myself. What a fool I'd been! I'd been so young and innocent – my folly had been virtuous, but was folly just the same. But what did I feel today? The Queen, I realised, had given me back my conscience: bruised, even scarred, but all the tougher for it. With each plodding step the bullocks took, and each creaking revolution of our wagon's wheels, my heart grew heavier. I began to dread the prospect of Le Mans. If the Princess was with Marian, what would I do?

At last, like all days, the day came round. Le Mans, wedged between the rivers Sarthe and Huisne, lay before us, St Julian's Cathedral rising above it from a promontory. It is an ancient place, for the Romans had a city here, Vindinium, whose walls – deviating from the modern here and there – could still be seen. Formerly, it had been seat to the Count of Maine, but thirty years before the Old Duke had seized it from them. Henry, King Richard's father, had been born here, and in his battle with his sons he'd made this his base, razing the town behind him in his last retreat. You could still see the effects of this: tumbled walls; the charred shells of dwellings; and the bustle of new building everywhere.

The Fair, quite a large one, was set up between the town walls and the Sarthe. We arrived early, found a decent stall, passed the usual day of haggling; then, as the clouds of a winter's afternoon closed in, I rented a palfrey from an ostler and trotted east, half in dread, toward the Abbey at L'Epau. It was an easy ride that would have been pleasant in other circumstances – beside the winding river, the track ran between soft, crouched hills enclosed with a silence that clung like a mist. I arrived just as dusk began to fall. The Abbey, surrounded by meadows whose hollows were brushed with snow, was a modest establishment: looking beyond the rubble wall, I could see a plain parish church, whitewashed, with a red tile roof, and a thatched refectory. The gates were already closed, but the monk who opened was polite enough, and led me across a silent, empty court to the outer parlour of the cloister. There, I gave the porter a coin and a message to take to Marian. Almost instantly the porter returned, led me through the parlour and unlatched the door leading to the cloister just beyond.

Marian was alone – thank God: and though it seemed a lifetime since I'd seen her, she was just the same. She sat bolt upright on a bench, her head uncovered. Her cloak had been hastily thrown on and she gripped it at her throat. She came forward – slowly, and then half-running; and then we hugged each other. "Dear, dear brother," she murmured, "thank God you're safe."

I eased her back and smiled. "You have no faith. Surely you never doubted it."

"No? When I didn't hear for months on end?" She squeezed my arm. "And Jean?" she asked. "Has he come with you?"

I shook my head. "He's travelling with Queen Eleanor's body-guard to Mainz. He'll reach the Rhine before us."

"I've seen him so little. It was horrible at Kirklees, meeting as we did, but this is even worse."

"Don't worry. This will all be over soon. With the King back home in England, all our old lives can begin again."

"I tell myself that, but I'm so afraid. Sometimes I think Jean's the biggest fool on earth – because he thinks that nothing on earth can hurt a man as big as him."

"Well, you know, he's *almost* right." She laughed at this and we began to walk around the cloister. The air was mild, but a light snow had begun to fall, the flakes lazily drifting through the gloom. We seemed to be alone: but I pitched my voice low. "How much did Queen Eleanor tell you?"

"That you had the ransom. When you might arrive. That Maud was dead – she knew how that would please me . . . And the details about the guard she's sent to meet you."

"Everything, then. She trusts you. I met her at Windsor – that's when I became a merchant's clerk – and she spoke well of you."

Marian hesitated, her step crunching lightly on the gravel. "She's a very remarkable woman."

I raised an eyebrow. "That's not so warm."

Taking my arm, she stepped ahead. "I don't mean that. Not quite, at least. She treated me kindly enough at Poitiers, but I suspect she was being politic: she wished to stay friendly with her strange ally, Robin Hood of Sherwood."

"She must be politic. She's a queen, remember."

"But that's all and everything she is. Mother, woman, friend – all her other qualities are poured into her crown as if it was a sort of vessel." I didn't argue; indeed, I didn't disagree. For a time, in silence, we walked along. Then Marian let go my hand and said: "There's one person we haven't talked about. When you first saw me – when you saw I was by myself – I thought you were relieved. You say Queen Eleanor trusts me. But so does another queen . . . though she still calls herself a Princess –"

"She's here?"

Marian shook her head. "Don't ask me where she is. But she sends a message. I'm to tell you that her spirit was long ago pledged to God, her title to a king, but her heart –"

"Dear God, don't say this. I beg you."

"Robert –" She stopped; glanced down. "I've grown to love her. If you were to make her my sister you wouldn't only please yourself. We've talked nights away about you, about what she feels, and about the King. She loves you –"

"*And I love her. But she is still the Queen.*"

"But she's not the Queen. Richard doesn't notice her, he has no use for her. You know she's not to be there when he's ransomed? In the Holy Land, she told me, she was locked up in a castle and never saw him once. When we came here, she said, 'We'll live in a nunnery since you are forced to live like one and I shall always be one.' With her, you can't commit adultery – she's never married."

"That can't be true."

"I swear it is. She's as innocent as these monks. The King, it seems, is a faithful Sodomite."

"He has a bastard son. I can't —"

"They say so, but I wonder. In any case, he'll get no heirs with her. He tried. He got drunk one night and tried. She told me that he kissed her and squeezed her breast, but all the time she could see it in his eyes — it was his mother that he wanted. And in the end he failed, so she's as much a maid today as the day she was born . . . Robert, love her as she loves you. You won't disserve the King. By God, he'll thank you for it since it's a service he has no wish to perform himself."

Perhaps. But what would his mother think? Or did she even have the right to say? I was about to speak, but just then the parlour door swung open; a monk, cloaked and hooded, stepped toward us. I whispered, "I should go before they get suspicious. What about the guard?"

"You're not angry at the way I've spoken?"

"No. Truthfully."

She took my hand. "Your guard has been here three days. Their leader is Sir Etienne Vizier, one of the Queen's household knights. Since they couldn't be sure precisely when you'd come, I told them to wait each evening at a spot not far from here. It's an abandoned mill down by the river. Just go east along the bank and you won't miss it. He'll stay there from compline to matins."

I leaned forward and kissed her on the cheek. "All right. Stay here now. You'll be safe, and I'll send word as soon as the King is ransomed."

She squeezed my hand and nodded. "Be careful, brother. Go with God."

Leaving the Abbey as I'd come, I rode toward the river; a path ran along beside it. Night had fallen. Snow still drifted through the stillness and my breath hung about my face in misty clouds. The path was little used — at times, the horse had to shoulder his way between the bushes — but after a league or so it opened out. Here there was a gully, a glinting stream rushing noisily along it to join the river, and once upon a time the trees must have been cut back, away from the bank, though now the space was overgrown with poplar and tall rushes. In the middle of this, the mill loomed up, a low, lumpy shade. I rode slowly closer. Details swelled in shadows and I could see that the great undershot wheel was still. As well, there was no rattle from the damsel and I caught the tang of wet, charred wood — the place must have burned and been abandoned. Hooves sucking, the horse now crossed a patch of muck, which showed the slots of other animals. But they'd not been made tonight: there was still an hour before compline.

Since I had no tinder, I didn't even try to go inside, but waited with the horse, shivering in the damp. Gathered in my cloak, I stamped my feet and watched the movement of my thoughts against the night. Snow, glistening in the air, gave the Princess ghostly form. Thank God she'd not been there. No. That was a lie. I'd felt relief but disappointment too. *Don't ask me where she is.* Why not? Where could she be? The wet ash smell filled my nostrils and memories swirled. Locksley Hall; its burnt-out shell; but also some childhood vision of yellow sun against a wall . . . A life had ended there, a life not tied to kings, which Marian still tried to live. Could I? Did I want to? It was a life that included love and happiness as naturally as spring and autumn. I could have it. The Princess loved me and I loved her. Richard, assuming reasonable discretion on our part, would hardly care. His mother might be a different matter. But did Eleanor, in truth, control my life, my fate? The snow drifted, tumbling, tickling down and melted, gleaming, on the horse's flanks. Time trickled by.

And then, in the distance I heard the Abbey bells and almost instantly I saw them on the gully's ridge, three riders framed against the gloom. A glint of mail: a knight. Two others, perhaps with crossbows – it was too dark to tell. Then, snickering softly to each other, our horses introduced us. The knight, lifting his hand, came forward, the other hanging back. Cautiously, he stopped well off on the far side of that patch of ooze. "Good evening, sir."

"I seek a knight, Sir Etienne Vizier."

"I am he . . . Lord Locksley?"

"Yes."

"Thank God . . . At least tonight we won't have to freeze till matins." Turning, he waved the others forward, then trotted toward me and swung down. He was an older man; his cowl was thrown back and I could see that his short, stiff hair was the colour of his mail. Removing his glove, he shook my hand. "Go in, my lord," he said, "go in. Tonight we came prepared."

Indeed they had; from their saddle-bags, they took flint and tinder, tapers, candles, bread, cheese and wine. Soon light flickered off the old stone walls and glistened on the black, charred beams. The mill's worn kingpin and two stones still stood in a corner and one of the stones became our hearth. Huddled about the blaze, we passed a wineskin round. Vizier said, "So tell me, lord, are you watched or followed?"

"No, sir. No one has the slightest idea who we are. If we can just avoid attracting attention to ourselves I think they'll never know."

"Good, then. I wouldn't think that we'll have been noticed either. You said to be discreet, so we're four knights travelling between the tournaments held beside the Fairs – I may look a little past it, but my companions are much younger so it works out well. Each of us has the usual esquire, but they are really knights themselves."

"So that makes eight of you?"

"Eight knights. But we also have our servants – these gentlemen – who are four of Aquitaine's finest arbalesters." I was pleased by all this. It had been done more neatly than I'd thought possible, and they'd make a handy force. I told Vizier so, and he went on, "The only difficulty will be time, my lord. The Queen has been delaying in Rouen, but she'll leave tomorrow. For her, it's a quick march, but for ourselves . . ."

I'd thought of that too, and said, "Yes, but since no one's following we can be less cautious. Let's move on between the Fairs but never stop at any – we'll always be on our way to the next along. And I'll sell my bullocks and buy horses; that should pick up our pace."

"Excellent," said Vizier. "And our route?"

"My lord, I'd prefer you to decide – you know the country better."

He was pleased, I think, and nodded. "Well, sir, I'd say the safest route would take us to Ostend and from there to Metz. Once across the Saar we'd head north to Mainz. That way we'll never have to cross Philip's lands, though I'm sure he'll have his spies about."

"Very good, my lord. And if we marched quickly, when do you think we'd reach Germany?"

He smiled. "When we do, Lord Locksley, when we do." I nodded, deciding I liked the man. I was relieved to have him with me. But even as I thought this, I saw his face cloud over. Since we seemed to have no problem, I couldn't think why. Frowning, he appeared to ponder, and then, with irritation, made up his mind. With an impatient gesture, he sent his two crossbowmen outside the mill. Then, speaking low, he said, "I wasn't going to tell you, Locksley, but I think I must. I said we were twelve, but that's not quite true. We have – we have one extra." He turned to face me. "A yeoman," he went on, "carrying one of your English bows."

"To hunt, you mean?"

"Yes, if she can actually shoot the thing she might do that."

I stared, my heart seeming to hang within my breast.

He said, "The Queen, my lord. *Your* Queen – King Richard's wife. She's cut her hair and put on mail, and now she rides with us – and she *can* ride, I'll own to that –"

"My lord, you can't be serious. This is impossible."

"No, sir. If it is, then what is happening is a miracle and I'll swear to God it isn't that."

"You mean she's coming with us?"

"So she says."

"She can't. . . . She mustn't. Good God, you have to send her back."

"How? She's Queen. She says she's going to see her husband ransomed and nothing on this earth can stop her." He hesitated. "God knows why she wants to go. They say he never –"

"Send a message to Queen Eleanor. She must be told –"

"Think, my lord . . . by your leave. My Lady is surrounded with spies. A messenger, riding from us, will only tell them everything we've tried so hard to hide."

I took a breath. All at once, a dozen emotions swelled within me – anger, pain and disbelief – but as they subsided I felt . . . only tenderness. I even smiled; and Vizier looked at me. "Surely you see my fear, my lord? There's the disgrace of it, but even more, what happens if we *are* attacked? King Philip, you know, has never forgiven Richard for throwing over his sister. How perfect this would be for him. He would take Richard's ransom – thus leaving him captive – and revenge himself on the Queen as well." With his toe, he prodded the fire. "This roll, my lord, we lose whatever shows. Dear God, even if we get her safely into Germany, Richard will only hate us for it."

He was right. Thus, why did she go? Why risk herself? Even if she succeeded, she'd only earn a public snub. But I was afraid I knew the answer.

"My lord," I said, "you know she's my sister's friend. Tomorrow, I'll speak with her myself, and if that doesn't work, I'll ask Marian to."

He nodded. "I wish you luck, but I don't think you'll have it." He paused. "Still, this fast pace we'll make may do the trick. A week in the saddle might have her begging us to take her home."

Of course with her, it wouldn't – she'd endure agonies before she'd beg. But I said, "We'll see, my lord."

"We will indeed. Nonetheless, I'm glad I spoke about it. Whatever happens, the consequences will fall on both our heads." I smiled. Again, he tried to stir the fire, but now it was dying down. He slapped his hands together. "Time to go, perhaps."

"Very well, my lord. I'll let you get well on, then follow."

We said farewells; shook hands again. But then, as Vizier stepped through the doorway, I called out, "The Queen, my lord . . . where is she now?"

"Le Mans. She's left the Abbey."

"With your men?"

In the gloom, I saw him shake his head. "I insisted on some decencies. She's at an inn, but I try to watch her."

Except now, I felt, she was watching me . . .

Quickly, Vizier and his men moved off, and I stepped outside the mill myself. Now the snow had stopped; the sky had cleared a little and a few stars were out, but the air was colder. Frost prickled in my nose. I rubbed the horse, wishing I had a blanket for him. Somewhere, an owl hooted and the breeze, rising now, rattled through the stalks of rushes. Searching round, my eyes probed the night. I felt her; somehow, I knew she was nearby, I knew she'd come. Because I was here. Again, time trickled by . . .

Until, at last, I heard the jingling of a bridle, a bright, sharp sound playing above the rushing of the stream. Then, a velvet gleam against the woolly night, I saw the horse's nostrils and the harder glint of starlight on the mail she wore. At an easy walk, her horse came forward, a lovely sorrel gelding – which made me smile, for even as a yeoman she remained a Princess. As he stopped, I whispered, "My Lady, is it you?"

Her voice was low. "Dear Locksley, yes."

And then I saw her face, a gentle oval coiffed in steel. In the darkness, at this distance, she might have been the most beautiful boy in all the world, except for the wide, soft darkness of her eyes. "You must be cold," I whispered.

"The ride was warming. You're the one who's had to wait."

"For years, My Lady. But this hour, knowing you would come, was the easiest part."

"You knew I'd come?"

"I knew." Her horse stretched out his neck, and shifted on his haunches. "I knew you'd come, My Lady, but you can go no farther. You mustn't . . . I know why you do –"

"To be near the one I love."

"Of course. Your husband."

"My true husband, yes. You know, My Lord, what I offer him?"

"I do, My Lady. And we both know that such an offer can never be accepted, and we both know why."

"My Lord, not ever?"

"My Lady . . ."

But now she only stared down upon my face, her vision moving like a breath upon my cheek: and she saw me, I knew, as no one else had ever seen me. Then, quite slowly, she drew the horse's reins up. "Don't be afraid," she whispered, "I'm just your life, come to rescue you from Fate."

And then, before I could stop her, she jerked the horse's head around and rode him up the path, away in darkness.

CHAPTER NINE

Across Flanders, across three freezing weeks, she haunted me. My life, she called herself; my ghost, she seemed. And indeed she followed our slow progress like a ghostly shadow. We rarely met or spoke, but I'd see her by the road or along the forest's edge, her image blurred by the jolting of the cart and shuttered by the trees. Or, passing round a bend, we'd come upon her standing in a snowy field, all clear, wreathed in that sorrel gelding's breath. Or, again, lifting up my eyes, I'd glimpse her shape against the slate grey sky, watching from a hillside.

Present always, she still kept her distance, like a dream I couldn't quite remember. Not just a dream of love, I thought, or even peace, but a dream of life exactly as she'd said. It was this dream, as delicate as a chain of flowers, that led back to Garth and Marian, to Locksley, to the hills we'd climbed, to a thousand memories . . . At some point, I knew, this chaplet had parted – perhaps the moment when Falaise had tossed his dice – or been transformed, hardened to a chain of steel, imprisoning me to Richard, Eleanor, the world of kings. By now, the links had tarnished, God only knew; not even the old Queen's polishing could hide the rust. It only held me – or so I told myself – because I didn't strain against my bonds. But did I want to? Did I truly wish to free myself? And if I did, would my freedom only seem an exile, a banishment from the Great World that Eleanor had called my fate?

League after league, the road and my questions rattled by; and, after a time – perhaps like the Princess who followed me – I no longer struggled, but just continued on. If I really possessed a fate, I thought, the journey itself would find an answer. And one day, at least, the journey ended. More than a month had passed since we'd left England, and the cold that had kept us huddled in our cloaks had given way to a muddy thaw. From dawn to dusk the sky was leaden; only your belly marked the passing of the hours. By that judge, it was a little before noon when a horse, with a heavy rider, drove splashing through the ooze toward us. It was Vizier. And despite our weeks of misery, he was beaming.

"We have them in sight, my lord. Two leagues on. But they've camped well off the road – a nasty pull for you."

I'd been taking my turn as driver; now, I passed the reins along to Allen, mounted one of our palfreys and waded down the road. The villages here were poor and half-deserted: a few rude huts clustered round a ford; some "lord's" bailey, guarding a wretched moitie, perched upon a distant hill. Now, swinging into the trees, we followed an easy path, climbing slowly up a hill and pausing on the crest. Far off, on the far side of the valley below us, we could see another road – and, much nearer, the loop of a wide stream. It was here, protected on two sides by water, that the Queen's men were pitching camp. Her own pavilion, Richard's lions flying before it, was already up, and some way behind I saw a large fly tent sheltering men in litters. "They've been attacked," I said.

"So it seems, my lord. Does that change our plans? We might keep separate from them even now, tell them we're here but quietly tag along behind."

I shook my head. "By your leave, I think not. The Queen has two score knights at least. Now that we're this close, and travelling just behind her, a force big enough to defeat hers would be bound to stumble on us. I'd say that our disguise is finished."

He considered a moment, then nodded. "You're likely right. Agreed."

I pointed. "The road we can see must cross the one we're on. We'll take the cart along it, then cross their stream. I suppose we can let them worry how."

"Aye . . ." He paused then, with a frown. "You know, though, there's one problem we must solve ourselves. What on God's Earth do we do about Richard's Queen? If we take her down there, My Lady Eleanor – someone – is bound to know her. She may even wish to join their party."

I thought a moment; it was, I supposed, a problem that would fall on his head more than mine. But then I said, "I'm not sure you have to worry, my lord. Keep her with your men, and keep them quiet. I think the Queen may just wish to watch. She has her own purposes – and I'm sure she doesn't wish to make you trouble. And if she wishes to present herself to the King, we can hardly –"

But then I stopped myself. To our left, there was a sudden crashing in the bushes; Vizier's hand instantly gripped his sword, and I tugged back my cloak, revealing my own. But then we both relaxed. We'd been speaking of the Queen and here she was: though in no condition to present herself to anyone. Her face was scratched and muddy; she was out of breath and even that great horse of hers was blowing.

"My Lady –"

"Thank God it's you . . . I thought it was." She took a breath, and looked at me. "My lord, I saw his shield – argent, a lion rampant gules – do you know those arms?"

I felt my eyes go wide. "Gisbourne's?"

"So I remembered right, then. Yes . . . his. I saw three men wearing them just now. And a fourth man – a huge man – was riding after them." She looked at me. "He was so large, my lord, he made me think of your sister's friend –"

"Jean Neuilly?"

"Yes. He looked just like that. And he wore Richard's arms."

"And which way did they go, my lady?"

"They crossed the road about a league behind our cart. I was riding in the woods on this side and saw them go. They drove their horses hard, down a little track –"

Vizier broke in then. "Locksley, who are these men?"

"Three enemies, my lord. And a friend. This track . . . ?"

"It's behind us, south, and heads west, toward the river. It's too hard to say. I'll have to show you. Quickly."

"My Lady –"

"Quickly." And then she turned her horse. I hesitated; but then jerked my arm at Vizier and followed after. We zigzagged down the ridge, bulled through the bush and waded a stream, clambering up the other side. There was no real way, except for the little openings the deer had made, and for an exhausting league we struggled on. The trees were oak and elm, or pine where the soil gave way to rock along the hillsides; in their shade the snow lay thick but across the open spaces the turf had turned to muck. Finally, we cut across the path: and I would have turned the Princess back but she'd already spurred along it and with that horse of hers was pounding up ahead, so far ahead that, after a moment, she had to hold him in. Now, for a good hour, we eased our mounts between a gallop and a canter, slowly strung out – Vizier's animal lumbering along behind – but then, having looped south, the track swung north, picking up the road Queen Eleanor had marched along, and we thudded on together. After a time, the land opened up a little – small steadings timorously hugged the road – but soon a track turned back toward the woods, and we could see four riders heading down it – three bunched up, the fourth pursuing. We plunged on behind them, closing up for now their destination was obvious; they were heading toward the Vale of Mainz where King Richard would be ransomed and where Henry, the Holy Roman Emperor, would have his camp. As we galloped after them, I knew that the gap between us had to shorten. Our horses were hardly fresh, but they must have been flaying theirs for days.

We caught them in a stony clearing, a sort of gully.

Or we caught two of them at least.

The third, close chased by Little John – for I was now certain it was him – swept round the gully's edge and headed toward a thicket. But by the time we reached the spot, the other two had turned and blocked our way. Viciously, Vizier pulled up his mount and I clattered to a halt beside him. I glanced toward him. He was a household knight. Some of these, I knew, were old hounds allowed to doze away their dotage before the hearth. But, if that was true of Vizier, he must once have been a fearsome brute. He had his lance; he and his horse had struggled with it (like some great war engine) through all the leagues and brush behind us. Now he bellowed, "My lord, you'll let me do the leading!" and before I could reply he nosed his shield and dropped the weapon's point. Up ahead – this spot was like an old stream bed with steep banks of shale and frozen mud – Gisbourne's men were turning round. They were not knights but sergeants, carrying swords and spears; yet the old knight showed no mercy. The one closest wasn't even set as he began his charge. Quartering away in panic, the sergeant's horse opened up his flank, and though he managed to toss his spear it was still in the air as Vizier's lance pierced his flimsy ox-hide shield and spitted him. Torn free by the tremendous impact, the pike tumbled along the ground, landing in some bushes, where the body seemed to cling like a shrike's prey upon a thorn. Now, seeing his chance, the second man dug in his spurs, but the old knight just calmly swung his horse's head around and galloped back toward me – so that I, driving ahead myself, met his pursuer as though in a list. I swung; he parried and cut back, the blow glancing against my quillon. But, at the sound of steel, Vizier had turned again and now took him from the other side. With a grunt, the old man swung; and this blow, blocked, left our opponent open, and my sword slashed across his mouth. For a second, a bloody grin creased his face; and then, like the lid of a tankard flipping back, his head was gone.

Vizier, flushed and panting, reared his mount beside me. "Well struck, my lord. But by God I hope these men have died for a reason."

"They have, I promise you." I looked around. "Where is the Princess – the Queen?"

Vizier twisted in his saddle. "By Christ's thorns . . . She's gone after those other two! Your friend and the last of these!"

Our bits tore our horses' mouths as we drove them up the gully. The path swung, slithering, up its bank. Then we levelled with a plain that was wedged between two forks of forest and covered by the darkening sky. Against this background it was hard to see, but then Vizier – old eyes or no – gave a shout and charged off to our left. I followed hard and soon made out three figures moving on a little rise – three figures that became three horses as we galloped closer. But I could only see two riders, and as Vizier and I pulled up, we saw the reason why. Little John had ridden down Gisbourne's man, but to no avail for the soldier had somehow captured Berengaria. Now he had her in front of him on his saddle, his spear point jabbed against her neck.

"No closer!" he shouted at us. "Another step and your squire's dead!"

Vizier went pale. "Dear God . . ."

Little John – who could not have known who the "squire" was – flashed me a welcoming grin. "Good evening, Robin. I wondered if it wasn't you." Then, not waiting for an answer, he shouted across to our opponent. "My friend, kill the little fellow and you'll have no shield – we'll hack you down. Turn and run and you'll be dead before you've gone a hundred paces. Put down your spear! We'll give you mercy!"

But the soldier shook his head and tightened his grip on Berengaria. "Back off I say! All of you back off!"

And then Berengaria shouted: "My lord! He has a cylinder like the one you found in Sicily! It's in –" She broke off. The soldier brought his spear up, she tried to struggle free, and then – but the next instant was so full that it seemed to hold, not end, a lifetime. My mouth hung open, for I'd been about to tell my friend who his "little fellow" was. But there was no need. Her voice had told him – told him, at least, her sex. And it was this that drove him forward before I could even tighten on my horse's reins. Jean Neuilly was not a knight. But no knight in Christendom was more chivalrous than he. I remember he once told me that during those years in Sherwood, those years of hunger, filth and cruelty, it was only his gentleness to women which proved, even for himself, that he remained a man. And he was such a man! The great roar he bellowed now shook the plain. The soldier stopped his spear. Twisted in his saddle. Pulled his arm back. Made his cast . . . I saw it glitter. Arc. I almost screamed. He tried to dodge. But he was so large, so close, a target. The spear took him high up in the chest and his bolting charge passed the point right through his body. Yet he didn't fall. Not then. He kept on coming and even got his right arm up for one last enormous buffet that toppled Gisbourne's soldier to the ground. And then Little John was down as well, lying in the dust.

In horror and dismay, I raced toward him. He was twisted on his side, his teeth drawn back in agony. The spear's bloody point jutted from his back and I pulled out my knife to cut the haft, but he reached up and gripped my arm.

"Dear Robin, don't. I beg you. I'm dying anyway." I moaned in wordless agony and he squeezed my arm again, as if it was me who needed comforting. "'Little John'," he said, "and 'Robin'. It's strange we always used those names."

"For each other, friend, that's who we always were."

"Yes. And that was everything." But then the pain tightened across his face and he fought for breath. When he spoke again, his voice was just a whisper. "The girl, the little squire . . . She's the one? She's your . . . ?" And though I couldn't speak, he must have read the answer on my face, for now he whispered: "Ah, that's good then. You must tell Marian that I —"

But then, with love forming on his lips, he closed his eyes and died. For a second longer, I held his head up; then gently laid it down. The Princess knelt beside me. "Poor, dear Marian," she whispered. A terrible choking grief swept over me. The Princess held me then, as she might have held a child, and at length Vizier led me off. It was now getting dark; he lit a fire, fed me a little bread and cheese and wine. I was half insensible and scarcely realised what was happening. The world only began again when Vizier, in his old soldier's fashion, knelt before me and seized my shoulders.

"My lord," he said, his voice a little gruff, "you have to rouse yourself. Your friend is gone; there's nothing you can do for him. But you and I still have work to do."

He was right, I knew, and I struggled to find my wits. "The Princess," I began, "the Queen – she said there was a message?"

"We found it in a cylinder, my lord. The Queen understands the cipher it was written in and has worked it out. John and Philip, both together, are asking the Emperor Henry to keep Richard captive, and in return they offer him an army of five thousand knights and soldiers to help seize Sicily for his Empire." Gently, now, he let go my shoulders, and added kindly: "Your friend didn't die in vain. At least this bribe hasn't been delivered."

I drew myself up then and tried to find my voice. "I thank you, my lord. Someone must take this news to Eleanor. May I ask you to? Tell her what has happened, and tell her to keep guard. We've found one piece of treachery; there may be more."

"And where are you in this, my lord?"

"I'll stay and scout the ground. Out there is where the ransoming takes place – it may be ambushed."

"My lord, I'd rather be with you."

I reached out and touched his shoulder. My voice was low, uncertain once again. "On any other night, my lord, I'd want you with me . . . But now – I ask you not to take offence – I'd rather be alone. Take my friend and the Queen safely back to Eleanor's camp and warn her. If all goes well, I'll see you in the morning."

He was about to speak, but stopped himself and turned away. I heard him get the horses, and saddle them; and I thanked God he didn't ask me to help him tie on Little John. He kicked the fire out and in the darkness we shook each other by the arm. I saw him smile. "You're a strange man, Locksley. Not many of us are lettered and none I know like you. In Poitiers, I have some of the finest pierrefitte you've ever tasted. Some night, when you have time, I'd like to feed it to you and hear your story."

I smiled, and tried to seem more cheerful. "I'll happily accept your wine and company, Vizier, but the story is much too long. You'd only fall asleep."

The Princess had been standing a little apart; now, tugging her horse along, she drew closer. In the darkness, her eyes were glistening and her voice was low: "My lord . . . He was your friend, and he died to save me. I could never take his place, but I ask you – let me be as great a friend in my own way."

I nodded; I wished to thank her but my voice was stiff. "You are my Queen, My Lady, just as you were his. At the end –"

"My lord, I beg you, don't be cruel – to me or him. He saved me because I was a woman, and he saw in me and you what you refuse to see. He was a soldier, my lord, in the service of his liege and because we have the message, that soldier didn't die in vain. But he was your friend. And as your friend his death will be vain unless –" But then Vizier came nearer and she stopped herself. She turned a little, stroking the muzzle of her gelding. Reaching out, she handed me the reins. "My lord, your horse is tired. Please take mine. Tonight you may need him more than me."

"My Lady, I will bring him back unharmed."

She smiled. "Just let him have his head, and he'll come straight to me."

She stepped back, and then I heard the creak of leather as she and Vizier mounted. The old soldier's voice clucked softly, their horses snorted, they softly called goodbye; then the darkness swallowed them and only the gelding's quivering nostrils followed his mistress's vanished scent. I waited for a time, then tugged the gelding's bridle and struck out across the plain. Easily, letting the great horse stay warm, I walked along. Soon, stars began to twinkle behind the clouds. We found a pool, a shallow puddle, and I let the horse kick through the ice and drink before I tugged him on again. Walking, I found some strength myself and began to think. I'd told Vizier that my story was a long one, but now I wondered if it wasn't coming to an end. It wasn't simply that Little John was dead; rather that his death – which filled me with a sadness I hadn't felt since Garth's – marked the closing of a circle. I was back to my beginning: a strange country, full of danger; a messenger, crossed by chance; a chessmen cipher and Prince John's treachery . . .

And then, as the night wore on, the rest of what had happened also seemed told again. A wind came up; frost iced the ground beneath my feet; and though there were no hounds chasing me, I still huddled within my cloak, without a fire, as I'd done those first desperate weeks in Sherwood. All this, I told myself, was a sign that my story was done, that I was free; my fate, my duty – call it what you will – had now been satisfied. I'd set out to serve the King, and if I now more served the crown he wore, the dawn should see both safe. His fate, *its* fate, would be in his hands, not mine. Everything else was thus an afterthought . . . but then I smiled a little ruefully for "everything else" meant my whole life. What would I do with it? Lord, outlaw, merchant in disguise – how would I choose to live? And how, too, would I choose to love?

The dawn rose; the earth gave up a mist. If there was any danger lurking on that plain, I couldn't see it; only a fox, like a scuttling shadow beneath a swirl of fog, and a flock of blackbirds swarming overhead, and then a gentle rain. I felt as though I hadn't slept in weeks, but now peace mingled with fatigue. Slowly, I walked the Princess's horse to the top of a little mound of earth, a lump upon the plain: here there was a huge boulder, covered with crumbly moss, and a tattered pine – a perfect seat, I thought, for the retiring spectator. To the east, where the light spread up, I could see the Emperor's camp, protected by an earthworks and a palisade: within lay five long rows of tents, a great marquee studded round with the pennons of the Empire's screaming eagles, and a smaller canopy with Richard's lions flying from it. An hour passed; inside the German camp, smoke began to curl, thickening the fog; and finally the palisade gates swung open and a procession of knights rode out. They crossed the plain below me, then stopped in line, their pennons hanging limply in the rain. Everything looked grey: the grey dawn light, the cold glint of armour, the silvery curtain of the rain. Gradually, within that light, the day unfurled. From the west, a procession of Eleanor's knights appeared, and then, behind both lines, tents were erected to shelter kings and knights and treasure.

Now came the hours of diplomatic waiting; of bows, kissed hands, and lances dipped. At length a party from Henry's side crossed between the lines and disappeared – presumably to count the ransom; and then a similar group, under Eleanor's banner, rode to the German camp, I suppose to see that Richard was still safe. Noon came and went before each was satisfied. But finally the lines of Eleanor's knights opened once again, and a man appeared. For a moment, at that distance and in the rain, I didn't know him, but then I saw his banner – it was Hubert Walter, archbishop of Rouen. He stepped ahead; and behind him, staggering in the mud, came a procession bearing the ransom on a score of litters. I wondered – now Henry had both King and Ransom. But the time for treachery had passed – to betray Richard now would only earn his excommunication – and soon the gates of the Emperor's palisade swung open. I think, from my vantage point, that I must have seen him before the others: a single man, alone, riding an ordinary sorrel palfrey, his hair longer than I remembered and blowing in the wind. He wore no armour, and his azure coat bore no arms. He trotted forward. The German lines swung open . . . and at last I heard the cheer.

The King was safe.

And that night, as I followed the long procession across the plain, I was finally free to think about myself, what I would do, where I would go, what my life meant now. The great train of men and horses wound along. Alone, I hung back and kept away. Dusk fell and I watched them pitch their camp, and then, as night drew in, I saw the bonfires blaze and listened to their singing. But still I stayed outside, beyond the circle of their guard. What would bring me in? What lay there now? Only one thing, I knew, one person. Was it not all I had? Was it not my just reward, a love beyond allegiance? Thus, slowly, I slipped between their lines. I stared about, but among the leaping fires saw only leaping shadows and of the faces that watched me as I passed, none knew mine. But remembering what she'd said, I let her horse's reins go slack, and step by step he took me to her: along a stream, through a frozen grove of naked trees, down behind a little bank. Here, off by themselves, a few fires and tents were scattered. The horse stopped; announced us softly. A moment passed. Faintly, I could hear the singing in the camp; a horn sounded, awkwardly – some drunken fool; a branch cracked in the fire . . . The tent flap opened. As she emerged, I saw she'd taken off her mail and clutched a cloak about her. It parted as she moved and the fire's ruddy light glowed against her skin, cast the softest shadow between her breasts.

She whispered: "So he found me, my lord, just as I said he would."

"And as I said, Your Highness, I've brought him safely back."

She smiled again. "'Your Highness'? A princess here? I hardly think so, my lord." Then, without the slightest trace of shame, as easily as a child, she let her cloak slip back so I saw her body shine, as soft and smooth as silk. Proudly, her eyes looked up to me. "My lord," she said, "I'm just a woman. Only that."

I stepped down and stood before her, my voice trembling in my throat: "My Lady, I thought you were a princess, but if you're not, if you only look like one, then I don't know you."

"No one does, my lord. I'm too far from home, lost in a land where I have few friends."

"Then I'll be one . . . if I can know your name."

"My name is Berenguela, in my mother's tongue."

I smiled. "My Lady, I'm just a simple Englishman, so by your leave I'll call you . . . Gala."

"Gala."

She said it once, against my cheek, and then I kissed her; and followed her inside.

The King was safe. Now at last I claimed my queen.

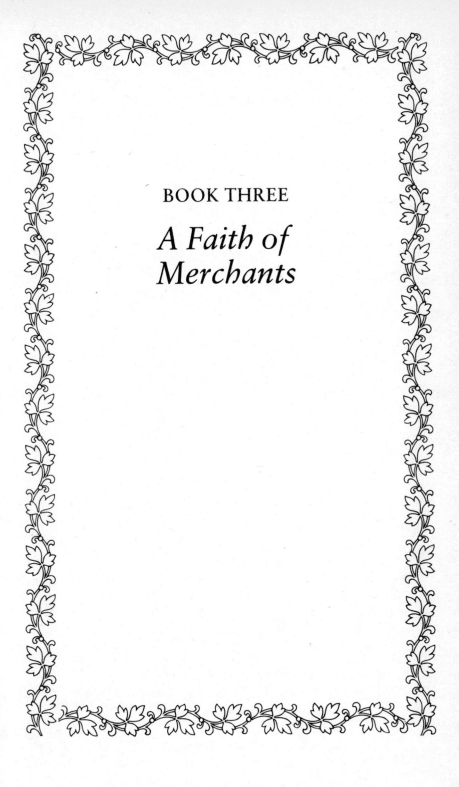

BOOK THREE

A Faith of Merchants

CHAPTER ONE

You live your life by days and weeks and months; but then, having lived it out, you discover that the memory of a year passes in a moment, a decade in the blinking of an eye. Thus, memory is like a currency; its value falls and rises for a hundred reasons, and weighed in its scale the end of kingdoms may seem nothing while a fleeting instant – the smell of bread on a winter's afternoon – sinks the balance like purest gold.

By this standard, my memories of the time between King Richard's homecoming and his death are worthless, mere leaden dross.

Of course, I know what happened in those years; I have the chronicles. But they stir me less than an ancient tally book, and the years themselves seem dead. Perhaps, indeed, I have nothing to remember because we didn't really live them. The King was dead already – his heart went out of him before Jerusalem's gate – while his brother still waited to be born: impatiently, he roamed the country, busied himself with plots and projects and kept his ear cocked for the tolling church bell that would make him king. And I was little better. I shuttled back and forth between sham king and pretending prince, a spy in both their houses: as Sir Robert Atheling, Lord Locksley, I played the part of courtier to the Prince while giving my true loyalties to his brother – whom I then betrayed, at every opportunity, with his wife. Thus, all our lives were mummery and even our falseness was false itself since everybody knew it. John, certainly, knew I was his brother's spy; returning home, the King had publicly pardoned him and then – with equal openness – had set a number of us to report on his princely conspirings. As for Gala and myself, he all but thanked me for assuming the burden of her happiness and only asked discretion – which was provided, easily enough, by Gala staying in Le Mans with Marian, whom I then visited as a loving brother.

Thus, the years passed by. I lived, more or less unhappily, at Windsor, and spent most of my time at Court: days of boredom, nights of wine and lies. Trusting even fewer people than trusted me, I had few friends, for the Sherwood men had gone their various ways: Allen became a bowyer again, in Nottingham; Much got back his mill – a few years later, I loaned him a little money; and I found Richard Lee a place with Vizier as a varlet. Of them all, only Mercury still stayed with me. I called him steward, but he was my advisor, jester and closest friend – "Locksley's Longchamp" as everybody said. He never failed me; indeed, if my spying was of any use to King Richard the credit should be his. His lips were always smacking with the latest gossip and every night his fornications discovered fresh conspiracies. When I think of it, perhaps he's the one to recall those years – he almost seemed to relish them.

But then, so suddenly, they were over. The waiting ended; Richard died and the rest of us began to live again.

Over the years, as I have told, my vision of the King had faded. Whenever I thought of him, I could feel a little smile play across my face: of affection always, but also of mockery – mockery against myself. Why did I still serve him? The answer, I suppose, was that I served a memory, a principle, an obligation – or perhaps, as I'd thought before, it was just my fate. But the King himself seemed dead. One winter's night, as I'd huddled within my skins in Sherwood, he'd finally perished; or so I thought . . . But even at the end, it seemed, something deep still drew us to each other. One night in early April I awoke with pounding heart and a mind filled with premonitions. I was in danger; I didn't know why, or how, but it swelled in the darkness all around me. I summoned Mercury at once, but he only smiled, offered to mix a draught, told me, as a conjuring sorcerer himself, never to believe in spirits. I listened . . . but then, that single time, ignored his counsel. Ordering our horses, we whipped up through the night like a pair of thieves, reaching London as the dawn came up. There, a sennight later, we learned the King had died that very night.

What was I to do?

This question, to some degree, turned upon another: who would be the king? There were two claimants to the throne. John, the Prince, was Eleanor's youngest son. All his older brothers were now dead, but one of them, Geoffrey, had left a child – Arthur of Brittany – who'd been raised as King Philip's ward. Hubert Walter first favoured him, or so people said, but I suspected that John would win in the end, if only because his mother wished it so. Despite myself, I was inclined to agree with her – Arthur was just a boy and would only be France's proxy – though I could scarcely imagine my own future if John assumed the throne. A ruthless man, he would be specially ruthless toward his brother's friends, and though Eleanor might wish to give me some protection, she was now very old and spent all her time in Aquitaine. Of course, I could go there myself, for Gala was now free, but that would only draw attention and danger to her. So, cautiously, I waited; then, following Mercury's advice, decided to do nothing. London, he said, would be our second Sherwood. Hidden in its crowds, we'd watch and wait; scent the air; wait for dust to settle . . . By the time it did, a year had passed, and John was King, and I was an outlaw once again.

But this time there was a difference: the difference silver makes. As Lord Locksley, I made back our family's fortune and I had a chest with me on that midnight ride from Windsor, and there was more with Gala and Marian at Le Mans. Now, I can't remember how much it came to, but there was enough to buy me comfort and protection. The only question was where these valuable commodities could be bought most cheaply. Mercury argued for Genoa – the language and the climate suited him though I knew I'd find it much too strange; I thought of France again, and even Navarre, but Gala was certain that her father would just lock her in a convent and she'd never see me (or light of day) again. So, in the end, prudence prevailed once more, and I moved more modestly: across the Thames, to Southwark. I would only be a stone's throw from Westminster and John's new Court, but in theory I was safe. In 1181, by order of the Justiciar Ranulf Glanville, Southward Sokes had been given a borough's rights, including that of sanctuary – anyone resident there for a year and a day was quit of all offence; and even if John might not be inclined to honour this, I knew the inhabitants would – for most of them were criminals. Then, as now, the area was London's whorehouse, a maze of stews, ale-houses and cheap lodgings for Flemish sailors, a society in which it was a simple matter to lose oneself. Thus, I became "Daniel Delore", outlaw-in-disguise. Using my silver, I bought a great man's house, The Tabard, that had fallen into disrepair, and made it presentable as an inn, used especially by pilgrims on their way to Canterbury, and merchants up from Dover. Less reputably (though no one ever claimed they were outside the law) I invested in a string of stews, which Mercury managed, and with their profits set myself up in the wool trade, thereby giving myself an excellent reason to pass through Le Mans at least three times a year. Life was easy. By leaps and bounds, my fortune grew. The stews – The Cardinal's Cap, Three Tuns, The Unicorn, The Swanne, all in prime locations on the Bankside – had a reputation for fairness and freedom from the pox, while my merchanting soon included everything from mustard to the finest

Venice cloth. Deniers piled up until my income was counted in hundreds of pounds, and soon Daniel Delore, merchant and whoremonger, was far richer than Lord Locksley had ever been.

But what of my fate? What of the Great World that had drawn me in so many times before? I forgot it – and assumed it had forgotten me. My only contact with it now was Gala, but even she preferred to let it go. She was my princess but no one's queen; her only visions, like my own, were of a time when we could always be together. Together, indeed, time flew; apart, it crawled. And thus, by jerks and starts, the months passed by. If I didn't quite forget the past, it nonetheless became like a strange, exciting dream. Kings and queens . . . great combats . . . conspiracies and secret ciphers . . . None of it made the same, sharp clicking sense of the abacus in my tally room. But then, one day in May, I awoke to find . . .

Light, like the inside of a golden bowl, glowed beyond my eyes. I didn't open them: but lay, as though upon a sunny hillside, with the brightness shining on my face. Above me, pigeons nestled in the thatch and softly cooed; in the High Street, cart wheels rumbled by and someone gave a shout . . . It was very early. With a contented sigh, I pressed my face against the pillow. A good day was dawning. Winter had been hard, but at last spring was warming into summer. Peacefully, drifting between sleep and waking, I contemplated what lay ahead. Lord Locksley was Daniel Delore; he had no lands or titles, but in fact his life was perfect except for his separation from a certain lady. A problem. Today, I'd try to find its remedy. With money, anything was surely possible. But then I must have fallen asleep once more; or perhaps not; perhaps the bowl was merely lifted from my head and the world outside came clamouring in. Below, I could hear my innkeeper, Tom Lugersdale, calling to the pot scrubbers and the scullery maids. Outside, the hens we kept for meat and eggs began to squawk, the breadman's cart rumbled into the yard, and old Blind Jack's nose flute began to trill while his dog boy, Will, shrieked out his hideous ballad – that same, unchanging tune, those same, unchanging words, the same dull tale of a whore on a cucking-stool. Finally, giving in, my eyes blinked open. The sun, at least, had been no dream. It filled the room; golden dust, descending from the thatch, drifted in the gentle breeze that wafted through the window. I smelled frying bacon and hot butter. The flute, with its horrible tune, continued – and then, thankfully, the slop boy's bucket dispersed our tormentors with shouts and cries. Reaching beyond the bed, I found my stick and added to the din: three thumps that alerted the servants in the buttery below that their master was up and rousing, that another day had now begun.

Breakfast, brought by Tom's daughter, Rachel, was bread and cheese and ale; I washed – a habit city filth had forced me to; then dressed in fresh hose and a belted tunic. Strapping on my purse, I set out on my morning round, the daily tour I took of my domain. I never learned the history of The Tabard before I owned it, but at some point it must have belonged to a prelate or a great lord, for it had always been large. Addition leaned upon addition; rooms divided within themselves like warrens; gables and pitches made the roof an alps. My own room, on the upper storey, gave onto the covered porch that surrounded three sides of the courtyard; within, it connected to a winding passage leading by the other guest rooms. At the end of this lay a double stair that connected to a minstrel's landing and then led down to the Pilgrims' Hall, called this in honour of our most constant customers, who all slept together on feather mattresses before the enormous stone hearth that dominated one end of it. Now, the bedding was all rolled and stored, and four of our servants were scrubbing down the planks. Each gave me good morning and a curtsy, while little Geoffrey, shovelling out the ashes from last night's fire, smiled hugely through the grime. He was less than ten – Tom's youngest – but worked with vigour, for I let him sell the ashes to the mercer's boiling house in Grasse Street on the London side.

Leaving the Hall, I walked through the kitchen and the scullery to the yard. This was broad and cobbled, and now filled with pleasant sunshine. A party of merchants, with loaded mules, was just arriving, and I watched Tom and the ostlers lead their mounts away. By now, Daniel Delore had a proper innkeeper's eye and ear; I judged my new guests' accent to be Flemish, and their bearing to be high – they wore velvet cloaks and doeskin leggings – while their trade would have been obvious to anyone. The mules, six of them, were burdened with iron-strapped chests and the merchants' servants made it clear that none of our men should touch them. As I came up, Tom gave me a little smile and a knowing nod. "Good morning, Master. I think we've more custom for Foster's Lane."

"Let's treat them well then, and hope they leave most of their silver here."

Tom smiled. "Not most, I think. Their chests look heavy. But I've given them the big rooms at the back – they said the best, and they'll be private there."

"What about our pilgrims?"

"They were on their way by prime. But they said there's plenty more behind them who should be here by nightfall."

That was our advantage: lying on the river's southern bank, pilgrims from the north could be quickly on their way to Canterbury, while travellers from Dover, and the south, reached us before they came to London proper.

With a nod, I let Tom go, then set off on my own business, passing through our gate into Southwark High Street. By now, the whole of Bankside was up and doing – which, for us, meant selling. The street churned like a basket of eels. Hawkers and mongers were minding their stalls and barrows, buyers fought each other as they searched out bargains, and shouted cries beat against each other in a deafening din: "Hot codlings! Hot codlings! Milk below, Mio! Brass pots! Brass pots to mend! What do ye lack? What do ye lack?" If I lacked anything, I often thought, it wasn't for lack of my neighbours trying. Wiggling through the crowds, I pushed along the street beside hunched and sagging buildings, many of which were now half a century old and seemed about to collapse beneath their own weight – houses, tenements, a hundred inns competing with my own – The Mermaid, Three Tuns, The Queen's Head, The Talbot, King's Bench . . . They stretched along both sides of the street, and God only knew how we all found custom. At last reaching Maid Lane, I cut through the vegetable market, then entered the Bankside backs. This was in a sense the city's dungeon or perhaps its midden: a nightmare of tumbled tenements and wattle hovels, a wormy maze of lanes and passageways, a bog of vapours. In the gutters, the children were fierce as rats, the rats the size of dogs. My stomach churned. Yet, I knew, this cesspool protected us more than any borough charter. Knights, even John, were countrymen. They preferred to stay in Windsor and when they had to come to London, stuck close to the Tower or Westminster. Southwark, to them, was just a den of thieves, a swamp of plague and cripple. A few might cross the river to gamble in the bear yards, or sample the better stews; but most left us alone. I didn't blame them. Even I, who was used to it, heaved a sigh of relief, and drew fresh breath, as I reached the water's edge.

I had come out at Horseshoe Alley stairs, and now could see the yellowish, smoky pall that cloaked the city. From here, for three pennies, a bargeman would pole you over, and I settled myself on a thwart. The river was beautiful; bright blue, cool to a trailing hand, sparkling in the sun. Fair weather had brought out the fishermen, who netted barbel and speared the last of the salmon run. Beside their little boats, the water was crowded with wherries and barges heaped with wool, coal from Tyne, enormous slabs of Kentish rag. Leaning back and watching them, I then looked toward the Bridge: only from the water could you see its true dimensions. Its piers loomed like cliffs; the covered sections gaped like caves. When I'd first come to London, it had already been underway; even now, only twelve of its twenty piers were finished, and only some of these were joined but already you could imagine its final shape – and understand why it would be a greater bridge than even the Romans built.

We landed at Swan Steps, beneath a row of warehouses, and I was assailed by a clangour that might even have drowned out Southwark's; the bells of fifty steeples ringing terce, the clanging hammers of the blacksmiths in the Steelyard farther down the bank, and then the crowing and squawking of ten thousand fowl as I reached the Poultry: chicken in cages, pigeons dangling from thongs, geese hunched and hissing in their baskets, ducks wired together at the neck. I kept my eyes open but mingled easily among the crowds of hawkers and their prey, not really expecting to find any of the King's men among them, and made a leisurely way to Jews Street. I'd never been up it before, though I'd passed it once or twice. Broader than the alleys, the way was cobbled and the high, spiked walls around the houses cast a cooling shade. The houses, like the walls, were stone, and most were large: the Jews' money bought only enemies and their street proclaimed it. As I started down, I felt a little chill pass across my neck. Never, face to face, had I met a Jew, and some said they were sorcerers, or even devils. Men without a country, their only loyalty was to their money; having God, but scorning Christ, they were born deformed. Still, no one had ever attacked their wits, and they were alchemists with silver – as I was not, and readily confessed. I could make money with the inn, and by my other ventures, but I only heaped it up: the Jews, lacking Christian consciences, rented money out, like land, and claimed the godless tithe called "interest". Now, as I walked along their street, I wondered if my own hopes weren't tainted by their skin. For my plan – designed to let me live in peace and comfort with Gala – was to place my money in the hands of a Jew called Jacob, who might, for a fee, rent it out on my behalf. I knew that some men did this, and claimed it was the most certain path to wealth, for you even found a profit in the misfortunes of others. I hardly wanted that, but wondered if this mightn't be a way to live in security regardless of the whims of kings.

Walking on, I counted off the houses. Each gate bore a painted sign and attached to most was a brass cylinder, or case, that Mercury had told me was called *mezuzah* – a sort of charm Jews used to ward away ill luck. The house I wanted, near the Lothbury end, bore one, highly polished and inscribed with Hebrew letters. I paused before it. And then, just as I reached up to strike the bell, I heard a door slam within, and voices raised in anger.

"I'll pay what's fair and nothing more!" screamed a courtly accent.

"You'll pay what's been written, sir, and duly witnessed."

"By God's throat, I'll not! And I'll pay only when I'm ready."

"Then remember, sir. My master will not advance you more until –"

But these words, more calmly uttered, were never finished. The gate in front of me was suddenly flung open and a figure came storming through, almost tumbling me into the gutter as he did so. In his fury, he scarcely suffered me a glance and probably wouldn't have known me anyway. But I recognised him at once.

It was John de Birkin.

CHAPTER TWO

As de Birkin stalked away, the Jew's gate began to swing shut and I stepped quickly forward.

"A moment, if you please. I've come to see a Jew, Jacob Mancère. Is this his house?"

The man within hesitated. I could barely see him in the shadows. Young. Short-cut hair. A long, plain gown. A clerk, perhaps, though not a Jew since he had neither their features nor the long side locks they favoured. His voice was soft. "Your name, sir?"

"Daniel Delore, innkeeper and merchant."

"And may I ask who sent you to us, sir?"

"Mercurio, a dwarf from Bankside."

Recognition flickered in his eyes, and his hand relaxed upon the gate. He opened it. I stepped ahead, entering a large yard or court; so large, in fact, that enough sunlight found its way here for apple and pear trees to grow and an arbour of roses to bloom across the path. The house these plantings decorated was also very large; indeed, for London, where space is the dearest commodity of them all, it was immense: thirty paces long, three storeys high, the whole topped by a slanting slate roof. It was built entirely of stone: which, alone, would have told me it was home to a Jew, with all the enemies their kind collected. To make it even more defensible, the ground floor was as blank as a baillie's wall, though the two storeys above it were set with perfectly arched windows, their lintels carved with intricate designs.

Following the clerk, I went up to the front door, which was as stout as the gate. Inside was a vestibule and another door, the clerk opening it with a key and then barring it solidly behind us. I was now in a large, open hall, dimly lit by high, narrow windows of oiled parchment at either end. A stone hearth and chimney stood on the opposite wall, fuelled from a large coal bucket though now the fire was cold. The floor was tiled – I'd seen this once in Canterbury:

squares of clay, baked hard as stone, set in mortar and arranged in patterns. The room, despite its size, was sparsely furnished; two couches, with cushions, drawn near the fire, and in the centre of the room a large table with two carved chairs, one in front, the other behind. On the table, I noticed a balance with a tray of weights and the most beautiful chess set I had ever seen – the pieces were very small and intricately worked, one army in gold, the other in silver. The clerk murmured at my back, "If you would sit, sir, I will fetch my master."

I nodded, and he passed through a door behind the desk. I didn't sit – I felt, in truth, a little nervous. And then this feeling, in its turn, made me feel more than foolish. Jacob Mancere was a Jew, but I'd been prepared to cross half the world to battle Saracens. Could he be any worse? After all, he was only a special kind of merchant, and I played the part myself. In any case, even if he was a devil he could only assume the guise of an evil man, and God only knew I'd met that kind before. Besides –

But then my speculations ceased, for the door swung open.

Jacob Mancere . . . Jacob of London . . . Jacob the Jew . . . My first view of him was one I would never forget. Gold and silver were his business, and he was a little metal man; he was short, and springy as a wire. Long wisps of silvery hair trailed around his face, while his skin was the colour of old copper and his eyes were black as iron. I put his age at nearly sixty, but he came forward briskly, regarding me with a darting glance – and then, suddenly, he stopped. And smiled. It was this smile that disconcerted me, though I hardly knew why. It was just a flash, and no less metallic than the rest of him. But his amusement, though restrained so instantly, was nonetheless immense – large enough to include me, himself, the world. It took me aback and made me stammer.

"You are Jacob Mancere?"

"I am. Jacob the Jew, men call me. Was it not I you wished to see?" Before I could reply, his smile flashed again. "I'm sorry to disappoint you. I'm an old man now, so all my fangs are pulled, I use sandalwood as perfume, never sulphur, and my only potion is the wine Bodwin is bringing – a red one, from Auxerre."

I eyed him carefully. "I didn't come here, sir" – I forced the word out – "to have you laugh at me."

"Nor do I. Only at your expression."

"Whatever that may be, I won't have it mocked . . . and perhaps you wouldn't if you knew I hadn't come to beg a loan. I owe you nothing now, nor will I."

He held up one hand. "Peace, my friend. I know you don't need my silver; in fact, you want to give me yours. But isn't that the finest jest of all? Men call me the Devil but trust me with their money: I can only hope that God makes an equal profit on their souls. Here, though, sit, and Bodwin can pour our wine."

The clerk had just come through the door, carrying a tray: a pitcher, goblets, a tray of cakes. The cups were silver, beautifully chased in golden filigree – I hadn't seen their like since that day in Windsor. Leaning forward, Jacob himself set a goblet before me. Then he murmured, "My clerk tells me you are a friend of Mercurio, the Lombard dwarf?"

"Yes."

Jacob, looking down, ran a single finger along the table-edge before him. "There's a bawdy riddle he sometimes tells . . . about how a whoremonger is like a vintner."

As he glanced up, I met his eyes. "And if I know the answer, you'll know I am who I say I am?"

"You will forgive me, but neither myself nor my clerk have ever seen your face. Even if we don't like each other, there must be a certain trust between us."

"Then Mercury would say: you make payment for both whores and wine before either are uncorked . . . and thus only learn they're vinegar when it's far too late to profit."

With a smile, Jacob raised his goblet. "Just so. And hopefully this wine will not be vinegar, but will only foretaste handsome profits for us both."

I sipped; and what I sipped was the finest wine I'd ever tasted, very sweet, just smooth enough, and so cold it bit my teeth. I realised he must have a well within the house, but then that would only be another strong point in his stout defences. With the goblet in my hand, I ran my thumb around its rim. The design was grape vines and leaves all intertwined, and so finely worked I couldn't see a join between the metals. It hadn't been done in London, I would have wagered. Venice, perhaps. Or Florence.

Jacob smiled. "Firenza."

I gave a little nod. "You read my thoughts."

"Ah, Master Delore, but we Jews are renowned for sorcery."

"Perhaps, then, you've already divined my business?"

He put down his cup. "There, I'm not so sure. You're something of a mystery. You own the stews that our dwarf friend runs, and The Tabard Inn as well, even if the deeds are in another's name. Also, from time to time, you take an interest in merchant cargoes bound for France. Beyond that no one can be sure about you. Some say you are an angel fallen from King Richard's court, others claim you as an outlaw. As for me, I just admit my ignorance."

My blood had run cold as he'd spoken. How had he learned or

guessed so much about my past? My voice turned hard. "I would not have called your knowledge ignorance, especially in a man who's never seen my face."

He held up his hand again. "Master Delore – though I know that's not your name – don't be afraid. A mason has a hundred tools, but I have only one – what I know. But that tool is useless if others share my knowledge. Don't trust me, just my greed: surely you believe in it." He sat back and sipped his wine. Then, putting down his cup, he shook his finger at me and went on. "In fact, now that I have seen your face, I know a little more. For instance, you have a Norman look, but speak English as well as any Saxon, and from that scar along your jaw, I'd say you fight like one as well. Yet you must be a gentleman, if not noble, for I've seen you looking at my chess game with understanding."

I smiled – for I *had* been glancing at the game. "Your sorcery, then, is just a practised eye?"

"No more than that. My eye, my ear for gossip, my tongue for asking questions. I said that I knew you didn't want a loan, but wished to leave some money with me. Why? Because Bodwin has used your stews and says they're the best in London, while many visitors to me have said The Tabard is both fair and honest. It would be neither if you needed money bad enough to pay Jews' interest."

I smiled again. And that was the moment, I think, when I began to like him. For the moment, what I felt was grudging; a respect for his wit, the quickness of his mind, his forthright manner. Then, I assumed that my change of feeling was due to his reassurance, for he'd convinced me that I needn't fear him. Later, however, I understood that the truth was just the opposite: I began to like him because he had no fear of me. He'd already seen beyond my Christian's hatred of the Jew – a hatred I only thought I felt – and thus, long before I knew it, he understood that we might be friends. That first morning, however, I merely nodded. "Your sorcery is right enough. I do want to leave some money with you."

"How much?"

"Three hundred pounds of silver."

"For a simple innkeeper, Master Delore, that is a substantial sum."

"It is everything I have."

He shook his head. "Then only leave me half and keep the rest."

I hesitated. "Why? You spoke of trust. If I can trust you with half my fortune, surely I can trust you with it all."

He was going to argue, but then simply shrugged. "As you wish. But trust, remember, isn't the only question. You have to think of risk. The higher the risk, the greater the profit. A safe return is always small."

I thought for a moment. Returns and profits, rents, interests, bills, exchequers . . . To me, Jacob's world was totally strange. I knew little of money; all my training and expectation had concerned land and crops, the duties owed – and required – of vassals. Only in these past few years, and always with Mercury's help, had I learned anything of commerce. I thanked God I knew numbers; some said *they* were sorcery, but at least I understood their spell. Finally, feeling my way through this mystery, I said, "If I understand you right, you will take my money and let it out for rent?"

"Yes."

"So my money will multiply as yours does?"

"If you like. Certainly the rent I pay you will be drawn from the rents I take in myself."

I smiled. "Thus, Jacob, I will be a usurer at second hand."

He shrugged. "The Torah says, 'Unto a stranger thou mayest lend upon usury; but unto thy brother thou shalt not lend upon usury, that the Lord thy God may bless thee.' Jew to Jew, Christian to a Christian – everyone agrees that such is usury. But a Jew lending to a Christian, or a Christian leaving his money with a Jew, breaks no one's law."

I knew he was right; it made me uneasy, but no priest could forbid what we were doing. I said, "Then that leaves only one question. How much rent do men pay you for your money, and how much will you pay me?"

Another shrug. "But I have told you, Master Delore, that depends upon the risk. Who is the man I am lending to? Why does he want my money? How long will he keep it for? To lend men money, you have to know their characters and businesses better than they do themselves. For a man I know well, or who leaves some chattel with me, I may only charge three or four pennies in the pound each week. For others, it could be as much as six or seven." He leaned back and sipped his wine, then eyed me carefully. "I would say that the safest loan is to a merchant, upon his bill. He will use the money that I loan him as a tool, to make yet more – and, by his making more, my payment is assured. Next in order I would put the King, or any other man who borrows constantly. To borrow afresh he must pay what he already owes, in an endless circle. Lastly I would put the man of virtuous character, honest and frugal, who borrows only as a last resort. No matter how great the usury you charge him, it is the money he takes that you'll most likely never see again."

For a moment, I wondered about de Birkin. Had he reached his last resort? But his character hardly seemed as noble as Jacob had described; more likely, on the Jew's scale of risk, he weighed somewhere in between.

Tilting my glass, I finished my wine, then said, "I'll leave you to judge such risks. I've only one: how can I be sure that you'll keep my money safe?"

He smiled. "But there's no risk there, Master Delore. If I don't, you'll tell all the world that I'm a thieving Jew, and no one will come to Jacob's door again. So have no fear. Your Christian silver will be guarded to the last drop of this old Jew's blood."

What should I do? I'd spoken honestly. My silver was my fortune. If I lost it, I'd be back to where I'd started. Yet, on the other hand, if I didn't leave my money with him, I'd be little better off. Lacking both land and title, I had only one demesne: the silver in my money chest. The usury I got from it would have to be my tithe, and Jacob would become my steward. According to the ancients, gold was barren, but if Jacob, with a Jew's perversity, could make it multiply unnaturally, I might have my freedom. But I hesitated. Could I truly trust him? I met his eyes, and tried to read his character in them. They were calm. At peace. But his gaze was steady and unflinching. Not unfriendly . . . in fact, they sparkled with a hint of curiosity, as though he'd judged me, made some secret estimation, and now waited to see if I would prove it for him. For some reason this thought made me smile a little, and perhaps, in the end, decided me.

I nodded.

"All right," I said, "you'll have my silver. Tell your servant to wait beside your gate, tomorrow before prime."

That was the first time I visited Jacob, but far from the last.

Every week, once a week, I would attend him, sip that perfect wine, and received his accounting of my money. Slowly – as I think he'd guessed – I came to trust him: partly, because he simply lost his strangeness; partly, because my money grew; and partly because Mercury scolded my suspicions. My fears of Jews, he said, were all illusions, no more than the foolish magic I gave them credit for practising themselves. "They're only Lombards," he told me with a laugh, "who refuse to kiss the bishop's ring." Yet, though all this was true, my education was mainly due to Jacob's teaching; he was so polite, so elegant, so straightforward in his dealings. Though I'd made it plain that I knew numbers, hoping to frighten him into honesty, I soon saw there was no need: his honour, in accounting for each part of every penny, was greater than any man I'd known. Gradually, my suspicion turned to shame; and when, in a dozen small ways – nothing being said – he extended his forgiveness, I took it gladly. I now looked forward to my weekly visit. I realised how much I'd missed elegant speech and manners, knowledge, interest, conversation that reached beyond The Tabard's yard. In his house – as nowhere else in England – I could be myself.

And then, one day, the trust I'd begun to feel gave way to something closer.

Every week, we met in that same room with its tile floor and cold stone hearth. Jacob would sit behind his table, I before it, and between us would lie our wine, the parchment with the record of our dealings, and the golden chessboard. I'd noticed it the first time I'd come, and one week I noticed it again. I was certain that the pieces had been moved – they were arranged as though in the middle of a game. "I could come another time," I told him, "there's no need to disturb your play."

He looked puzzled, but then, following my eye, he laughed. "No, no. You're not disturbing anything. I'm playing with an old friend, Ben Isaac, who lives in Troyes. Some merchants whose bills we both accept carry the moves between us. It's gone on three years. If we both live long enough, perhaps we'll finish it."

For a second, a little dizzily, I marvelled: a chess game played across a continent. But then he'd already told me that he'd been born in Wawel, on a river called the Vistula, and had come to London slowly, by way of Krakov, Rome and Paris. His life, his mind, his business, stretched everywhere.

I said, "You have the white?"

"Yes; the silver pieces. It will end a draw. Not the worst result between two friends."

"But perhaps it won't," I said. "Your bishop is in danger."

"Yes, but I'll just move him . . . here."

"In which case he only needs . . ." My fingers moved a pawn, which threatened no one: but the file thus opened allowed a castle to attack. "Instead," I said, "you should leave your bishop but move your knight. That will protect you, but at the same time attack his queen."

Jacob frowned. Then laughed. "You've saved me, Daniel. But I'm not sure I can accept your deliverance with honour. Two against one is hardly fair."

"Why not?" I answered. "I'm sure your friend in Troyes has friends to help him also."

"Friends": for an instant, the word hung between us, and then he moved the piece. Nothing more was said. But the next week, the day before my usual visit, he sent Bodwin to me, at The Tabard, with an invitation to come later in the day and dine with him. Now, for the first time, I was led through his outer chamber to his withdrawing room. This was more elaborate, and much more comfortable.

Bright carpets were laid across the floor, and couches were piled high with cushions. At the back stood a row of shelves laden with a variety of treasures in pawn and not redeemed: boxes of gold and silver, rings, pendants, brooches and torques. Beside this was an ambry which he opened with a key and displayed most proudly: it contained fourteen books, the most I'd ever known a single man to own – the laws of his religion; histories in Latin, and two books from the Low Countries he called "ruttiers" that gave directions for travel on land and sea. Our meal, in keeping with all this, was rich, a little strange, and served with elegance. Afterwards, he gave me brandy and then, with a slight smile, asked me if I'd like a game of chess . . . a challenge I accepted and promptly lost.

But that meal, and that game, were only the first of many. My weekly routine was changed and the counting of my silver became secondary to our growing friendship. It was a friendship based upon respect, keen competition (our chess games could be fierce) and perhaps, as well, the difference in our ages. I came to love him as one loves a grandfather, or a special teacher. In fact, he was my teacher – every friendship is an education, but I've never learned more from any man. To begin, he taught me a little about his faith. I had always known that Jews believe in God but refused our Christ. Now, I learned that their religion was, above all else, a faith of laws: laws that governed every aspect of their lives, their food, their dress, their business. "For us," he said, "a good man is a *lawful* man. We express our faith more by what we do than what we feel. If a Christian murders with righteousness in his heart, he may still hope to find forgiveness – but not a Jew."

"So your God is fierce?"

"Is not yours? I would say the difference comes more from our belief that we are God's chosen people. We've made a pact with him, a contract, and must keep it to the letter. There lies our salvation."

"While a Christian, by his suffering, is already saved."

"Yes. No matter what he does. Even on his death bed, a Christian can still repent." He smiled. "Laws and contracts – they're our whole life. You can see why a Jew is so easily a merchant."

"But why are you all so drawn to money and usury?"

"Ah well . . . would we lend if you refused to borrow? As well, I think, we have more optimism. For a Christian the World is over. Man has Fallen; Christ has Come. You're always looking back. But we Jews are still awaiting our Messiah. We have a faith in the future that you don't have. If we live and judge aright, we *expect* to be repaid, and so are not afraid to lend."

For hours on my visits, we'd talk like this. I learned the details of

194

his life, his faith, his business: calculations, laws and charters I'd never seen before. Gradually, I came to understand the strange position the Jews now occupied: secure and powerful, yet constantly endangered. They built their houses of stone because of the mobs that sometimes attacked them; at the same time, they enjoyed the special favour of the King. In London, and all the other great towns, special exchequers had been established – chests with triple locks – for the securing of their bonds, and a record of their loans was kept by the King himself. All this gave them some protection. But what a price they paid. When Henry, Richard's father, had gone on Crusade, he'd tithed a tenth of his Christian subjects' chattels, but took a fourth from every Jew. And when a Jew money-lender died, all his goods and loans were forfeit to the Crown. As Jacob said, "A Jew leaves no inheritance. If I had a son, he would have to buy this house, everything I own, and all the loans men owed me from the King."

"But why? Why do you think men so hate the Jews?"

He smiled and shrugged. "Why did you?"

I flushed with shame. "Because I didn't know you."

"Yes, and because you didn't know me you believed the worst – that we're devils, murderers of Christian children. Your Church preaches this all the time, mainly because they fear our power with the King. In this land, who can read or write, or number? Keep accounts? Advise on taxes? The Christian priests and the devil Jews; we're the only ones. And because we have the right to lend the King our money, the priests always fear we may gain more favour than they enjoy. Now, I'm afraid, it grows even worse. Every day, more and more Christians trade and lend, especially the Lombards and the Genovese – Italians, men who have such a special influence in the Church. Fearing our competition in the market-place, they'll use their power with the Pope to drive us out."

Drive us out. That was his fear, his special worry, though he rarely spoke about it openly. Once, however, he told me about the butchery of the Jews at the time of Richard's Coronation. Wishing to bring their new King presents, they appeared outside Westminster's walls, where the crowds – made jealous by the lavish gifts they bore – fell upon them. Many were killed or wounded, and then the rampage spread to London where houses were burned and plundered.

"The streets ran red, they told me. My neighbours on both sides were murdered."

"Yet you saved yourself."

He shook his head. "I wasn't here. That was ten years ago, remember; more. I was younger then and sometimes travelled with my cargoes. I was in Troyes that month. By the time I returned, the fire had raged on: Lynn, Norwich, Lincoln . . . If towns had Jews, they died. The worst was in the spring, in York, because the mob there was led by barons, men who owed Jews money and wished to destroy their records. They beseiged them in a castle and more than a hundred had to kill themselves like Maccabbees. I lost many friends that night."

I'd heard about this, but only as a rumour. Now Jacob explained that it was this disaster that had forced the King to establish his Jews' Exchequer. For some years, this had given them a measure of protection – from everyone, that is, except the King himself. But soon enough I learned that even this safeguard was less real than it first seemed. Many months had passed; the fall had come. Within the city, the dusk rushed in at evening and we ate and played our games of chess by candle-light – for Jacob had the riches to burn fat tallow candles the way other men light tapers. Having played one match, we were starting on another when Bodwin came running in, pale and out of breath.

"Master," he gasped.

"What is it?"

"A mob, with torches. They're approaching up the street, crying against the Jew."

The old man's face turned white. "You think they're coming here?"

"Yes, sir . . ." He glanced at me and hesitated, but then hurried on. "De Birkin leads them, Master. I saw him clearly."

I leaned back. "De Birkin . . ."

Jacob turned toward me. "A man I've loaned to. He has claims to an estate near Nottingham, and once – so I was told – had enough favour with King John to make it good."

I held up my hand, half smiling. "I know a little of his story. But why this mob? He may burn your house, but your records are safe with the King."

Jacob shook his head. "Not in his case. He paid an extra interest to keep his debt a secret for that's why he wants the money – to make his petition at the Court."

I listened. Faintly, in the distance, I could hear the mob. "Burn the Jew!" they shouted. "Clean the Plague!"

I rose. "Jacob . . . Bodwin. You'll both have to come with me. Your gate will hold them long enough to let us climb your wall. I'll take you to The Tabard."

Jacob shook his head again. "Take Bodwin, but I'm too old for scrambling through the night. I'll bar the door and hope –"

"They'll burn you, Master," Bodwin moaned.

I could hear them plainly now and knew that the old man was right. They were too close; he'd never get away. I took his arm. "Listen, my friend – here's what we'll do. Bodwin – run ahead and find de Birkin. Tell him to hold back his mob and come ahead himself. Then, let him in, alone. Jacob . . . when he's here, you must show him your exchequer."

"But even if he has the book, he'll kill me."

"Perhaps. But your exchequer will be empty. *I'll* have your book safely in The Tabard. And de Birkin will know that if you die, all your loans are forfeit to the King – and, by God, that would be one debt I'd make certain John collected."

Now the old man looked at me, and for a second I saw doubt, suspicion, flicker in his eyes. I didn't blame him. Why, in truth, should he have trusted me or any other man? But we had no time to argue. Gently, I laid my hand on his.

"Jacob," I said softly, "I think your exchequer is your life."

"You know it is, my friend."

"Then trust me with it, and I'll trust you with mine. My name, my true identity, is Robert Atheling, and I am the rightful heir to all the Locksley lands. Just whisper this to anyone and *my* life is forfeit."

His eyes looked into mine and believed the truth they saw.

He turned to Bodwin. "Bring it," he commanded.

And soon, as torches flickered through the streets of Jewry, I was running through the night, the old man's book pressed tight against my breast.

CHAPTER THREE

A week passed before I received a message from Jacob.

Looking back, I can see that this time was crucial to me. I spent it alone, in The Tabard, consumed with a sort of angry restlessness. I had a sense, an intuition, that my life was greatly changing, and I wanted to hurry that change along. Apparently, little happened. But my thoughts began to find new patterns. In a way I hadn't done before, I began to recognise the realities of my life. The world of kings and queens had thrown me overboard; like a desperate sailor, I'd scrambled ashore on a strange, wild coast called "London". Yet, despite its strangeness (and my own best efforts) I'd continued to see it with the eyes of the past, and speak about it with the same old words. But landscape and language had changed: and at last I was able to admit it. As the days passed, I even began to understand why. I'd called myself Locksley to Jacob. "Locksley." The syllables had earned the old man's trust. But now I wondered if they truly sounded my name. Surely "Locksley's" time was gone, that person was dead; only his burial was left to perform. To make a new life I had to face this truth. I had to forget my name, my titles, all my ancient claims and loyalties. I had one goal: Gala and our happiness. And that week I finally accepted how I must accomplish it. The past few years, and my more recent friendship with Jacob, had taught me a great deal, and now I saw that it was time to put the lessons to work. I had no land, but I didn't need it. The blood of the world – and certainly the world of kings – was money. *There* lay liberty and happiness. When I'd first gone to Jacob, I'd already realised this, at least dimly; now I saw it as plainly as the sun. Three hundred marks! A substantial sum for an innkeeper, as Jacob had said. But it was nothing. To live the life I wanted, I needed more. The question was: how to get it?

By the time that week was up, and I had returned Jacob's book, I thought I could see a way.

He met me outside his gate – which was charred and splintered, though still solidly on its hinges – and kissed me on the cheeks. "It's good to see you, friend."

"And you, Jacob." But he looked older; frailer. As I hugged him, I could feel his bones beneath his tunic. "Here's your book," I said, "all safe."

He took it and we passed through the gate, Jacob touching his *mezuzah* as he did so. "It's madness," he said, "but de Birkin's mob made me feel more a Jew than ever, and less inclined to be anything else."

I understood: whatever he might suffer as a Jew, he would at least never have to join that mob. Together, we walked up the path, through the quiet garden, and then entered the house, where I greeted Bodwin. I looked around his counting chamber, but it seemed no different. "You kept them out entirely?"

He nodded. "They were really de Birkin's men, bought and paid for. He was able to turn them back."

"Thank God, then."

"Yes, but you as well. If I'm safe, you're the reason."

I smiled. "It was a case of love joining with necessity. You're the only man on earth I can beat at chess."

He laughed. "That game . . . it brought us together, didn't it?" Walking round the table, he stood before that magnificent golden set I remembered from my first visit; it was still laid out, for the game with Ben Isaac of Troyes was far from over. Now, Jacob held up the queen; and then held it out to me. "Here. Take this as a token of my love."

I waved his hand away. "Moses would curse you, Jacob. I have your love itself. I don't need its idol."

"Please . . . That night, you saw my eyes. For a moment, I mistrusted you."

"Perhaps you did. But who would blame you for it? And if I took your piece, the whole game would be destroyed."

"My friend, I blame myself – and perhaps we should all have a reminder that, without trust, nothing has any value."

He came around the table and pressed it into my hand, then hugged me once again. Releasing him, I smiled. "You make me feel more guilty. I have my own sins to confess."

"Ah, very good. For a Jew, I make an excellent priest."

"Then, dear Father, I have sinned. Curiosity overcame me. I read your book – the record of all your loans."

Smiling, he took my arm and drew me toward the inner chamber. "Is that a sin? It sounds too tedious."

"Hardly. Every line excited avarice."

"Then your penance will be an extra jug of wine for supper."

It was a penance, I think, that I managed with good grace. But when we'd finished eating, and Bodwin had retired, I murmured across our empty cups "I remind you, dear Jacob . . . I read your book."

"So you said."

"Most of it, I think, I understood."

"But not all?"

"The records of the loans were clear enough, but beside some entries – whose names were always Jewish – I saw the sign *au*. If I recall my Latin, that means gold."

He eyed me. And the flash in his eye was somehow cheering – a spark of life. "I was forgetting . . . Daniel Delore, owner of The Tabard, was schooled by Atheling, Lord Locksley."

"So he was. And Locksley now reminds him that Fitz Alewin, and the other leaders of the Goldsmith's Hall, have kept their trade from Jews by inducing the King to rule it illegal for Jews, or anyone outside the Guild, to import gold into London."

Jacob smiled. "A plea, I've often thought, that wasn't harmed by Fitz Alewin's position as Lord Mayor."

I grinned. "Jacob, now I'll be priest. Confess: you smuggle gold and sell it to the Jews."

Pouring us each more wine, he murmured, "Perhaps I do. A little . . . After all, Jews have worked in gold for a thousand years, and work it better than any other race. Who is Fitz Alewin to turn that history? Besides, the quantities are very small, never enough to harm the Lord Mayor and his guildsmen. No one will sell gold to a Jew in England, and few enough abroad."

I remembered the morning I'd first visited him and said, "But Lombards and Flanders men bring in whole trains of it. I've seen them at The Tabard."

"Oh yes. Indeed they do. They sell in Foster's Lane and the rest is taken by the Mint. But we see none of it. The Lombards, remember, hate us more than any other men alive.'

"So how do you get it, then?" I set the chess queen before me on the table. "*That* is gold. It had to come from somewhere."

"We're Jews, my lord. They force us to be sly. Our gold comes from coins that no one else will take. At the Fairs, when the money-changers get debased coins, they are required to take them out of trade and give them to the King. His smiths then melt them down, extract the pure metal and mint new coins . . . or at least that is the law. But the Crown only pays for the value of the gold they get – which is always less than the value on the coin, which the money-changer paid. Thus, by offering a little more, they give their coins to us."

Bad money; good gold; the profit skimmed like alloy. It could have stood, I thought, for the way Jews eked out their lives. But I said, "There are few gold coins in Europe, more in England. You can't get very much like this."

Old Jacob shrugged. "Six or seven pounds a year. Our artisans use it to make what our people wish to buy – small items like that chess set, as you've guessed."

I thought again. "Six or seven pounds . . . Not much. If you could get a little more, could you use it? I'm remembering, you see, that all gold is registered at the Goldsmiths' Hall and the Guild controls its trade."

"They do in London, yes. But London isn't England, and England is not the whole world –"

"So if a Christian were to purchase gold in France or Flanders and smuggle it to London, you would buy? Your people would?"

Jacob watched me for a moment. Then smiled. Then laughed. "Dear God . . . You Christians! Some day, you may drive us out of trade."

Scholar, Crusader, knight – now, as my life took another turn, I became chief smuggler to the Jews.

My strategy was simple. In a small way, as I've mentioned, I was already established as a merchant, if only to make easier my visits to Gala and Marian in Le Mans. Now, this business was just expanded: taking my accustomed route, I journeyed south to Tours, Le Mans and Bordeaux, exchanging my English wool for dates and figs, then struck out east to Lyons where my fruit was traded, in its turn, for silk and other textiles. Next I headed north to Champagne and Troyes – the largest of the Fairs. There, lost among the crowds, I made two purchases, both of them quite legal: sheet gold, brought from Nuremberg and Vienna, and sword blanks from Toledo. Taking these to Bruges, I gave them to a Jewish smith – Jacob had supplied his name – who cunningly combined them. In a secret forge, he worked the sword blanks to fine honed blades, then fitted them with hollow hilts of gold: in the hand, they felt like ordinary swords, and when the hilts were wrapped in leather the gold was completely hidden.

That first trip, in this manner, I brought back six pounds; the second, nine; the third, fourteen.

My profits were substantial: and by the fourth trip, they were doubled. Now, in leaving England, I had more than wool – I also carried gold torques and bracelets made by Jacob's artisans. Purchased jointly by Jacob and myself, these wares were sold more safely in France than England, and their revenues were used to buy yet more metal. So the months passed; our sales piled up; and soon enough I was making so much money that it grew unsafe to carry it back to England, so I began leaving part of it in Troyes, with Jacob's old chess friend Ben Isaac. He let it out to rent – and thus, contrary to the ancients, gold bred more gold, ceaselessly.

As the profits mounted, Gala counted them. I saw her on every trip, and now the trips were much more frequent. Lying in each other's arms, we planned our future. When we'd amassed our treasure, so much that we'd need no more throughout our lives, we intended to move to Rome or Florence – so Mercury, in the end, would triumph. And indeed we planned to take both he and Marian with us. In Italy, despite the strangeness, we could live at peace, and though departing England would be hateful, I was certain now that it was the only way we could ever live together. Besides, it seemed plain that my country and my King no longer had a use for me. Even if they had, would I wish to serve them? For, like everyone else, I'd been filled with loathing by John's reign. I granted him a little: his roads were safe, his Courts well run. But his own character and life were a sermon of vice and wickedness, a Royal sedition against State and Crown. Bullying his bishops, he'd voided his first marriage and taken as his second wife a girl, Isabelle of Angoulême, who was barely twelve years old. She was already betrothed to Hugo Lusignan, who naturally rebelled and who – just as naturally – found instant support from Philip; thus, as the months passed, and I went from fair to fair, I watched as the empire of old Henry, Eleanor and Richard was allowed to crumble, all on account of John's lust for his rutting little nymph. Still, to me, all this seemed the background: a world I'd once been part of but had now forgotten. As war began to smoulder in Poitou, Aquitaine and Normandy, it soon grew clear that my smuggling trips would have to end, but even that seemed of small importance. By now, I had gold enough, and more, and by the spring of 1202 all that seemed required was to make our final plans. Thus for one last time, I set out from Dover across the Channel, reaching Avranches on the 1st of May.

At the best of times, Avranches is a mean port, small and under-used, poor cousin to the great centres of Calais and Honfleur. Its facilities are crude, a single quay of crushed stone and a few tumbled warehouses open to the weather and barely thatched. Now, if anything, the quay was even emptier than usual – trade always falling with the rising tide of war – and, as I got down from my ship, there were only a few piles of baled-up goods to impede my way. I started toward the town. It was very small, no more than a hundred citizens, mostly fishermen, but there was a good inn where I usually stayed a night before heading to Le Mans. My heels crunched on the gravel of the quay – and then stopped dead.

At the end of the pier two figures stood, who seemed summoned from a dream: a woman, in a grey, hooded cloak, her hair blowing in the wind; beside her, a soldier in a hauberk.

The woman I recognised at once as Marian, my sister. She smiled as my eyes fell on her, a gentle, joyful glance, though nothing could smooth completely the lines of sadness that had tightened on her face at Little John's death. Knowing her, however, allowed me to recognise her companion as well: it was Gala, dressed as she'd been on that long-ago march to Richard's ransoming.

I stepped quickly forward, almost running up to them, but then a sign from Marian stopped me. "My lord," she murmured, as I approached, "don't seem to know us. Walk on as you normally would, and we'll fall in beside you."

Dumbfounded but obedient, I continued up the road, whose muddy ruts were drying to a crumbling dust. Anxiously, I looked around. A few people were about, drawn to the quay by the ship's arrival. They were mainly old folk and the wives of fishermen, and though a few glanced our way, no one paid us real attention.

In a moment, Marian was at my right hand, Gala on my left.

I whispered "I love you both, but in the name of God what has brought you here – like this?"

"You, of course," Gala said. "We wanted to see you secretly before you reached Le Mans."

"In secret? I can't think how you could have drawn more attention to yourselves. You know Philip has his spies on you."

She nodded. "Of course he watches me, but no one troubles over Marian. Thus I became her escort. As you know, it's a position I've been well trained for."

I smiled. "You're both enjoying this – too much, I think. In any case, what's the object of the game?"

"To warn you – of war."

"You don't need to warn me of something the whole world has known about for months."

Marian leaned toward me and whispered, "Listen to us, Robert. It's not a game. Philip has made a treaty with Arthur, who's now betrothed to his infant daughter. Her dowry – so it seems – are all the Angevin fiefs outside of Normandy."

I laughed. "Arthur will have to fight to get them – and if John's no warrior, Arthur is even less of one."

"But he may not need to fight. He may get them as a ransom."

"Who? Who can be ransomed for half a kingdom?"

"Eleanor," said Gala. "They plan to besiege her in Mirebeau. And it's not half a kingdom, but all of it. Philip is still trying to sit young Arthur on the English throne."

I stopped dead. Arthur was nothing; a mere boy; powerless. But as Philip's figure-head . . . I took a breath: it had finally happened. The ancient plot had been resurrected. Once France had conspired with John against his brother; now he used the nephew, and the former friend was victim. But what did it mean to me? What could it? And did I wish it to mean anything?

I said, "You're sure of this?"

Gala nodded. "The Archbishop of Paris told us, without meaning to. He visited L'Epau and talked about it with the Prior, speaking in Latin which he assumed I didn't understand."

"Has Eleanor been warned?"

"It's too late for that. Arthur's army – which is really Philip's – is already on the march."

"Then it's too late for anything. There's nothing we can do."

"No – Robert. She could withstand a siege. For a month, at any rate."

I took another breath. "Dear God, I've served them long enough. We both have. We've given them more than anyone could have asked, more indeed than they demanded. We have our lives to live. That's why I'm here. Let them fight for their crown and lands. In a month, all of us can be in Rome with enough gold . . ." But my voice gave out. Neither of them spoke; and in their eyes, I suppose, I saw only what was in my heart. Doubt . . . uncertainty . . . a little guilt . . . But perhaps they didn't feel my anger.

Gala touched my arm. "Robert, think of Eleanor. Think what will happen. And not just to her, or England, but to yourself. If we leave now, you may live out your life and always feel –"

I stopped her with a curse. A curse so vile it startled me. And in the silence which followed I finally realised something – that it was a curse, not fate, that had governed my life for all these years.

Marian whispered, "Robert . . . what you do, you must do it for yourself."

Myself . . .

I turned, looking toward the sea, blue and brittle beneath the morning sun; and then I started walking toward it.

Loyalty with a heavy heart; allegiance weighted by foreboding. As we returned to England, I suppose that described my mood. But at least the trip was quick. Hiring the same vessel that had brought me, I turned her round and we sailed on the evening tide. Then in Pevensey I hired the best mounts available and we rode hard for

London, making a five-day trip in three. But there was no time to lose. In London, leaving Marian and the Princess in Mercury's care at The Tabard, I went straight to Jacob and told him what I'd found. There was no need to convince him of the importance of my news.

"For you, for England – for everyone – this is disaster. If Arthur captures Eleanor, and takes John's fiefs in France, an invasion of England can't be far behind."

"An invasion, old friend, that might well succeed. Half John's barons would welcome it already. And John's no general. At the first reverse, the other half would swing around."

The old man nodded. "Even if it failed, trade would be destroyed. For my people, that would be catastrophe. And if such an invasion did succeed, catastrophe would be doubled and re-doubled. Few hate the Jews like Philip."

I took a grateful breath, relieved that I hadn't had to make this final point: for I didn't want to seem to bully him. "You can guess, then, why I've come to you."

"Oh yes. As you say, John would be hard pressed to raise an army."

"Partly that. But even if he could, it wouldn't help. We must move quickly, nip this in the bud by stopping Arthur from capturing Eleanor. An army *here* would be no use. He'd have to take it across the Channel – and by then he'd be too late."

"And an army *there* would have to be bought and paid for?"

I nodded. "Yes. A *routier* army drawn from Flanders. The question is: could you buy it?"

He smiled crookedly. "Croesus, my friend, was not a Jew. I couldn't finance a half of it . . ."

"But your people, Jacob? If you all put your gold together . . . ?"

He thought a moment. "It would be money well spent, God knows – if we don't keep Philip out, he'll only take it from us." He nodded. "All right. I'll ask. I'll need a week –"

"Three days, no more."

He reached out, took his bell, and rang for Bodwin.

It took four days, in fact: but in the end he got agreement and summoned me. Now we faced a thorny problem. How would we obtain an audience with the King? I realised how many years had passed: I no longer had a single friend at Court.

"There is one way," said Jacob with a frown. "At least, I think we might get a message to him. The Jewish Exchequer is run by three officials and one, the Arch-Presbyter, is a Jew himself, Elizar of Norwich. I know him well."

"And trust him?"

"Yes . . . but any message might pass through another's hands."

I smiled. "That's all right. I'll cipher it."

"A cipher? But the King must read it."

"Don't worry. He'll read it plain enough. I'll just need your chess set . . ."

So, with parchment and that golden chess set placed before me, I wrote a message to my king, the king I'd battled against so many times before. As I worked, I felt almost giddy. It was as though my life had come full circle. But where, on that circle, was I standing now? Was I like Gisbourne, a knight traitor to his king? Or was I St Denis, an opportunist, eyes fixed firmly on the rise and fall of my private fortunes? Or was I just a simple pawn, a clumsy piece ready to be sacrificed to gain the least advantage? And, in the end, did it really matter? The questions didn't, anyway, for I could hardly answer them. I just worked away, and when I had it finished, Jacob sent it off. Two days passed by; and then a week. And finally, returned by Jacob's friend, our reply came through, couched in the strangest form – an invitation to join His Majesty for dinner at his apartments in Westminster.

We all went together – Jacob, Gala, Marian and myself. Of course, I'd argued against Gala's coming, for it could only put her in danger, but she'd insisted, claiming that her presence would give me safety: she was under Eleanor's protection and I was under hers. She may have been right; then again, we may all have been quite safe. John had many faults, and I could have easily listed them, but he also had his virtues. One of these was curiosity. His mind was quick – too quick: sometimes it shied at shadows and even imagined shadows it could shy at – but that night, I think, he was eager to meet me again after so many years, and even more eager to meet his brother's queen. In any case, we were led discreetly, but politely, through the guarded gates beyond William's massive Abbey, then past the great expanse of Westminster Hall to the Royal Offices and Chambers. From there, by a dozen silent halls and flights of stairs, the yeoman of the guard led us up to the King's Royal Apartments, high above the Privy Staircase leading down to the Thames below. The room was large, though not much greater than the outer chambers of Jacob's house. The walls were hung with tapestries, the floor strewn with carpets – the Prince had always liked his comfort – and at either end fires crackled brightly, though the night was warm enough. John was seated at a long, linen-covered table; beside him, a young, fair-haired woman, presumably his queen. As the door was shut behind us, I dropped to one knee, Jacob beside me, while Marian curtsied deeply. Both she and Gala had managed to find silk gowns for this royal evening, Gala's being azure shot with threads of gold. I watched her from the corner of my eye: and she made no show of homage, only smiled. John, after a moment, nodded and then smiled himself. Gesturing us up, he grunted, "Locksley . . . before I have your head, you may introduce me to your friends."

I hesitated; it was possible, indeed, that he was serious. But I said, "Sire, my poor head would be a pitiful substitute for your own. As for my friends, Sire, they are Jacob, a Jew from London, my sister, the Lady Marian, and Berengaria, Princess of Navarre and your brother Richard's queen."

He eyed us coldly; for a moment, the air was very still and quiet. He was making up his mind: to kill us, or let us live. At length he gave another grunt. "Since they are with you, Locksley, I presume they are all spies?"

"Yes, Sire . . . in your enemy's camp."

A smile touched the corner of his lips. "I'm a coward, Locksley. Thus, I admire courage in others. But sometimes what we envy, and cannot have, we happily destroy. Your bravery might be better tempered with humility."

For some reason – not, I think the point he took – my eyes flickered momentarily toward his little queen. And John, following my gaze, laughed aloud. "Indeed, you may envy her, my lord, but I swear you cannot have her and no one will destroy her – except myself perhaps." Then, reaching forward with a jerk, he rang his bell. "Come. Sit. I invited you to supper, so let us eat."

I felt relieved and disconcerted, both at once: relieved at still being alive, disconcerted because I hadn't really taken his invitation seriously. But I'd forgotten John. For him, nothing was more serious than food, and since I'd seen him last he'd grown immensely fat, flesh weighing down his cheeks, his glistening lips, his belly. But, as the servants entered, we found our places at the table, which was soon groaning beneath a feast fit for sixty more than six. The courses came on and on, like surf upon a beach. Piles of bread, dishes of whipped butter; jellied fish and sausage hedgehogs, then Paris pies and gilded chicken, a loin of pork in boar's tail sauce, grilled fish, rice and oysters all mixed together, a roasted tongue, creamed leeks and chestnut turnips. Girding up our loins – or rather loosening them – we forced it down, all the while cringing in dread at the prospect of the sideboard which was piled high with rich desserts – strawberry custard tart, fig pudding, honey candies and the King's well-known favourite, pears in thick wine syrup.

As we ate, conversation was strictly limited and pointedly neutral, which forced Jacob to bear the greatest weight of it.

"I like your race, Jacob," the King said to him. "Do you know why?"

"Sire, I know that you protect us, and I am most grateful."

"Speak plainly. I command you. Why? Because I like your money?"

"Sire, all men like money, of necessity. It is our privilege to provide it to you."

"Ah, but you're wrong, you see. I like your race because you can read and write, keep records and give advice, and yet you never preach at me the way my priests do – because, I suppose, you've already assigned me to some Jewish Hell. – Don't touch that; it's the pork. But pass it to me."

"Sire –"

"You do think I'm bound to Hell, for eating it?"

"No, Sire, but a Jew would be. A Christian doesn't sin by not keeping Jewish laws –"

"Nor a Jew by keeping Christian ones, and so usury was born. Let us both thank God for it . . ."

As they chatted on, I watched the King, trying to guess his mood. I mentioned the dark quickness of his mind, and some men claimed that he was mad. I didn't believe this; he was only crafty. In his talk, in this whole scene there was a kind of playfulness that frightened me. How would he bring the game to its conclusion? In my message, I'd given him no details, only hints, thinking that this would best assure our hearing. Now I wasn't sure: we mightn't even get a chance to speak, and it was plain he didn't want us to do so now. Perhaps the reason was his queen. She *was* a child; beautiful; fair-haired; with a gentle, oval face. But though she ate with relish, it was clear our conversation bored her, and as the meal dragged on, she even dozed. Finally, toward matins, the King nudged her off to bed. I waited then, expectantly, and even cleared my throat; but still the King delayed, and ringing his bell impatiently called for the servants to bring the subtlety.

It was brought in, balanced on a board, a huge pastry sheeted to form crenellated walls, with round towers at the corner. In the centre, a plum pudding had been shaped into a Keep and crossing a drawbridge was a sugar figure on a wafer horse – by the little crown it wore, I imagined that this represented the King himself. With care, this glutton's treasure was set before the King, and indeed it was so large that I could barely see his head above it. The thing delighted him. He clapped his hands, then dipped two fingers into one of the corner towers, which proved to be filled with cream. Gleefully, he sucked and licked.

"Try it," he announced. "I command you all. Only leave the figure on the drawbridge. It makes me queasy to see someone chew me down – it's a privilege I only allow the Queen." He belched.

208

Normally, despite his gluttony and lust, he wasn't vulgar – I realised he was drunk. Carefully, I said, "Your Highness, you've set us a most lavish table. We might best thank you by telling you why we've come."

With a spoon, he razed the upper storey of the keep, and eyed me over it. "It must be important, Locksley, to bring you out of hiding – and not just you, but a Jew, an orphan lady, and a widowed queen. You realise, lord, that I could simply clap you in the Tower, and there starve you slowly. *That* would be a fitting ending to this meal."

I paused; and then, just as I was about to speak, Gala said, "You could, sir, but you won't. You are many things, but not an utter fool."

No one moved; her voice had cut like steel. Even the King stopped chewing. Then he said, "You're right, My Lady. I am not a fool – but those who hint that I might be, are."

"Good, Sir. Then no one here is foolish. For only a fool would threaten a man who has come to warn him of the gravest peril."

"Himself, you mean? He has come to confess his treason?"

Now I broke in. "No, Sire. The traitors are your nephew, Arthur and your former ally, Philip. *They* are now allied, and even as we speak are besieging your mother, Eleanor, at Mirebeau." This staggered him; and before he could recover, I delivered the other blows, and told him everything we knew. It left him white. His hand began to tremble, and with an angry gesture he threw his spoon against the subtlety, knocking the little king and horse into a pastry moat. Blustering, he said:

"And you expect me to thank you for this? A useless warning? A warning that comes too late?"

"Sire, not too late –"

"By whatever God you worship, Locksley, you know I have no army. And even if I could raise one, there's no chance that I could get it there in time." Quickly, then, I tried to tell him of our plan, but he cut me off. "Pay for mercenaries? With what, I ask you? The throne my brother left me was a legacy of debt."

"Sire . . ." Now Jacob spoke. "That's why I'm here, My Lord. Myself, Aaron Ben-Aaron of York, Ben-Judah of Lincoln, the Arch-Presbyter Elizar – the ten greatest money-lenders of your realm – are prepared to advance enough to buy your army."

He licked his lips. "Jews, advancing money for a Christian cause . . ."

Jacob smiled. "Your father, Sire, took a fourth of all we had on his Crusade."

"Took –"

"We would advance this, Sire, as a loan. There would be no interest. The term would run five years."

He grunted, his eyes narrowing. "Why?"

"An expression of our loyalty, Your —"

"Jew, we've all agreed: there are no fools here. Loyalty is purchased. What is your price?"

Jacob shrugged. "Your continued protection, My Lord. Nothing more. If you wish to find our interest, just ask anyone how Jews are treated under Philip."

He paused; threw me a glance. Licked his lips again. Reached out, plucking up his fallen pastry king. "This, I will admit, is a handsome gift . . ."

Jacob's face assumed a fixed, polite expression. "The offer, Sire, is indeed a gift, but the money itself would be a loan. As I said —"

"I heard you. But what's the sum? An army of Flemish mercenaries will be expensive. I'll need at least five thousand men."

I broke in again, trying to stem his greed before it reached full flood. "Sire, I think not quite so much. Arthur will have a thousand men at most, perhaps three hundred knights. His purpose is to take a hostage, not fight a war."

"Still . . . I'd need twice his force. Two thousand men, six hundred knights . . ."

These, more or less, were the numbers I'd already settled on. "Agreed, Sire. Two thousand pounds would purchase such a force and provision it for a month. If there's a need to keep them longer, I'm sure Jacob and his friends would honour the amount."

He looked me in the eye. "My lord, you think this could be done?"

"I do, Your Highness."

"And so you'd be prepared to fight beside me?"

"It would be an honour, Sire."

"An honour!" He laughed. "Dear God, I never thought I'd see the day when anyone would call me honourable. But it's settled then . . . except one thing."

"Sire?"

He jerked his head toward Gala. "If my dead brother's queen goes back to France, she'll be in danger. Arthur might even take her in preference to my mother. She should stay with me, my lord — wouldn't you like that, My Lady?"

I felt myself turn pale. When is a guest a hostage? Not such a riddle: When she's staying with King John . . . Quickly I replied: "Sire, I'm sure your hospitality would be most welcome, but I'm not sure it's wise. If the Queen stays away too long, Arthur and Philip might grow suspicious."

"My Liege," said Gala, "they'll track me here and everything we've planned will fail."

John grunted, picked up his wine. Something – the taste; the dancing firelight; some other scheme – perhaps distracted him. For the dangerous moment passed. He laughed and banged his cup down and grinned at me. "An honour! An honour, you call it Locksley! Admit it to yourself – you think I am the Devil, but now you're Mephistopheles!"

Outside, standing in the yard, we waited for the grooms to bring our horses.

The watch clanked around the battlements. A few torches flared. In the stables, across the way, I heard a gentle laugh. The night was cool, but Jacob's shiver had another cause. "We're well out of that, my lord."

"He's mad," said Gala.

"Sometimes. Or he likes to act that way. At the end, it was very close."

Marian touched my arm. In the darkness, with her cloak wrapped round, I could scarcely see her face. But now, even in her low-pitched voice, I could hear more life than I had in months. "Robert, I was thinking something. You know, the King is right. At Le Mans, Gala *is* in danger."

I'd been pondering this as well. For both sides, Richard's queen was still a tempting prize. But what were the alternatives? Stay in London? The narrow escape she'd had tonight just showed the danger. Her family in Navarre? She'd be safe there, but I knew she didn't want this. Nor did I. Besides, the point I'd made was true as well. For our plans to work, she should return. "She's not safe anywhere," I finally replied. "But safer there than here."

But then, with even greater animation, Marian whispered: "I have another plan. Listen, both of you. Why isn't Gala safe in London? Because she's Berengaria, Richard's queen –"

"I can't change that," she said.

"No? Think a moment. No one's ever seen your face in London, except the King and a few men at Court. If people didn't *know* you were here, they'd never recognise you – it would never cross their minds."

"But I can't be in both London and Le Mans. I could pretend to go back, then hide here – but I wouldn't *be* back."

"You could be, though. L'Epau is cloistered. Almost no one knows you there as well. If I were to return in your place – saying Marian Atheling had remained behind – no one would guess. Especially if you stayed here as me."

"That's impossible!" said Gala.

"Why? Who would know the difference? Queen Eleanor – she knows us both – but she'd keep the secret. You'd have to stay away from Locksley Hall, where people know me, but here in London you could live with Robert as his sister. Just stay out of King John's sight."

"But you'd be in cloisters, Marian, shut up –"

"I wouldn't care! Don't deny me. It's the life I'll lead in any case. I've lost my love, but I can give you yours. I don't want another man, so why stay in the world to look for one? I'd be as happy in Le Mans as I can ever be."

I turned to Gala, but she reached out and took Marian's hands. "You're sure?" she whispered. "You know how happy this would make me, make us both. But I couldn't bear the thought that our joy was bought at your expense."

Marian laughed, and kissed her cheek. "No, no. Your happiness will make me happy. Why shouldn't it? You'll be an outlaw's sister – I'll become a queen."

CHAPTER FOUR

With a grunt, and a muttered curse, King John shifted forward in his saddle. His horse stamped testily. I pitied the poor beast, though the hard night's riding that had almost killed him had left me respecting his rider more. The King readily confessed that he had no courage but, at least in fits, he possessed something near as valuable: great energy. Despite his obese bulk – made even more ridiculous in mail – and despite his love of comfort and indulgence, he'd left his army of hardened Flemish *routiers* in a straggling, exhausted line behind us. Now he coughed and spat. And, with his frequent, disconcerting accuracy, seemed to read my thoughts.

"You keep up with me, Locksley, I give you that."

"Henceforth, Sire, it shall be a special boast of mine."

He smiled, never being one to disdain a little flattery, though I always suspected he knew it for what it was. Catching my breath, I squinted forward in the obscure, grey light of the false dawn. We were on a ridge, screened by a stand of cypress. Below us lay Mirebeau, a scattering of streets and dwellings behind a low, crumbling, ancient wall.

"By God," the King said, "it scarcely deserves the name of castle. Whatever possessed the woman to stop here?"

I had been wondering this myself; but just then we heard horses coming up behind us and swivelled in our saddles. Three riders . . . Our arms . . . Dew glistened on their mail . . . I recognised des Roches, seneschal of Anjou, now acting as our captain. He was as bulky as the King, but solid muscle, and wore a bushy beard, rare decoration in these parts.

"Sire," he announced.

John grunted out a greeting. "This isn't much. I can't even see where the boy has put his army."

"Within the town, Sire. Behind the walls. The Queen has retired to the keep."

"But they have no engines."

"Aye, they could only wait and starve her out."

"Your advice?"

"Sire, our scouts have been questioning some serfs. They say Arthur's left one gate open for supplies, and though he understands we're in the country, he thinks we're at least a week away. Sire, if we strike at once, we can take them by surprise."

"But my wretched Flemards won't be here till noon."

Des Roches shook his head emphatically. "I won't need an army, Sire. I'd rather use the men who're up with us, break through the open gate, and take them while they sleep – it would make for more prisoners and less blood."

The King squinted in the gloom. Then, taking a skin from his saddle-bag, he filled his mouth with wine till his cheeks were bulging. He gargled with it; then, with a retching sound, spat it on the ground. "This whole land is sour . . ." We waited; and I reflected again that John could never decide his mind unless his mouth was full. He sipped once more; this time swallowed. "So," he finally said, "the army I've bought and paid for will get its silver for marching peacefully across Maine. Not such a bargain."

"Sire," said des Roches, "by the time our main force reaches us, Arthur will –"

The King waved him into silence. "All right. Do it as you will. But if you fail, my lord, remember – I'll have your head."

Des Roches smiled fleetingly. "Your Highness . . . By your leave, I would only ask that you recall the remainder of my commission: I am to take Arthur and his men alive, so far as possible, and our captives will be released when they sign a truce, not be held for ransom."

The King eyed him with a surly look. "Just do it, my lord."

Des Roches flashed a glance at me – which I accepted with the stoniest indifference. If he wished to believe the King, he was welcome to; as for myself . . . Then, without replying, des Roches turned his horse away. I began to follow, but the King held up his hand. "Stay, Locksley, we'll watch together . . . and I need someone to help me down from this wretched, bony brute."

Thus, that was my position as the "battle" for Mirebeau unfolded: seated by my Sire, leaning back against a cypress tree, with a skinful of royal wine held ready on my lap. In truth, the wine was not unwelcome; the false dawn seeped away and the air turned chill. After a time, the King dozed off, snoring in a vinous bliss, and when the fighting started, it scarcely roused him.

Des Roches, leading barely fifty knights, struck just as the dawn came up, and was through the undefended gate before the slightest alarm was raised. Later, we learned that most of Arthur's army had been asleep, almost all his knights had put aside their armour while the boy himself was beginning a breakfast of roasted pigeons. There was virtually no combat, at least that we could see: a skirmish as a few of Arthur's men tried to escape across the walls, a wisp of smoke as a cart was set on fire, a brief glinting flash of arrows.

"Sire," I said, "the day is ours."

John laughed. "I'm not my brother, Locksley. As a battle, I'd say this was less a spectacle than you might find in a Southwark bear-garden."

"Perhaps, Your Majesty. But this skirmish may have saved Westminster. Sire – des Roches is riding out, I think to come to us."

He grunted. "Then get me on that horse. I suppose I should assume a little dignity."

He was still grumbling and shifting in his saddle as his seneschal came up. "Sire, the town is ours. We have taken most of Arthur's knights, de Lusignan, Hugh le Brun, Châtellerault . . ."

"And Arthur?"

"Sire, he has escaped into the keep with your mother."

The King was not easily left speechless but now his mouth dropped open. "You jest, des Roches."

"Sire, I swear not."

"Dear God, the boy is worse than me! He fights with a slapstick not a sword. Is my mother safe? He's not got a dagger at her throat?"

"No, Your Highness. He pleads with her for sanctuary."

"My mother, I assure you, is no nun. She'll not grant sanctuary to anyone. We'll dig him out."

"Sire . . . by your leave, you promised to release him, unharmed, in my protection. He's but a boy."

John laughed. "Unharmed, des Roches? By all that's holy, I'll not harm a single one of his childish locks. But he'll not come under your protection. If Philip thought my mother was worth half my kingdom, his little friend should be worth a box of gold." He turned to me. "Take someone . . . de Braose, he's loyal – and go and get him."

I reined up my horse as des Roches' face flushed angrily. "Sire . . . Locksley – you are a knight."

"A knight in service of the King," I muttered, then dug in my spurs and rode toward Mirebeau.

De Braose came galloping after me and together we rode through the open gate. Already, the town was quiet. Swords, spears, armour were heaped in piles; Arthur's army, such as it was, was already penned up in sheds and under guard. Cautiously, the townspeople were appearing – their faces nervous, but relieved, at the virtually bloodless victory. I knew de Braose of Brecon only slightly. A close friend of John's, he was known to be both loyal and ruthless, and no doubt his heart was easier than mine was. Still, I confess, my own misgivings were hardly strong. John had broken his word, but des Roches had been a fool to think he'd do anything else. And the concern des Roches felt for Arthur was one I needn't share. Arthur was Duke of Brittany, which lay beside Anjou, where des Roches was seneschal. Mistreating the Duke of such a powerful neighbour could only cause him trouble; but that trouble would come on this side of the Channel, not in England. I might hope that it could be prevented – but that hope wouldn't lead me to cross the King.

We off-saddled before the keep, but the portcullis was still firmly shut and we had to bang, announce ourselves, then wait. About half an hour passed before the captain let us enter. Inside, our noses twitched at the stench of siege: dung; the heated smell of animals penned up together; stagnant water; rushes that hadn't been changed for weeks. The garrison remained on a war footing; having been besieged by her grandson, the old Queen, perhaps, distrusted her son all the more. Under guard, we were led up the stairs to the hall. This was small and very crowded: Eleanor's knights and soldiers had all been sleeping here, and all sorts of possessions of the town – hoes to harps – were heaped up in piles. Again we waited as the yeoman ascended to the Queen's bower.

De Braose eyed me. He had a long, thin, mournful face; and the mournfulness was little relieved as a faint smile flickered. "I'm surprised to see you trusted in this way, my lord. You're not known as loyal to John."

I saw no point in quibbling about my loyalty, so merely shrugged. "I know the Queen."

A single eyebrow lifted. "In truth? I've never met her. Will she make trouble, do you think?"

"Why should she?"

He smiled again. "Des Roches doesn't want Arthur ransomed, perhaps she may not. He's sought sanctuary from her, after all, and she may feel compelled to grant it." I doubted that. She was forgiving of her sons, but why extend her mercy to a second generation? Besides, Arthur was a tool; it would be strange if she didn't put him to some use. "In any case," de Braose went on, "if she doesn't let us have him, what do you propose to do?"

Whatever I answered, I suspected, would get back to John; so I was carefully neutral. "We'll tell our king, my lord. We're talking of his mother and nephew, so the decision must surely be his."

Then, before he could press me further, the yeoman came down the stairs. We both rose from our bench, but the man gave us a little bow and declared, "My lords, the Queen asks to see Lord Locksley first, alone."

Taking this as a slight, de Braose shot me a wicked glance, but I ignored it and followed the yeoman up the stairs. At the top, holding back the curtain, he announced me, and I stepped forward into the besieged bower of the Queen. It was long and narrow, divided in two by a folding screen. The windows and shutters were now thrown open, but the air had a musty smell and the light was dim. Eleanor, flanked by two maids, was standing in the gloomy centre of the room and I sank down to my knee.

She smiled. "Rise, my lord. It is truly good to see you. Today, hearing no other name could have given me such pleasure."

I stood. "Your Highness, I thank you for your kindness."

She'd aged; but then, for years she'd aged and never quite seemed old. The maids beside her were barely girls but rather than contrasting sadly with their mistress, they only set her off. Now she smiled at them. "Ladies, old age permits immodesty. If you'll excuse us, I'll speak with Lord Locksley in my little chamber."

They curtsied; gave me smiles. Then the Queen turned – a little haltingly; she was leaning heavily on her ebony stick – and stepped around the screen. Here she had her private chambers, her couch, a table with goblets and a jug of wine, another covered with her sewing. At the very back, two plain wooden chairs had been set beneath the window.

"We'll talk there," she said, "and keep our voices low. They're good girls, but even the best girls gossip." Settling herself, she smiled. "I said I was glad to see you, and I am. Very glad – but not surprised."

"If you're not surprised, Your Highness, I'm sure you're the only one. Few people on this earth ever expected me to ride beside King John."

She laughed. "Ah, now, *his* presence, I confess, is astonishing. He's the most unlikely rescuer a lady could imagine. But still, your being here is no surprise. I need you, and when I need you, you always seem at hand."

My fate . . . Would I have believed it if she hadn't put it in my head? I wondered again how many torments might have passed me by if I'd missed that sunrise on Kyrenia's harbour. But even as I recalled that moment, the Queen softly murmured, "You're remembering, Locksley."

"Yes, I am."

"And regretting, my lord?"

"No . . . No, I don't regret." I smiled. "You always ask . . ."

"So I do, my lord, though if you did regret, you'd be too discreet to tell me. But you're tired, I expect . . . You'll admit to that?"

"Willingly, Your Highness."

She nodded. "Then we're one. My mind, my heart, my very bones – I'm tired in every part of me. If I ask a service now, my lord – if I call upon you once again – you may be sure it will be the last."

I paused. The simple, obvious question breathed behind my lips. Did I want to ask it? Yet, in her presence, the will I exercised was never quite the same. "Your Highness, what service can I do?"

"It concerns my grandson, Arthur. I take it he's why you're here?"

"Yes . . . The King wishes us to fetch him. He wants to ransom him to Philip."

She nodded. "I thought that might be in his mind. Two things drive men mad: women, and empty coffers." She looked hard at me. "You *do* realise it would be madness?"

"Your Highness, the seneschal des Roches fought hard against it and even had the King's word pledged."

"Which meant what it always does, precisely nothing . . . And even so, des Roches has only petty worries. He's concerned to have an enemy on his western border. Reasonable enough; but that war would be nothing in comparison to what could come. If Arthur's ransomed, Philip will only take him to his bosom again and try once more to sit him on John's throne. Already Brittany, Maine and Poitou accept him as their King."

I hesitated. "But surely, Your Highness, even if he's not held for ransom that's bound to happen. He *has* a claim – the whole world knows it. And he was virtually raised by Philip as a second son. They're natural allies."

"Oh, yes. And his mother hated all Plantagenets. I know all that. Worse: he's just a boy, a mere sixteen. If he's released, the Franks might use his claim against us for fifty years."

For a moment, I couldn't meet her eye and glanced at the window. Her logic was impregnable. But if I did not get Arthur back, John would be furious. Of course, he was a king and had an army; he could easily come before his mother and plead his case. In the end, my wager would have been on Eleanor, but even if he was convinced, John would begrudge a fortune lost – and I'd be blamed. I cleared my throat. "Your Highness, if you hold him prisoner –"

"My lord, that's not in question. Even as a captive, Arthur would live on, the *idea* of him, the constant possibility. Since he was born, he's been like a viper crawling near our feet. Now I've pinched him beneath my stick. Why should I let him wriggle free?"

"Dear Jesus . . ."

"Ah, I've found it. Locksley's sticking point."

"Your Highness, he's just a boy."

"So he is. A boy, halfway an idiot, and so weak that he couldn't capture an ancient woman in a crumbling keep. Locksley, understand – that's why he's so dangerous. Sitting on the throne, he'd just be Philip's shadow."

"But my God . . . Your Highness, to murder him? I am a knight . . . How can you ask me to?"

"How? Just because you are a knight, my lord. *My* knight. *My* son's liege. *My* servant . . . My lord, you are my man, and I ask you only to do the dirty work of men." She laughed. "Sir Knight, would you have this ancient woman do it?"

My heart began to pound with horror. I could feel my stomach start to heave. But I fought to keep it down; strived to find my senses. "Your Highness, you see your grandson as a danger to your kingdom, but killing him will only start the fiercest wars against it. Brittany, Maine, Poitou, Anjou . . . Philip would declare openly against you."

She'd scarcely moved as we'd been talking, or changed expression: her back was as rigid as a bolt, her head as level as a scale. Now, she leaned back slightly in her chair, a shaft of sunshine falling through the window on her face; one half was silver, the other black as pitch. And then she softly murmured, "You're right, my lord, so right. Philip would declare against us, there'd be war . . . and he might well win. And if he didn't win on that day, they'd find another. Oh, yes. He'll win . . . Does that surprise you? Let me tell you something, my lord. I'm an old, old woman and I'll tell you what my years have taught me. I could never leave this land. It's in my bones and soon enough my bones shall lie in it. But one day, I know it will be French. We've failed, you see. From the first, old Duke William – William, The Great Conqueror – feared precisely what has happened, and so he scattered his barons' land from Normandy to Kent, Vexin to Gloucester. But the water's too broad for a man to straddle. Look at yourself, my lord. You're neither Norman nor Saxon but something in between. You came from *that* land, not *this*. And just as there are two lands divided by the sea, so there must be two kingdoms. We have to choose. And here, I am afraid, we cannot hold. For a time, perhaps – till I'm in my grave, I trust. But the Franks are much too strong; in the end we'll lose. But in your native land we have a chance – as long as Arthur, Philip's puppet, doesn't gain our throne . . ." Her eyes now moved across my face and I felt them seize me. "In the end, Lord Locksley, I ask you not to murder but only to defend yourself – to preserve who and what you are."

I was silent; I might have been entranced. She was right, I knew: in some great, deep way I scarcely understood. But how could right be so evil? I couldn't hold her gaze for it froze my blood and my hand seemed to tremble at her will. Indeed, with a horrifying shudder, I knew then that I would do her will. But how could such an act, so darkly evil, be also right and in my own defence? For I would only wound myself. If I murdered Arthur, what would be the Princess's fate, and Marian's? I almost groaned aloud. "Your Highness, God would curse me if I did it – not for Arthur's blood alone but . . ." I paused. "The King . . ."

She cocked her head. "He has some hold on you? Let's break it, then, my lord. More: we can reverse it. Secure a hold on him that can bend him to our wills."

She rose; went to her table; pulled back some cloth where she'd been sewing and revealed a box, shut with three bands of iron and three separate locks. She brought it to me and took a ring of keys from within her girdle. The locks snapped open one by one and she lifted back the lid. From inside she lifted up a dagger, and as it caught the light I saw John's crest embossed in gold upon the pommel. "Do you see, my lord? Kill the boy with this. Stab him through the tunic and when he's dead cut the front away. That cloth, its rents, this dagger – they'll be proof enough of guilt to keep poor John under both our thumbs forever. Kill Arthur, my lord, and you can free yourself from any fear of John."

My hand was trembling . . . but held firm enough to seize the blade. And then I swore a curse beneath my breath, or thought I did, or perhaps it was just the rustling of the old Queen's dress as she bent forward and lightly kissed my cheek.

"My lord," she whispered, "you'll need another man. Not to kill him, certainly, but to remove the body. Do you know de Braose, the lord who's come with you?"

"Your Highness, I don't trust him. No one can."

"Then John can't either. Leave him to me – I know he is ambitious and that's enough."

"All right. But how must we do it?"

"Carefully, my lord. We'll kill him now, but in such a way that no one shall find his body, and for a time we'll say we're only holding him in prison . . . Here's what to do. At dusk go to the granary inside the town, the upper chamber. Wait there. De Braose will lead the boy, who'll think you're taking him to safety. Kill him, then throw him down the well behind the building – his own men poisoned it in their siege and no one will be using it for years. Then bring the shirt and dagger back to me. I'll put them in this box, and leave it with the monks in Vezelay. Each of us will have a key – so each of us must trust the other."

I squeezed the dagger's pommel; for one instant I thought to plunge it through my breast.

She whispered low, "You'll do it, Locksley?"

Like a rat I crouched among the mouldy piles of grain. The setting sun squeaked through the granary's roofboards and dust motes swirled like wraiths. I strained my ears. A real rat scratched along a beam; bats, roused by dusk, rustled in the eaves. Then hoofbeats . . . or conscience thudding in my ears? A moment passed. Below me, a door scraped open and, peering down, I saw a wedge of hazy shadow pry apart the dark. Two figures. A single voice: as normal as "good morning".

"My Prince, straight up the ladder. We'll hide in the upper chamber till it's dark, then sneak away."

De Braose. His spurs were jangling. Softer, stroking under them, were the Prince's boots against the rungs: as smooth as the golden pommel, sweat-slick, that nudged against my palm.

Step by step, they climbed up closer. My eyes darted round the room, I pressed my body as flat as it could get: but there was no escape, no hiding place. A blood-red shaft of sunlight angled from the roof in prophecy and then, with the shifting of a cloud, that silvery, smoky haze swirled round me once again. And there they were: men of blood and bone trapped in this ethereal light. They scrambled up: the Prince ahead, de Braose in behind: he reached out at once and grabbed the Prince, pinning back his arms. I rose. I struck. And oddly, both together, we made a little grunt and then blood sprayed like rain across my breast.

"Dear God!" he murmured.

Stepping back, unsticking him, my shadow moved away. I saw him then. His face, in life, had been as pale as death: a smooth white boyish face. Now his lips formed a childish O and his eyes were bright as morning.

"Once more, my lord!" de Braose shouted.

"Oh Christ!" I answered. And then I struck again, and de Braose let him go. He slumped forward to the floor. Kneeled a moment. Toppled to one side. He'd cried out to God, I'd called upon the Son: now, rising in a silvery, swirling cloud of dust I felt the Holy Ghost.

Quickly now, greedy for our spoils, de Braose got down beside him and cut all around his tunic – with his bloodied arms, the rents that this knife fitted – and held it up.

"My lord," he grinned, "the ticket to our fortunes."

I shuddered. He was right, I knew, if our fortunes lay in Hell.

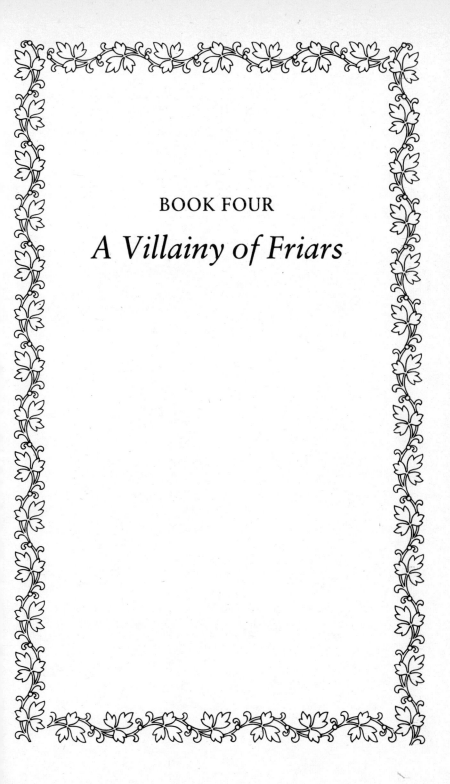

BOOK FOUR

A Villainy of Friars

CHAPTER ONE

"Now we are all Jews," I said.

"You'll survive," said Jacob. "We always do."

"Even prosper?"

"Why not?" He smiled. "You must admit the Interdict has kept our taxes down; now John's excommunication may eliminate them altogether. Too great a price to pay for making the kingdom heathen?"

I laughed. Perhaps he had a point – though prosperity seemed an unlikely consequence of the turmoil we'd been suffering and living through. When Robert Walter, the old Archbishop of Canterbury, had finally died, King John and his good prelates had quarrelled over the appointment of a new one – a quarrel that Pope Innocent had neatly settled by giving the job to Stephen Langton, one of his oldest friends. A regal-papal jousting match had then ensued. First stroke: King John had sequestrated all the lands owned by the monks at Canterbury. Parry: a papal Interdict, closing all our churches. Next, John had made a lightning thrust, taking over *all* Church lands and so filling his treasury that he had little need of ordinary taxes. And now we'd learned of Innocent's answering buffet: King John was excommunicated . . . an act, I thought, whose consequences would be more political than economic. John's subjects gave him little loyalty at the best of times; now, as his kingdom teetered on the brink of Hell, their loyalty was further undermined. So trouble was coming. You could sniff it in the air – a thousand old discontents and angers would find fresh life in this. I asked my old friend:

"When the knives come out, who will you support?"

"John, of course." He smiled. "God save the King."

"You don't like Langton?"

He made a face. "Liking has little to do with it, but better a bad king on the throne than none at all. As a matter of fact, I *do* like

Langton. I even met him once – he visited an old friend of mine, David Ben-Isaac of Pontigny. You know that Langton was the man who divided your Bible into chapters?"

I nodded.

"Well, Ben-Isaac is a great student of the Jewish Pentateuch which makes up the first books of your Old Testament. Langton often came to him to talk."

"And your friend thought well of him?"

"Yes. But, as I say, that makes little difference. I'll support the King. We already know his failings and can discount them. And though he's no great lover of the Jews, at least he doesn't hate us in that evil, senseless way some Christians do. Besides – just check your purse – he has a feel for trade."

Stephen Langton . . . John . . . Pope Innocent . . .

That afternoon, as I walked home through the streets of London, I told myself that it made no difference which side you favoured. For most men, victor and vanquished would be like the wind and rain, scarcely separable elements in the storm that overwhelmed them. And that storm, I was all the more convinced, was coming. The streets still rang with the cries of trade, but there was an uneasy undertone as well, the buzz of rumour from the Vatican and Court. The people edgy, and full of furtive looks: like rabbits ready to make a sudden dash for shelter. Would they find it? Could I?

I wondered. I was exposed in some ways, protected in others. I had money, at least, for old Jacob had been right: King John did have a feel for trade. Even as he lost his own domains in Normandy, commerce in his English kingdom flourished. Wisely, he'd regulated goods coming from abroad, insisted on licences for foreign merchants and taxed their goods two shillings in the pound. As a consequence of this, the merchanting I'd started while hiding out in Southwark had prospered and by this time there was no way I could avoid the title "rich man". In addition – another weight on safety's scale – I now lived exclusively in London. Gala and I had built a manor on the Strand – we called it Sherwood Hall – and almost all the old Locksley lands were let out. Within the City's walls, we were fairly safe: safe from the King, who was hated by most Londoners and rarely ventured here; and safe from the more ordinary ravages of war. Though still a knight in name, I had no men; my service was done entirely in scutage.

But balancing this were certain constant dangers. John hated me; and though I kept myself strictly from his sight, everyone knew how long he held his grudges. Worse, if he'd only known it, he could have had a terrible hold on me. Luckily, he had never learned that Marian had returned to France as Berengaria, while Gala stayed with me in London, living as my sister. But if he ever did so . . . It was something I hated even thinking of, for I knew John's dungeons were full of hostages, and half the pages at his court were the children of his enemies, their presence a ruthless check against their parents' opposition. Still, I had one surety: the "evidence" that the king was guilty of his nephew's murder. That awful day! Even now I'd sometimes wake at night, sweating with the horror of it; but then, looking at Gala, calmly sleeping at my side, I'd think, "At least *she's* safe . . ." But at heart I knew my reassurance wasn't quite so certain; the sword I could lay against John's throat was double-edged, as the fate of William de Braose had amply proved. Like a fool, he'd used our hold upon the King to further his own ambitions, demanding numerous "favours" to hold his peace. For a time, this succeeded well enough (in those days he'd sometimes mock my caution), but then the rumours began to spread – what special power did de Braose have against the Crown? – and John grew more and more embarrassed. Finally, when a quarrel broke out between them, some business about debts and lands, John seized the chance to prove his independence: he demanded that one of de Braose's children come to Court, ostensibly as a page, in truth a hostage. God knows what he should have done; he was a shaken, frightened man, and I spent one awful evening with him trying to plot a course. But before he could act, his wife – a foolish, hot-headed woman named Maud de Valery – actually said in public that she'd send no child of hers to a man who'd slaughtered his own nephew. A dare. Which proved unwise. John, I'd always thought, was like wild pig; an erratic boldness was the most dangerous element within his character – and the grounds for my own caution. Now, instead of running, he turned and called their bluff. Seizing their lands, he ordered the arrest of the entire family. Maud, the wife, was caught, imprisoned, and starved to death: some said in Corfe, Ireland, but I knew (through Mercury) that she'd actually died in Windsor. As for poor William, he got to France, intending to use the evidence the old Queen had deposited at Vezelay to threaten John and free his wife. For that he needed all three keys. He had his own; on her death, as we'd all agreed, Eleanor's had been given to the monks with instructions to use it if the other two were present; and so only mine was lacking. But I hesitated. I pitied de Braose but had no great love for him – it's hard to love a fool; and once the evidence was used, I knew, it could not be used again: it would grant *me* no protection. So I wrote him cautiously, made promises, then took my time. And by the time I reluctantly reached France, the poor man had already learned that his wife was dead and was expiring himself near Paris. For me, I confess, his passing only made things easier. Now the secret was in my hands alone. But I also learned a lesson; some threats are better never uttered. The power I held over John was strictly limited, no more than a last-resort defence. Yes, I thought, as I reached my door: in the coming storm, caution must be my watchword. Keep down; keep out of sight; hold silent.

Were all these thoughts a sort of premonition? Later, I sometimes thought so. That night, I know, Gala caught my sober mood, but then she would have been a trifle gloomy anyway. By this time, I spent almost all my time in London, letting my hirelings do the travelling, but the yearly Fair at Troyes was important enough to go myself and I'd be leaving within the week. So, subdued and quiet, she took my hand and led me through our gardens and then along the Thames embankment. We often walked here and sometimes quite a distance: in our own quarter we were careful to remain Lord Locksley and his sister, but in the City we dropped pretence. Now, among the other strollers, we seemed a normal couple, and as the dusk thickened, and the crickets started, she leaned against me.

"You're worried, Robert."

"Just a little."

"Not because you're leaving me, I know." She squeezed my arm but then looked serious. "Are you afraid John's excommunication will bring us trouble?"

"Not us, I hope. Not here. But *he'll* have trouble."

"Which bothers you?" She smiled. "You miss it, don't you? Kings and queens, plots and courts . . . What we used to call your fate . . ."

"Oh, I think I escaped all that long ago. Richard and the old Queen are dead, after all, and no one on this earth could serve King John from love. Besides, even Eleanor didn't see . . ." I hesitated then. What had she failed to see? She'd seen so much: the failings of herself, her children, the disintegration of her family's Norman kingdom, its shrinking to the English side. But perhaps, I thought, she hadn't seen *this*: for now we stopped beside a railing, near the new London Bridge, and stared toward the southern side of town. How huge the City was! How different this world was from the world the old Queen knew. For her, the lord and manor were the kingdom's heart, and cities were strange, mysterious places scarcely known. What held all these people, massed together, and bound them to their King? And what bound the King to them? As a boy, I now understood I'd served a man – Richard – who was a king, but Eleanor had taught me to see that kingship was something in itself, something separate from the person who possessed it. Yet now I sensed a vision beyond even this; an idea she had never seen and which I could scarcely glimpse myself.

Gala broke up my thoughts. "How peculiar," she said, "to live in the middle of a bridge."

I smiled. The huge stone structure, which we'd watched them building for so long, was now surmounted by rickety, wooden shops and houses – two, three, four storeys high – that formed a kind of commercial battlement. "A great place for hawkers," I said. "Half the traffic into London passes by your door."

"But how cold they'll be this winter, the water under them, the wind blowing down the river."

I nodded, but was thinking of something else: that bridge was a little city within the larger one, a double world the old Queen had never contemplated.

Just then, a little along from us, a man gasped and pointed. "Dear God, look!"

Taking our eyes from the bridge, we looked toward the southern bank. I saw a curl of smoke; then Gala picked out the flame. "Just there . . . That steeple . . . I think Our Lady of the Canons . . ." I squinted toward the church, which lay near the bridge's Southwark Gate. I saw it for an instant – but then it was hidden by a cloud of smoke. We stared ahead; crowds pushed and jostled; and people appeared on the roofs and balconies of the buildings near us. For a time, the smoke was so black and heavy that we couldn't see, but I'd lived in Southwark long enough to imagine the horror of a fire among those stews and aleshops, the flames racing up the narrow alleys and licking at the close-packed houses. And then the wind came up; the smoke swirled and parted. The crowd, now huge, let out a groan – for against the deepening night, we could see that the farther bank was a curtain of shooting flame. Now the wind came round. We choked on smoke; soot set our eyes to streaming; and embers, drifting down, made a burning rain. Everyone began to scream. Those who lived nearby ran in panic toward their homes, each with its thick, thatched roof. Safest where we were, we clung to the embankment railing, and the Princess seized my arm. She pointed down the river: pointed at the sight that filled us all with horror. For the red hot coals, drifting on the wind, had fallen on the bridge. In barely the time it took to draw a breath, the bridge was burning at both ends. Both banks, the river, the very sky, glowed red. We were close enough to hear the screams: see the final, desperate plunges into the frigid current. . . It was a Hell before our eyes and at length, half-sick, we struggled clear of those around us and turned away, all thoughts of popes and kings and ancient fates driven from our minds. But that night I dreamed of fire; woke, all sweaty, with the heat of it; saw, against the darkness, torches flickering in Kyrenia's square, the blaze of Nottingham's Great Hall . . .

Portents: at heart, to tell the truth, I don't believe them. We think they tell the future but we only ever see them afterwards. Weeks passed; my nightmares, and my talk with Jacob, were all forgotten. I set off for Troyes . . . Yet, to give those signs their due, something of their feeling travelled with me. I felt gloomy and drawn in, like someone waiting for the worst to happen, and when I looked about, seeking reassurance, even the most normal sights seemed threatening: villeins at work in their seigneurs' fields, fishermen bringing their catch to port, merchants grumbling over prices in the inns – were they not more sullen, wary, fretful? No one spoke directly: the world pretended that the world was just the same . . . but everyone knew that trouble was on its way. God knows, I was scarcely different: I went about my business just as usual, as if popes and interdicts and the acts of foolish kings weighed nothing in comparison to the bargain I was trying to make.

I felt all this, thought some of it, as I finally made my way towards home. Trouble. Riding up that familiar, winding road from Dover, I could sense it everywhere: closing in, like dusk, as I came through the City gates; settling, like the smoky fog, between the elms along the Strand. The air was chill; I drew my cloak about me. It was a night for witches, I told myself, a perfect night for these poor times, and, uneasily, as if to insure a normal homecoming, I sent my servant on ahead so a dozen hands were at my horse's bridle as I reached the gates of Sherwood Hall. Which made no difference. Peering down through clouds of frosting breath, I saw the worry on my steward's face.

"What is it, Martin?"

"My lord, this can't be a happy welcome. We have trouble."

I felt no surprise – just nodded, swung down, then clattered across the yard and climbed the double stairs to Gala's chambers. She made me smile, as she always did. Valiantly, with half a dozen candles and a roaring hearth, she'd tried to disperse the gloom. I kissed her and held her for a moment; but then she whispered in my ear. "I hate this, Robert. But something's happened."

I eased her back. "I know. Don't worry. Just tell me what."

"It's Jacob. The King has taken him."

My guts went cold. "When?"

"Three nights ago. They took him to Windsor gaol – we can't be certain, but we think he's still alive."

For that, I drew a thankful breath. "Did they have a warrant?"

She shook her head. "No. But they took his books as well. His clerk says they wanted them as much as him."

That made sense. If the King had Jacob's books, and could read the cipher they were written in, he had a lever that could move some

230

of the most powerful men in England. But why put a weak old man in prison? The hopeful answer was just to keep him silent. But I knew there was another: when a Jew money-lender died, the debts owing him were collected by the King . . . a tempting way for John to fatten up his treasury. Trying to brush away this thought, I squeezed Gala's hand. "Don't worry. We'll get him out."

She smiled slightly, but didn't speak. She was fond of Jacob and knew how much we owed him. But she also knew that saving him – or trying to – would put us in great danger.

"You'll see the King?" she finally asked.

"I'll have to."

This broke our firmest rule: removing ourselves entirely from John's regal sight. Trying to reassure her, I added: "Remember, I'm not entirely powerless when it comes to our dear liege."

"So de Braose thought."

"Never fear. Having his example, I won't make his mistake."

She held my eyes a moment, her features firm; but then her face filled again with worry and she leaned against me. "I'm so frightened, Robert. Since you left for France, everything is worse. The whole city is filled with rumours of rebellion. John's trapped – the French and the Pope on one side, his own barons on the other. Now's just the time when he'll be most dangerous."

She was right, and I knew it. That night, I dreamed more portents: I was in Cyprus with Garth again, and we were puzzling the French king's ciphered message – in some dream-like fashion this was supposed to help me save old Jacob. Waking, however, I felt only a throbbing head and no great confidence. Full of caution, I sent Gala across the river to stay with Mercury – I was afraid that John might use my "sister" to strike at me – then set out alone for Windsor. Bringing no attention to myself, I rode quite slowly, and it was late afternoon before I reached the castle. Within its walls, I was as discreet as possible. I still had friends in the Court, or at least men who knew me, but I deliberately sought out one of the lesser clerks whom I'd once lent money to and had him take my petition in; and since his answer might well be my arrest, I didn't loiter but rode back to my inn and waited there. An hour passed. Then, as dusk tightened into night, a messenger rode up – alone. Neutral glance; a civil voice . . . which might only mean that John was setting his trap with care. But from this point on I had to walk straight into it regardless. He had no torch. We rode silently, in darkness. He took me through a side gate, then up back passages and winding stairs: cold, wet channels in the stone, like the meanderings of a cave. I didn't like it. Our footsteps clattered. Far-off voices echoed hollowly. If these corridors ended at the dungeons, no one would be the wiser. But suddenly, with no warning, my guide halted before a plain wooden door. There was no guard, and he didn't knock: just opened it and moved aside.

I stepped forward into a small stone room, a sort of vault. It had no lights or windows or decoration; only a huge fire roaring in a hearth, two chairs and a small table with wine. John, slouched beneath a black fur cloak, had a goblet at his lips. Years had passed since I'd last seen him. He was now immensely fat. His cheeks had burst like roses from too much drinking, and even the rings on his fingers were buried in flesh. His face glistened sweatily, and I was suddenly aware of the crackling fire's heat. But then that fitted: Pope Innocent, after all, had banished John to Hell.

He grunted as he set his goblet down. "You said a private meeting, Locksley. I trust this suits?"

"Perfectly, My Liege."

Another grunt. "We no longer see you much at Court, my lord."

"No, Sire . . . I regret that I have little business there."

"Unlike de Braose?"

"Exactly, Sire. Unlike de Braose."

De Braose . . . So that's what he'd thought I wanted.

No doubt a touch surprised by my response, he raised his eyebrows, then gestured with his hand. "In my banished state, I care less for ceremony. Sit, my lord. And this wine is excellent." I nodded, and came across the room. But my hand hesitated as I reached toward the flagon. John smiled – at times, I'll admit, he showed a sense of manners. Snatching up the jug, he filled his goblet to the rim and chuckled. "If it's poisoned, sir, we'll die together . . . and perhaps my soul will take some good from the company of yours."

"I doubt that, Sire. Mine's not so pure."

"Ah yes. I was forgetting. *You* killed sweet Arthur – I'm just the one who can be blamed for it." He laughed again. "That's why I like you, Locksley. You're proof, at least for myself, that I'm actually better than the world believes."

I sipped the warm, spiced wine and murmured: "Sire, I'm sure the world thinks well of you."

At once, his eyes jerked toward me, flashing red with the fire's light. "Don't flatter me, my lord. They hate me and I know it. The world loved my father for his wisdom, my brother for his bravery, but I am neither wise nor brave, nor . . ." He gulped his wine then smiled down at his cup. "God knows what I am. Perhaps you can say – what quality marks me out from them?"

Taking more wine, I watched him carefully. I couldn't gauge his mood. He was half-drunk, no doubt, mellow with wine and drowsy with this roasting heat. But this made him like certain seas: beneath the rolling, oily waves of his self-pity lay a violent turbulence. I must not provoke . . . yet he clearly had no taste for flattery to-night.

His eyes, meeting mine, called for an answer, so I said: "Ambition, Sire."

He frowned, and then he snarled. "Ambition? Is there something wrong in that?"

"No, My Liege."

His glistening jowls began to shake. "And what am I ambitious for? *The Throne?* It's mine by right of birth."

"Of course, Sire."

"So how am I ambitious? How can I grasp at what is mine already?"

Luckily, I didn't have to answer. Throwing off his robe, he staggered from his chair and went closer to the fire, splashing his wine across the flames with an angry gesture. I waited, silent. He grew a little calmer. Then he grunted: "You're right of course, my lord. Ambition. Greed. That's what I'm stained with. That's what they hold against me. What they gave Richard without a thought they give me only grudgingly – because I was fool enough to ask for it."

"And what is that, Sire?"

He turned his face a little. "Loyalty. What else does a king require? But instead of giving it, they'll let an Italian Pope appoint their priests and sit a French king on my throne."

With an effort, my face stayed rigid. John and loyalty – what a nerve he had to complain like this. On Cyprus, as I well knew, he'd plotted Richard's death with Philip, and I'd seen how he'd tried to prevent his brother's ransoming. *Loyalty.* I was surprised he knew how to say the word. But I held my tongue and he turned away. His back was to me and the fire, leaping up, made him a silhouette, a kind of effigy. And I saw something then; in his shadowy presence, or in the fire or in myself – I wasn't sure. But it was what I'd almost glimpsed that day when I'd looked out, with Gala, at London Bridge. I'd grown and changed with all of them, Richard, Eleanor and John. My loyalties had shifted from the man who wore the crown to the crown itself; and now I felt them shifting once again. What bound the people to their King? Loyalty – as John said. But what bound *him* to *them*? Did he even know them? Did he have any feelings that stretched outside this room? Count of Poitou, Duke of Aquitaine . . . for me all that meant nothing now. John was King of England . . . and as between the King and England, I knew where my loyalties lay.

But then he turned and I could see his face again: his lips held a sardonic twist. "Once, weren't you intended to be a priest?"

"A long time ago, My Liege."

He grunted. "All the same, something about you brings out confession. I ask your pardon. You didn't come to hear me talk. You wanted something."

"Only a small favour, Sire. Not for myself. A friend."

"Again, unlike de Braose?"

"As you say, My Liege."

"But – correct me if I'm wrong – if I don't grant this little boon the world might be given cause to think me even worse than it does now?"

"Sire, if you'll permit me . . . The man I ask this for already has a claim upon your gratitude."

This suggestion, I think, caused genuine surprise and the royal brow furrowed. "Whoever are you speaking of? No one does me favours – which at least has one advantage. I don't owe any in return."

"The man is a Jew, Sire. Jacob Mancere. He's in your gaol."

He still seemed puzzled.

"You remember, Sire, when we dined –"

"Ah . . . I didn't realise. But I don't intend him any harm, my lord. I only wished to see his ledgers. He lends money to some of my greatest enemies and I was curious to see which had suddenly cleared their debts – with Philip's gold."

"Sire, he's a weak old man. If you keep him –"

"I only want his silence."

"He'll give it, Sire. I promise you."

He shrugged. For a second, holding my breath, I thought . . . but then a look passed across his face. His eyes glinted and then he smiled. "Locksley, you love this man?"

"I owe him a great deal, Sire."

"Then – since he's a money-lender – you should pay your debt. And I'll give you the means to do so." I didn't speak, just tried to fix his eye; but he shifted it away. "And if you don't accept those means, I'll kill him, and the guilt will be squarely on your head for I certainly shouldn't do so otherwise."

"My Liege, if you so much –"

"Ah, your threat! I fear it, truly. My barons would weep with joy if you could prove I was a murderer. They'd hurry Philip so quickly to my throne that he'd be out of breath. But that may happen anyway. And think – would it save your friend?" He leaned toward me, and his hand reached out and tapped my knee. "Besides, dear Locksley, I don't ask so much. Nothing you haven't done before."

My throat was dry. Carefully, I leaned away from him and sipped some wine. Finally, deliberately, I asked: "What do you want of me, My Liege?"

"Murder." He spat out the word but instantly began to shake his head. "No . . . That may not be right. Living with the Devil, I obviously know nothing of morality. Perhaps if you take one life to save another, it's not murder but something different. Indeed, it may earn you grace."

"You can't earn that, My Liege. God gives it or he doesn't."

"I was forgetting: you went to school. But see? Even Arthur's murderer can still have hope. In the sight of God's great mercy, another bloody knife will scarcely make a difference."

Again, I tried to fix his eye. And this time he let me: to see in its fiercely narrowed gaze that he was in earnest. He slowly smiled. "Come, my lord. You have to ask the question."

My head began to spin and the taste of that cloying wine rose back up my throat.

He laughed. "Come, come. See? I've taken up your challenge. Do your worst. Expose me. I'll laugh so hard, my lord – I might lose my crown for the single crime I'm not guilty of. It almost pleases me! But that won't save your friend . . . So ask me, Locksley. Ask me."

My voice became a whisper, I could barely hear myself. "Who? Who, then . . . My Liege?"

"But guess – who could it be? Who's the single man whose murder might save me yet?"

For a mad second in that fetid room, with the wine gagging in my throat I thought he meant the Pope himself. But then, sickeningly, I understood. Stephen Langton . . .

"Sire, he is a priest."

"So he is, by God. But not yet an archbishop."

"I cannot, Sire."

"But certainly you can. Was Arthur not a prince?"

"Sire –"

"And your friend is an ancient Jew. Priest, prince or Jew – which do you value most?"

My mind was racing, trying to find some exit, but every door seemed locked. I felt terror then, terror such as I'd never felt before. Because I'd do it? Because I'd be unable to? Horror spread across me, a heat that blistered on my skin. I could hear Arthur crying out. I could see his blood, blood that flowed to join a bloody river, Garth's blood, Thomas Hoade's, Jean Neuilly's and a hundred others. I prayed. In my heart, I begged for God to help me . . . And then, quite casually, as easily as another breath, my prayer was answered and I saw what I must do. As John pressed his face a finger's width from mine and his hot breath pressed against my cheek, my heart went out to him in pity.

"You'll do it, Locksley, won't you? You'll serve me just as you served my brother, just as you served my mother. By the blood of Christ you will!"

Then he pulled his face away and began to laugh, half-crazed with glee. To serve him as I'd served Eleanor: serve the fate that had brought me here. But no, I thought; no more. I whispered: "No, My Liege. I'll not serve you. At long last I'll serve myself."

But he was laughing now too hard to hear, laughing and shouting all at once, calling to the messenger who finally came to lead me out.

CHAPTER TWO

Mercury said, "Now, my friends, we must all decide what masks we'll wear."

"Perhaps I'll be Marian again," Marian replied.

Gala smiled. "You can't be. If you are Marian, then I must be the Princess Berengaria and I've forgotten all the ways of court."

We paused at the top of a hill, coming to the end of a trip which, if not exactly happy, at least we'd kept from being doleful. Or perhaps that wasn't so surprising. Marian, so long cloistered in Le Mans, had enjoyed a glimpse of the outside world. As for Gala, she always loved to get on a horse and it had taken some persuasion to keep her out of chain-mail. And for Mercury and myself it was like old times. Guessing my thoughts, he smiled. "This brings back memories of our youth."

Saddle-sore, I grunted. "But not our youth itself."

"Be grateful. At least this time you don't have to be a gong-farmer."

Indeed. Our approach to Stephen Langton would be more subtle, following a plan suggested by the King and which, since I could imagine no greater master of treachery, I'd readily accepted. Besides, it had a comical side as well. For years, John told me, he'd been negotiating with Gala's family in Navarre about the jointure due her after Richard's death. Various plans had been agreed, revised, reneged on, and at length the Pope had even intervened, taking Gala's part. Of course, unbeknownst to John, I was already aware of this; in fact, on one occasion, my 'sister' had been forced to resume her real identity and travel home. In any case, the King now said that I should go as his secret emissary to Le Mans and propose – since the Pope could no longer be considered neutral – that they submit their dispute to Otto, Duke of Saxony. The princess was naive, John said; it was possible she might accept this. But I was to claim to be her friend, and remind her that Richard had once entrusted her to my protection. Accordingly, I was to point out the truth: that Otto was John's nephew and ally, and that John had supported him in a dispute with Philip, the Hohenstaufen. "You know I only met her once," the King had said, "that time you came here with that Jew. She's a trusting girl, I think. If it wasn't for her brother and that cursed Pope our quarrel might have been settled years ago. So use your guile. Paint me black. Tell her that Otto would surely side with me and she'd get nothing. Instead, advise her to see Langton and through Langton strive to see the Pope. You see? She'll get you in to see him privately." He'd grinned at me, delighted at his ingenuity. No wonder! I'd kill his archbishop and stain Gala into the bargain – he'd have an excuse never to pay her anything. Of course, he had no way of knowing the double ingenuity it held for me. Carefully, I retained a serious face, accepted his suggestion and followed it to the letter: travelled to Le Mans with his spies tagging along behind; saw the cloistered "princess"; duly persuaded her – miracle of miracles! – to send her letter off to Langton.

Now our journey was at an end: we seemed just an innocent group of pilgrims, waiting for their servants to catch up, staring across the valley toward the spires of Vezelay. Clinging to the brow of a rounded granite scarp, the town looked serenely down on the rolling countryside of Burgundy. Far below, the river Cure twisted like a silver ribbon through a narrow valley that was dotted with vineyards, orchards and grassy fields. Seeming to stretch its shadow across this peaceful scene – and clearly visible to us – was the tallest spire in the town, rising from the cathedral of St Mary Magdalene. I'd seen it several times before; even so, it made me catch my breath, for of all the shrines in Christendom, save Rome and Jerusalem itself, the crypt of this gentle saint is the most important. Huddling about the church and the monastery walls, even the shops and houses of the town itself had the appearance of humble supplicants. Yet, as I well knew, Vezelay wasn't just a pilgrim's destination: that craggy, granite cliff made it one of the Holy Church's most powerful redoubts. Never in history had any king, or duke, or lord dared to try to breach its walls; for Langton – like Becket before him – there could have been no safer refuge.

Turning to Mercury, I said, "A Holy Fortress."

Crossing himself, he nodded. "You could leaguer it for years and never enter." Then he grinned. "But these ladies – though which is which I wouldn't like to say – should get us in speedily enough."

In truth, as we started down the valley's side and drew nearer the place, I began to appreciate the deviousness of the King's plan. At the base of a scarp was a hamlet, La Grangeotte, and from here we had to climb a steep, sharply winding path toward the town itself.

This ascent was unguarded, though there was a gauntlet to be run of hawkers peddling pilgrims' wares, figures of the Saint and scraps of leather purportedly from her sandals, but at the top of the hill stood a high stone wall with a guarded, narrow portal. Stout defences, or so they must have thought . . . but useless against John's cunning. Within a few hours of our arrival, I was standing in front of Langton and could have murdered him as easily as spit.

Looking around his room, I wondered if he cared.

In exile, the great archbishop lived no better than a hermit. His 'palace' was a small stone chamber off the monastery's inner court. The glory of his office consisted of one plain table, bare except for writing instruments; a stool with a seat of woven rush; a hard bed without a canopy. His entourage was three old clerks; and there was no guard, save God, at all.

"He must not remember Becket," Marian whispered as we waited.

No, I thought. But then again, perhaps he did. They say Becket welcomed the knives, knowing that his death would prove a curse to Henry; conceivably Langton thought his own martyrdom might gain him a similar victory over Henry's son. But even as I thought this, Marian touched my hand. Heavily cloaked and veiled, she might have been a nun; and her ears were tuned to the rustlings of the cloister. "Brother, he's coming now . . ."

There was no announcement. The latch just lifted and there he was, stepping across the threshold all alone. An old man, short and slight. Finely sculpted features outlined by clear, pale skin stretched smooth. A French face or Italian, though I knew he was more English than myself . . . "Your Grace."

Long hands, hollowed at the palm, lifted us from our knees. He smiled. And then I *felt* his grace: for the gentleness in that smile was matched by its calm authority, a most determined will. Taking Marian's hand, he murmured, "Your Highness, the whole world speaks of the blessings you bring L'Epau, and thanks you for it. You prove that perfect marriage is the model for our love of God."

I noted the hint of friendliness in this: John claimed that Richard had never married the Princess properly, and therefore the jointure wasn't owned. Acknowledging this as well, Marian inclined her head. In the end, we'd decided that she should play her customary role as 'Princess'. Langton didn't know her face; behind her veil he couldn't see it anyway; and if we actually had to discuss her argument with John, she was more familiar with its details. But now I realised that her act, at least in its inward aspects, was more than this. "Your Grace," she whispered, "the only difference is that our love for God may last through all eternity." What else, indeed, would the grieving, cloistered Princess say?

Langton nodded, then turned to me and shook my hand. "My lord, let me welcome you, though I confess it's strange to see an English knight in Philip's France."

"As surprising, Your Grace, that England's archbishop should be dwelling here."

He laughed at this – and showed he did remember Becket. "I'm not so certain. Around Vezelay, at least, they're growing used to us."

"I'm sure the monks love you very well, Your Grace, and I wouldn't wish to bring them sorrow. Nonetheless, I trust you'll soon be bidding them farewell."

He nodded, and for a second his face looked grave. "I thank you, my lord." But then he brightened. "Still, let's not speak of my problems with the King. I know you have your own." He turned toward Marian. "Your Highness, I read your letter with great sympathy."

We had rehearsed this moment many times. But now, departing from everything we'd talked about, Marian stunned me – and drew back her veil. I drew in my breath; but knew that this was precisely what a princess would have done. Her face, revealed, was utterly calm. Her voice was low but level:

"Your Grace, I feel ashamed. That letter was false. A lie."

The revelation of her face had been as startling for Langton as for myself; for a second, he was so fixed by Marian's eyes that he didn't speak. I broke in: "Your Grace, the letter was a ruse, suggested by King John, to enable me to see you privately."

Slowly, frowning, Langton turned to me. "For what purpose, my lord?"

"Your Grace . . . to murder you."

It had been essential that he not cry out, and Marian's face – so calm and placid – had accomplished this. I'm not sure he knew what to think. But then he smiled and said: "Do you intend to?"

"No."

He raised an eyebrow. "Then let me thank God for both of us."

"Archbishop, I ask your pardon. But I'm not mad. Nor is this a game. At this very moment, an old man is imprisoned in the King's dungeons at Windsor. The price of his freedom was my knife through your heart. And to see that the bargain was kept, John's spies have followed me all the way from England. If you cry out now, or let it be known I've failed, then that old man will die – and his blood will be on your hands as surely as if you'd murdered him yourself."

For a long second, Langton stared at me, then slowly he turned toward Marian whose veil had dropped again. "My Lady, does he speak the truth?"

"Your Grace, believe him. He's trying to save your life."

Walking a little away from us, he turned aside and whispered, "Dear God . . . The man he holds – is it your father?"

"No, Your Grace. A friend."

"Poor John. How like him. Not simply murder, but the extortion of a murder . . ." But then, recovering himself a little, he turned back and met my eyes. "I thank you, my lord: for my life, for keeping your own conscience from damnation, for trying to save the King's."

"Your Grace, that is uncertain. I trust John in few things, but to take revenge . . ."

"I understand. What can we do? I've never hated him. I've only wanted loyally to serve him. So why does he hate me?"

"You stand in his way, Your Grace."

"Dear God, I don't. His pride opposes him."

"He thinks that you're in league with Philip."

"Why?"

I shrugged. "Because you've lived so long in France. Because the Pope is close to Philip and you are Innocent's oldest friend."

"Do you believe him?"

I hesitated. It was, after all, a sensible question. Langton *had* lived for years in Paris, and it was there indeed that he'd first met Lothario di Segni – nephew of Clement III, a cardinal at twenty-nine, elected Pope at thirty-seven. Innocent had promptly made his old friend Cardinal, now archbishop, so that in these quarrels Stephen Langton stood to lose very little and gain much. But I didn't truly doubt him. Or at least I didn't think that he'd conspire with Philip. But at the same time I understood that his true loyalties lay not with any temporal throne, but with the Church.

Carefully, I qualified my answer: "Your Grace, I would say that all John's fears are just his conscience talking. Until King Richard died, John spent all his time conspiring with Philip to take the throne. He knows those conspiracies were real. And he knows that Philip's ambitions are all real enough."

"So he does, my lord. But I wonder if he knows how successful they may be."

"Your Grace?"

His hands clasped behind his back, his face turned grim. "My lord, you say I am a friend of Innocent's. You're right. So let me tell you that I know his patience has worn out. He's ready to declare John's disobedience a justification for Philip deposing him. He may *order* France to do it . . . and there's one command, my lord, that will be speedily obeyed."

I was aghast. I had scarcely voice enough to stammer, "Your Grace, you can't let this happen?"

He cocked his head. "Can't I? Tell me how to stop it."

"Your Grace, you'd be purchasing your throne with England's!"

"My throne? You think I care what hat I wear? England is a nation outside the sacraments. To save a kingdom from the Devil is worth paying any price – and we both can name one king who's worse than Philip." My head began to spin. Here it was, at last: the nightmare that Richard, Eleanor, myself, had struggled to avoid. How cruelly fitting it would be. John had conspired so long with Philip to get the English throne – now, having it at last, he would lose it to him. And by losing it I would lose as well: half the meaning of my life. The old priest must have seen the horror that this held for me because he reached out now and gently touched my arm. "My lord, I know what you are feeling, for I've felt it all myself. Only remember this, my lord. If the Pope chooses to use Philip to bring England back to Christ, we should be grateful to them both."

"But if there's another way?"

"Which way is that, my lord?"

"Your Grace . . . can I ask you for your trust?"

His lips curved in the faintest smile. "My lord, it seems that I can trust you with my life."

"Then take me to the Pope, your friend. I have a plan. Let me tell it to him."

Now he frowned a little. "A plan to . . . ?"

"Regain England for the church without losing it to France."

He hesitated; and then the smile came back, perhaps a trifle mocking. "All right, my lord. If you can save my life, who knows? Perhaps you can save England's."

I held his eye. "And there's one other yet, Your Grace. My friend – John's hostage."

His face turned entirely serious. "As you say, my lord, his blood would be partly on my hands. What would you have me do?"

"If you agree, Your Grace, we'll leave secretly for Rome tonight. Tell no one. Not even your own people. Tomorrow your disappearance will be a great mystery in the town, and John's spy will carry the story back to England. The King will assume I've kept our bargain."

He considered this, then nodded. "Very well. If playing at my death can save a life, I'll do it gladly."

So that was how we rode to Rome – a not-quite archbishop

242

travelling as a simple priest; an English lord, calling himself Robin Hood again; one pretending princess with a false sister as her maid; and a dwarf named after a pagan god. But on the road to Lyons, even such an odd procession went unnoticed and by the time we reached the town I was confident our trick had worked. Continuing south, we reached Marseilles, sailed to Ostia, then rode the last few miles to Rome. As a merchant, I'd made this journey half a dozen times, but for Marian and even Gala it was all a wonder, while Mercury was in heaven, babbling in his native tongue to everyone we passed. For his part, Langton was quiet, uncomplaining and always courteous. I suspected he was sceptical about my efforts and he was an old man as well, near sixty; but he still seemed tough as chain and I could never say he slowed our pace. And that pace, God knows, was quick enough. By the first week of November we'd come in sight of the greatest city in the world. It was raining hard, as it usually does that time of year. The Tiber, swirling with yellow mud, rushed on beside the road. But as I lifted my gaze and peered ahead, I could just make out the bastion of Hadrian's Tomb looming like the city's sentinel through the mist. As we came closer, Marian's eyes were fairly bulging out. "Such a place! I've never seen a town so great!"

Her waiting maid smiled broadly. "But you have, my lady. You stayed here with your mother Eleanor when you journeyed to Sicily to marry Richard."

"Ah yes, Maid Marian," Marian said, "but I was so young then my eyes didn't know what they were seeing."

The real Princess laughed. "Since my eyes were yours then, let me say it's true."

Mercury was bulging with his pride. "No wonder, dear ladies. You poor people don't know what a city is. You could put ten Londons into Rome. It's half as old as time and holds a million souls."

"And they're all like you," said Gala, "filled with wine and talk, like those Irishmen our poor King is always trying to conquer."

Langton, and the one other servant I'd brought with us, was riding up ahead. Now, as we entered a maze of criss-crossed streets and alleys, jammed with carts and people, we pulled up together to keep from getting lost. All around us, buildings rose like mountains; houses of brick and wood and wattle, church after church — Della Fratte, Apostoli, Balbina — so that floor rose over floor, roof surmounted roof, and the glittering spires out-reached each other. Despite the rain, after the greys and browns of London the City's colours were astounding; Rome was a holy city but hardly modest. Men wore velvet tunics of the brightest scarlet, the women seemed to favour the most gaudy purple and even the houses were painted blue and yellow. Matching this was the City's raucous din; with his horse jostling against my own, Langton still had to strain his voice:

"My lord, do we stay in our disguises?"

"We're safe enough, Your Grace, but we may as well be cautious."

"As you say, my lord. There's an inn by here. If you agree, stay here with the others and I'll ride ahead to arrange your meeting with His Holiness."

"How long?"

"An hour . . . a week. You understand, my lord, I'll not be the one to say."

He took us to the inn, and returned that afternoon – with a set look on his face that made me ask at once about our prospects.

"They're not good, my lord. I think his mind is settled. And I had to tell him how we met, which hardly made him more forgiving toward the King."

"But he'll see me?"

"Yes. And listen. He's always curious, which doesn't hurt, and I told him you'd taken the Cross with Richard, which gains you a certain favour."

"And if you're still his friend, Your Grace, he may even want to thank me for saving you."

Langton smiled that little smile he had. "My lord, I trust you won't count too much on that."

In truth, I didn't. Innocent, as the whole world knew, was both prince and priest; indeed, some said, more prince than priest. The cardinals had actually made him Pope before he was ordained and his first acts had been to drive the Germans out of Italy and Sicily. I knew, therefore, that my appeal to him could not be personal, but would have to touch both his sense of holiness and power.

Dressing carefully, I followed the archbishop to the Lateran. It is an enormous place; and if I wished to address the holiness and power of the Church, here I found both aspects perfectly embodied, for the Lateran is not so much a palace as a fortress whose keep is an enormous monastery. About the size of Southwark, it is built on an enormous square, or *piazza* as the Romans call it, that they've named for St John. Huge carved gates admit you. To the left, you first see the Lateran Schools, where the priests are trained, and beyond this the hospices and inns erected to receive pilgrims and emissaries to the Holy See; on the right, in a tumble of white-plastered buildings, more than a thousand clerks and priests work constantly at the business of the Church. But it is the far side of the square that draws your eye, for here is the Lateran Palace itself, the monastery-fortress: a heavy wall, broken at odd places with the higher walls of buildings and overlooked by squat, tiled towers with narrow windows. Before its gates a caterwauling crowd was milling: pilgrims in wide-brimmed hats, rich men in sweeping cloaks of silk, crusader knights and a thousand merchants: from carts and stalls, or just from their pockets, they sold wooden statues of the saints, Holy Marys, and pilgrims' seals made of anything from lead to gold. Some of these men would see the Pope, a few might hear him: but all felt a little closer to their souls just by being there.

I followed after Langton. At the gate, a guard admitted us and another took our horses. Climbing a broad set of stone stairs, we passed beneath a portal and entered a long, cool hall whose bright mosaic floor told the story of the gospels. This hall led to another, then another after that, until they became a maze: halls, cloisters, columned vestibules, more passageways. Clutching Langton's sleeve like a frightened child, I followed along in silence. In fact, the place was silent as the grave; two priests passed us in a hall, I glimpsed a room filled with cowled Benedictines writing at long tables, but there were no sounds louder than a slipping sandal, a swishing robe, a scratching quill. At length, as we approached a vaulted portal, Langton tugged my arm:

"We go in here, my lord. His Holiness' audience chamber."

Oddly, there was no guard. But then, as we stepped across the threshold, I realised the room was empty. It was a round chamber, the domed roof arching high above my head. Galleries ran all around it, marble columns supporting alabaster spans, with tall windows behind filtering the sun to the softest milky white. Opposite the entrance stood the Holy Throne, canopied with a marble dome supported by four columns of black porphyry.

Langton whispered: "He holds his public audiences here, but he'll see you privately in the room behind. Wait a moment. I'll see if he is ready to receive us."

Confident, moving easily in this familiar place, he strode past the throne and opened a door in the wall beyond. Waiting, I wondered if I should pray – and then decided I'd do better to fix my arguments firmly in my mind. Some moments passed. Then Langton was standing in the doorway, beckoning me to come.

I stepped forward; crossed the threshold; hesitated. I was in a long, narrow room. The light was very dim; it seemed to hang in the air and swirl, like the finest silver dust. To left and right were high-backed wooden benches, as cold and empty as granite gravestones; beyond, arched galleries, still as crypts, draped in dusky crimson velvet. I glimpsed Langton through the gloom and saw him make a little gesture with his hand. I stepped forward down the marble aisle which ended in a marble dais. Langton stood there, a little to one side, and on the top of it was raised a gold and silver throne, canopied by a gilded dome above. Here Innocent sat, a soft, silky gleam in that smoky light. Reaching the dais, I sank to my knees and Langton murmured:

"Your Holiness . . . I present Lord Locksley, journeyed here from England."

The Holy arm extended. Stepping up, I knelt again and kissed St Peter's ring. I kept my head bowed. When he spoke, I didn't see the parting of his lips but his voice was very soft:

"My lord . . . the dear archbishop has told me some of your adventures. He claims you travelled in disguise. He was a simple priest named John, while you were . . . ?"

"Your Holiness, I called myself Robin Hood."

"An English name? A Saxon name?"

"A man, Your Holiness, that I knew many years ago."

"I trust a good man, since you took his name."

"Your Holiness, I must confess . . . not quite."

I looked up then. He had a round, plump face but his lips were very thin and his eyebrows were so fair you could barely see them. *Innocent*. Indeed, he did look like a baby – but the oldest baby in the world. Now he nodded: the slightest gesture, but it seemed to set that silvery hair to swirling so his smile was like a sickle moon.

"I won't hold that against you, lord. What's in a name? Segni I was born; Scotti I was called, after my mother's family. And I took the name of Innocent because the second Innocent, Guidoni, gave Italy to the Germans and I thought another Innocent should take it back. Even Locksley can't be your true name since you're a lord."

"Your Holiness, I am Robert Atheling."

"Your father was a knight?"

"Yes."

"King Richard's knight?"

"And King Henry's, in his time."

"And who knighted you, my lord?"

"The Lionheart, Your Holiness. On Cyprus."

"So you are a knight, made so by King Richard, but you are loyal to John?"

"He is my king, Your Holiness."

"A king who holds your friend as ransom – his price the murdering of a priest. I am amazed by such allegiance, my lord. Langton even tells me you come to plead John's case."

"I plead his kingdom's case. I plead for his subjects, whose souls and lives are in your care as well."

"Ah. But then you will support my policy. In the name of God, and of God's Church, Philip of France will return the English people to the Sacraments."

My heart sank, but I controlled my voice: "Your Holiness . . . you have ordered this?"

"I have ordered it, my lord. With great relief."

"Then they will return to the Church beneath a foreign king . . . unwillingly . . . by force . . ."

"Foreign to you, my lord. But not to God. Or me."

"Your Holiness, by this conquest he will be the most powerful king in all of Europe, a king more powerful . . ." But then I thought to be discreet. Innocent would know precisely what I meant: by conquering England, Philip's power would certainly overbear his own. I waited, peering through the gloom. And suddenly realised that the Pope had closed his eyes. A long moment passed. Slowly, his eyes flickered open once again, now with a sharper gleam:

"My dear lord, I have given John every chance. Ask my cardinals and bishops. On my bended knees I've prayed to God to save his soul and open up his heart. But his will is plain. He denies Christ and myself . . . What else can I do? If he is not deposed, his people will be damned."

I tried to catch that gleaming eye, but in that shadowy room, where every beam of light seemed reflected from some infinite point, it was hard to know. "Your Holiness," I said, "if he must be deposed, so be it. But why use Philip as your instrument? Should his lust be so rewarded? I ask you . . . why not use another way?"

"Ah yes. *That* way . . . the way my eyes have failed to see."

I drew a breath. I was gambling now and the dice were in my hands. "Your Holiness, John's kingdom is seething with rebellion for a hundred reasons. The common people hate him. His barons distrust him totally. If you gave your support – if you let me carry back that word – King John's own knights would throw him over. *This* is the other way, Your Holiness. John would be deposed, the true archbishop would sit in Canterbury . . . and Philip would be no stronger than he is today."

His eyes grew wider; then, like a sleepy reptile's, narrowed. "Who then would be your king, my lord?"

"Henry. John's son. An English king."

"He is a child. Not five years old."

My heart lifted – he must have thought this out. I rushed ahead: "A mere boy, Your Holiness, so there would have to be a Regency . . . in which the Church would have great influence."

His eyes fell shut again. I had tempted him. But then, abruptly, he stood up and with a soft swishing of his robes – the light swirling round him like a silent whirlpool – he stepped down from the dais. I stood aside, caught Langton's frightened eye. Yet still the voice was soft, the syllables all coiled and murmuring:

"Lord Locksley, tell me. Where does power come from?"

A knife. A lance. A bowstring. A bulging treasury . . . But not here: "From God," I answered.

"And who does God give it to?"

"To kings, Your Holiness."

"Not priests?"

"And priests."

"Is it not true, my lord, that princes rule the material world – the world of clay – while priests rule over souls?"

"It is so, Your Holiness."

"But the body is mortal, is it not?"

"Yes."

"While the soul exists eternally?"

"Of course, Your Holiness."

"By this token, then, the soul is superior to the body, and the power of priests is superior to that of kings. The King of Kings gave power to princes here on earth, but a priest has power that extends even up to Heaven. Do you not agree?"

"Your Holiness –"

"And of all priests, Lord Locksley, is not the Pope, Christ's Vicar, the most powerful?"

"He is, Your Holiness."

"Good, my lord. Remember. This order was ordained by God. He so established kingship and the priesthood that kingship should be holy and priesthood royal – thereby setting Christ's Vicar on this earth above all other priests and kings. But also remember this, my lord. God's order goes much farther. Just as the Vicar of Christ must demand the allegiance of all princes, so those princes must demand the allegiance of their barons – and their barons of their villeins. You are a knight. Is that not how you fight your tournaments? Knight fights knight, you don't contest your squires. *And only kings fight kings.* It is this holy connection of allegiances, ordained by God, that you now ask me to help you break."

My heart sank then; I'd lost. But I'd not lose easily, so I took a breath – the deepest breath I could – and said: "Your Holiness, your logic surely errs. You yourself have cast out John. In God's sight he is no king – nor a baron, nor the humblest lord, but only a soul damned for all eternity."

"And what you ask of me, my lord, will damn my soul with just that certainty."

Behind me, Langton whispered: "I beg you, lord . . . some arguments are better lost."

But what had I to lose? What had John, or England? I pressed ahead: "Your Holiness, you speak of allegiances ordained by God, but I ask you: will Philip's rule of England fall within them? Will he recognise the authority you claim? In the name of Christ's mercy, I ask you to give John one more chance. Let me return to England as your emissary. Let me say, from you, that you will take him back within the Church and stay Philip's hand providing . . ." My mind raced now. What could I give him? *"Providing that he accepts your overlordship and agrees to hold all his kingdoms as fiefs of the Holy See."*

Behind me, Langton gasped.

And then all was silent.

Like a misty dawn reflected on the water, that shadowy light swirled and eddied; and then a distant smile spread over Innocent's face.

"My lord Locksley . . . if John were to agree with what you've just proposed it could only be the purest expression of the will of God. I am a priest. I will not obstruct it. Go, my lord, and be my emissary."

And then, like shadows folding into shadows, he was gone.

Silence. It was so perfect that I dared not breathe. I stood quite still, and that light, like the ancient dust of tombs, settled all around me. What did it remind me of? This light? This stillness? This long waiting with my breath frozen in my chest? And then I seemed to hear the echo of a scream. My God. Oh my God have mercy –

"You traitor, Locksley! For this your wretched Jew will die and so –"

"Will you, my liege."

"By Christ's blood, my lord, I'll have you gutted like a fish."

"Think again, sire. If I am touched, I promise that the evidence of Arthur's murder will go straight to Philip, who loved the boy almost like a son. And remember – Philip, with the Pope beside him, stands ready to invade."

"I'm innocent!"

"You are. So kill me then. And trust King Philip to believe you."

"By God, you are the Devil!"

"Choose, my liege. Choose! Bow to Innocent or kneel down to Philip's chopping block. Kill me, and we both shall die. If your soul flies up to Heaven and mine burns in Hell, so be it. But we'll both be dead!"

Yes, that's what I'd have to say: Mephistopheles would deliver his message to the Devil.

Behind me, in that terrible gloom, Langton murmured: "You have promised much, my lord . . . more, some would say, than any king has the right to give."

I turned. "I promised what I had to."

"But you can give it to him?"

Did I smile? Did my face fill up with horror? My voice was just a whisper: "Oh yes, Your Grace, I can."

Langton stepped back, as if in dread, and slowly crossed himself.

CHAPTER THREE

John, I always felt, gloried in his own humiliations. Mixing anger, resentment and shame, he produced the brew of self-pity that was his favourite drink.

His submission to Innocent was a perfect example of this.

Gathering his barons together, he put on his finest ermine cloak and broadest greasy smile, and made a magnificent spectacle of his own debasement. The scene was the Templars' Church in London. The altar of sacrifice was lit brilliantly with a hundred flickering candles and a dozen blazing torches, and the air was perfumed with the richest incense. On John's instructions, his clerks had arranged us carefully, so that no one would miss a single detail of his shame. Of course, there was another side of that. He wanted to see *us* as well. That's what gave him pleasure. His own humiliations became a challenge to us all, even a sort of victory for him. *You didn't believe I'd do it, did you? You didn't think I'd bow this low!* That morning, as he lifted up the scroll, he glanced around, trying to catch the eye of the assembled throng. But all eyes turned down, ashamed to witness his glorious mortification – all eyes, that is, save mine. Had I not produced this moment? Was it not my victory as well? Yet his eyes weren't filled with hate, as you might expect; rather, there was a sort of satisfaction, almost a contentment. He needed me; I needed him: in some strange way, since Mirebeau I think, we'd been like brothers, for each provided for the other a connection to the past – the world of Eleanor and Richard, Garth and Jean Neuilly, Guy de Gisbourne and Maud de Caux. They were all gone now, and only we were left, each knowing the other's secret heart. And our most terrible secret, Arthur's murder, was part of it as well. I think he almost took delight in the irony of this. I had driven him to this moment because of the crime that lay on my conscience but which the world would lay on his. In a strange way, as he lifted that scroll to read, he was almost forgiving me:

"My lords," he began, his voice smooth and rich as honey, "We have deeply offended our Holy Mother and Church and it will be hard to draw now upon the mercy of Heaven. Therefore we would humble ourselves and without constraint and of our own free will, and by the consent of our barons, give and confer on God, on the Holy Apostles St Peter and St Paul, on our Mother Church and on Pope Innocent the Third and his Catholic successors, the whole Kingdom of England and Ireland with all their rights and dependencies, for the remission of our sins. Henceforth, we will hold them as a fief and in token we swear allegiance" – he looked up now, and glanced around the room – "we *happily* swear allegiance in the presence of Pandulfo, Legate of the Holy See."

The gasp that this produced – for no one but myself had known that it was coming – was as sharp as a sword thrust into flesh. And the silence that followed was as complete as death. With a smile, John shuffled to the altar. Clerks held down the parchment. There was a hiss, and the smell of burning, as the seal was made . . . Behind me, William of Warren whispered in my ear:

"My lord, how cunning this all is. Tomorrow is Ascension Day. If Innocent can arrange to die, he'll rise straight up like Christ and with that parchment in his hand St Peter will give him the most honoured place in Heaven."

I smiled. But I wanted no one to suspect my role in what had happened, so I whispered: "You're not angry, baron, that he's given away the land beneath your feet?"

He chuckled. "I don't know. My serfs have always thought me partly God; now I can say so truthfully." Then he muttered: "It's not so bad, my lord. John's shrewd enough. He understands, I think, that Rome's farther off than Paris."

A voice hissed: *"Aye, lords, but that'll do us no good – for Windsor's no farther by a mile than it was a week ago."*

I didn't know this latter voice – and it was quickly hushed – but in fact he echoed my thoughts perfectly. I watched the King kneel before Pandulfo, hand across the scroll, and take his pledge. Then, I suppose, someone gave a signal, for bells began to ring. But did we have reason to rejoice?

That spring morning, as Pandulfo and John walked in procession down the aisle – like some bride and groom obscenely married – I had my doubts; and even as the weeks passed by, and a kind of normality returned, I didn't lose them. True, the priests were back in their churches (handsomely recompensed by John's treasury) and the King himself welcomed Langton back to England. True, Innocent kept his word, forbidding Philip's invasion on threat of excommunication. True, we even had a little victory: the Earl of Salisbury, in a daring raid, descended on the French fleet at Damme and burned the half of it. But still I worried. Neither my fate nor England's was yet concluded. I'd gained a little time, and the French threat had been postponed, but the greatest problem remained unsolved, for that problem was the King. Later that spring, I finally sent word to Rome that Gala should return to London and Marian to Le Mans; but I did so very reluctantly. I knew this wasn't over. All around, I could feel the trouble stirring.

That trouble . . . how can I describe it? You might say it was just the same old trouble, coming back again as if nothing had changed at all. But, in a sense, that was the trouble, for *everything* had changed. I had changed. The world had changed. It was this that poor John never understood. His kingdom was now entirely different but he was trying to be a king in the same old way. He so wanted to be king! He'd yearned so long for it! But those years of waiting, when the rest of us were living, hadn't changed him a jot – except, perhaps, to sharpen his rancour and resentment. He'd not seen what we had seen, or learned what we had learned. He was still living in a past which everyone (even his ancient mother) had long since understood was gone. They say that dying men see their whole lives flash before them in an instant. Well, this time was just like that. Everything came back, but speeded up, so that everything was twisted into a kind of mockery of itself. Poor John put on his armour and tried to be his brother. The person *he* had been – conspiring in the shadows – was taken by two barons, Fitzwalter and de Vesci, and trying to keep both sides from each other's throats was Stephen Langton, dressed up in robes like a manly Eleanor. Only a single figure remained unchanged: King Philip. He was bald and fat, they said, and his son Louis was jogging at his elbow, but he still played the ancient game – How could France take England?

As for myself, I watched and waited, as indeed I'd done so many years before. But this time my vantage point was my hall in London, not a ditch in Sherwood Forest; I was safe and comfortable. Londoners were as shrewd then as they are today and I knew they'd pick the winner, and as a peep-hole the town was excellent. In London, you hear everything. Windsor was an excellent source of gossip, even when the king was absent; Langton, nearby at Canterbury, was now my special friend; and travellers passing through my counting-rooms brought me all the news from the world outside. Their story, as I've said, was one I'd heard before, but this time I seemed to hear it from a madman in a dream. It went this way:

My ruse, the threat of Arthur's blood, had tipped the balance, and against all the odds our King had accepted reason and made his peace with Innocent. But with John, reason was like wine to an abstaining man, all the more powerful for being strange. In July, Langton ended John's excommunication and the Interdict – by August, with the church bells ringing through his English kingdom, he was deciding to retake his Norman realms. This was madness. Years before, his own mother had told me that a kingdom divided by the Channel was impossible: a mark of her great wisdom then, but now even the most ordinary men were wise. But John was never ordinary. No. Not wise – he was a fool – nor ordinary: he was the King. So he blew his trumpets, made levies on his barons, planted the Royal Standard on Plymouth shore – and then had the audacity to be surprised when no one came. His fury was exceeded only by embarrassment. I wasn't there, and didn't see it myself, but I was told that he actually boarded his ship, *without an army*, and ordered his fleet to sail, only turning back when he reached Jersey. This humiliation then provoked a different kind of folly. Since his barons wouldn't help him fight the French, he'd fight his barons, and promptly marched off to do so. Only Langton stopped him; he threatened to renew the Interdict and excommunication.

"I'm surprised that worked," I told him afterward.

"In truth, my lord, so was I. But sometimes I think he does mad things, knowing it perfectly, and *wants* someone to stop him."

"Like a runaway horse, Your Grace?"

He smiled. "You're right, my lord. It could be dangerous work – for thanks, you'd find yourself trampled beneath his hooves."

I eyed him. Above all, Langton wanted peace; he was ready to take any chance, even reckless ones, to get it. I said: "Not just the *King's* hooves, I'm inclined to think."

His eyes didn't quite meet mine, proving he'd followed my train of thought; but then he smiled again. "It might be blasphemy, Lord Locksley, to compare His Holiness to a horse. A lion would be closer. Or a falcon."

"All right. But then you must accept the talons. *Would* Innocent have supported you in another excommunication?" When he didn't answer, I added: "Be careful, Stephen. I think he wouldn't and those talons would be sharp. Remember what he told us – popes are overlords of kings, and kings of barons, so that in revolting against the King, the barons attack the Pope himself. Now that they are reconciled, Innocent will support the King in every way, no matter what his archbishop says."

He didn't respond directly.

"My lord, the King was too hot for reasoning. He raved and ranted. The barons would have obeyed old Henry, he said, or Richard, so why not him?"

I snorted. "Because he's not his father or his brother."

"A point, my lord, I was careful not to make."

"But you could have said that *his* barons weren't Henry's or Richard's either. They're English, not Norman, Frenchmen are as strange to them as Scots."

Langton made a face. "Not quite, I trust. But I *did* say that. What profit would his barons find in an invasion of Poitou? Distant lands, impossible to administer, which would only drain them dry . . . And the barons themselves have said that they're not obligated to support their king in a campaign on foreign soil. Except, in law, they're wrong – as John heatedly pointed out."

"But surely," I said, "it's more important that they *see* those lands as foreign?"

"Perhaps." He sighed. "In any case, I managed to distract him."

This was only partly true. John changed his methods but not his aims. His barons wouldn't fight for him, so instead he taxed them fiercely to buy a mercenary army. And since these Englishmen could see no profit in reducing France, he began conspiring with those who could: the lords of Poitou, on King Philip's western flank; the counts of Boulogne and Flanders to the north; and finally with Otto, the Holy Roman Emperor, in Germany. John's plan was cunning. His own army, lacking the English barons, was too small to threaten Philip; but by landing at Poitou and striking north, he hoped to draw the French king out to meet him. Then, while Philip's back was turned, Otto and the other allies would strike at Paris. It was a good plan and it almost worked. But not quite: for Otto wasn't quick enough. Philip had time enough to realise that John's attack was just a feint, left his son to deal with it, and wheeled his forces round. Meeting the allied armies at Bouvines, he destroyed it utterly. Otto abandoned the Imperial Eagle in the field; Salisbury and the Count of Boulogne were captured; and poor John came scuttling home.

I can imagine the rejoicing Philip's victory caused in Paris: but it was scarcely less in London. By now John's barons hated him like death, and delighted to see him weakened. To make this bad situation worse – John's usual effect – he now levied an additional scutage against those who hadn't followed him against the French. Everybody groaned. *I* groaned: and I had more silver money than many others.

As Jacob said, "You're paying dearly for your title, my lord. When the King's tax collectors come passing by, I'd rather be an old Jew than an earl."

I cursed. "Old friend, we'd all be better as Mohammedans. I

wouldn't pay another denier if I didn't want to stay out of his ugly sight."

This last desire, in fact, remained my principal aim. My fate had summoned me when John had demanded that I murder Langton: but I'd seized it then, taken it into my own two hands. I served no one now except myself and I knew I'd act again – but until that moment came, I wanted to remain invisible. This wasn't easy. AD 1214 was the year of treason and rebellion; you sucked it in with every breath, felt it grip your boots with every step. On St Luke's day, for example, an interesting party assembled at my hall in London. This was entirely an accident; certainly I wanted to avoid the appearance of conspiracy. Indeed, I'd invited Warenne (still one of John's closest friends and much in demand that year as a kind of proof of good intentions) and Langton had come up from Canterbury – in all these affairs, he was studiously neutral. But few of the others, I'll admit, were exactly devoted to the throne: Robert Fitzwalter was there, and de Vesci; Robert de Vere; de Mandeville; half a dozen others. It was a miserable day, cold and wet, but we built up the hearth fire, roasted an ox in honour of the saint, and didn't stint the wine. Gala, as my modest sister Marian, was hostess, and for a time her presence kept the conversation steady – though, in the end, it was her question to Fitzwalter that ruffled it:

"My lord," she innocently asked, "how is your sister?"

Fitzwalter, an enormous, fleshy man, had a soft, droopy mouth inclined to sulking. Now, with a twitch, his lips gathered in a smile: "She's much occupied, my lady. Our dear King keeps trying to seduce her. She says he is persistent, and as handsome as a bloat fly."

Inwardly, I groaned. John's designs on his sister made one of Fitzwalter's sorest grievances, though no one could be sure how real it was. It was a story I'd heard a dozen times before, and I wasn't inclined to hear it all again. Perhaps someone else agreed, for a voice down the table muttered:

"Fitzwalter, you love your sister better than you ever could a wife."

Quickly taking up this change of subject, de Vere put in: "Doesn't everyone, my lord? Sisters are so superior to wives. They can't betray us, nor we them."

We laughed at this – an expression of relief on my part – but then de Vesci said: "When you talk of betrayal, I think of kings not wives."

By this time, such a remark didn't cause the briefest ripple. De Vere replied: "No, Eustace, there's a difference. When a wife betrays a man, he can at least appeal – to her sense of honour, or her family's. Or her sense of shame. And in the last resort you have a marriage contract."

Setting down his wine, Fitzwalter grunted: "Our John may be a woman, but he has neither shame nor honour."

With a glance of apology toward myself for having begun it all, Gala now tried to steer sedition towards humour: "So you need a contract, lords, if we're all married to the King. My brother's trading means he knows about the law. He might draw it up."

We began to smile at this, now Langton spoke. "Why not, my lords? Isn't that precisely what we need? A contract with the King? Not exactly a contract, for this is not a question of trade or money. But an agreement, a charter, setting out his rights and obligations."

Now there was a pause: which, naturally, Fitzwalter broke. "Your Grace, you will pardon me, but agreements with John are worthless. He breaks them as easily as his wind."

Langton bestowed that little smile he had. "But at least, my lord, if you had an agreement written down, there'd be no argument about who made the evil smell."

De Vere, who was always reasonable, leaned back and said: "With respect, Your Grace, a king will always say that he must rule by his will alone."

"His will, yes . . . but all wills are bounded. A father is king to his son, but in raising him up, he will rule by custom, advice, affection, what others think. All governance is like that. From time to time, I'm told, even the Pope consults his cardinals."

De Mandeville smiled at this, and looked up the table toward Langton. "All right, Your Grace, but how do you make good this contract? If a father neglects all reason in bringing up his son, what can that son do but fight him or run away?"

Langton, on the other side of Gala, lifted his wine and motioned to me. "According to Lady Marian, our host will write this contract so we should ask him that."

I shrugged. "Contracts are enforced by law, Your Grace. This means the King would judge himself – surely the very meaning of a will unbounded."

"There's no other way?"

"Well . . . most contracts say that you can distrain or distress a person, except upon his body, to make good your claim. And I suppose, in the end, you can quit doing business with him, and tell the world to do the same."

"And wouldn't that," said Langton, "be an effective bounding of the King?"

This was the first I'd heard of Langton's famous charter, his "contract with the King". He claimed himself that it had a precedent in Henry's reign, but that was just his caution: the idea was truly his alone. And like most great ideas it was very simple. At Runnymede, while the bargaining was going on, he told me impatiently: "The barons don't understand, my lord. It almost makes no difference what this charter says – if the king seals it, that's enough. He will be accepting that his power is conditional."

"And if he rejects it later?"

Langton shook his head in irritation. "It will be too late then, my lord. Remember: men used to fight to see who'd be the king, but then someone thought of passing the crown from fathers to their sons. Ever since, men have tried to eradicate that notion, but they never can for long. Ideas are like souls. They have a kind of immortality."

Which was right, and cunning. But he was even more cunning with the barons than the king. A small group of them, led by Fitzwalter and de Vesci, wanted anarchy: a land in which every baron would be a little king. This group and John were impossible to reconcile. But there was a much larger party who were more moderate; their grievances were reasonable, and they wanted only ordinary justice. By writing his charter the way he did – generally and moderately – he appealed to just those men: and hoped to use their weight, not only to counterpoise the King, but to balance the hardest barons.

That was Langton's plan in any case, and through the winter he worked to make it real. By November, the barons had agreed to a list of grievances, issued at Bury St Edmunds, but John, against the advice of William Marshall (so Langton said), put them off till Easter. A cold winter shuddered by. The barons grumbled; John manoeuvred. He appealed to Innocent and even promised to take the Cross. Uneasily, the barons repeated their demands and sent de Vesci off to Rome to plead their case. I wished him luck but doubted that he'd find it; and he was quickly home, arriving just before Innocent's letter that threatened the barons with excommunication. Then events moved quickly. At Stamford, the barons formed an army captained by Fitzwalter (putting on his usual airs, he called himself "marshal of God and Holy Church") and marched south toward London. John, to counter this, granted London a great list of rights and liberties, but he was just too late. Before we knew about it, the barons appeared before our gates and we let them in. Furious, John then hid himself in Windsor. He was safe there: as safe as the barons were in London. But neither party dared come out . . . which was just the sort of stalemate Langton had been waiting for and he moved at once. Within hours, clerks and priests were rushing back and forth with messages. Rumours flashed like lightning through the town. Peace? War? A siege? Fire ships set drifting down the Thames? Through much of this, I knew little more than other people, but near the end of May the archbishop asked me to arrange a secret meeting at my hall: himself, Warenne, William Marshall, Fitzwalter and de Vere. Gala, carefully watering their wine, kept them tolerably sober, and they argued heatedly for hours. The upshot was: more argument. But now they agreed to do it publicly and asked me to name a place. There were a dozen I could have chosen, but I said: "Along the Thames, near Staines, there's a water meadow the local people call Runnymede. It would do as neutral ground. The land's so open that no one could bring up soldiers secretly."

So they met there and argued and everyone grew bored. A week passed, then another. After seeing one draft, John threw it over and another was drawn up. This was the time when Langton told me that all these details didn't matter, but Marshall and de Vesci argued over them like clerks: laws, fines, the forests, merchants, Jews, hostages, Welshmen and the Scots – everything was touched on. But finally they were done and on a bright summer morning the whole city rode out to see the charter signed and sealed.

Of the two sides, it was undoubtedly the barons who made the best procession. There must have been a hundred of them – Bigod, Bohun, Percy, Lacey, de Vere, de Vesci, Quincy, dozens I couldn't name – and they'd brought with them four thousand knights and a mass of followers. By contrast, the King's force was much less splendid, though John bravely led the way, rocking and teetering in his saddle like some enormous egg. His retinue, following on, reminded me of coffin-bearers; they had the faces for it: Amaury, the Grand Master of the Templars; Pembroke; Warenne; Longes-pee; the faithful Marshall; perhaps a hundred lesser knights. Assembling in a line, everybody waited while Langton and Pandulfo led up their bishops. Next came confusion: the ceremony, though brief, was necessarily unrehearsed. But finally someone read out the charter (scraps of badly spoken Latin among the snapping of the pennons) and John and a group of barons stepped forward to a trestle and made their seals. A bugle blew. The barons stepped backward from the King. One knelt. Thought better of it . . . but finally, in fair unison, the whole mass of them shouted their oath of allegiance to their king. After this, an awkward silence fell. People glanced around a little sheepishly. Then, since there's nothing to do at Runnymede except sign charters or graze sheep, they all turned and went.

I'd ridden up on the barons' side, but my shield, discreetly, was without a blazon. Letting the others jostle past me, I made my way to Langton. He smiled broadly, without his usual reserve – but then this was his greatest day.

"I'm glad you came, Lord Locksley. If there's blame for this, you deserve a little."

"May I read it, Your Grace?"

He handed me a copy. I unrolled it, and read it through. I wondered, then, if all the "details" were as unimportant as he thought: restricting the royal forests, regulating fines and punishments, redressing grievances against the sheriffs – if any of my friends from Sherwood Forest were still alive, they wouldn't think so. And all merchants, including Daniel Delore, Jacob Mancere and Robert Atheling would say good riddance to His Majesty's "evil tolls". Turning the Latin into English, I then read aloud: "'No freeman shall be arrested, or detained in prison, or deprived of his freehold, or outlawed, or banished, or in any way molested; nor shall we set forth against him, nor shall we send against him, except by the lawful judgement of his peers and by the law of the land.'" Looking up, I asked: "And who wrote *that*, Your Grace?"

"William Marshall."

I wasn't entirely surprised, and smiled. "He's tightly bound his king, my lord. The law governs now, not John."

He nodded, but then his face grew clouded. "I know, my lord," he said. "It's what we wanted – but will it work?"

I handed him the parchment, feeling its slippery touch against my fingers. But then the breeze riffled through my hair and I felt the springy loam beneath my boots. In the distance, the barons were a cloud of dust and a glint of steel.

I shook my head. "Truthfully, Your Grace, I think not. Your words are right – your thought is born – but these men are not. Fitzwalter still wants war. John won't give his power to a piece of paper. And I'm afraid his Holiness won't abide with this."

"Yes. I've wondered that myself."

Smiling at the memory, I said: "Answer me, Your Grace. Where does power come from?"

He laughed then, very faintly. "From God, my lord – as you well know."

"From God, who gave it to priests and Christian princes. Thus, by bounding that prince as you have done, you bound the Pope and even God himself. No, Your Grace. Your charter is a heresy."

His face went grave again.

"We'll see, my friend."

He saw all right. Within days John tore his charter into tatters. He wrote to the Pope, claiming it had been forced upon him, and

Innocent absolved him from his oath and excommunicated all "Troublers of the King and Kingdom". When Langton refused to pronounce the sentences, he was removed from Canterbury, summoned to Rome, and Pandulfo took his place. Using his mercenaries, John now struck quickly. With the Earl of Salisbury guarding London, he besieged Rochester castle, took it, then marched up and down his kingdom, ravaging – from St Albans to York, the Scots border down to Colchester. The barons panicked. They still held London, but little else. Their troops were wavering, even their leaders: Oxford had already gone over to the King. So now – repeating and repeating – they did what such conspirators had always done before . . .

I found out in April, a rainy night, as cold as winter. A single horse came clattering across the yard, a fist pounded on the door. I knew, I think. In any case, I stopped the servants and opened it myself. A single figure stood there, mailed, buckled, glistening with wet. His face was white as chalk and for a moment I didn't recognise him. But then I did. Fitzwalter . . .

"Sir Robert . . . I didn't know you were still in London. Please –"

"My lord, I have no time. I'm riding to the Channel, then to France. We've no choice, Locksley. We're asking Philip to send his son as King of England."

"This is all decided? He agrees?"

He nodded. "We've had letters from him . . . My lord, we ask for your support."

"I'm a lord, but I have no knights. You know that."

He hesitated, taking off his glove and wiping his dripping face. "My lord – you must know about the rumours. They say that you can prove that John slew his nephew, Arthur. This is the pretext Philip seeks for deposing John."

I smiled then. "A pretext? My lord, he's never needed one before."

"He fears the Pope. He wants some just excuse –"

"Believe me, the Pope won't blame John for killing Arthur. Arthur was rebelling against his overlord – his mother, after all – and to Innocent that means his death was just."

"Locksley . . . I beg you. Let us be the judge of that. Do you have the proof?"

I shrugged. "I do. And it proves John completely innocent."

"Locksley –"

"Believe me, sir. Of *that* he's innocent."

"You lie . . . My lord, listen –"

"Fitzwalter, I am a knight, knighted by King Richard. Do you doubt my word?"

His eyes faltered then, and he slowly nodded. "I ask your pardon, my lord. If you say —"

"And I do say —"

"Then I accept your word."

He began to go, his face now more ashen than before. As he turned, he said: "In what follows, Locksley, who will you support?"

Inside, I was ice cold.

"Not John," I said, ". . . but England."

His face looked quizzical: but I knew exactly what I had to do. If England was to live, one man had to die.

CHAPTER FOUR

Sky: low, knotted clouds that drag across the land, weeping over it like a keening widow by a grave.

Marsh: ditch-water glistening like ice; mud; grey, grassy hummocks hunched like frightened animals; the far, flat glitter of the sea.

These are "The Fens": a paradise for robbers, but not the sort of land a soldier likes; ambushes hide in potholes beneath your very feet and the unwary die with their mouths full of muck. Nervously, I looked around. The land here lies so flat you'd think it would be easy to keep watch, but the muddle of ditches and ponds, brackish pools and muddy flats – never precisely the same, but never really changing as the miles pass by – half blinds the eye. For the second time, I stared hard at a dune. I thought something might have moved there but now I wasn't certain.

"It's just the wind," said a voice behind me, "passing through the furze."

I half turned and nodded. At Runnymede, I'd wondered if any of the men from Sherwood were still alive. Mercury had turned up too: Richard Lee, who now edged his horse up to me, and Alan Dale, our bowyer. In the old days, Richard had been our messenger, and when I'd left the Forest, I'd found him a place with old Etienne Vizier. He was still tall and thin, a runner; but Vizier had made a soldier of him. He even looked like one: which was more than I could say of Alan – though I didn't doubt his old man's leathery toughness – or any of the others I'd brought with me: my old steward and a stable boy from London, and a heavy-mitted brawler from one of Mercury's stews. Indeed, in comparison to these, even Gala in her chain mail seemed a more military man. And in fact it was my 'squire' who pointed now: "There, my lord – just there!"

I squinted. Something *had* been moving behind that dune.

Richard laughed at his mistake. "So I was right, my lord. Isn't Mercury the wind?"

I smiled: Vizier had done wonders with our country lad. "Just remember," I replied, "if you see any arrows in the air, they won't be from Cupid's bow."

We watched as Mercury scuttled toward us. He was black with mud and came up shaking like a little terrier.

"Did you find them, then?"

"Half a mile along this track, my lord. The same as before, I think. I counted eight. They've strung ropes across the road to trip our horses."

"Can we go around them?"

We'd done this once, but now Mercury shook his head. "On foot we might, but not with horses. The mud just sucks you down."

I cursed. We'd met this band twice before: 'robbers' I suppose you had to call them, but they were more like half-starved scavengers. King's men and barons' men had marched through these lands half a dozen times leaving little for plain men behind.

"What weapons?"

"Staves, my lord. I think the leader has an ancient broadsword."

"Bows?"

He shook his head. "Where would they find the trees?"

He was right enough. Men here fished, or fowled with nets; and from where I stood, I could scarcely see a tree much taller than a man – though we were only two days' ride from Sherwood.

"My lord," Mercury went on, "I think we have no choice."

I cursed softly; I would rather have avoided them; but then turned to Gala. "Go back to the others. Tell them to wait until you hear our signal."

She hesitated, her face anxious; she knew what I was thinking, knew what we had to do. But then she nodded and pulled her horse around. As she trotted back along the track, Mercury scrambled aboard his pony: a small, shaggy beast that perfectly fitted him and turned him into a little knight. I unslung my bow – that Turkish bow I hadn't bent for so many years – and Richard unsheathed his sword: with a show of force, we might frighten them away, though this was more hope than expectation. We moved ahead. The track twisted here, ascending a range of dunes – a veritable alps on this muddy plain – then slithered into a grove of stunted trees and shrubs; as cover for an ambush, it was obvious.

Mercury murmured, "My lord, I'll ride ahead and cut their ropes."

With a nod to Richard, I reined in, and Mercury's pony raced ahead. A dwarf! The poor wretches had been spying on us, so they must have seen him, but they couldn't have foreseen how his presence changed their plan. Their ropes, pulleyed taut around trees on opposite sides of the road, jerked up: the lowest, at a height to trip a full-grown horse around the knees, was conveniently placed for Mercury, leaning forward slightly, to cut it neatly; while the highest, designed to catch a rider across the chest, passed right over him. Wheeling back, he severed it with a single stroke, so that Richard and myself rode up unimpeded. Backing our horses round, we covered the ditch on either side.

I watched three men, hairy as goats, emerge from the cover of the brush.

They hesitated dumbly; since we weren't lying stunned across the track, they were uncertain what to do. But then another shaggy brute rose up. Skins and leathers covered him like scales, and his hair twisted from his scalp like Medusa's locks. He must have been their leader for he carried a great sword, its ancient blade as ragged as a saw.

"My lord!" called Richard Lee.

"I see him."

I nocked an arrow. Drew it to my ear. He saw me then; I caught his eye; and I prayed that he might run. But with a bellowed cry, like some angry animal's, he exhorted the others to a charge. Did he know? I wondered. Did he prefer this end? I loosed. The arrow thumped his chest like a hatchet striking into wood, sitting him down on a patch of mud. Then, quite neatly, he folded back, all ready for his grave.

On my side of the road, his followers fled at once.

But the others hadn't seen him fall and came on grimly. Richard, wading in with his broadsword, slashed an arm, sliced staves like kindling; but then the last of them, catching Mercury grappling with his startled pony, struck him a tremendous blow across the back and shoulder. Spinning like a quintain, he toppled from his saddle. At once his attacker drew a knife. I nocked an arrow, loosed: too quick to aim, but sure enough to pierce his shoulder. With a scream, he staggered backwards, spilling in the ditch. And that – so quickly – was the wretched end of it.

I caught my breath and calmed my horse. A panting, snorting moment passed. Standing in my stirrups, I squinted all around, but nothing moved. The clouds, drizzling since the previous day, summoned up the energy to rain. Far off, a vee of ducks skidded toward the sea . . .

Then, with a little burst of energy, Mercury chased down his pony and Richard, sword-drawn, dug up the man I'd wounded almost like a clam. A short fellow, he had reddish hair and was hard and filthy as a rusted nail. His eyes were wild with pain and fear, but he had courage enough to stand up straight before me. "Turn round!" I ordered. Warily, his eye on Richard's sword, he did so. "You're lucky, friend. The head's passed cleanly through." I snapped it off. "This way now." He turned back and with one quick lunge I pulled the shaft out – at which he didn't groan or grunt; indeed, his face hardly changed expression. Mercury, back atop his pony, now trotted up. His right arm was hanging limp but he laughed to see our prisoner.

"My lord Robin Hood – I can remember times when you didn't look much better!"

"I've been thinking that." I nodded at his shoulder. "I pulled my arrow out. Do you think he'll live?"

"Oh, I'd say he's tough enough. What's his name?"

His eyes met mine, then looked away. "Hardwin . . . my lord."

Hardwin. Alan Dale. Jean Neuilly . . . Oh yes, I thought in the old days he would have done. I opened up my saddle-bag and handed him a loaf and a square of cheese wrapped up in a cloth, then took a silver denier from my purse and slapped it in his palm. "There's your reward," I said, "for . . . being who you are." He was struck dumb; his eyes went wide; and I felt afraid – afraid for his poor dignity – that he might fall at my feet and blubber. But he merely swallowed and said firmly, "I thank you, sir. You are a Christian."

I said: "Are you from these parts?"

"Yes, sir. I am."

"King's Lynn?"

"Not from the town, my lord, but thereabouts."

"Do you know if King John's there?"

"He was. But they've left now, my lord. They're waiting at St Andrew's for the tide."

"The tide?"

"When the tide is out, sir, there's a ford across The Wash there, much shorter than going round the shore."

"And where is this place?"

"It's near a church, my lord. If you follow this track along you'll reach it."

I sent Richard back to fetch the others and thought very carefully. For months, I'd watched and waited, as the balance swung this way and that. The French held London; William, Earl of Salisbury, had come over to their side; indeed, almost all the greatest lords except for William Marshall and the Earl of Chester had deserted John. Yet the King was undefeated: Lincoln, Durham, Barnard Castle; Windsor, Dover, the Cinque Ports – all these were loyal. But what difference did it make? The kingdom John was fighting for was dying from his very sword. Thus, as the summer ended, I'd known I had to act. All I needed was the moment, and for these last weeks, like the King's dark shadow, I'd followed after him. Now, I wondered, had that moment come?

I said nothing, even to myself, but in Mercury's face I saw he knew the answer. As the others caught us up, I turned my horse along that filthy track. A few miles of mud passed by. Then we saw the sea; then a spire near the shore; then sodden pennons stiffened by the breeze. At last, two knights rode out to meet us:

"Who's man are you?" one called.

"The King's," I lied.

But we'd made a mistake.

These were the King's men, all right, but the King wasn't with them. Leaving King's Lynn that morning, John was travelling first to Wisbech and then going on to Swineshead Abbey, this route taking him around The Wash. The group we'd stumbled on – his household, exchequer, baggage train – intended to take the shorter route, across the ford, and arrive ahead of him.

Mercury didn't like it. "He's so unpredictable, my lord. If he's angry, he might take a fancy to revenge – and now you're much too handy."

"I know. But we can't leave them now. And it might be for the best. By the time we reach the King, no one will notice us at all."

In fact, no one was paying us much attention as it was. A king's household may be royal but it's still a household: a confusion of servants snaggling with each other. Like so many angry crows, John's clerks hopped around his baggage. Everything was here: his treasury; the crown jewels and all the royal regalia; John's chapel, with his altar; his armour; clothes; bedding; casks of special wine; boxes of royal papers . . . They'd apparently been carrying a lot of this in waggons, but now it was being transferred to a string of rouncies who protested, in their usual fashion, at the assumption of the burden. None of this confusion was aided by the pelting rain or the dreariness of the spot. A brown-grey world of mud and sea surrounded us. Only the church stood out, a sharp black silhouette half a mile away. It occupied a little stony rise; sloping down from this was a narrow vein of gravel, providing the pebbly beach where we were standing, which then continued across The Wash and made the ford. Or so I guessed: for if there was a ford, it was invisible. The tide, though clearly ebbing, still had a way to go; mud flats, cut and carved by the retreating water, were exposed along the shore, but then disappeared beneath the waves. Concluding from this that we'd have a while to wait, I told Alan to unload our brazier and warm some wine, but no sooner had he done so than one of the royal clerks came running up. I knew him slightly – Bernard Vigot, one of the keepers of John's tax rolls. His face bore that harried, self-important aspect such men so love.

"My lord, I bid you welcome. You're travelling with us?"

"If we may."

He smiled – a fleeting, humourless expression that was more a grimace. "We're all surprised to see you, lord, but I think you know the King's in no position to spurn anyone who claims to be his friend."

"I don't love him, Vigot, or pretend to. But I hate the French." This, I knew, was the explanation of my presence that would provoke the least suspicion. More than one man that year had swallowed his pride and rallied to the King because – at least – he wasn't Philip. I added: "I can't offer much. For years I've paid the scutage rather than train soldiers. But I'm still a knight, I've three good yeomen – one might make a sergeant – and this little man's the Devil's brother."

His smile twitched again. "We're glad to have you all, my lord. I only ask you, be ready to leave at once. As soon as those packs are lashed, we'll be on our way."

I nodded toward the sea. "The tide will ebb a long way yet."

"My lord, we'll leave before it's run. We have two guides who can find the ford even when it's covered. Just remember – follow carefully. There's enough muck out there to drown us all."

With this warning, he hurried off. Obediently, we doused our fire. And shortly, with the rain slacking off as a kind of parting gift, our party began to form. The two guides were clearly local men, and with three armed knights they led the way: they were to find the ford, test the footing, and mark it out with staves. When they were a hundred paces out, the first of the rouncies followed, tied nose-to-tail in groups of three. After the fifth string had gone, a steward waved us into line and we splashed ahead: myself, Mercury, Gala, Alan, the London men and Richard Lee bringing up our rear. Shallow to begin with, the water quickly deepened: over the horse's knees, then lapping at their bellies. After a time, Mercury's pony was almost swimming and I pulled the little fellow up behind me. No one talked. The horses splashed and waded. Uncertain of their footing, they plunged and whinnied at every slip; and each step they took brought up the smell of muck. Then the rain began again, and the wind came with it. Our sodden clothes were turned to ice against our skin and the sea began to chop. I squinted across my horse's ears. Grey seas. Grey rain. The shadowy shape of the rider next ahead. Turning, I looked behind. Gala bravely smiled. I could make out Alan . . . but Richard and the others were completely lost. I shivered; and not just with cold: the sea stretched grey and endless roundabout us, and our only connection to the land was this line of sticks bobbing through the waves. Where was it leading?

We discovered soon enough.

It was nothing, to begin with. As the rain grew heavier, I began to lose sight of the rider next ahead. I didn't like this, but it wasn't disastrous, for the markers were fairly easy to see: each bore a tuft of branches that stood out well against the waves. But then, just as I came up to one, I saw it bob and start to drift. I shoved it down, only thinking that the current had tugged it loose. And the next was firm. But the one beyond this was drifting. I cursed. The rider in front of me must have brushed against it, or the guides weren't shoving them down deep enough. I drew in my reins, using my knees to edge the horse slowly forward. The ground seemed solid. But the next marker was drifting free and after that . . .

I pulled up hard. Gala's horse, behind, nudged mine and snorted. She clucked it quiet. I tried to listen. The rain hissed against the water. Ahead, a horse began to whinny. Someone shouted: loud but indistinct.

"My lord . . . ?"

Richard had now come up behind us. I shouted back:

"Stay where you are! Don't move!"

And then someone behind us in the line began to shout. A horn blew. Another answered. A violent gust of wind whipped the rain away and I thought I saw a shape . . . too formless to be certain, but on our right. And then another horse began to neigh – a horn blew stridently, then again – and then the whinnying grew shrill and fearful: the awful, desperate call of frightened animals. My own mount shuddered and put his ears back, and I stroked his neck. The rain was swirling all around, making ghostly shapes of riders and plunging horses, that rose up before my eyes and vanished in an instant.

An awful scream.

Another horn blew – long and desperate.

Richard went to answer but I shouted, "No!"

"Robert – what is happening?"

Gala was edging up beside me. I reached out, seizing her horse's bridle, for his nostrils were now flared in panic as he scented the deaths of horses near him.

"We've lost the markers. Instead of stopping, I think the men ahead are trying to come back to us. There's quicksand all around here."

And then it happened. The horror that we'd only heard about

269

now appeared before us. I saw them first: three rouncies, still roped together, plunging through the sea. Despite the great boxes on their backs, they were running as hard as I'd seen horses run before: necks stretched out and straining, forelegs lunging, eyes wild, muzzles flecked with foam. They were no more than thirty paces off, and for a moment the ground seemed solid under them. But then the leading horse plunged down; the two others whipped and slewed. They kicked and bucked, hooves flailing the sea to foam, and tried to rise. Staggered. One made it up . . . then tried to lift his feet.

"Dear God," breathed Gala.

It was a sickening sight. Somehow, they all got standing; for a second, they were almost steady. But then the sands began to suck . . . We were so close we could see the terror in their eyes, feel the ground tugging at their feet. Whinnying with panic, they tried to free themselves. One got his front legs up, and up again: but each time he rose, the sands sucked his haunches down till he was half sitting in the water. Then the poor creatures began to bray and screech, and our horses began to dance and blow. Mercury, now aboard his pony, grabbed my arm. "My lord, your bow – or these horses will be bolting under us!"

He was right. I grabbed three arrows, gave him my reins, and jumped down in the water, which was now below my waist. I nocked an arrow. The rouncies were floundering pitifully, and one had somehow turned over on its back so its legs kicked and thrashed like a tipped-up turtle's. I stretched my bow and loosed – they were so close I hardly had to aim: three arrows that put them out of misery. Dying, one seemed to stretch toward me gratefully, then calmly settled its neck along the water and closed its eyes.

I turned toward the others then and said: "Listen carefully. We're safe here. The ground is firm – if we don't move, we've only got a soaking from the rain. And once the tide's gone out, we can find our way. Don't move for anything, and if your horse bolts, jump straight off him and let him go. You understand?"

They nodded, though hardly happily: there's nothing worse on earth than to be cold and wet and frightened.

After a moment, Alan Dale moved up toward me. Squinting against the rain, he said: "Robin – my lord – do you know what's in those boxes?"

I shook my head. "I hadn't thought."

Quietly, no more excited than an old man sitting before a fire, he cleared his throat. "John's treasure. All his jewels. That second horse you killed, the roan mare with the blaze? His crown's on that one. I heard them talking as they loaded her."

Dumbfounded, I stared across the water.

"Dear Christ," I murmured, "all swallowed by a bog."

Alan spat. "Not yet it's not."

I smiled and swore by Christ, "Do you think you're Him and can walk across the water to fetch it back?"

"No, but I can swim."

I shook my head. "Too shallow. And getting shallower. You'd never make it."

Then Mercury said, "I'm no Christ, my lord, but I'm lighter than a man . . . I might be able to walk across the sand itself."

"So you might – and your coffin might be elm or oak. You couldn't risk it."

We all fell silent. The horses lay there, humped like whales: slowly sinking. But it was hard to tell how much, for the ebbing waters had exposed their bodies more. I finally said, "I could put an arrow into one of them, with a rope attached, and we might try to pull it out. But I'm afraid the sand's too strong; the arrow would just jerk free."

"Yes, but think," said Alan, "think of your sending your rope out like you say and we use it as a kind of railing. Hanging onto it, someone light enough might walk out there."

I thought a moment. It just might work . . . I turned to Mercury. "Could you do it? What about your arm?"

Flexing it, he grimaced. "That's the trouble. It's numb as January. I could walk all right, but as for hanging on –"

I shook my head again. "It's too much risk."

"Robert . . ." Gala reached out and touched my arm. "Let me do it . . . No – think a moment. Listen. I weigh even less than Mercury. And you could tie another rope around my waist. That way, if I fall, you can simply pull me in. I'll get wet and muddy but nothing more. And think again. What a chance this is . . . Think what you plan to do. If you fail, if anything goes amiss, that crown – Richard's crown, Henry's crown, the crown of England – would be your ransom."

I hesitated.

Mercury murmured, "Robin, I think she can."

"I know I can."

Still I hesitated. But did I have the right to be afraid for her? She could ride as well as any man, and think much better, and God knows she had courage enough for two. I'd wanted her with me because, in London with the French, she'd not be safe and because I knew that this adventure – win or lose – must be my last. Now that she was here, was it strange that she'd found this part to play? *Richard's crown* . . . that crown she'd tried to marry and which I'd tried to serve. Should we not, together, attempt to save it?

"All right. Get out the ropes."

We had to splice several lengths together, but in the end we had enough. The first we looped round Gala's waist, then cinched on Alan's saddle; the second I wound around my heaviest arrow. My first try fell a little short; I was still a little out of practice, and the rope's weight dragged it down. But then I aimed a little higher and hit my mark: that poor mare's outstretched neck. I'd wanted the shaft to pierce right through, becoming an enormous barb when I pulled back the rope, and this must have worked: I leaned back in my saddle, the rope's free end looped round my waist, and stretched it taut as a fiddle string. Now Gala gave me a smile, slipped from her saddle, and splashed into the water, which was growing shallower by the moment. We'd taught them all to call her "boy" or "squire" but Mercury whispered, "Careful now, my lady . . ." She waded forward. Feeling with her toes, she crossed the width of the ford — then stopped and grabbed the rope and called:

"Now it's sand . . . you can't . . ."

Her voice was shaking at the awful feel of ooze beneath her feet. I glanced at Alan and he nodded; he held the second rope quite taut, paying it out slowly. She inched ahead. But this first part, once she'd gained a little confidence, proved easy; because I was on my horse, the rope, angling down, was well above the water: almost draped across her "railing" her feet only trailed across the bog. But the nearer to the dead mare she came, the more her weight was taken by the sand. Finally, a body's length away, she began to flounder, but with a desperate lunge grabbed the horse's mane and dragged herself atop the slowly sinking body.

She waved.

We gave a little cheer; she caught her breath; I eased back the tension on the rope. The mare had died with its legs splayed out, and Gala was able to sit astride its back and begin working at the crates. She pried one open. Dug about. Then held something up . . . the crown. And then some jewels — even in that gloomy light they glittered. But now the horse, burdened with her extra weight, was sinking fast: gruesomely, we saw the head sucked down. I leaned back against the rope, stringing it taut again, and in a dive Gala launched herself toward it. I grunted as her weight came down, felt the cords digging round my middle — but she'd grabbed it, and now fought to kick her legs out of the muck. I turned to Alan but he'd already begun to pull: firmly, to lift her free; but not so hard as to pull her from my rope. And then her foot came loose and she made a lunge, draping herself across the rope so that it passed beneath her armpits . . .

"Alan – pull her in!"

He tightened up the slack. She began to slide, almost like a pulley:

closer, foot by foot; higher, inch by inch. But then I felt the dead mare, our anchor, begin to slip: the weight around my waist suddenly increased as the poor beast was sucked down some more. Alan, seeing this, reeled faster . . . but with an awful gurgling noise the horse sank beneath the water and I was toppled from my saddle.

Gala splashed, kicking and flailing into the sea, and even as I struck the water I was trying to stand and run toward her.

But then, a little shakily, she stood.

We'd pulled her far enough; she'd landed in the ford. Everyone gave a shout and Mercury splashed towards her on his little horse. And then, arms trembling, she lifted something up above her head.

King Richard's crown.

I stood there, wet and shivering. In the distance, frightened trumpets blew.

I ask you: were the signs not clear?

I'd taken my fate into my own two hands: now, as if that fate was blessed, it had delivered me the crown as well. I could feel it as I rode along, hard and heavy in my purse, jostling at my knee. Old Henry's crown . . . The Lionheart's . . . Poor John Lackland's . . . Now only I possessed it. But what a mockery this was. John had gone and lost it in a bog: but if he'd not, he'd only have melted it to pay his *routiers* – who were already losing that same crown to a foreign king. *Serve the crown rather than the man who wears it*: time and time again, I'd remembered Eleanor's advice. But now both man and crown meant nothing. It was only England, the poor wretched kingdom, that tore my heart.

And there, God knows, was another dreadful sign.

When the tide had fully ebbed, when at last we could see our way, we passed through a valley of death that would have made the psalmist cringe. I had never seen such terrible desolation: smooth, glistening hills of stinking mud, rivulets of ooze, deep-cut ravines; and strewn across this was the flotsam of our king, each a sign of the shattered land he ruled. Horses were still dying everywhere. Trapped, sucked down to their very necks, they brayed and struggled, fighting for a final breath. Here and there, lying in brackish pools, shrouded in their courtly finery, dead men floated: and these were the lucky ones, for mostly we could pull them out and give them decent burial. But all along the way we saw poor helpless souls that would suffocate in Hell: arms stuck up, and legs; obscene plantings in the slime; desperate, distorted limbs testifying to the horror of their final agonies. Who could believe that this was not a judgement? John's train . . . John's household . . . This was what it had become.

Haunted, stricken, we reached Swineshead Abbey late that day and made an exhausted camp beneath its walls. Next morning, leaving late, we moved to Sleaford. John was so angry that he saw no one, and I only caught a glimpse of him. Some said he'd fallen sick, but he was only desperate – so desperate he sent a party back to search along the ford. When they returned next day with only two trunks of sodden clothes, the party left for Newark: John in such despair that he refused to ride and was carried on a litter. No one noticed us; asked who we were or what we did there. After all, such questions could have been asked equally of themselves. Now, men only followed John from habit, or because they had nowhere else to go. Riding cautiously up that disconsolate cavalcade, catching sight of William Marshall, I thought he made the best example of them all: faithful to his sense of faithfulness; loyal to loyalty itself. Step by step, he rode along, just waiting for the end.

But still, through those days, I dallied.

I knew what I had to do. I'd even known before that night I'd spoken to Fitzwalter – hadn't I asked the Pope to depose the King and put young Prince Henry in his place? I knew; but something held me back. Was I afraid? Did I balk from pity or from conscience? Seeing the signs so clearly, didn't I believe them?

Then, that first night in Newark Castle, I had a dream and understood.

Some say that dreams are the Devil's work, but I'm not so sure; that night my dream was like a way of talking to myself. I could have dreamed of some many people, times, and places. I could have asked a phantom Stephen Langton for advice, or Eleanor, or Jean Neuilly. I could have asked Richard for forgiveness, or Marian for sympathy. But I dreamed of none of them. I dreamed of Garth instead, of Cyprus and that day he died. I saw the Turk's huge axe swing up and hack his neck, and then the blinding halo of Richard's face as he saved me. There was the simple truth: Garth had died and I had lived. There was the true beginning of my fate – I'd been allowed to live to reach this day. And all at once I understood my fear, and was so startled that I woke. I'd been allowed to live only for this day – but once it passed, even if I was spared again, what would I have to live for? But how mad that was! Reaching out, I put my arm round Gala: here was the answer as it had always been, for the fate of kings and queens hadn't reckoned on this different life.

So, decided and serene, I waited for the dawn, and when it came I announced my plan. I'd act that night. Mercury and the others would leave that afternoon and ride to Sherwood, to our old camp at The Eagle's Nest, and I'd try to join them there. If I failed, they'd run for safety, and bury the crown as they saw fit: bury it, that is, except for a single golden point. I hacked this off and sewed it in a piece of leather, making a magic talisman that would lead me to the King.

The day passed slowly. I knew Gala was afraid but she didn't show it, and I told her that we shouldn't say good-bye for we'd meet too soon. Quietly, at noontime, they drifted off. Newark Castle was large enough that no one saw them going; and even if they had, the discreet desertion of the King, under present circumstances, could hardly arouse suspicion. At length, dusk fell. I ate alone, outside the hall. When I was sure that the others were finished with their suppers and dozing over wine, I went inside. I searched for Vigot – a survivor of our grisly stranding in The Wash.

"I thought you'd gone, my lord."

"Yes, my men have, and I plan to leave tomorrow morning."

He shrugged. "No one will blame you. The King is now virtually abandoned."

"If I could, I'd like to say farewell."

His eyebrows lifted. "To the King?"

"Of course."

His smile twitched sarcastically. "You've more courage than some others I could name, but it'll not be tested. He's seeing no one."

"Could I try?"

He shrugged again, then pointed to the stairs leading above the hall. "Gualo, the Pope's new legate, has the first apartment. Only with his permission does anyone see John."

No one watched as I climbed the stairs. At the top, the passage was lit with guttering, smoky cressets. Indeed, I thought, John really was abandoned: there were no guards at any of the doors, and I saw nothing to prevent me opening each in turn till I found the King's. But I resisted that temptation and continued with my plan, knocking softly on the legate's door. A servant let me in. I'd met Gualo once; he pretended to remember. As I stated my purpose, he politely listened, then shook his head.

"My lord, your desire to see him speaks very well of you, and I will say so, but the King wishes to be left alone."

"Some say he's ill, Your Excellency."

He shook his head. "His gout. Fatigue. Nothing more than that."

"Then might I ask you to give him this? Tell him it comes from me, and say I'd like to see him." I held out my scrap of leather with the piece of gold inside. Gualo, puzzled, took it hesitantly, and I added: "Your Excellency, I think he'll want to have it."

Frowning, he beckoned to a servant, then waved him off and went out the door himself. He returned a moment later – obviously wanting to ask a dozen questions, but leading me in silence to the King's apartment. I stepped inside. Gualo had said John wasn't sick: but that room was like a sick-room. There was a fetid, sweaty odour with a smell of smoking herbs laid over it. And the room was very hot, a fire roaring in the hearth, a brazier burning near the bed. The King, propped up on pillows, buried under rugs and blankets, looked sick as well. His face was grey. His campaigns, his worries, this sweltering heat – something had melted the fat away, and the skin hung from his face in two wrinkled dewlaps.

"Out," he muttered. "You, I mean. Locksley – stay."

I didn't move. Gualo, bowing, passed backwards out the door.

Reflecting the brazier's flames, John's eyes made two yellow points as he moved them over me. "Vigot told me you were here," he said, "but I'd no wish to see you gloat."

"That's not why I came, My Liege."

"'My Liege' . . . You're sure that's what you mean, my lord? I'm 'liege' for few men now. I was John Lackland once and now I'm John Lackeverything. I've no kingdom, army, treasury, no . . . crown." But then his fist sprang open and I saw the glint of gold. "Or perhaps that isn't true. Where did you get this?"

"From your crown, Sire. I hacked it off."

Slowly, I edged across the room. He wasn't sick: but, in drawing closer, I could see how sick at heart he was. With every breath, he sucked in despair, breathed out self-pity. Seeing me approach, he whispered:

"Where did you find it?"

"In The Wash. Lying in the mud."

"You betrayed me, then?"

"No, Sire. I rescued it. Your guides –"

"You swear?"

"I swear."

Feebly, he smiled. "For some reason, I believe you. Tell me: where is it now?"

"Buried, My Liege. I don't know where – deliberately."

Another smile. "So there'd be no point in torturing you?"

"Precisely."

"Ah yes . . . John the torturer. Do you know what the peasants say? I'm such a glutton I gnaw on children's bones." He looked earnestly toward me. "Do you believe that?"

"No."

He laughed. "Perhaps you should. I'm such a pig I might try it yet." He began to grin, and I remembered what I'd thought before: that John found his greatest pleasure in his own humiliation. Now he added: "I suppose, dear Locksley, you want to make a bargain – I

276

grant another of your favours to get back my crown. All right –
I agree. Just don't ask too much. These days, I'm not sure how much
I want it."

"Sire . . . would you give it up?" Perhaps I felt a twitch of hope.
"You could abdicate, My Liege. Then –"

"No king has ever abdicated, no king ever will."

"Sire, your son could rule –"

"Don't tell me, Locksley. Of course I've made a will. When I die,
Henry will be king and William Marshall regent. But only *when* I
die."

"You'll fight, then, to the end? No matter what it costs your
kingdom?"

"My kingdom! This wretched place . . . What has it ever given me
that I should care for it? Complaint. Rebellion. Treachery. My
brother spent one half his time fighting in Jerusalem, the other
heaving at some pageboy's arse. What did the kingdom give him?
Loyalty and treasure . . . My old father killed his own archbishop
and what did his penance earn him? Rich fiefs, from Aquitaine to
Wales . . . By God I owe this kingdom nothing, which is precisely
what it's given me."

His eyes were wild now; he was utterly distracted. Poor John,
swaddled like a whining baby. Poor John, mad within himself. Poor
John, rotting with self-pity. I drew my right hand from beneath my
cloak. He saw the knife; saw it glitter in the firelight. I raised it high
and with both hands he grabbed my arm. And opened his mouth to
shout. And then my left hand, bearing a vial of poison Mercury had
mixed for me, clamped hard against his lips.

He struggled. Twisted. I pressed down harder: leaning my breast
against my hand, pinning him against the pillow. Then his mouth
began to work, as if he wished to gnaw right through my palm and
eat my heart. Grunting, I pushed down with all my strength . . . and
felt him weaken. A spasm shook his body. His fingers opened
around my arm. He drew a terrible rasping breath . . .

I moved away. Now his eyes were shut and his chest was heaving.
Mercury had told me that the poison would quickly render him
unconscious but then kill him slowly, like a sickness. This, in fact,
was exactly how it looked. Sweat was beading on his brow; his lips
were frothing. Putting my knife away, I wiped my hands inside my
tunic and arranged the covers naturally on the bed, erasing any signs
of struggle. His breath, as I bent over him, brushed against my
cheek. Poor King, I thought. Who never should have been the King.
Poor John. Who should not have had to die like this. But I knew his
death would save the kingdom; there was no need for rebellion or a
French king now. England could be England's once again . . .

But now I had to save myself.

I was very calm, but inside that room, horror was easily feigned and when I cried out I almost believed myself: "Lords! Your Excellency . . . The King!" I rushed outside, meeting the legate in the hall. Leading him to the bed, he found nothing to blame me for.

"He was sick then," he whispered.

"We must find a doctor."

"The abbot of Croxton — he's in the hall. Fetch him instantly."

I did as I was told; and once he was in the room, with Marshall, Vigot and a few others, it was easy for me to slip away. My horse was waiting. The sergeant didn't want to raise the gate, but I whispered him the news and said I'd been dispatched to London. I fled across the night, miles unwinding through the blackness. The dawn came up, and then I was pursued, the tolling of a hundred bells chasing me across the land. "The King. The King. You've killed the King." After a time, that was what those mournful notes began to say. But it wasn't regicide that led me to the church, but simple murder: the murder of an ordinary man that made me feel the guilt that any man can feel. So I found a priest, confessed, and heard my penance:

"Do you know God, my son?"

"Father, I swear I do."

"Then every year upon this day, no matter what you've done on all the other days, you must find a church and beg God's forgiveness at its altar."

"Father, I will."

"Do you know love, my son?"

"Father, I truly do."

"Then every year upon this day, no matter what you've done on all the other days, you must pledge your love, your faithfulness."

"Father, I swear I will."

"And now, my son, I ask you to feel with all your heart and soul. You have God and love, you say. But after these, what do you treasure most? Gold? Some special pleasure? Perhaps some very ordinary thing. Don't answer — only your heart and Christ need ever know it. But throughout the year, for every day *except* this day, you must forego it. And on this single day, the only day each year when you can feel or taste or sense that treasure, you will think of the terrible sin you've done."

What did he mean? Could this be a penance? To beg my God's forgiveness one day a year, annually to pledge my faithfulness to the only woman I could ever love? Then, as I left his church, I didn't know. But I had his absolution. Riding on, I entered Sherwood

Forest and soon began to recognise the old, familiar paths; each hillside, stream and valley brought back a rush of memory. I crossed the ford near Locksley Hall; jumped ditches where I'd once crouched in fear; climbed hills where we'd lain in ambush. And that evening, as dusk was falling, I reached the camp . . .

The others had all arrived safely; fires were lit and burning, shelters made, and they'd even shot a buck, fat and heavy after a summer's feeding. So we had a feast and Mercury – performing his usual magic – even produced some wine. As we drank it and crouched close beside the fire, Richard Lee put into words the thought we'd all been thinking:

"What happens next, my lord?"

"For us, I don't know. But I think the kingdom's safe. They'll do as John wished, I think – make Henry king, with Marshall to stand beside the throne."

"Which means," said Mercury, "that Henry will be King, but the barons'll rule."

"Maybe . . . But not for long. They *need* a king. What nation doesn't? But everyone will learn what we've learned – that kingship must be different."

Old Alan cleared his throat. "That leaves John's crown, my lord. What do you want to do with it?"

Mercury chuckled quietly. "I know what you want, old man. You want to melt it down."

"Dear Christ," he said, "you know I don't. That gold is cursed."

"No – no gold is cursed."

But then Gala said: "Robert's right, I think. Henry, Richard, John . . . That crown was worn by kings whose kind we'll never see again. They're all dead and buried. I say their crown should be buried with them."

So, in the end, that's what we did.

Next morning, on a hillside, near a stand of ancient oaks, we dug out a little hole and laid it there. Then, leading our horses higher, we stood upon the hilltop and gazed out across the valley, so peaceful now, green and gold and russet in the sun. What a sweet and perfect place, I thought, what a lovely treasure . . . But then tears started in my eyes, for all at once I understood the cunning of that priest and the meaning of his penance. I'd won my victory; my fate had freed me. I had both God and love. After these, what could any man desire? Only the great Land that is spread out before me now. This was the love my penance commanded that I forego, except for a single day each year: and that day, when I might glimpse this love, this land again, would only remind me of all I'd lost. Thus, even as my fate released me, it won the final victory. At night, before the sun went down, Gala and I rode off together – to live our life, to find my exile.

So memory fades, my voice grows faint, and what I have to tell is told.

So many words, so many years . . . Did it really happen? It almost seems impossible. Locksley – who is he? Daniel Delore? Such an outlandish name! If I lived *their* lives at all it was only to live this *one*: here, in Calais, with Gala at my side.

Yet I know it happened, for every year I do my penance. Even now, even in my dotage, I obey that priest's command. October comes, I find a ship, sail across the English Sea. Then, holding Gala's hand, I pledge my love again and find a church and pray. And I remember: just as I was told. Besides, if I do not, who else will? The others are all dead, except for Mercury, and my name dies with them. Not that it makes much difference. Vanity's one fault I've never had, and it's fruitless anyway. Men raise statues to kings and great men only to pull them down again, and the glory that attaches to a name usually has little to do with the man who bore it. Last year, indeed, I had a dreadful proof of this. We were making my annual penance – contrary winds had even extended it a day or two – and we were staying at an inn in Dover. As we waited by the fire, a minstrel began to strum and sing, whining out an ill-rhymed ballad about a chivalrous outlaw whose name was Robin Hood. Robin Hood! Gala had to prod me before I understood, but then how hard I laughed. If that was fame, I said to her, I would happily accept obscurity, and quietly thanked God that the "immortality" granted by a song is fleeting. After all, I tell myself, how long can a ballad last?